"Sometimes in the face of perversity, neglect, and growing up in a rundown Moscow flat one bedroom too small, one needs to do their own mythmaking. And in this unflinching, yet achingly humorous look at millennial Russia, Katya Kazbek celebrates a wonderfully heroic self-deification. Proving we can become the gods and goddesses this world truly needs."

—**PAUL BEATTY**, *The Sellout*

"Katya Kazbek's *Little Foxes Took Up Matches* is a stunning and transformative novel that shows us the playful possibility and subversive quality of queer mythmaking. With humor, heart, and expansiveness, Kazbek forges a new language to belong inside and reinvents storytelling. This book will swallow you and shelter you. It's pure magic and will rearrange you from the inside out."

—**K-MING CHANG**, *Bestiary*

"Many have tried and failed to summon the magic Katya Kazbek wields here as matter of factly as a switchblade. A relief, really, to read a debut novel as original as this—as cunning, wild, and free."

—**ALEXANDER CHEE**, *How to Write an Autobiographical Novel*

"A luscious, modern queer fable drawn in post-Soviet Russian red lipstick. Kazbek's dreamy family of misfits forged in the feminine occult will stay with you forever. Brava!"

—**SOPHIA SHALMIYEV**, *Mother Winter*

"A Russian satire, a queer myth, an enchanting coming-of-age story— *Little Foxes Took Up Matches* is one of the most original, and charming, debuts I've read in some time. Katya Kazbek writes with wit, heart, and the needle-prick of life."

—**DAVID EBERSHOFF**, *The 19th Wife*

"I am in love! *Little Foxes Took Up Matches* is an utterly spectacular modern myth. This rapturous coming of age, equal parts wit and grit, weaves a spellbinding tale about having the courage to incite a revolution in oneself. With this debut Katya Kazbek proves she is an absolute legend in her own right."

—**AFIA ATAKORA**, *Conjure Women*

"Katya Kazbek's first novel is a book borne out of her experience of living in a world in which nothing is fixed but struggle, humor, and the unreality to be found in the reality of everyday life. Told with precision, empathy, and a non-jaundiced eye for the absurdity inherent in being different in a world that doesn't necessarily cherish it, *Little Foxes Took Up Matches* is an auspicious debut, eminently cherishable."

—**HILTON ALS**, *White Girls*

"An unpredictable love story that is mesmeric, totally original, and deeply, deeply touching, *Little Foxes Took Up Matches* examines our competing human instincts to belong and to escape. Kazbek has reinvented—and bewitched—the coming-of-age genre, and I can't wait to succumb to whatever magic she writes next."

—**COURTNEY MAUM**, *Costalegre*

"Absorbing and unremittingly honest, *Little Foxes Took Up Matches* is a magnificent journey with a thunderous effect that both injures and mends. Kazbek writes this fascinating story with eloquence, human understanding, and compassion. She illuminates post-Soviet Russia's contradictions in prose as undeflected and fearless as the contradictions themselves are piercing and violent. It's nothing short of exceptional that anyone can write original, brilliant, and witty prose in a language not their own; we marvel at a Vladimir Nabokov, a Joseph Conrad, a Jhumpa Lahiri, a Katya Kazbek."

—**JAMES CAÑÓN**, *Tales from the Town of Widows*

LITTLE

FOXES

TOOK

UP

MATCHES

KATYA KAZBEK

TIN HOUSE / Portland, Oregon

Published by Tin House, Portland, Oregon

Distributed by W. W. Norton & Company
Library of Congress Cataloging-in-Publication Data

Names: Kazbek, Katya, author.
Title: Little foxes took up matches / Katya Kazbek.
Description: Portland, Oregon : Tin House, [2022]
Identifiers: LCCN 2021046893 | ISBN 9781953534026 (hardcover) |
  ISBN 9781953534088 (ebook)
Subjects: LCGFT: Bildungsromans. | Novels.
Classification: LCC PS3611.A957 L58 2022 | DDC 813/.6—dc23
LC record available at https://lccn.loc.gov/2021046893

First US Edition 2022
Printed in the USA
Interior design by Jakob Vala

www.tinhouse.com

Cover images: ©KsushaFineArt / Shutterstock, ⊕Ivan Bilibin, © Rawpixel

In memory of Ritoozik, my real-life Semargl

For Tanechka and Yurochka

Begot Tsarina in the night
Neither a boy, nor a girl child,
Not a mouse and not a toad,
A beast of which one's never heard.

—Alexander Pushkin,
The Tale of Tsar Saltan, 1831

A horse saw a camel, and its remark was coarse:
"What a weird-looking bastard spawn of a horse."
"You're not a horse either," responded the camel.
"Just another camel but underdeveloped."
And only the god with his gray and long beard
Knew they were animals of different breeds.

—Vladimir Mayakovsky,
"A Poem on the Difference in Tastes," 1928

ONE

Have you ever heard about Koschei the Deathless? Koschei is a villain, in possession of many treasures that he hoards. He may not be killed unless someone breaks the needle that is his death. That's way more convenient than having a lousy heel, like Achilles, or vulnerable locks, like Samson. And it's better than being mortal. You take the death needle, and you store it in a place where no one can find it. Then you live forever, or as long as you want to live. In the fairy tale, the needle is concealed within an egg. The egg is within a duck, the duck is within a hare, and the hare is inside a chest suspended on a branch on a tree growing on a cliff that overlooks the stormy sea.

So what does this have to do with a skinny young boy who packs lipsticks into a jar, then puts the jar beneath his shirt so that he can try to get it halfway across the city of Moscow undetected? It's 1999, everything is covered in asphalt, and while it may seem too late for any folklore myth to be unfolding, in Russia fairy tales predetermine reality. The boy's name is Mitya and he's twelve. He has a needle somewhere deep inside his body, which he believes makes him invincible. His dreams are full of sticky, viscous fairy tales, where he is Koschei. But there's no resolution yet, whether he's the villain or the hero. Perhaps Mitya should decide, but he doesn't like making decisions. He can't even decide if he's a boy or a girl.

This is why he has the jar of lipsticks. And many more jars, in fact: his treasures, some with colorful clothes inside them, some with other kinds of makeup. And he's taken them from the pre-revolutionary apartment building on the Old Arbat street, where he grew up, and where there were many convenient nooks to hide things, to a new apartment in one of the superblocks in the residential area called Chertanovo in the south of Moscow. It's a much smaller space, and Mitya is still figuring out how to store these jars in a way that his parents won't discover them.

Mitya has had some fascinating events occur in his life lately. He almost solved a murder, almost committed another murder, almost moved to a new country.

At one point in school, they studied fractions, and Mitya had a tough time understanding that halves are just that, halves, 0.5, 50%, ½. What if one of them is bigger than the other? Mitya is not good at math, as you can see. But he's good at imagination. Mitya is utterly convinced that no one has ever looked at two halves long enough, or attentively enough.

Now that his family is moving—because his parents have lost a lot of money in the recession and had to sell the apartment—Mitya is secretly excited. He knows that the other half of his life is starting and that it's going to be better than the previous one. Besides, he's going to be thirteen soon. Everyone is always so dismissive of the number thirteen, giving it a bad name, that Mitya knows for sure: the overlooked number is bitter. Recognize it, and it will make you happy. So Mitya thinks that at thirteen he will be the happiest. After all, why shouldn't he be? He's moving and leaving some nasty things behind. Like his cousin, Vovka. Terrible Vovka. Mitya's father, Dmitriy Fyodorovich, who is also Vovka's uncle, says that Vovka is staying behind so he can rot. Mitya silently agrees with his father, which doesn't happen often. It also makes him sad that the better half of Vovka's life is behind him.

This is where it's about time to start wondering: How does an almost-thirteen-year-old boy live with a needle inside of his body? Shouldn't he see a doctor? How did the needle get there in the first place? Well, this is a long story, which needs to be told from the beginning. It's hard to say whether anything exciting would happen to Mitya at all, if not for the incident with the needle. Maybe Mitya would not be hiding lipsticks in a jar beneath his T-shirt now. So listen to the tale closely, and don't interrupt. Whoever interrupts will have a snake crawl down their throat and will not live longer than three days from now.

1

It all began when the Soviet Union was still united, which was, by the accounts of everyone around Mitya, a much better time. He couldn't know for sure because the events surrounding the USSR's collapse were about as dim as anything that happens in one's childhood. So Mitya was forced to trust the words of adults until he knew better. Mitya's grandmother, Alyssa Vitalyevna, liked retelling the events that occurred one night when Mitya was two years old, which made Mitya believe that what happened that night was a fateful, life-altering accident.

According to Alyssa Vitalyevna, Mitya was weak and frail as a toddler but had the stamina of a scavenger bird when it came to picking up small objects that had fallen on the floor, or even on the ground outside. His mother, Yelena Viktorovna, once had to pry a morsel of moldy bread from his tightly shut mouth. She then escorted Mitya off the playground as the other mothers, not even trying to conceal their voices, declared, "That Mowgli."

Yelena Viktorovna and Mitya never returned to that playground. "These other mothers aren't worth the soles on my shoes," Yelena Viktorovna hissed. She was of an utmost conviction that she, the daughter of a distinguished space scientist and a graduate of the Moscow State Institute of International Relations, was far superior to the other women.

After that, she did not let Mitya out of his stroller on walks. He was allowed to go on slides and swings only when escorted by his father, Dmitriy Fyodorovich. After all, Dmitriy Fyodorovich was an Afghan War veteran, and his army brand of discipline was reliable in preventing any mishap.

That one evening, Mitya's parents went out to dinner at the home of their colleagues from the Rubin factory. Dmitriy Fyodorovich made televisions at Rubin, and Yelena Viktorovna provided bookkeeping services. The colleagues lived in a room in faraway Medvedkovo, and so his parents left Mitya with Babushka, who lived with them in the apartment. Nothing could go wrong.

Alyssa Vitalyevna, who was, by the way, a fourth-generation Muscovite, did not consider herself a natural-born caretaker. She didn't mind looking after Mitya, of course: he was a lovely, docile child with eyes like blue buttons and blond curls. Most importantly, he looked nothing like his father, whom Alyssa Vitalyevna loathed. She went to great lengths to avoid addressing Dmitriy Fyodorovich in the second person and referred to him as "indyuk," turkey cock, or "armeysky sapog," army boot.

Alyssa Vitalyevna was not that kind of Russian grandmother who dedicates herself to baking pies and knitting socks for the grandchildren. She had better things to do than babysit. She had phone calls to make; she had stitch patterns to finish and, maybe, to gift. She had a boyfriend, the Greek Dr. Khristofor Khristofor-ovich Kherentzis, who would not survive without her guidance and instruction.

Reluctantly, Alyssa Vitalyevna joined Mitya in the living room, which doubled as his bedroom. The Communist Party had given the apartment to Alyssa Vitalyevna's recently deceased husband, Mitya's grandfather. He was one of the scientists who invented the first space toilet for the Soyuz spacecraft: a suction cup and a tube for urinating, a small bucket for defecating, all connected to a vacuum pump. "I am the woman who made cos-monauts stop shitting into diapers," Babushka said when she felt that life was treating her unfairly. It was her utmost conviction that without being inspired by her, Dedushka and his colleagues would never have been able to invent the space toilet. She kept a prototype of the device in her credenza and sometimes took it out. Alyssa Vitalyevna always mentioned how she was a cru-cial part of the prototyping process—and Mitya never dared ask what this implied, afraid it might have been something intimate, like her trying out the toilet before the cosmonauts.

Alyssa Vitalyevna, regal and flushed with menopause, sat on Mitya's mustard-yellow sofa that evening wearing a red mohair beret that she never took off in the colder months for fear of drafts. Behind her was a rug tapestry depicting Peresvet, a Rus-sian monk, fighting Tatar warrior Chelubey. Beneath her was another rug, a Middle Eastern red-and-black pattern of crows' feet and geometric flower shapes. Mitya was crawling on it, try-ing to find something to put in his mouth. There was nothing but crumbs. He licked them off the carpet and tasted kurabie biscuits and three-kopeck bread rolls with a touch of wet dog.

Alyssa Vitalyevna paid her grandson no mind. She was working on an embroidery: Dr. Khristofor Khristoforovich Kherentzis's initials on an off-white handkerchief. She was also talking on the phone to her best friend and occasional nemesis, Cleopatra. The TV in front of her was on, at full volume, and both ladies were discussing the events of *Santa Barbara*, an American soap opera that was all the rage. The main character, C. C. Capwell, a gray-haired millionaire, was splitting from his much younger wife, Gina. In protest, Gina took off her jewelry, got undressed, and left the Capwell mansion naked.

Alyssa Vitalyevna gasped into the receiver. She briefly glanced at Mitya to check if he had seen the impropriety, but the boy was busy studying the rug. Unseen, the needle had detached from the embroidery. And as Alyssa Vitalyevna was shuffling the receiver, she caused the needle to fall off the sofa and onto the rug. Mitya picked up the needle with his little hand. It was thin, shiny, small—Alyssa Vitalyevna was working on the tiniest details, using her most delicate needle.

It was like nothing Mitya had seen before. Maybe if he had stung himself with it, he would have broken down in tears and thrown the needle back on the floor. But it stayed firmly in the boy's fist. He put the needle into his mouth and swallowed.

Or at least, that's what Alyssa Vitalyevna figured had happened.

While the end credits were rolling, she realized that something was amiss. She looked at her embroidery, couldn't find the needle, and gasped. She patted the area on the couch around her, looking. She searched beneath her feet. Then Babushka stood up and explored the area where her buttocks had been. When she couldn't see the needle there, she bent down and started looking beneath the couch. She moved her open palm across the floor, but all she could find were dust bunnies.

Her attention shifted to Mitya.

"Mitya, did you swallow the needle?" she asked him.

And he replied: "Yes, Baba."

Alyssa Vitalyevna believed that once a person swallowed a needle or even as much as stepped on it, the sharp little piece of steel would immediately get absorbed into the flesh and it would be mere hours before it reached the bloodstream and set on its way to the heart to kill the person. Babushka knew that she had to rush Mitya to the emergency room, but not until she relayed all that to Cleopatra on the other end of the phone line.

Fortunately, it was mid-October, and it was not snowing yet. Alyssa Vitalyevna put on her lambswool coat, grabbed her pocketbook, and rushed down in the elevator with Mitya in tow. As soon as she ran out of the building and stepped into a puddle, Alyssa Vitalyevna realized that she was still wearing her slippers. It was too late to turn back. She ran through the inner courtyard and out into the street. Mitya held on to the front of her cardigan and felt the cold wind brush against his naked calves.

Outside, Alyssa Vitalyevna stopped a car by jumping in front of it.

"Quickly, or the child will perish," she shouted at the driver, a middle-aged Georgian man in a cat fur hat, as she got into the passenger seat. The man had no option but to obey. Babushka had quite a commanding presence. She propped Mitya against the front panel and gave out instructions on how to get to the hospital. It was about thirty minutes away, on Leninskiy Prospect.

When they reached the hospital, a converted pre-Soviet mansion, Alyssa Vitalyevna barely waited for the car to stop. She jumped out and rushed Mitya to the entrance. The driver shouted his phone number after them. His name was Vakhtang. He must have liked Alyssa Vitalyevna, she later surmised.

The receptionist told Alyssa Vitalyevna and Mitya to wait in line to be helped. The waiting room was full of adults who did not look sick enough to be tended to earlier than Mitya. There were no empty spaces on the benches upholstered in cheap brown pleather along the walls. A wailing preschooler latched on to her mother, who kept shoving a whole peeled onion into her daughter's mouth. The air smelled of the eternal tug-of-war between urine and chlorine.

Babushka rotated on the barely existent heels of her slippers to face the receptionist once again.

"This child is dying," she announced.

"You have to wait, zhenshina," the woman said, oblivious to Alyssa Vitalyevna's dominating charms.

Babushka had no patience for bureaucracy. She took hold of the phone on the receptionist's desk and ferociously spun the rotary dial.

"Khristik?" she asked as soon as the call was connected. The usage of a diminutive conveyed the urgency of the situation. "Khristik, dear, Mitya is about to perish, and they will not see him at your hospital!"

Dr. Khristofor Khristoforovich Kherentzis, one of the chief surgeons of the hospital, was not expecting to hear from his beloved Alyssa that evening. His brother-in-law Zhora was visiting from Sukhumi and mercilessly winning at backgammon.

"Can I maybe put you in touch with my friend Alexei?" he offered.

"But Khristik! You must come right away! I am here alone, and I see no help from anyone!"

Babushka glared at the receptionist.

It was quite pleasant at Khristofor Khristoforovich's apartment. He and Zhora were halfway through the second bottle, and there was some lamb and ajapsandali left over for a snack later that night. But he also knew that going against Alyssa Vitalyevna's will could propel him to visit the ER himself.

"I am coming, Alyssa," Khristofor Khristoforovich sighed.

They waited for him in the corner, Alyssa Vitalyevna perched on the windowsill and quite magnificent in her lambswool. Mitya tried to reach the nearby ficus plant and treat himself to its luscious, dust-absorbent foliage, but his arms were too short.

Dr. Khristofor Khristoforovich Kherentzis arrived disheveled in his white undershirt and loosened suspenders beneath his winter coat, smelling like homemade wine. The receptionist immediately began collecting the necessary information to get Mitya's medical record out of the archive.

"Year of birth?" she asked his grandmother.

"1937," Alyssa Vitalyevna exclaimed proudly. Now the younger woman had no way of ignoring the importance of her plea.

The receptionist looked at Babushka over her thick-rimmed glasses with a question in her eyes.

"Not you, Alyssa, the boy," Khristofor Khristoforovich crooned.

"Oh," Babushka replied. "1986."

"And the name?"

"Dmitriy Dmitriyevich." She propped Mitya on her chest.

"Last name?" the receptionist asked.

"Noskov," Alyssa Vitalyevna replied less enthusiastically.

She had always disliked Mitya's last name. Not only did it signify the fact that both her daughter and her grandson belonged to that ridiculous indyuk, but it also came from the word *nosok*, sock. Whenever she thought of that last name, she could sense the odor of dirty feet in her nose. And the smell, albeit imaginary, had to come from Dmitriy Fyodorovich's army boots, there could be no doubt about that.

The receptionist retrieved Mitya's medical record, a thin stack of papers bound in a frivolous floral fabric and filled with illegible doctors' writing. They were admitted to the X-ray room immediately, and Babushka paraded, proudly, in front of all the ailing patients still waiting in line. She was greeted by the radiologist, an old drinking buddy of Khristofor Khristoforovich. He must have heard about Babushka because he steered away from her cautiously as she entered. He had a bald white head and a red face. Both looked entertaining to Mitya, who tried to lick the doctor's forehead and then his cheek and compare the taste of the colors. Unfortunately, the doctor never came close enough.

The bald doctor took X-rays of Mitya's digestive system but found nothing.

"The needle has already reached the bloodstream and could be practically anywhere!" Alyssa Vitalyevna insisted.

"But madam," the bald doctor started. "It's not scientifically sound . . ."

Khristofor Khristoforovich gave him a telling glance. It meant that following Babushka's lead was the top medical priority at the moment.

The doctor proceeded to take X-rays of Mitya's whole body. Babushka was in awe of how small and neatly arranged the bones inside of him were. The needle was nowhere to be found.

"What a krokhotka," Alyssa Vitalyevna thought. "And I did not protect him. How small must the coffin be for such a tiny child? And what does one put inside it as a keepsake? A volume of Pushkin's verse?"

Because the needle remained undetected, the bald doctor let them go. Khristofor Khristoforovich made Babushka promise that she'd carefully observe Mitya's stool for the needle. If she had the smallest suspicion that he was unwell, she'd call.

She put Mitya on the windowsill in the reception area and hugged Khristofor Khristoforovich in gratitude. Mitya finally managed to get his hands on the ficus plant and ate quite a few leaves off it. Afterward, he had diarrhea. Because of it, observing the excrement inside his potty became both messier and less complicated. Of course, Alyssa Vitalyevna didn't do it herself. She delegated the ordeal to Yelena Viktorovna, who obediently went through her son's feces with rubber gloves.

Though the needle was never retrieved, Mitya didn't die. And so the grown-ups came to the conclusion that it must have gotten stuck somewhere, and would ultimately kill Mitya. Alyssa Vitalyevna realized that she had been complicit in the damage that her only grandson had incurred. She was not religious, but she made a promise to the forces that be. As long as they both remained alive, she would help the boy in everything. As she said these words, she imagined herself, slightly older but as glamorous, pushing the boy in a wheelchair. Passersby stopped in awe, as they noticed the graceful petite woman who so selflessly took care of her infirm son. (He couldn't be her grandson, could he? Such a young, elegant lady!) Alyssa Vitalyevna was ready for her life to become a sacrifice. She would make it appear effortless. Making sure that the boy would make it in life to the fullest extent of her ability would be her mission.

Meanwhile, Mitya himself did not feel the effects of the needle in his body, or his mind. He was still frail, but comparatively healthy. His limbs grew. He learned to read at four years old, with some assistance from Alyssa Vitalyevna. And in one of the fairy tale books, he discovered Koschei. The coincidence was striking, and it did not take long for Mitya to figure out that the needle was his blessing. It would always shield him from harm and make him special; he was convinced.

It didn't matter, though. Mitya could talk all he wanted of how the needle was right for him, or of how he couldn't feel a single symptom: none of it mattered. Mitya was a child, and children, though they quite often possess the clearest, least obstructed view of reality, are never asked to present it.

2

The Old Arbat, the street where the Noskovs lived, was one of the oldest, most historical and beautiful streets in Moscow. However, in his earliest childhood, Mitya did not get to see any of it much. His world was confined to the apartment. More precisely, to his room, which was also the living room, and the kitchen, where he saw Yelena Viktorovna cook and clean. There was also a narrow space between the wall and the bookshelf, where he liked to stand and tug at the loose piece of wallpaper, to reveal old newspaper. Mitya did not know which time, exactly, it came from. There were some young women in old-fashioned dresses in front of a movie theater, and the text below that advertised the theater's opening.

Having the boy at home was a hindrance for all concerned, but there was no other choice. Mitya would get sick right when the grown-ups attempted to place him in a kindergarten. It was as if the boy learned about the plan, and absorbed the bacteria from the air in the apartment with all the urgency of his little, weak lungs. The minute Mama came to him to offer help packing up for kindergarten, Mitya responded with a thread of brown snot hanging from his nose.

Whenever he had the flu, Mitya lay down on the living room sofa that doubled as his bed, swaddled in many blankets to sweat it out. Sticking to her promise, Alyssa Vitalyevna nursed him. She brought Mitya glasses of warm milk with raspberry jam, vodka, and pepper, and put her lips against his forehead to measure his temperature. Everything around Mitya swam in a fever, and halfway between dreaming and waking, he distinguished his babushka's soothing whispers. Sometimes she read Pushkin to him. Sometimes she read Tolstoy. Sometimes she talked on the phone. Sometimes she hissed at the TV screen, where another soap opera was unwrapping.

When Yelena Viktorovna came home in the evening, she relieved Alyssa Vitalyevna. She lacked her mother's force of spirit and had a much grimmer outlook on her son's fate. She knew she couldn't have more children—she had had a hysterectomy—and so Mitya was her only bet on motherhood. She enjoyed him when he was an infant, but the older he grew, the more she realized that her son was becoming an entity separate from her. She did not like that. She had no control over her temperamental mother, and though she achieved a bit more success with her husband, controlling him took careful planning and skillful manipulation. And since a foreign object had overtaken her toddler's body, he simply became a ticking time bomb, over which she had no say.

So Mama came up with the best idea she could. She came to terms with his inevitable death. "I can't do anything, so I'll do my best in the circumstances, and he will pass away, slowly," she mentioned to a colleague. The role of a mother who had lost her child in his prime was, to her, a romantic one, noble, one she could learn to enjoy. So even while the child was still alive, she began practicing.

When nursing sick Mitya, Yelena Viktorovna started out sweet and dreamy. She would talk about Mitya as a baby, perfect in every way. But grief was always lurking around the corner. If she stayed by Mitya's side long enough, Yelena Viktorovna mentioned the future loss, her whispers breaking down into sobs. "Bedniy moy detochka," she cried. My poor baby.

Mitya did not die. And then, shortly before he was four, he made it out of the apartment, to kindergarten. Mama's hand firmly held his as they made their way through the 7:00 AM dusk of the Old Arbat. The world lay around them in its sleepy splendor. Mitya raised his eyes to see the bluish-yellow sky above the buildings of painted yellow brick. He saw a woman on a balcony, her ample breasts spilling across the railing. A man shook violently from behind. Mitya told his mother of the dangerous situation, but Mama led him farther and told him not to look.

The children in kindergarten were the first ones Mitya had encountered closely. His overzealous parents were not pulling him away from the kids this time. The realization that there were real lives outside their apartment, and that people functioned there, and formed their own opinions of him, was a strange discovery. He did not know what to make of the people he met. Two women, Olga and Yevgeniya, took care of the children in his group and helped everyone change into room shoes. All the children were wearing chunky tights like Mitya, in various muted colors, with shorts or dresses or nothing but a sweater, always sagging and bubbling at the knee.

Mitya had spent the morning staring at himself in the mirror that hung by the entrance to the apartment. The tights, the shorts, the flannel of his shirt were all so sad, and his ugliness petrified him. Yelena Viktorovna had cut his hair and she wasn't any good. She told him not to scratch the red rash on his cheeks, but he couldn't resist. Now, he saw other children as ugly as him. The kindergarten was enveloped in the dim fluorescent light and in the sour cabbage smell that emanated from the kitchen. It seemed so deliciously disgusting that his little heart started beating faster. He was fascinated with the symmetry of existence.

As Olga and Yevgeniya helped him change into the brown Mary Janes, they summoned a small girl that Mitya had seen before.

"Your mother said Zhenya lives in your building, so you'll be friends," Olga said. "Zhenya, you know everything; show Mitya around."

Zhenya looked at him with the eyes of a calf. She had uneven bangs and green snot in her nose. He knew that her father was in the city police, militsia.

"Zhenya's mother is our cook, so you listen to her," Yevgeniya told Mitya with a smirk. "By the way, Zhenya, can you please tell your mother to cook us some green instead of all that cabbage?"

Zhenya stared, still silent.

"She means money," Olga explained. "Our wages are too low; she should start cooking up some rubles or, even better, bucks so that we can live! Otherwise, we'll have to start prostituting ourselves!"

Mitya did not know what "prostituting" meant, but he knew that it was impossible to cook money. Otherwise his mother would be doing that instead of complaining about wages, which had been going down lately. Zhenya shrugged and put a finger up her nostril, right into the green.

She did not heed the instructions and did not show Mitya anything. She kept to herself throughout breakfast, class time, drawing time, and outside time, and barely spoke. Mitya started to suspect she didn't like him.

Mitya didn't feel like talking to the other children, but it seemed to be the purpose of kindergarten, so he decided to try during playtime.

"Can I be the mother of this doll?" Mitya asked a pony-tailed girl playing house.

"You're a durak," she responded loudly. "Only girls can be mothers."

Mitya had never thought about it, but it made sense. His mother was a girl. He sat down on the bench, watching the others frolic with naked dolls, whose hair looked like loofah sponges, and misshapen plush animals. Suddenly, Zhenya, who was left out of the game too, gestured for him to follow her. Because there was nothing better to do, and out of curiosity, Mitya did.

They went into what must have been a bathroom. At least, there were tiles on the walls and potties on the floor. There were twenty of them, all positioned in a circle. The realization crept into Mitya's head: one of the minders, Olga or Yevgeniya—he wasn't sure which—had mentioned that there was to be toilet time. Mitya imagined the children sitting on the potties in a circle, and something started tugging at his stomach. Whenever

Alyssa Vitalyevna disliked something, she said it wasn't "digni-
fied." This setup wasn't.

Meanwhile, Zhenya, as silent as ever, went up to him. She
pulled her tights down and showed him what lay beneath (she was
not wearing underwear, unlike Mitya): two folds, a duck's mouth,
bunny ears. Mitya was fascinated. He had something completely
different inside his tights: swollen, outward, rounded.

"Why do you have a different thing?" he asked. It was just
the two of them, and he didn't expect Zhenya to answer him.

"I'm a girl, and you're a boy," she said, her voice oddly gut-
tural for such a small body.

Mitya saw that Zhenya had green snot in her nose again,
slowly climbing down out of one nostril. He watched, not sure
if he was to look into the nose, or down there. He had never
before considered the things inside his pants, though they tickled nicely sometimes. But now, when Zhenya revealed hers to
him with her utter conviction, he realized that this couldn't be
normal. It couldn't be a thing people did all the time. And yet
it beguiled him.

As plainly as she had revealed it, Zhenya pulled her tights back
on and led him back to the playroom, where the house was in full
play. Boys pretended to come back from work, to dinners cooked
by girls, to kiss their doll children. Mitya looked at everyone with
a newfound curiosity. Boys had outie things, and girls had innie
things. There were no other distinctions, as far as he could see.
Boys wore shorts more often, and girls, dresses. Girls had longer
hair. Boys were more often acknowledged, and heard. Not Mitya,
though. He spent the rest of the day silently, watching, pensive,
trying to understand. He observed children through playtime

and during mealtime, as they ate the disgusting food that smelled like boiled cabbage. He didn't want to eat it but forced himself to, so as not to offend Zhenya by refusing her mother's labors.

During lunch hour, not able to figure out if he was allowed to go to the collective bathroom for individual concern, he pooped his pants. Olga and Yevgeniya found out and reluctantly washed him off with household soap in a sink. His mother had not packed him extra clothes. While his freshly washed tights, shorts, and briefs dried on the radiator, he had to wear his shirt on his bottom: legs inside sleeves, his privates, suddenly so full of meaning, dangling in the buttoned-up neckhole.

Olga and Yevgeniya left before Yelena Viktorovna picked Mitya up. They reminded him to tell his mother about his little accident. Mitya didn't. Why would he ever speak of something so undignified?

The next day Mitya had the stomach flu. He wasn't sure if it was from the kindergarten food or the thought of it, but it abruptly ended his kindergarten career. The grown-ups considered Mitya old and self-sufficient enough to be able to stay at home on his own.

———

Mitya was alone in the apartment when the putsch started. The word reminded him of cabbage, the smell of kindergarten. Maybe it was because it sounded similar to the word *puchit*. *Puchit* meant that someone had gas in their stomach and was about to fart. He turned the TV on to watch something, and there was ballet on all three channels. With nothing better to do, Mitya set out to explore the secret lives of his parents and grandmother.

Going through Dmitriy Fyodorovich's stuff was not fun. Everything he kept was connected to the army in one way or another. There were his medals, photographs of him with his buddies, his army electric razor in a travel case. And of course, his set of army clothes, which he wore for celebrations, including portyanki, long pieces of fabric that soldiers used instead of socks, wrapping them around their feet. There were photographs of Dmitriy Fyodorovich as a boy, too, with his brother. The brother, Uncle Seryozha, had died in the war before Mitya was born, and was not to be mentioned.

Babushka's belongings were more varied and exciting. Mitya carefully held the space toilet in his hands and tried to imagine how the cosmonauts used it inside the spaceship. He opened her medicine bottles and played with the pills, scanned through the old letters in yellow envelopes in search of juicy details and photographs. Babushka was young and beautiful in them, and often accompanied by Dedushka or small Yelena Viktorovna, who both looked a lot like Mitya.

There was Alyssa Vitalyevna's bribery compartment, an essential lifeline for anything she wanted done: stacks of candy boxes and sprat tins, rounds of caviar in glass and sealed brand lipsticks. No visit to the doctor, no government bureaucracy proceeding, nothing in life could be accomplished without a voluntary donation to the executor's family table. In her head, Alyssa Vitalyevna had a clear outline of what deed warranted what delicacy. It usually took her only a second to establish what to take with her to the government office or the dentist. Some more exquisite, particularly laborious occasions also required oiling with the liquids produced by Moscow's own distillery, Kristall, or, in more delicate cases still, foreign liquors. Alyssa Vitalyevna kept them in a separate compartment, as Mitya knew. The door to that compartment was locked with a key, to protect the precious spirits from Dmitriy Fyodorovich. When anyone mentioned the concealed alcohol, Dmitriy Fyodorovich always denied being interested. Instead, he complained that Alyssa Vitalyevna's love for corruption was the force driving the country into the ground. In response, she never hesitated to mention that her son-in-law sometimes came home very inebriated, "crawling on his eyebrows," as Alyssa Vitalyevna put it.

The prettiest things in Babushka's credenza were her perfume bottles and makeup boxes. Babushka used a lot of makeup; it was evident by the way her skin was always powdery pale, and her cheeks flushed with rouge. And she loved to smell nice. Her perfume bottles were numerous but old, and most of them contained a small splash of yellow liquid on the bottom. Mitya opened and smelled them, then applied the perfume to his skin and put droplets on his tongue to get a taste. They were all the same this way, and only burned his tongue.

What makeup she didn't carry in her pocketbook dated back to her younger years, maybe the years in which she appeared in the photographs. The boxes were lovely, with interesting pictures, but they had not aged well. Ones that were made from paper had wrinkled. The plastic ones were dirty, and their labels faded. The metallic parts had rusted through, sometimes sealed shut. Mitya opened powder cases and took in the stale, dusty aroma, though the remnants at the bottom were almost inexistent. The powder puffs had dirty stains on them and smelled musty. He wanted to try applying the powder but the odor put him off.

Mama's makeup was newer. She didn't have a lot of it, but what she had, Mitya didn't mind touching. The things she used herself were inside the bottom cabinet of the dresser in his parents' room. There were a few lipsticks and a compact powder with a dirty mirror that had been used enough for the metal tray to peep through the cake.

Mitya was most impressed by a blue plastic chest with a gold rim. His grandfather had received it as part of his official rations and gifted it to Yelena Viktorovna on her eighteenth birthday. It had everything: a palette of gray, blue, purple, and green eye shadows, cream concealers in different tones, a variety of cream blushes that could double as lipsticks. Mitya liked the two minuscule mascaras in black and brown best. His mother had barely used any, so the small black applicators were clean, and most of the little mounds of blush, eye shadow and lipstick were intact.

He decided to give it a try. He had not been planning, had not thought about it until that moment. But once the tidy pressed cakes of pigment were in front of him, it was apparent that he had to put them on his face.

Mitya had no idea how to apply makeup and sought to figure out what to do with each of the textures and colors. The eye makeup was intuitive: he put some blue and green in thick strokes on his upper eyelids and then darkened his lashes by holding the black mascara on the brush against them, gingerly, so as not to poke an eye out.

With a dusty-pink lipstick, Mitya covered his lips, connecting the lower to the upper in a thick line that disappeared as soon as he closed his mouth. The top lip was challenging: there were two little peaks at the top that he couldn't make even, so he kept adding more color until the new lip line was halfway toward his nostrils. It looked messy, but as Mitya stepped away from the mirror and squinted, he could see that his lips were now full, voluptuous.

He started to apply the rouge to his cheek with the applicator but soon realized it was much easier with his fingertips. Mitya dipped them in the paint and swept the sticky blush across the apples. The bright pink of his cheeks made him look like he had been running, and he liked the effortlessness of it.

Mitya took off the T-shirt he was wearing and threw it on the floor. Using his thumbs and index fingers, he grabbed at the flesh around his nipples and brought them forward slightly. They were small and pale—he was only five years old, after all— but reminded him of Mama's breasts, which he sometimes saw when she changed after work. He took off the sweatpants he was wearing, and then his socks and briefs, and threw them all into a pile on the floor, shaking his head and swaying his arms around, as if he were a beautiful, haughty lady.

What he saw in the mirror was not a boy or a girl; it was a woman. Mitya bent his back, put his hands on his hips, and turned around, sticking his butt out so that his outie thing was not reflected in the mirror anymore. He was a beautiful woman, independent and powerful.

Yelena Viktorovna came home a little earlier than her husband that day. They traveled from the factory together, but Dmitriy

Fyodorovich had gotten caught up chatting with their next-door neighbor Grishka about the events of the day. Grishka was a talkative man, and even Dmitriy Fyodorovich, who was not someone known for his diplomacy, could be ambushed for a good thirty minutes if Grishka was in the mood and smoking in the stairway enclosure. And now that there was a coup d'état and blockades all over the streets, Dmitriy Fyodorovich struck up the conversation first.

When she entered and saw Mitya in war paint, Yelena Viktorovna was first of all amazed at the level of artistry. She had never been one with an eye for makeup, but her five-year-old son's face looked more polished than even her colleague Lyudmila's—and Lyudmila took out her powder puff and mascara every twenty minutes or so.

Yelena Viktorovna was so impressed that she didn't even consider the deviancy of it all. But, intuitively, she knew she had to do something before Dmitriy Fyodorovich had had enough and returned to the apartment. So she rubbed the makeup off Mitya's face with soap and Dmitriy Fyodorovich's vodka. Mitya felt a sharp pain in his eyeballs, as if someone were poking them with a knife, and even thought for a second that the needle must have come out, it hurt so much. But he didn't mind. He was happy. He had become someone.

When Dmitriy Fyodorovich finally came home after his discussion with Grishka, Mitya listened in on his parents' conversation. In this way, he learned that he was not the only one going through changes that day. There was something called *putsch*, and people were putting barricades in the streets. Mitya knew only one meaning of the word *barricades*: Barricades was the name of a movie theater where Alyssa Vitalyevna sometimes let him join her and Dr. Khristofor Khristoforovich Kherentzis on their early afternoon dates. It was usually a fun outing: Khristofor Khristoforovich bought Mitya ice cream, and then they watched cartoons or children's films, or Indian films where people always danced.

Mitya couldn't figure out how people would be able to take the cinema apart and put it in the streets. He was concerned that his grandmother and her doctor would not have a place for dates anymore, and Mitya would not get his ice cream. Besides, Khristofor Khristoforovich was nice to sit next to. He smelled like tobacco and unfamiliar herbs, and Mitya liked inhaling that. But his parents were discussing the putsch so energetically that Mitya couldn't even tell if they liked it or not, if they agreed with each other or not. He wanted to wait until Alyssa Vitalyevna came back home, to ask her.

Alyssa Vitalyevna announced her arrival by proclaiming that she had been to the barricades. That made Mitya stop worrying: surely his grandmother would not let anything happen to her beloved cinema. But for some reason Yelena Viktorovna was worried.

"Mama, why did you go?" she asked Alyssa Vitalyevna. "There are tanks and it's dangerous."

"I can't let them take over my country now that it's on the precipice of something good," Alyssa Vitalyevna replied.

Now that he had stopped worrying about the movie theater, Mitya had to start worrying about the whole country.

His father and grandmother did not seem to agree in their opinions of the situation, and they started arguing, talking about someone named Yeltsin, although they couldn't agree if he was a president or not, and something abbreviated with the letters GKChP. Mitya had no idea what it was, but he knew that ChP was short for chrezvychaynoye proishestviye, an emergency, like when there was a big car crash. Alyssa Vitalyevna also said that there was a ChP whenever Mitya wet himself.

At the dinner table, everyone kept throwing glances at the ballet still on the TV, to see when the emergency news report would come on again. Mitya's father and grandmother kept bickering.

"An old communist like your late husband would never approve of Yeltsin," Dmitriy Fyodorovich said to Alyssa Vitalyevna.

"You are a lumpen lacking perspective, and you cannot even imagine the breadth of views that my late husband possessed," she responded.

"I will go shopping for supplies early tomorrow morning before work," Yelena Viktorovna said. "Food is always the first to go. I should buy buckwheat and oats, things that keep well. Candles and matches too."

Mitya thought that if tanks were in the streets, people were arguing, and there was no TV and no food, then, perhaps, everything that had existed in the world before would be no more. And he was right—to a point. In a few months, the USSR, the country in which Mitya was born, ceased to exist. Now he lived in Russia.

TWO

Quickly the fairy tale is told, but slowly the deed is done.

So, there was this villain called Koschei, and he swallowed a needle and couldn't be killed.

Back in his day, everyone was living within an egg. It wasn't a regular egg: it was a golden egg laid by an ambitious little duck that belonged to an elderly rural couple. The couple was likely more hungry than curious, so they didn't try to investigate what it was that made the duck lay golden eggs. All they wanted was to try to get to the delicious yolk and the creamy white.

But no one could break this egg: neither the man nor the woman. So the couple sat and stared vacantly into space, resigned to their fate, apathetic, listless. And when they were least expecting it, the touch of a mouse's tail caused the egg to fall and the shell to break.

The man and the woman were devastated that they had no say in the egg's demise and couldn't even partake of its contents. They

29

started crying and cried so much, and for so long, they didn't even notice that there was a whole world inside of the egg. As they cried, this world became one with their world, and chaos ensued. Their village burned to the ground, and their granddaughter hanged herself from grief over the surrounding misery. They didn't notice the whole realm descend into darkness, as poverty and suicides permeated the landscape and indistinctive, quiet men robbed the land until nothing was left. The couple stopped crying only when they realized that there was a way to use the duck to alleviate their hunger. They took her and killed her, put her on a spit, and started roasting her over the charred remains of their village hall.

This was when Koschei, full of villainous thoughts and despicable aspirations, happened to be passing by. He smelled the delicious tang of fatty duck skin roasting, of course, but being a respectful villain, didn't ask about it.

"Come closer," a tiny voice suddenly said.

There was no one around the barbecue at that point, so it took Koschei a while until he finally figured out that it was the duck speaking to him from its spit.

"I know that you are of the needle, and I want to help. You must ask the elderly couple for my head and heart and eat them. Then you will be the luckiest of all."

"But I don't want to eat you after we've had a conversation," Koschei countered. "I only want to eat the meat of animals I didn't know personally and never saw killed."

"If you don't partake, I'll burn to a crisp right now, and the elderly couple will starve to death," the duck threatened.

Koschei knew that denying the duck the agency to be eaten was not nice of him. He asked the couple for the duck's head and heart, and though secretly they knew those were the best parts, they agreed, because you're not supposed to mess with villains.

So Koschei ate the heart and the head. He was done with the meat and was now chewing on the beak cartilage. What would happen now? he wondered. Perhaps he'd become a tsar, because that was what always happened around him at a certain point: everyone became a tsar. Perhaps he'd start belching money: he'd seen something of the kind on TV, where a bespectacled duck swam around in coins.

But nothing of the sort happened. Instead, Koschei noticed that he was now becoming drawn to women's gowns. His patterns of hoarding, a known necessity for the Koschei family, changed too: he'd fall for absolutely useless objects, which somehow seemed beautiful. Nothing of value interested him anymore.

The main purpose of any self-respecting Koschei is to begin to kidnap young female royalty, the tsarevnas. Our Koschei was told how to spy on tsarevnas, how to tell them bad things that would make them doubt themselves, how to make them fall in love with him so he could bring them to his dungeon and stack them for hoarding purposes. This was what every other, older Koschei, already worthy of being called tsar, was doing.

But now that accumulating value was not one of his goals, young Koschei realized that he did not want to say mean things to tsarevnas. Instead, he wanted to be more like them, with their beautiful dresses, ruby lips, and emerald lids.

And that's when young Koschei knew he was in trouble.

3

By 1992, Dmitriy Fyodorovich had been laid off from the Rubin factory. Despite rumors that the workers would have a chance to buy it out for themselves, it had been privatized and was doing worse with each passing day. To add insult to his injury, Yelena Viktorovna was still employed. And because Alyssa Vitalyevna led a vibrant social life elsewhere, it was mostly Dmitriy Fyodorovich and Mitya stuck together at home.

Dmitriy Fyodorovich's late older brother had left behind a perfectly manly, well-developed male heir, Vovka, and Dmitriy Fyodorovich wanted to accomplish the same. But he understood swiftly that Mitya was not growing up to be the son he had wished to have. Mitya did not like playing with the three toy guns that his father had bought for him. Once, Dmitriy Fyodorovich gave his son a toy tank. It was an accurate, scale model of the tank that he had operated in the Afghan War. Dmitriy Fyodorovich found it a week later, behind the fridge, covered in dust, next to a rotting chicken drumstick. Behind the fridge was where Dmitriy Fyodorovich kept his extra money so that Yelena Viktorovna wouldn't find it. That was also the place where Mitya deposited unwanted food and toys.

Mitya did not like helping Papa with his chores or participating in his pastimes. Once given a hammer, he immediately hurt his pinkie and cried for a whole hour without Mama to comfort him, getting on Papa's nerves. Once, Dmitriy Fyodorovich poured some beer into a glass for him, and Mitya broke down in tears after tasting the bitter liquid. Another time Papa took him to a soccer match, the army's sports team, CSKA, against the visiting Shakhter from Donetsk. Mitya feasted on the sunflower seed shells and cigarette butts that the large scary men spat out, and then started vomiting halfway through the second halftime. Because Dmitriy Fyodorovich had to hold his son over the squat toilet as he threw up, they missed Papa's team's two defining goals. CSKA was leading, and he wasn't there to see it. When father and son returned from the restrooms, there were twenty minutes of the game left. In these twenty minutes, CSKA was defeated three to four, and it was quite clear that it was all Mitya's fault.

After that, whenever Dmitriy Fyodorovich asked his son to join him in yet another endeavor, Mitya made a sad face, and Papa proclaimed that he was a devchonka, a girl.

If Mama, Babushka, or anyone else was around, he would add: "My son is an idiot, an invalid, a sissy."

But there were some advantages to the situation. The fact that his mother-in-law had made his son mentally incapacitated presented Dmitriy Fyodorovich with constant power over her. Alyssa Vitalyevna liked complaining of how arrogant and ridiculous her son-in-law was, how unworthy of her higher-class, educated daughter. But whenever she started, he reminded her of the time she almost killed his only child. The pangs of guilt forced Alyssa Vitalyevna to her room.

Now that father and son were stuck together, Mitya's deviance, ripening, swelling, was too hard to ignore. When Dmitriy Fyodorovich walked in on Mitya drawing pictures on the kitchen table, he saw little animals in dresses frolicking on the pages of his drawing pad. The drawings were meticulous, but so unmanly. When passersby in the park on the weekend asked Mitya who he wanted to become when he grew up, Dmitriy Fyodorovich heard his son respond, "Alla Pugacheva." She was the country's biggest pop star and, unforgivably, a woman, all curls and kaftans.

And Mitya cried too much. He cried when he fell and scraped a knee. He cried when he didn't want to eat soup. He cried when he saw war films. He cried when he saw fairy tale movies. He cried when he saw cartoons.

"Devchonka!" Papa growled again when he saw Mitya—before he even had a chance to find out what unmanly activity his son was engrossed with at a given time. The word *devchonka* was everything to Mitya. It sounded like a magical spell, like something that was not to be said out loud. And once his father, that giant with his booming voice, pronounced the truth, there was no way to back away from it.

"Devchonka," Mitya whispered whenever he put on makeup.

The older Mitya got, the more Devchonka became a part of his life. He quickly learned that his dressing up was not a universally admired thing. So he mostly became Devchonka when he stayed at home alone, and then made sure to remove every trace of her from his body, using soap and vodka.

———

Seasons changed, the country changed. A little before his eighth birthday, in 1993, Mitya heard gunshots outside and a woman in the opposite building spent the whole night swearing at Yeltsin from her window. Alyssa Vitalyevna and Dmitriy Fyodorovich fought about him again. The next day, they showed the white house where the parliament sat on TV and it was blackened on the top, but Mitya did not understand why. It was as though the building's mascara got smudged.

A month before Mitya was eight, he started school. He was older than all the other children in first grade. The school was public but was considered better than most: they boasted in-depth foreign-language classes. Mitya was eligible based on address, but the trick was to get into the best class with the best teacher. Bribes were out of the question; the family's income had been severely depleted since the collapse of the USSR since the new government undertook various financial measures. But Dr. Khristofor Khristoforovich Kherentzis's little niece was going to that school, so he asked her parents to talk to the principal about admitting Mitya to a good class.

As his own grandchildren were already teenagers, no one could deny him the right to get a good education for the smallest ersatz grandson that he had. Besides, from the few times that Alyssa Vitalyevna had taken Mitya with her to Khristofor

Khristoforovich's relatives' Greek parties, everyone knew the timid little boy. He was pale and scrawny, unlike their beautiful sun-kissed children with dimples in their elbows. But there was something angelic about Mitya's blond curls, and the sad way he looked at everyone.

The Greek community and, in particular, its women did not enjoy the fact that the non-Greek Alyssa Vitalyevna was threatening Khristofor Khristoforovich's blissful widowhood. But they did feel pangs of affection for the outsider child. The Greek women talked behind Alyssa Vitalyevna's back and they fed Mitya more and more khachapuri smothered in cheese as if to atone for their intolerance.

Although his acceptance to the school's leading class was made through the systems of nepotism, Mitya was still a charity case. Most of the time, Mitya's classmates pretended he did not exist. Their homeroom teacher, Tatiana Ivanovna, did the same. Mitya's parents did not give her fancy gifts for her birthday; they were not friends with the principal; they didn't come to any of the parent-teacher meetings. Tatiana Ivanovna barely mentioned his name during roll call. She never failed to call out the Nariyan twins, who came before him on the alphabetical list, and Orlanova, after him. The Nariyan twins came from a flower trade family and gave great discounts. Orlanova's aunt was a teacher in the attached middle school.

The only person at school who never failed to notice Mitya was the decrepit custodian, Semenovna, who took to washing the floors on the ground floor at the same moment classes were over, but that was mostly because Mitya had a habit of loitering in the way of her broom.

Mitya was absent from the class photos for the first three years of school: it was as if he never existed at all. He missed the first time by accident and, as Tatiana Ivanovna was distributing the school photographs to those who had paid for them, peeked at the glossy portraits that his classmates received. Everyone was so beautiful: girls in expensive, puffy dresses or crisp blouses, boys in miniature suits and bow ties. In the following years, he purposely avoided the days when the photographer came. Mitya stood in front of the mirror in his boy clothes, a white turtleneck a few sizes too big and the itchy gray sweater with an X-pattern. He saw that he was ugly, poor, and not worthy of the class photo.

His memories of everything that happened during classes were dim too. He was too shy to read aloud or answer the teacher's questions in class and got bad grades. He had no friends. But the life that he had back at home was boundless. Mitya was left to his own devices once Papa left to look for a new job, Mama went to the factory, and Babushka went to the hospital. Dr. Khristofor Khristoforovich Kherentzis helped her get a position as a receptionist, after he assisted in firing one of the original receptionists for being mean to Alyssa Vitalyevna. Money was tighter than ever, and Alyssa Vitalyevna reveled in the fact of her increased participation in the family's income. She never failed to flaunt the fact in front of her unemployed son-in-law.

Once Mitya realized that the female garments found at home were not glamorous enough for his aspirations, he opted to create new outfits from scratch. At first, he glued things together using the skills from home economics class in school. Later, Mitya took advantage of Mama's sewing kit and sewing machine. He made utterly unwearable garments, spoiled most of the material and torn clothes he had stolen from the home economics classroom or found by the dumpster. But little by little, Mitya got better.

Because Mama and Babushka sometimes worked changing hours, they got to see him dressed as a woman a few times. Mama was not happy, but she didn't say much. She asked Mitya to be more careful with some of her lipsticks because he was leaving teeth marks on them. She didn't care what he did as long as he kept busy. As the Russian saying goes: "Whatever the child may do lest they hang themselves." Sometimes, while sitting at work, Yelena Viktorovna wondered whether, maybe, Mitya had hanged himself in her absence. She wanted to call home, but a calmness of not knowing overtook her, and she put the phone back down and smiled into the distance.

Babushka was more sympathetic. She had been struggling with the fact that her grandson was becoming homely with age: gone was the tender toddler she had known before the needle accident. Though it was too early for puberty to harden the boy's looks, he had somehow managed to become unappealing: like a skinny mouse bathed in soup. When she saw him in makeup and girl clothes that he must have made himself, she saw a pretty girl. The pastiness of a sickly winter child disappeared; his cheeks were now rosy, his lips plump and red, and his eyes well defined and wicked. Alyssa Vitalyevna had always had a weakness for the bohemian, and now she saw that her daughter's little offspring had the inclinations of an artist. Was it possible he could become an actor? Or a singer? Most importantly, he wouldn't follow in his father's proletarian footsteps.

She did not want to be too encouraging. After all, it was probably a phase, and it would pass once Mitya found a more fitting outlet for his talents. She made a mental note to ask Cleopatra about that woman who gave singing lessons to someone else's grandson. Alyssa Vitalyevna told Mitya to be careful not to appear like that in front of his father and gave him a book of Pushkin's poetry, her answer to everything.

———

The Rubin factory closed. Yelena Viktorovna did not stay unemployed for long. She asked the new factory owner if he needed a housekeeper, then ironed some shirts in front of his wife, and was hired. The hardest part was telling this to Alyssa Vitalyevna, who felt so humiliated by her daughter's downshifting, it would be a year before she could discuss it with her.

And then, finally, after two years of looking for a job, Dmitriy Fyodorovich found one, too. Or rather, Alyssa Vitalyevna found it for him, when he finally consented to her bribery schemes, which were even more effective in the new Russia than in the old country. The family had to skimp to afford them but a few bottles of champagne and imported whiskey later, Dmitriy Fyodorovich was again gainfully employed, through a kindness from a cosmonaut's ex-wife's nephew, who had recently opened an upscale supermarket and was looking for day guards.

The job kept Dmitriy Fyodorovich from seeing Devchonka. But it was bound to happen one day. Mitya was nine, and it was a September afternoon in 1995. The supermarket was shut down before closing time because of a power outage. Imported

French chickens, German cakes and pizzas, and Norwegian fish fillets were thawing in the freezers, so the manager made the employees buy everything perishable at half price. Dmitriy Fyodorovich came home with bags full of fancy food and found his son dressed as Ariel the mermaid from the foreign cartoon.

Mitya was wearing Babushka's red cardigan on his head, instead of a wig. He had on Mama's blue slacks, secured with a ribbon at the end to resemble a fishtail. On his chest was a bra of Yelena Viktorovna's that Mitya had enhanced with candy wrappers in different shades of blue—sky-blue Mishkas, navy Belochkas, snowflake-covered Snezhoks. He had also attached some red-and-white Rakovie Sheyki because they had crawfish on them. A mermaid needed sea creatures as her friends. But most importantly, Mitya's face was painted to the fullest, with bright red lips and green-and-blue eyelids.

When he saw Mitya, Dmitriy Fyodorovich did not drop his bags in surprise, cinematically. It wasn't a surprise at all: more like the worst that he could fathom coming to life. So instead, he held on to the bags and came at his son. He started hitting Mitya, the handles of the bags still wrapped around his wrists. It seemed, for the moment, that beating the femininity out of his son was possible. One more punch, and the needle that had crippled Mitya, and now also made him a deviant, would become detached and fall out on the floor between them.

Mitya could feel two frozen-solid chicken carcasses and a couple of cardboard boxes attack him from the sides as Papa beat him on the head.

"Suka, you want to be a devchonka? You paint your face like a blyad? You want to shame me? You're a pidoras?" Dmitriy

Fyodorovich bombarded Mitya with questions for which his small son didn't have answers.

It was the first time Papa had beaten him. It was also the first time Mitya had ever heard the words *blyad* and *pidoras*. He had no idea what they meant but suspected that it was something wrong. Mitya had never seen his father this angry before: he had never been a pleasant man, but mostly his temper was reserved. He had never beaten Yelena Viktorovna and steered clear of Alyssa Vitalyevna.

The beating hurt. It felt simultaneously like scalding-hot water and a heavy winter frost, like falling off the swing at the playground and running out of breath on a chilly day in autumn. Mitya held his breath and listened to the metal tinkling inside his head—was it the needle?—as each of his father's fists landed on the boy's head. It seemed like Mitya was becoming deaf and could only feel everything around him through the pain in his skull. Mitya wondered if he would hear the slight fall of the needle on the floor when it finally got detached.

"Petukh pozorniy," Papa spat at him when both of the bags had torn and spilled their insides out. Dmitriy Fyodorovich had let off steam, but not anger. It was still simmering inside him, and the punches brought no relief. He stopped and pointed at the mess on the floor: "Now clean this up."

Mitya picked up the fancy frozen food and felt a hot numbness where Papa had been hitting him. There was no needle to be found anywhere around him. It had protected him: maybe the pain was there, but the beating had stopped, and he had survived.

As he put everything in the freezer, Mitya wondered if what Papa had called him—"petukh pozorniy," a shameful rooster—had anything to do with the frozen chickens. When Papa left, Mitya took the chickens, still frozen but a little thawed out on the outside so that his fingers left indentations in the top layer beneath the plastic. He kissed the dead birds' carcasses one by one and left traces of lipstick on their white striped packaging.

───

Yelena Viktorovna was upset that Dmitriy Fyodorovich had let his fists fly free but did not intervene. It was not her fault and not her place. She was the best mother that she could be, but her son was not turning out as her husband had hoped, or as she had hoped—although she wasn't sure what it was they had hoped for.

A month or so after Dmitriy Fyodorovich's attack, Yelena Viktorovna took Mitya to the market, and he liked it. It smelled like blood and fermented cabbage, his two favorite things in the world, and the ceiling was so high above him, Mitya felt like he had lost the ground beneath his feet when he stared upward for too long. He felt small and insignificant.

Mitya saw many dead animals at the market. There were chickens, and bigger chickens, and the largest chickens of all. "Look, Mama, these chickens are huge," he said, pointing at them. Mama giggled. "They are cows, silly." There were also skinned rabbits with furry feet, which, Yelena Viktorovna explained, vendors kept to show the buyers that the smaller corpses were in fact rabbits, not cats. There were chebureki, juicy, deep-fried bubbly pies filled with meat. They smelled great, and Mitya wanted to try them, but Mama refused: they could be made from dogs. She didn't have any reason to think that they were. But that was the same excuse Alyssa Vitalyevna had given when Yelena Viktorovna was a child and needed to be lured away from street meat.

And then Mitya saw a pig's head. It was pink, with touches of red where the air had dried it out, and where the blood vessels appeared through the translucent skin. Its hairs were sparse, thin and white like an ancient man's, and on its lips was a smirk. The eyes were half-closed as if the pig were napping, eyelashes long and white, some crusty goo around them: dried tears, or gunk that one has to pick out from the corners of one's eyes in the morning. The pig's head looked like it belonged to a human, only a deformed, strange human, who had been given the porcine features as punishment by a witch.

Mitya stopped in front of the pig's head and stared at it. His mother did not notice at first, and proceeded to the cheese stalls to the right. They couldn't afford the expensive handmade cheese and had to stick to the factory Rossiyskiy from the grocery store.

When she noticed that Mitya had lagged, Yelena Viktorovna came back and waited for him patiently. She hoped he wouldn't get attached to something and ask her to buy it. They'd gotten soup bones, but the rest of the meat would have to come from the store: the market fare was way too expensive. She watched the butcher, dark-haired, perhaps Georgian or Armenian—Muslims wouldn't be handling pork, would they?—chop up a rib cage, wipe his hands with dry rags, and accept money from an older woman in a fur coat. Yelena Viktorovna squirmed. Animals, no sense of hygiene at all.

They stayed by the pig's head for a few minutes. It took Mitya a while to muster up the courage to feel the head with his hand. The skin felt human, too, only thicker. Mitya became braver and touched the bumpy snout and the droopy, torn ears. He did it with such ravishment, mouth agape, eyes as big as five-ruble coins.

"I want to take it home," Mitya said to his mother.

Just what she feared. Yelena Viktorovna shook her head, took hold of his hand, and pulled on it: "Poydem."

Mitya resisted.

"I want it," he repeated. It was rare for him to be this assertive, but the beckoning of the pig's head was too strong to deny.

The butcher, who had finished his transaction, turned to them. Yelena Viktorovna was prepared to be coldly polite, or maybe even rude if the man persisted. Georgians could be talkative, persuasive, that was why there were so many of them at the marketplace. She firmly held Mitya's hand, as if ready for a standoff.

Instead, the man smiled widely.

"I see that the boy likes the pig's head," he said, with a heavy accent. "I'll give it to you free of charge!"

As he wrapped the head, he laughed heartily and loudly relayed the story to his friends from the neighboring stalls.

Yelena Viktorovna thanked him, dryly, not ready to trust the unexpected kindness, aware that any minute she could be asked to give something in return.

All the way home, on the trolleybus, Mitya kept touching the yellowish flesh of the pig and comparing it to the rough surface of the parchment wrapped around it. The feeling it gave him was powerful, yet not erotic, akin to what he felt when he admired himself in the mirror in makeup and women's clothes—a loving admiration for texture. But also, for death.

He played with it at home, keeping it in the fridge. Each time Alyssa Vitalyevna discovered it there, she let out a scream. When the head had wilted enough to render it a dangerous toy for Mitya, Yelena Viktorovna made kholodets from it for a whole week. Dmitriy Fyodorovich ate it with horseradish, Alyssa Vitalyevna with mustard, and Mitya with a sullen fascination. He was, after all, mourning a beloved friend.

4

When Mitya was ten years old, in the spring of 1997, Vovka, Dmitriy Fyodorovich's nephew, came to live with the family after having served in the Chechen War. He was the son of Uncle Seryozha, Dmitriy Fyodorovich's brother, who had died in the Afghan War.

When the First Chechen War started in late 1994, Vovka was eighteen. He had been conscripted into the army and undergoing training. He was stationed in the South of the Russian Federation, close enough to the war zone, and in the spring of 1995 their infantry regiment was dispatched to Grozny, which had been finally taken by the federal forces after two and a half months of intense fighting. The city looked exactly how one would imagine a war-torn city to look: with rotting corpses everywhere and no one to dispose of them. Even though Vovka was full of fervor to avenge his father's death and fight the insurgents, the misery that surrounded him filled him with absolute terror. This terror permeated everything and everyone around him, even the seasoned fighters who had survived Afghanistan earlier and now tried their best to protect the newly arrived draftees from immediate danger. And it worked, Vovka made it through one whole year before his wartime was cut short by an unfortunate chain of events.

It was on a gray March day in 1996 that Vovka and some of the more experienced servicemen were crossing into a village in the Achkhoy-Martan region in a militsia car on a patrolling mission. As they approached, they saw a Chechen man praying on a rug, his feet in socks raised to the sky, his head facing Mecca. There was something suspicious about him to the seasoned fighters, and the men decided to investigate him. Vovka lost the coin toss, and he wanted to have a smoke anyway, so he got out of the car. It took no more than twenty seconds. Maybe thirty. As he lit his cigarette, the insurgents appeared out of nowhere and started shooting at them. It was later established that the three men inside the car were immediately struck and killed. However, when a bullet hit the almost-empty gas tank, the vehicle was engulfed in flames. Like in the Jean-Claude Van Damme movies, Vovka thought. He tried to save his comrades, not realizing that they were dead already. He was severely burned, lost his right arm, spent months in the hospital but pulled through, and was shipped back to Moscow. A few months after his demobilization, it was established that his mother, Aunt Sveta, could not take care of Vovka alone. At Mitya's home, someone in the family could always be around when Vovka had screaming fits during the night or when he needed someone to blast him with ice water during the day to stop the agitation. Vovka stayed in the living room with Mitya, and they had to sleep on the same sofa, head to toe, which made Mitya feel sick because

Vovka's feet smelled notoriously bad. The ripe socks he changed only once a week always ended up in places where Mitya had to pick them up.

Mitya was not used to being around someone all the time, and so this intrusion made him nervous. Vovka barely slept, and whenever he did, he had terrible nightmares. So whenever Mitya woke up at night to go to the bathroom, Vovka was either going out or returning from a cigarette break on the staircase. He wore the same dirty pair of sweatpants and a white sleeveless shirt. The only thing that remained of Vovka's arm was an awkward lump of flesh with stitching across, which was always in sight. It was always a curious sight to see Vovka smoke, as the end of his cigarette flickered red next to his scorched skin on the right side of his neck and face.

"Saved my life once," Vovka always said about his habit. "Will save it again."

Vovka didn't have to go anywhere. He refused to apply to universities because everyone there would be "sissies and botaniks who would never understand him." And unlike Dmitriy Fyodorovich, Vovka did not drink. So there was no hope that he would leave in the evening and return later, barely conscious.

It became problematic for Mitya to dress up and be Devchonka. With Vovka's arrival, there was never a time when Mitya was alone. Each day was the same: Mitya came back home after school to find Vovka in his shirt and pants sitting on the sofa. Sometimes he saw him earlier, by the window on the stairs, smoking. His cousin greeted him with a dull nod.

———

Summer vacation came, school was over, and Vovka and Mitya didn't spend a minute apart. Mitya had nowhere to go, and neither did Vovka. He didn't notice Mitya. His eyes were glassy, his stare absent. When Mitya asked Mama and Babushka about the vacancy in him, they shushed him and replied, their voices lowered: "Chechnya."

Vovka did not talk to Mitya outside of the scope of things related to his daily survival in their home, like when he needed his younger cousin to open up the sofa into a bed or heat some food on the stove.

"Vovka, tell me about Chechnya," Mitya asked Vovka one day as they were eating milk noodle soup.

"What do you want to know?" Vovka asked without looking up, as he spooned the murky liquid from his bowl.

"Why are you always so quiet? Mama and Babushka say it's because of Chechnya."

Vovka snickered. It was not a good snicker, and Mitya thought that his cousin might punch him.

"This isn't life here, Mitya. My comrades died, and I wish I died with them. I couldn't save them and I can't avenge them. Like I couldn't avenge my father. The evil won."

Mitya knew about the car fire, how his uncle Seryozha died in Afghanistan, how his and Vovka's grandfather was a Great Patriotic War veteran. Dmitriy Fyodorovich had told him about Grandfather defeating Hitler, and how he fought the mujahideen in Afghanistan, but by the time the Chechen War started he had already pulled away and never explained anything to Mitya. Mitya wasn't sure who the evil in question even was.

"Who killed your comrades, Vovka?" Mitya asked.

"The Chekhs," Vovka answered. "The Chechen insurgents. Who else, Russians?"

Vovka thought that his little cousin was incredibly naive for ten years of age.

"Did they want to hurt you?"

"What do you think, Mitya? It's war."

"But why did you go to the war if it's so dangerous? You could have died like your father."

Mitya's eyes were blue and innocent.

"Did I have a choice? Chechnya is part of our homeland. I had to protect it. That's what men in our family do. Fight terrorists, fight fascists."

Mitya knew that their grandfather was the only one of three brothers to return from the Great Patriotic War. The men in their family did not seem to be winning a lot.

"Do women fight in the war, Vovka?" Mitya asked his cousin before going to bed later that day.

"Not really, bratish, they're usually too gentle," Vovka answered, leaving for another smoke break.

Mitya resolved that he would stay out of the war along with the women, then.

That night he couldn't sleep. He noticed that Vovka was moving in place, bending his legs, which seemed to be arrested by a tremor, breathing heavily and groaning. Mitya thought that he was dying, so he jumped up from the sofa and at his cousin, and started shaking him with all his might.

"Get off me, debil," Vovka yelped. He had almost climaxed, thinking of his high school sweetheart, Mashka. He shook Mitya off to the floor with his healthy arm.

"Are you okay, Vovka?" Mitya asked from below.

"I'm all right," Vovka spat through his teeth as he got up from beneath the duvet they shared. He took his pants off the armchair and walked out of the room. It was dark, but a large slice of moonlight fell upon the bookshelves. As Vovka passed through there, Mitya saw that something was bulging inside his briefs. A gun!

Mitya sat on their bed until Vovka came back. He smelled like cigarettes.

"Vovka, I'm sorry, I didn't mean to scare you," Mitya told him.

Vovka did not respond; he took his pants off and lay down. He hadn't washed his hand, and now the smell, eggy, thick, lulled him back to sleep.

Mitya couldn't fall back asleep for a long time afterward and kept listening, but Vovka was silent and then started to snore loudly.

———

In June, some of Vovka's school friends were on summer break from university and Vovka was invited to a gathering. He didn't want to go and felt self-conscious about his arm. But Dmitriy Fyodorovich insisted that getting out of the apartment would do him good. The meetup was at a café on a sunny afternoon, and Vovka showered, shaved, drenched himself in cologne, and planned to get a haircut on his way. He put on Dmitriy Fyodorovich's suit, which was a bit big and hung loosely where his right arm was supposed to be. The empty sleeve bothered him. Vovka didn't want to look like someone who went around the metro trains begging for money. But if he turned around with the sleeve behind him, the way the striped fabric blended concealed his amputation. He almost looked handsome. He practiced his entrance and imagined how Mashka's face would cheer up when she saw him.

When the front door closed behind Vovka, Mitya was deliriously happy for him to be leaving: finally, he had the apartment to himself and was able to dress up as Devchonka.

That day, he would be Madonna, the singer. He put on the tape of her songs that he had bought at the kiosk near their building and walked flailing his arms around to "Vogue." He acted dramatically to "Take a Bow" and moved around like a sexy robot to "Human Nature." Mitya used his grandmother's curling iron on his hair, blackened his brows with mascara, and put on some red lipstick together with brown eye shadow to make his look more goth. He put on Mama's bra and filled it with pieces of bread so that it looked like he had perky breasts. He finished off the look by putting on some dozhdik, long thin strands of tinfoil that he had preserved after the New Year's celebration. It was exhilarating.

Way before Mitya had had enough with his dress-up and way before he had expected anyone to come home, the doorbell rang. Mitya sneaked closer to it, as softly as possible on bare feet, and crawled onto the stool nearby to look through the peephole. In it, he saw Vovka, disheveled and dirty. He was keeled over, holding himself against the wall with his left arm.

Mitya didn't know what else to do, so he opened the door. Vovka entered, pivoting from wall to wall, and with him came in vodka vapors and the smell of throw-up. Dmitriy Fyodorovich's suit was torn and covered in something yellow and disgusting, and from the top of Vovka's head, a trickle of blood descended onto his white shirt.

"Vovka, what happened?" Mitya asked as he closed the door.

"Bratish, they're sluts," Vovka answered and plunged to the floor. "They're dating Chekhs. My Mashka . . ."

Vovka had entered the café as he'd practiced, and Mashka's face had indeed cheered up when she saw him. Her hair was shorter and more blond, and her eyeliner heavier, but she was still his Mashka. She fussed all around Vovka as if he were a hero, and it didn't seem to matter that his arm was missing.

But then, her boyfriend showed up. He was a Chechen guy in expensive jeans and a T-shirt that hugged his two biceps. His skin was tanned, uncommon for a Chechen person, and he kept on talking about going on vacation to the Emirates with the family. His father must have been one of those city Chechens who do nothing and sell guns to the insurgents back home. As nausea came with the memory, Vovka tried to crawl toward the bathroom but instead painfully threw up into Alyssa Vitalyevna's slippers.

Dmitriy Fyodorovich showed up drunk often enough for Mitya to know that the best thing to do was to put the drunk person in the bathtub and give him a cold shower. Besides, Papa did this to Vovka whenever he started raving soberly about the horrors of Chechnya. So Mitya grasped Vovka's only hand and started pulling him to the bathroom. It wasn't easy, but after a while, he was able to get his cousin through the corridor. Vovka threw up once more, in front of Mitya's parents' bedroom door. But once in the bathroom, he was easier to get into the bathtub.

Back in the café, Vovka had tried to stay patient. So, Mashka didn't wait for him—they weren't engaged or anything, that was fine by him. She'd decided to become an inkpot, to have a Chechen's black khuy dip into her. Who could judge, Russia was a free country. But when her Chekh decided to pay for the whole table, in the end, Vovka lost it. There were four girls and four guys around the table, including the Chekh. The guys could pay for the girls. He didn't have to treat them all like he was their benevolent master. Like they owed him something.

Vovka jumped him and hit him with his only arm. It was surprisingly easy, as if his body were whole again. But then Vovka realized that the ease of movement stemmed from the Chekh not defending himself. When the Chekh finally threw a punch, it was precise, masterful. Vovka spat out a tooth. With the next one, he felt his brow split. In the background, Mashka shrieked. "He is a boxer," someone said.

Vovka did not remember leaving the café. Had anyone tried to go after him? Had Mashka cried? He recalled buying a bottle of vodka and walking home. He remembered buying a second bottle of vodka. It fell on the floor in the archway leading to their building's courtyard and broke.

Mitya turned on the water and started pouring it down on Vovka. The gray suit gradually darkened as it became covered with water, and the vomit was washing off bit by bit. As Mitya poured, Vovka's gaze became clearer. He asked Mitya to unbutton his shirt, then removed his clothes one by one until he was left in the bathtub wearing only his socks and his briefs.

Suddenly, Vovka's eyes went from vacant to evil, concentrated.

He noticed that his cousin had colorful makeup smudged all over his face and that he was wearing a bra. He snatched Mitya by the hair.

"Why are you wearing makeup?" he asked.

Mitya did not know what to answer. Vovka's stare, aimed at him, was horrifying.

"Do you want to look like a devchonka?"

Vovka felt the rage again. White-hot, scalding. Everything he loved, everything he fought for in the war had been spoiled, corrupted, taken away. He slid his arm behind Mitya's back, and with all his might forced his little cousin into the bathtub. His back was against the drain, so the water was not going anywhere, and Mitya found himself touching the cold, stinky water beneath Vovka.

Vovka pushed Mitya off himself to where his feet were in the tub, and Mitya could smell the wet hair on his legs and his wet socks. Vovka raised his hips above the water while propping himself up on his shoulders against the edge of the bathtub, and pulled his briefs down with his one hand. His thing came out, large, pink, hard, and Mitya felt the smell of his body enter the air.

"You've seen this, bratish?" Vovka asked Mitya as he grabbed him by the neck and pushed Mitya down toward his pipiska. "So, you want to be a devchonka?"

Mitya's face was a couple of centimeters away from the thing. The odor coming off it was unpleasant, and he tried to hold his breath.

"Mashka won't have it, she's got enough Chechen khuy," Vovka groaned. "But you will, right, Mitya?"

It seemed to Vovka as if he were watching himself from above. He felt desire take over his every remaining limb, and though his little cousin was not an object worthy of such excitement, he was the only option available.

"Sosi, Mitya," he said. "Suck it. Or I will tell your parents what you do. I'll tell them you're a rooster."

———

The vodka fumes evaporated from Vovka's blood and breath over the next day, as he slept until the afternoon. There was no yellow bile in the basin Alyssa Vitalyevna had put beneath the sofa where Mitya and Vovka both slept. Vovka's dreams were, as usual, ridden with anxiety and claustrophobia. Mitya's were worse.

Over the next few days, Vovka didn't seem to notice his younger cousin. He tried to avoid looking at him, out of guilt, but also out of fear that the soft girlish face might look attractive to him now.

Mitya wanted to escape Vovka's presence even more than before. His throat was sore, his jaw ached, and his body went numb whenever he smelled Vovka's fetid warmth as he collapsed into shallow sleep each night. After Vovka had fallen asleep, Mitya took a book and went to read it in the bathroom, inside the empty bathtub, his bare feet against the hollow enamel. It was the same place where it all happened, and yet it was also the safest, somehow.

Vovka had not touched him again. He looked at Mitya rarely, and his stare was glazed, gray eyes clouded with something dissolute. Everything seemed to fall back into place, slowly but surely. At times, Mitya started wondering if the scene in the bathroom was a product of his imagination or a nightmare. The bruises inside his throat had healed, his jaw didn't ache anymore, and nothing kept him connected to that night—except for the burning inside his rib cage that Mitya felt whenever Vovka's leg rubbed against his in sleep.

Sometimes Mitya woke up in the night and noticed Vovka convulse beneath the sheets. He didn't want to be kind to his cousin anymore or worry about him dying, so he watched him, pretending to be asleep. Vovka groaned and moaned and then, in a few minutes, went silent, wiping his hand on his thigh. Mitya recognized the noises and the stickiness of the liquid when he touched the spot on the sofa where Vovka's hand had been. It was the same pearly whiteness from the bathroom. So it must have happened, Mitya thought. But his cousin didn't mean it. He was drunk. He probably didn't understand what he was doing.

THREE

As soon as young Koschei's father, Koschei Senior, learned about his son's proclivities, he ordered his minions to put the boy into a barrel, nail it shut, tighten it with braces, waterproof it with tar, and throw it into the ocean so that he couldn't bring shame to the notoriously evil household. There are no female Koscheis, and baby Koscheis are born emerging from their fathers' testicles. So Koschei Junior didn't have a mother, and there was no one to argue with Koschei Senior's decision.

Koschei lay inside the barrel, looking at the blue sky through the hole between the planks, and wondered if splashing around in the middle of the ocean for an indefinite amount of time would be able to kill him.

He wasn't sure how much time had passed, but suddenly he spotted odd-looking birds scurrying around his peephole. The birds had naked pink bodies with no feathers on them, and it was hard to understand how they managed to flap their wings and fly given their condition. Because they had red crowns on top of their heads, Koschei realized that they must be chickens.

"Our comrade the duck sent us." One of the chickens, which was probably the leader, because his comb was the biggest, looked at Koschei through the hole. "She said you might be in trouble. How can we help?"

"I'm hungry," Koschei said.

The birds gathered and pecked around the peephole to make it bigger. And then Koschei almost didn't believe his eyes as the biggest chicken twisted his own leg out of the socket and squeezed it through the hole.

"Are you sure?" Koschei verified.

Then he ate it and became full.

"Now what do we do?" the chicken asked him.

"Maybe you can take me to land so I can take care of myself?" Koschei asked, humbly.

The chickens managed to lift the barrel with their beaks and began flying with it across the sky, the ocean left down below.

"We're sort of far away from anywhere," the head chicken said. "And now we're getting hungry from all this flying. Think you can return the favor?"

As the chicken said the words, a pocketknife appeared next to Koschei within the barrel. He knew immediately what to do and used it to cut a chunk of meat from his thigh. It was painful, but Koschei wanted their relationship to be fair. He then pressed the flesh through the hole, and the chickens gobbled it up.

They flew for a couple of days, and whenever the chickens got hungry, Koschei had to cut off slices of himself. He cut into both of his thighs, then his calves, then his buttocks, and even his heels. He kept losing consciousness whenever he leaned on the wounds, so he ended up lying on his stomach. He, too, got hungry throughout their journey, but he didn't tell the chickens so that he wouldn't cause them to lose more limbs.

Finally, they reached land and dropped the barrel, which burst open upon impact with the ground.

"Here, let us show you something." The main chicken led Koschei, who had to walk on tiptoe, to a spring. "This here is vitality water. Watch me."

The chicken dipped his drumstick stump into the water, and his leg instantly grew back. He then submerged his whole body into the spring, and beautiful, shiny feathers covered his entire frame. The other chickens joined their leader, and also emerged in full plumage, fluffy and dazzling.

"Now it's your turn," the chicken told Koschei.

He dipped his heel lightly into the water and felt flesh grow anew.

"Make yourself at home on this island," the chickens told Koschei and touched his forehead gently with their beaks before flying off.

Left alone, Koschei went to explore the island's abundant greenery. He encountered some tiny flies who were also talkative and friendly. They introduced him to the local flora and fauna, and explained what berries, weeds, and mushrooms to pick and which to avoid. Koschei wasn't sure how his life would work out on the island, but that night, sheltered by a wide branch of an oak tree, lulled by food and exciting new friendships, he felt safe.

5

The book Mitya was reading was called *Dinka*. It was his mama's favorite when she was a child, she said, as she gave it to Mitya. "Lena Trofimova," her maiden name, and "1968" were inscribed on it in a childish cursive, the letters so round they could burst. Mitya was reading it for the third time. Dinka, the main character, was a willful girl, growing up in a family of revolutionaries in pre-Soviet Russia. She was unlike her proper and well-behaved sisters; she didn't want to be what girls should be. Grown-ups often reprimanded Dinka for acting out, for swimming in the river without taking her dress off, for getting into trouble. She made a friend, a pauper boy, Lyonka. To make him like her more, she pretended to come from poverty too. Dinka wore a torn, dirty dress whenever she went to see her new friend. She also befriended an old man who played the barrel organ, and followed him around, singing songs, as orphans did.

Mitya read about Dinka with sweet abandon; he ached to set foot into the world in which she lived. He wanted nothing more than to go with Lyonka and her to look for the cliff where Stenka Razin, a Cossack rebel leader, had sat and plotted his uprising against the tsar. Dinka and Lyonka lived on the river Volga, and around them were fields, forests, birch trees—vast, unbounded freedom in which to lose themselves, in which to roam free. Mitya, on the other hand, had nothing. Even his room and his bed were not his own, invaded by a threatening presence.

Mitya wished he could befriend a pauper child and make money by singing songs, as Dinka did. This way, he wouldn't have to stay around Vovka in the daytime. Maybe he could wear a dress while singing. He didn't mind if it was a torn one. But he did not know how to do it alone. He was afraid to do it alone. He wanted someone.

His family was out of the question. He avoided Vovka and Papa, while Babushka and Mama had no time for him, too busy with their own things. Mitya had not made any friends at school, either, and it was too late to try: the relationships had been established. When Mitya came up to any of his class-mates, it was always unpleasant. In the best case, they made fun of the cracks in the corners of his mouth or his cheap shoes.

Zoya, the girl who shared her desk with him—pretty, always well dressed, with short hair and a mullet—responded to him politely when Mitya asked her about something, usually related to schoolwork. But Mitya could see her stare at the burn on his chin, squeamish. Mitya got it from spilling hot tea all over him-self when Papa struck him for not refilling the kettle. Mama blew on the burn and put Vaseline on it; she told Mitya always to ask if anyone else would be drinking tea besides himself. As if there were any behavior that would prevent Dmitriy Fyodorovich from getting angry with Mitya for the smallest things.

Alyssa Vitalyevna had stopped taking Mitya to school because it conflicted with her work. He was on his own, so he chose to stop going to classes half the time while it was still warm and walked around the streets. He knew Tatiana Ivanovna wouldn't care. He was looking for pauper boys, for regular boys alone in the street, for girls in dirty dresses, for anyone as lonely as himself.

Mitya saw Roma boys with dirty faces on the New Arbat, the more modern avenue running parallel to the Old Arbat. But they were always in groups, rowdy, loud, and he was too shy to talk to them. He saw a boy who played his violin close to their building, a couple of paper bills always in the violin case. But when Mitya approached him during a break he was taking, a woman came out of nowhere and told Mitya to go away.

On one of his truant walks, Mitya went into the Dobrolyubov Library on Novinskiy Boulevard. The sign said that it was the first multimedia library in the country. It had computers inside, and he decided that maybe computers would make him feel less lonely. The woman at the reception desk told him they could only admit minors after their parents signed them up. So he asked Mama, fearing that she would refuse. But he mentioned how he liked *Dinka* and wanted to read more books. Yelena Viktorovna didn't mind. In fact, she wished that everyone in the family would join a library so she would have more peaceful time to herself at home. She picked Mitya up after school the next day and took him there. From then on, Mitya spent a lot of time at the library, but quite soon found out that computers, just like books, were not exactly a substitute for human friends.

One day, while skipping school, Mitya went to the playground next to his building. It was always empty except for bomzh Valerka, the homeless man who slept in the communal hallways at night and tended to crows during the day. He had a puffy red face, which, Babushka explained, came from all the drinking. But despite his bad habits, he never stank up the hallway. That was why he was allowed to stay. Mitya never dared to go this close to home during class time. But he often sat on the bench in the corner of that playground after school, with a book.

"Would you like to meet the ladies?" Valerka asked him, pointing at the crows. Valerka used the polite form of *you*: he thought that being courteous was most important, even when one's hygiene was lacking. Mitya had never been addressed like that, in particular by a grown-up.

"Of course."

Some of the crows were perched on Valerka's shoulders; some sat on the green fence beneath where he stood.

"This is Avdotya Philippovna," Valerka said, introducing the crow on his right shoulder, then pointed to the left one. "This is Mariya Nikitichna. The ones on the fence are Evdokiya Matveyevna, Ekaterina Petrovna, and Lidiya Olegovna. You'll meet the others when they come back from scavenging."

The formal names of the crows amused Mitya immensely, but he did not ask Valerka why he named them this way. He also did not question why Valerka thought that all the crows were females. He thought that Valerka must have known. He could tell them apart somehow, after all.

Valerka found that telling apart birds and children was much easier than telling apart men walking home after work in their suits. This was why he respected birds and children much more than men in suits.

"How do you make them sit on your shoulders?" Mitya asked.

"By being kind," Valerka replied. "If you treat all god's creatures kindly, they will come to you."

He smiled and revealed the few teeth that were left in his mouth. His nose was swollen like a spud, and his lower lip hung low into his wiry beard. Valerka's hair was matted, his clothes dirty, and he smelled faintly of urine and strongly of alcohol. His face was soft, softer than any Mitya had seen.

"Do you promise to be kind to animals, druzhok?" Valerka asked. The child in front of him had kind and sad eyes, and he thought that he could trust such a child with the most important things.

Mitya nodded. He had no idea why he would want to be unkind to the beautiful crows that sat on Valerka's shoulders, or to any other animal at all. He did not wish to be cruel to anyone, not even Vovka. He also liked that Valerka didn't call him a boy or a girl but "druzhok," a genderless "little friend."

———

Valerka and Mitya became friends. Mitya saved bread from his meals and gave it to Valerka and the crows. Valerka thanked him profusely. He usually refused to eat the offering himself and said that he preferred the liquid bread, which, Mitya knew from Papa, was beer. But the crows ate the meal with gusto and allowed Mitya to pet them on their small heads. He did and felt their slick feathers beneath his fingers and their fragile skulls.

The crows liked the small person and his soft fingers.

Once, on the weekend, when Mitya came over to see Valerka earlier than usual, he found him without the crows.

They had flown home for a while and should return soon, Valerka explained. The crows did not tell him when they'd be returning, and he didn't ask, it was like that between them. But they would return. They always came back.

"Do you ever go home yourself?" Mitya asked Valerka.

"Oh, druzhok. I don't have one. Not anymore. Now my home is here."

"But what happened?"

"I lost our savings, and my wife told me to go away," he said, his face still kind. It was a while since anyone had asked him such questions. Everyone else, even when giving him money, or beer, would scrunch their noses and turn away quickly, hoping to avoid the smell.

"How did you lose the money? In the street?" Mitya wondered.

Valerka grinned.

"No, I was a partner in MMM—you know MMM, druzhok? With the advertisements on TV. Lyonya Golubkov, who got rich and bought a fur coat for his wife. Well, I didn't get to purchase the fur coat. I bought the shares and got nothing, and my wife kicked me out. It's been two years."

Mitya remembered the advertisements. Papa saw them, too, and he bought shares, but then Babushka heard that people were not getting their money from MMM, and she told him to stop investing. They were all fighting a lot at that time, Mama trying to reconcile her mother and husband. In the end, Vovka's mom, Aunt Sveta, had lost her dead husband's car because of MMM. She couldn't drive and didn't use it, but it was still pretty bad. There was no use in arguing anymore, so Papa stopped doing MMM, and Babushka stopped pestering him.

Mitya was sorry that nobody had told Valerka that MMM was crooked. He looked into the homeless man's sweet face, tears pooling up in his eyes, and thought that he must miss home a lot. Mitya wondered if maybe they could have him live with them. Vovka lived with them, and he hurt Mitya. Valerka had never hurt Mitya. Mitya would share his sofa with Valerka. He would take a bath if he had one, wouldn't he? He could drink beer with Papa and teach him some kindness too. And Mitya would even tell him about the needle.

Something told Mitya that his parents would never agree. But he made a decision to put away a percentage of the money that Mama gave him for sweet buns at the school cafeteria every day. He planned to give it to Valerka once he gathered a hefty sum.

———

One day, when Vovka had gone to visit his mother, and everyone else had left for work, Mitya rushed to his apartment and started dressing up. He did not want anything elaborate; a quick transformation into Devchonka. So he put on a dress, put on some lipstick and some eye shadow, and went out into the hallway. He was wary of someone else seeing him, so he did not take the elevator and walked down all fourteen flights of stairs.

Mitya made it to the front door and out into the courtyard, taking a left to the playground.

Valerka did not seem to see the difference. "Zdravstvuyte, druzhok," he greeted Mitya with a smile and went on to relay the news of the crows' health and exploits. A few of them had found colorful beads that Valerka had put in his pocket. Lidiya Olegovna had found a coin. Ekaterina Petrovna was not feeling well and stayed by his side. Mitya listened to Valerka talk, nervously tugging on the hem of his dress, waiting for any sign of hostility. Maybe Valerka talked like this to any child that came his way?

But then Valerka said: "You don't need to bring us bread today, druzhok. Someone threw a loaf of bread out, with some mold in the middle, so the ladies had a feast." And it was clear that he knew that it was Mitya in front of him.

The crows perched on Valerka's shoulders and the nearby fence, recognized Mitya too, and croaked happily. Avdotya Philippovna sat down on his shoulder for a while, tickling him with her claw. She was the friendliest bird, but would never do something like that to a person she didn't know from before. It had taken Mitya a few weeks to earn the privilege of Avdotya Philippovna's embrace.

Valerka enjoyed watching his child friend bond with the crows. He liked how the child's face was painted, and the dress too. It was festive, and there were so few festive things in his life.

Despite the warm welcome, Mitya couldn't stay outside wearing the dress for too long, in case someone else saw him and wasn't as friendly. He said his goodbye to Valerka and the crows and went back up the stairs, triumphant.

He had shown Devchonka to someone, to a whole crowd, and nothing terrible had happened. They still liked Mitya. Could it possibly mean that he wasn't deviant, wasn't bad or spoiled? Was he something different, unique, that grown-ups—at least, most of them—were not able to understand?

After that day, when Mitya went to the bathroom at night, he sat there thinking of all the possibilities were he to venture out into the world as Devchonka. He closed his eyes and imagined. Here he was wearing a beautiful lace-trimmed dress. He came to school, and everyone suddenly saw him for what he was, a beautiful girl, not a tiny boy. Everyone fell in love with him, the mean kids, his deskmate, pretty Zoya, Tatiana Ivanovna. The custodian Semenovna put down her push broom and admired the glow of Mitya's golden curls and his glossy red lips.

Mitya imagined going to the grocery store across the road from their building in a pink T-shirt, hot shorts, his hair in pigtails, and the woman at the cash register smiling at him and saying: "What a beautiful girl you are." Mitya imagined coming home from school in a skirt and a puffy fur coat, like Zoya's, and Alyssa Vitalyevna greeting him, calling him "vnuchka," granddaughter. She would tell him she had a doll for him, a late birthday gift. Wouldn't Mitya just look at how much alike he and the toy were!

6

Two months, one week, and four days after the first incident—
Mitya had counted—Vovka got drunk for the second time. Mitya
was not dressed up that day to make him angry, and there was no
sad story about his Mashka. Mitya's parents and Babushka were
at home, too, in their beds. It was late. And yet, it happened again.
Mitya was lying there, waiting for Vovka to doze off, himself in a
state of pre-slumber, almost able to fall asleep. He saw pre-dreams,
pictures beneath his eyelids, so real, yet so abstract—animals, like
those he had seen at the merry-go-round when Mama took him
to the amusement park for Victory Day while Papa was celebrating with his army buddies back at home.

At first, Mitya felt the weight on his chest. Then he felt the
coarseness against his cheeks. Then came the smell and the flesh.
He opened his eyes and saw Vovka sitting on top of him. Mitya
was suffocating, a crushing vacuum inside of him, and he closed
his eyes and saw the pictures come back.

When it was done, Vovka lay back as the realization what he had done crept in, slowly overtaking him like poison. Mitya's sobs had slowed down, and he would fall asleep any minute, leaving Vovka all alone with his terror. The terror that had started back in the war and refused to leave, that became the only mode of existence in this hell that was populated with rotting corpses, dead comrades, enemy combatants, and the worst monster of all, himself.

He wasn't just the one being tormented; he had become the tormentor. It wasn't even his personal hell: just part of the communal hell they all inhabited.

———

Vovka began drinking every day. Mitya would have run away from home if he hadn't seen what it had done to Valerka. You had to have a place to go. Besides, he saw that none of the grown-ups liked Vovka, especially now that he was permanently drunk, even around them. Babushka was the most outspoken about it; she told her friends on the phone how she "could not face this devil's negative influence on Mitya anymore, with all the drinking."

Vovka no longer ate anything Yelena Viktorovna cooked and subsisted on vafelniye stakanchiki, waffle cups filled with ice cream.

"Will Vovka always live with us?" Mitya asked Yelena Viktorovna once, as she swept the ice cream wrappers from beneath the shared sofa.

"Don't I wish I knew the same thing," she answered mysteriously, and that was the end of the conversation.

In the beginning, Dmitriy Fyodorovich always took Vovka's side.

"He's a real army man," was his favorite line of defense. "He suffered during the war. He has a medal for bravery."

But once Vovka had started drinking more than Dmitriy Fyodorovich himself, the approval became less enthusiastic.

Sometimes Dmitriy Fyodorovich took Vovka to the kitchen late in the evening, and they talked about life over a bottle of vodka. The more they drank, the louder they became. Smoke seeped beneath the kitchen door and filled the apartment. Dmitriy Fyodorovich tried to be delicate with his nephew, to make him see that there was life after war too. But Vovka saw through him.

"What do you have to show for your sacrifice? Living with your mother-in-law, working for kopecks, and your son is a sissy. I'd rather drink myself to death right now than have a life like this. Especially while the Chechens own our city and roll around in money."

On these nights, Yelena Viktorovna and Alyssa Vitalyevna stood outside the door. They listened and waited to jump in and try to take the fighting men apart. Alyssa Vitalyevna took Dmitriy Fyodorovich because he didn't dare touch her back, while Yelena Viktorovna blocked Vovka, whose skewed balance made him easy to topple. Mitya noticed how emaciated he looked, his collarbones sharp, his only arm stick-thin.

But Dmitriy Fyodorovich usually dropped out the door first and ran to his bedroom, fuming. Then Vovka finished the bottle off and set out into the streets in search of more. He sometimes drank with the older woman who lived in the building across the

street and swore at Yeltsin. She still liked to perform on the tri-
bune of her windowsill, and Vovka became her trusted partner.
They sang songs loudly and swore at the woman's son, who was
twice Vovka's age himself. All the drunks from the neighborhood
gathered in her apartment and didn't try to pretend that life was
something more than emptiness with an opportunity to fall into a
drunken stupor. It wasn't much, Vovka thought, but it was honest.

FOUR

Koschei's life on the island was quite splendid. Food was abundant: the forest provided a scrumptious vegetarian diet, and whenever he had a craving for some nice roast meat, Koschei could cut off a bit off himself and then heal it in the spring. Sometimes the animals he had befriended offered him their flesh, too, and it made for a nice change of pace, but he never asked first.

His shelter beneath an oak branch was quite comfortable, but one night it rained, and Koschei was soaked to the bone marrow. In the morning, he settled that it was time to start building something permanent. He had never built anything in his life before, and things weren't going great until a friendly hare approached him, carrying a saw.

"Are you trying to build a house?"

"I am, but it's turning out bad."

"I'm a carpenter, and I'll help you out," she said. "But you have to promise that your dwelling will always be open to the

*other inhabitants of this island, though the majority of us prefer
to sleep in burrows."*

Koschei agreed.

*They started working together and, in no time, built a spa-
cious dwelling, with whitewashed walls and colorful onion domes.
All the animals in the forest contributed, bringing pigments, tars,
mud, their dung, and hair for insulation. The house stood out in
front of the greenery: bright and cheerful, yet in harmony with
nature. Koschei was the primary occupant, but all the animals
were always welcome to stay.*

*There were leftover materials from the construction, and
with the pigments, sticks, bristles, and mud, Koschei began cre-
ating art. He wanted to make a portrait of each of the forest's
inhabitants, from the tiniest ant to the mightiest bison, and was
moving ahead with his project smoothly.*

*One day, as Koschei was doing calisthenics near his house, a
short man came out of the forest. He was naked, but most of his
body was covered with a long gray beard. On his head, he was wearing a mushroom cap, and in his hands was a scepter made from a
tiny knotty tree. By his side were a few small mushrooms who didn't
speak but seemed to accompany his speech with a high pitched hum.*

*"I'm Leshy," the man said, introducing himself. "The guardian
of the forest."*

*"Koschei." Our hero found himself unthinkingly curtsying to
Leshy. "I've never seen you before, but I hope you don't mind me
imposing with this structure. I have nowhere else to go."*

*"Neither do I," Leshy responded. "You've done a good job, and
you can stay. The forest clearly likes you. I came here to extend an
invitation to her depths to you, if you would be so kind."*

Koschei didn't have time to respond. Quickly the mushrooms surrounded him, lifted him, and started carrying Koschei into the dense thicket. All the while, they kept uttering their fairy hum.

They arrived in a clearing, where a large wardrobe, also of knotty wood, was standing with its doors flung open, and within it were unseen wonders. Dresses, skirts, petticoats, and blouses made from the most delicate mosses, spiderwebs, and flowers waited on the hangers. Elegant high-heeled shoes made out of bundled leaves and the choicest barks stood in rows, while an army of frogs was gathered in a circle nearby. As Koschei approached, they simultaneously unrolled their long tongues, each one revealing a priceless jewel. Some were made of fresh morning dew, others of amber drops with ancient remains, butterfly wings, or insect carapaces inside. Meanwhile, deer and moose gathered round, their eyes beckoning Koschei with a mysterious glint.

A gray gecko stepped out from among the frogs, carrying a small crown that had a sun on the front, a half moon on the back, and stars on the sides.

"Can I touch it?" Koschei asked as he reached for it.

"You must wear it immediately," Leshy said. He raised his beard, covered in fallen leaves, and showed the tips of his own high-heeled slippers the color of ripe blood. Right away, the mushrooms and frogs starting swarming Koschei with exquisite clothes and accessories in tow and dressed him up in all the finery. The fireflies arrived and began covering his face with pigments and pollens. Once they were done, the creatures procured a full-length mirror and allowed Koschei to look at himself.

"I'm a real tsarevna myself now," Koschei said with a gasp, and Leshy responded with a hearty, content laugh, which reverberated across the forest with the mushroom hum.

"It didn't seem right to have a castle without a tsarevna inside."

No one on the island minded it when Koschei dressed up as Tsarevna. They all embraced it. Soon, Koschei's original clothes became tattered, and he switched to wearing Tsarevna's clothes exclusively. And when he didn't feel like Tsarevna, and wanted to be Koschei for the day, he went naked. Growing up he had learned that nakedness was shameful, but here he basked in the sun among the animals, and it was the most natural thing.

7

Fall came, and so did fifth grade. Moscow was engrossed in the celebration of its 850th anniversary. It was a big deal for Mayor Luzhkov, everyone said, and he plunged into the beautification of the city, bald, round head first. There would be events, concerts, parades, and even though everything around seemed linked to the festivities, Mitya couldn't care less about any of it.

It was getting colder, yet Valerka still somehow made do. Mitya was used to seeing Valerka every day, and he felt as if they had established a family sort of routine. But one day in October, when Mitya came to the playground to talk to Valerka, he wasn't there. The crows were there, some of them keeping low, some hiding in the naked trees. Mitya took out the bread that he had brought that day and put it out on top of the fence. He retreated, to watch the crows from a distance. But they didn't touch the bread, and only the pigeons and sparrows pecked at it. Previously they had been afraid to show up and start a turf war.

But now the crows were not moving, so there was nothing to be scared of. The crows uttered a sad, long croak in a weird unison.

They never asked when Valerka was going to return. It was like that between them. But he would return. He always came back.

A week passed, and Valerka didn't come back. His meager possessions were still lying in the building's communal hallway. Mitya checked the other places he could have been: the queue by the liquor store, the entrance to McDonald's, where he sometimes begged. Valerka was nowhere to be found.

"Babushka, do you know where Valerka has gone?" Mitya asked Alyssa Vitalyevna once as she sat next to him and watched *A Próxima Vítima*, a Brazilian telenovela of crime and passion.

"Oh, they say a bunch of drunk youngsters beat him to death by Tsoi's Wall," Babushka replied. Tsoi's Wall was part of a building covered in graffiti farther up the Old Arbat, a fan monument to the memory of rock singer Viktor Tsoi. Mitya passed it often but never stopped to look. The people who hung out around it were usually fans, hippies who sang Tsoi's songs and worshipped the enclosure densely covered with unremarkable graffiti. But Mitya knew that there could be some dangerous elements there too.

Mitya froze. Valerka, his friend, was dead. It had always seemed to Mitya that there should be some complexity about death. But here the person he was used to seeing in the playground every day did not exist on earth anymore. And there was nothing to mark the occasion, not even a poof.

"Do you know who killed him?" Mitya finally asked. He was wondering if maybe it was Vovka or some of his drinking buddies. He wouldn't be surprised if the only friend he had in his life had disappeared through Vovka's interference. "Is the militsia looking for them?"

"Who knows, Mitya?" Babushka shrugged. "He's a bomzh. No one will ever try to solve this."

She was anxious to get back to her show, where a strong, beautiful middle-aged woman and a dark, handsome man shared a passionate romance. Alyssa Vitalyevna couldn't help drawing parallels with the story of herself and Dr. Khristofor Khristoforovich Kherentzis.

Mitya tried to imagine Valerka being beaten. Maybe even stabbed: there were a lot of stabbings in the criminal news. When he thought about the knife entering the flesh, he thought about the market, where the knives chopped meat, where the smell of fresh and stale blood mingled with the briny aroma of the pickles. Of course, he knew that the murder wouldn't actually smell like the meat rows, but the smell permeated him whenever he considered that Valerka had been stabbed to death.

He tried to rid himself of these thoughts, hoping, against what he knew, that Valerka was still alive. In a week, the last reminders of Valerka disappeared from the hallway. Mitya preferred to think that Valerka himself had come back to take them. He might have. Some other homeless man could have been the one beaten to death near Tsoi's Wall. There were plenty of them on the Old Arbat. But Mitya also realized that Valerka's possessions could have been taken by the other homeless, or disposed of by the groundskeeper or one of the residents. They were Valerka's life possessions, sure, but common trash to anyone else. And he couldn't go basing a theory on these things.

Mitya had to know the truth. He hated this feeling, as if he wanted to jump ahead but his body was holding him back.

He asked Babushka again in a few days, but she had no updates.

"Who told you that he was beaten to death?" Mitya asked.

"The cashier at the Dieta store," she replied. "She said she'd heard a rumor, and then I heard that he was dead from Petya the militsioner."

Uncle Petya was the father of Zhenya, the strange girl who'd showed her slit to Mitya in kindergarten.

Mitya asked his mother about Valerka, too, and she repeated what Alyssa Vitalyevna had told him, almost word for word. It turned out that they were together in the elevator when Uncle Petya told them. He liked to inform women of accidents that happened in the neighborhood: sometimes out of concern for their safety, sometimes out of a morbid desire to make them uncomfortable.

Mitya himself had always felt uncomfortable around Uncle Petya. He was a short man with a large, protruding stomach who often made jokes that Mitya did not understand.

Mitya had spent enough time seated next to his mama and babushka, doing his homework as they watched *A Próxima Vítima* to know that crimes were solved through painstaking investigation. A young woman in the telenovela was trying to find out who killed a bunch of people, including her relatives. She asked questions and revealed other people's secrets, and seemed to be closing in on the perpetrator. The only obstacle holding her back was the abundance of love triangles and illegitimate children that she discovered along the way.

Mitya decided that he, too, could be like that woman. Why couldn't he? Valerka had been his only friend. Valerka had accepted Mitya as Devchonka, and never asked any questions. For that kindness, Mitya owed him. He had to find Valerka and help him out of trouble—or, in the worst-case scenario, solve his murder.

That night in bed Mitya thought about the ways he could solve the mystery, the people he could see, the questions he could ask. It was much better than debating whether Valerka had indeed been killed, or if he was alive, rumination that had exhausted him the previous evenings. Everything around him was calm, Vovka, thankfully, absent. Mitya wondered if Vovka could be involved. Then Mitya could get rid of Vovka for good. The exciting possibility lulled Mitya to sleep, for a short while, until Vovka came home.

———

Now that it had been established that knowing Uncle Petya was Mitya's key to finding Valerka, he committed to rekindling his friendship with Zhenya. Mitya had considered this earlier—after all, they had their shared history. He hadn't done it; each time shyness had overcome him. But under the new circumstances, it could no longer be an excuse.

Mitya had not talked with Zhenya since he stopped going to kindergarten. He saw her often, in the elevator or the store on the corner, and said hello. Zhenya went to the same school as Mitya did, but since she had started middle school the previous year and he was still in elementary, they had been in different buildings for the past year. Now Mitya had joined her. From being the oldest children in the elementary school, Mitya and his classmates had gone to looking like preschoolers next to the big-breasted ninth graders and eleventh graders with facial hair. It did not bother Mitya. He preferred it, actually: there were now girls in makeup whom he could watch and copy, and boys who sometimes looked at him admiringly as he walked down the corridor. Some referred to him as "the maloletka" if they needed him to move or something, mistaking him for a girl, and it made Mitya happy.

Like Mitya, Zhenya was a loner. He noticed that, more often than not, she sat on a bench by herself and scribbled something in a notepad. Perhaps she was doing her homework, Mitya thought. What else could she be doing? Because he had a disappearance to investigate and, likely, a murder to solve, Mitya could not postpone approaching Zhenya any longer. So when he saw that class 6D was done with lessons for that day, and everyone was heading home, he followed Zhenya. The walk from school to home normally took about fifteen minutes, but Zhenya sauntered, which made it harder for indecisive Mitya to keep behind her.

He still had not approached her when they reached the yellow mansion of McDonald's near the Smolenskaya station on the navy line. Mitya thought that Zhenya would pass the yellow mansion and turn left on the Old Arbat, toward their building, but instead, she turned toward the restaurant and went in. Mitya came forward to the tall glass window to see her inside. Instead of proceeding to the register like the other customers, Zhenya stopped next to the entrance by the trash receptacle: a large box that came up to her neck. Zhenya looked around her while taking off her oversized men's jacket. She put it on the floor. Then she quickly pried open the door on the side of the garbage bin and started taking things out, speedily but methodically, putting some objects, like open cups, back in, and keeping only the things she considered useful. Mitya stared at her, fascinated, while other passersby kept on walking. Once there was a decent pile of half-eaten food and half-empty packaging on top of her jacket, Zhenya closed the garbage bin's door, wrapped her loot in the coat, left the restaurant, and started walking up the Old Arbat, holding her cargo in front of her chest. Now she was walking fast, at a pace that Mitya had not expected from her: he could barely keep up.

Once they reached the archway that led into their building's courtyard, it was difficult for Mitya to keep his distance, so he stayed in the shadows until Zhenya disappeared into the hallway. He then walked into the hall too but noticed that he couldn't hear the elevator. Zhenya lived on the sixth floor, and it was doubtful that she would walk all the way up with her load. She also wouldn't have been able to reach her apartment quickly enough for the elevator to stop the whirr. Mitya went to check the staircase, but once he stepped onto the first step, he heard sounds coming from beneath.

Below the stairwell was the common basement, to which Mitya had never been. He began descending into the darkness. Though the building's garbage chute had been out of order for a long time, and no one was supposed to throw garbage down there, the first smell he detected was of household waste, sweet rot, and fermentation. The second one was unfamiliar, salty, and somehow indecent, with a hint of urine. Then Mitya smelled the greasy deliciousness of the McDonald's food, a smell he recognized from his only visit there, and from passing by the restaurant.

Once Mitya made it down to the door, he saw that it was open by a few fingers. The smells emanated from within, along with a dim light. Mitya pushed the door and found himself inside a small, dirty room illuminated by a single light bulb. Pipes ran through the room's floor and walls, with brooms, buckets, plastic bottle crates, and other sorts of things scattered all over. There were two people inside. Zhenya sat on one of the pipes. Her jacket was lying on the ground in front of her, filled with the loot from the McDonald's trash can. Another girl, smaller than Zhenya, sat in front of her with her back to the door. They dug through the loot, unwrapping half-eaten burgers, taking out the remainders of fries from waxy white packets and red cardboard ones, and discarding the dirty napkins and empty wrappers to one side. What they managed to salvage they put to the other side in neat rows: fry to fry, bun piece to bun piece, ketchup packet to ketchup packet. There was half a milkshake in a paper cup in the corner.

There was no space at all for Mitya to remain unnoticed in the small room. Despite the dim light, Zhenya immediately saw and recognized him. The smaller girl turned to follow Zhenya's gaze, and Mitya recognized her as the daughter of the surrounding buildings' caretaker. The basement room must have been where he kept his cleaning equipment, and his daughter had access to the key.

"Please don't tell my papa," the girl squealed instead of hello, her eyes wet.

"He won't, don't fret," Zhenya reassured her. She seemed unfazed by Mitya's arrival, and he started wondering if she had seen him following her. Zhenya nodded to Mitya. "You can join us if you'd like. But I'm not sure if we have enough for all three of us and the little ones."

As she said that, Mitya noticed that something was moving inside the bucket that stood next to the spread. He came closer and peeked in. There were seven mini rats inside. They didn't look like newborns. Mitya knew it was typical for many species of mammals to be blind and bald after birth, and these had fur. But they were still pretty new, smaller than the rats he had seen lurking around the dumpsters in other courtyards, with miniature human hands in the front and pristine coats of gray, white, and brown fur.

"Their mother went somewhere, and they were blind and forgotten. We feed them so they can grow strong."

"And then, Zhenya says, my father will poison them with rat poison." The little girl wrinkled her face and her eyes dampened further.

"He might," Zhenya said nonchalantly. She was used to taking the truth of this world unflinchingly and wanted to teach her small friend to do the same.

Mitya was surprised at how calm Zhenya seemed to be about everything, from eating garbage to raising rats for slaughter.

"Do you think Valerka might be staying here now?" he asked the girls.

"You mean the man from the stairs? He is dead!" The little girl's eyes glistened.

"Are you sure, though?" Mitya was looking at Zhenya, who seemed to be the mouthpiece of reason in this room.

"My father said so," Zhenya said. "Why do you care?"

"We were friends, and I wanted to help him. Does your father know anything else?"

"I don't know; I didn't ask him."

"Can you ask?" Mitya uttered unexpectedly, astounded by his own daring.

"He won't tell me anything unless he is drunk." Zhenya shrugged as she continued going through the leftovers.

"Does your father get drunk often?"

"Mine does," the little girl pitched in.

"I know. My cousin drinks with your dad."

"Not anymore," the little girl said. "My parents said that he is bad and they don't want to associate with him anymore."

Mitya thought that he had never agreed with anything so wholeheartedly.

"My father loves to drink, but my mother does not allow him to do it that much," Zhenya answered. "But I could try to make him, if you want. Why should I?"

"Valerka was kind, and he also liked animals." Mitya pointed to the bucket of rats. "I want to know what happened to him so I can maybe avenge his death. Get rid of the bad people."

His words didn't make sense to Mitya himself, as he said them out loud, but the little girl nodded in agreement, and Zhenya raised her eyes from a wrapper that said "Big Mac."

"Like Sailor Moon. I like that."

"Yeah, like Sailor Moon."

"If you can get some vodka, we can try," Zhenya said, as she placed the last packet of ketchup in the row. "Or Dasha here can help you. Give her money, she'll buy it. She always buys for her parents, and everyone at the store knows her."

Dasha grinned at the recognition. She felt useful.

"Now, let's eat."

Mitya feared it would be impolite not to partake in the feast. Still, he felt queasy, looking at the pieces of sandwiches with the teeth marks of strangers. He took some of the fries and nibbled on them, squeezing lines of ketchup from a packet on a new napkin. The fries were cold and a bit stale, but still tasty. The girls ate with less discretion, taking alternating sips from the milkshake cup. They threw the smallest and most misshapen pieces of hamburger into the bucket, where the rats rushed to their lunch with glee.

"You shouldn't touch them, though," Mitya said, when the jacket's lining was empty, except for the greasy stains that covered it. "They could have the plague." He had read about it on the internet in the library recently.

"My mama calls me the plague," Zhenya said as she put her jacket back on. "You know the saying? 'A disease doesn't stick to disease.'"

8

Mitya did not want to take any money out of his Valerka cash to buy the vodka demanded by Zhenya. He was still hopeful that all of this could be a misunderstanding, and Valerka would come back. Still, he took out 50,000 rubles from the money he had saved, which he was sure would be more than enough. The next day after school he gave it to Dasha.

"It's too much. Vodka costs 40,000," she said, counting the 1,000-ruble notes.

"Keep the change. You can buy some chocolate," Mitya said. It seemed only fair that the skinny thing get something for herself. Mitya had never felt more affluent than next to Dasha.

"I know something better," she said and went to the store. "I'll be back!"

Mitya and Zhenya were left alone in the caretaker's room. As on the previous day, Zhenya was going through her Mc-Donald's loot, and the rats squirmed in the bucket. Mitya was used to the smells in the room, and the half-eaten food did not make him as queasy. There was something tender about the way Zhenya brought the leftovers to feed her small friend and the animal children.

When Dasha returned, she was carrying a bottle of vodka and some type of candy bar.

"I got Hematogen!" she exclaimed.

Zhenya squirmed.

Mitya had no idea what it was, but when Dasha opened the packaging and stretched out her hand with it inside, he saw what looked like chocolate, only more porous and thicker. Mitya broke a square off and put it in his mouth. It was not excessively sweet but still tasted quite like candy, only dustier, grainy on the tongue.

"I like it." Mitya was glad that he didn't have to lie out of politeness and could honestly attest to his happy palate.

"Do you know it has blood in it?" Zhenya asked.

"What do you mean?"

"They make it from bulls' blood. And they sell it at the pharmacy."

"They sell a lot of good stuff at the pharmacy! Don't you like askorbinka?" Dasha said through a mouthful.

"You should have bought some instead," Zhenya scolded.

Mitya knew what askorbinka was, but he had never eaten it for pleasure. It made sense: the miniature round pills of vitamin C that you were supposed to eat whenever you felt the flu coming on were covered in something white, likely melted sugar, and exploded in sourness when you sucked to the center. He resolved to get some from the medicine shelf when he returned home and bring it to his new friends the next day. But not before Zhenya went through with getting her father drunk.

———

Mitya went over to Zhenya's place after dinner. He passed Vovka smoking on the stairs. Already tipsy, Vovka cast a mean glance in Mitya's direction.

"I'm going to see a friend," Mitya responded. "I'll be back soon."

Vovka nodded and turned away. He didn't care where the boy was going, but he wanted a reason to be angry. Mitya was also not the best person to pick on, because every glimpse of him raised anxiety in Vovka that elevated bitterly, like acid reflux. He could face Mitya only when he had had enough to drink, and the urge, the necessity took over his mind, not leaving space for reflection.

Mitya reached the sixth floor and rang, and soon Zhenya opened the door, wearing tights and what looked like her father's oversized T-shirt.

"You're lucky; my mama is working, making food for a wedding tonight, so she'll be back late. Nothing stood between Papa and the bottle. He's pretty well licked already."

The apartment was smaller than theirs and had two rooms, one occupied by Zhenya's family, the other by a single woman named Larissa whom Mitya didn't know but liked a lot. She always smelled of some exciting fragrance, had colorful lipsticks, and wore the sought-after Dolchiki, crocheted tights that were advertised on TV with a memorable slogan: "Dolchiki! Devilishly good." Mitya had often wondered what it would be like to be able to go through Larissa's wardrobe. He would have wanted to do it. Maybe if he and Zhenya became better friends, he would be able to cozy up to Larissa too?

Uncle Petya was sitting on the unmade sofa that also served as the bed for him and his wife. A smaller bed in the other corner must have been Zhenya's. Uncle Petya was watching what looked like a recording of a concert: the bottle-blonde singer Tanya Bulanova was singing a lullaby.

Don't call the teddy bear your daddy
And don't tug on his paw.
It is my fault.
Not all families are full.

Sleep, my little boy,
Sleep, my son.
I'm not crying anymore.
All the pain is gone.

Uncle Petya was crying large round tears as he sang along.

"Papa, here is Mitya, from the seventh floor. He's my friend from school. He's wondering if you can tell him something."

Uncle Petya turned his wet face to the children. He recognized the boy. Mitya's father was a stand-up man, as far as Petya was concerned, and he wanted to know whether the boy was of the same mettle.

"Mitya, do you cherish and honor your batenka?"

Mitya had not heard anyone use the words "cherish," "honor," or "batenka" in real life. They were more suited to Pushkin's fairy tales, where people referred to the tsar as their collective father whom to honor. But Mitya understood that Uncle Petya was rolling along with the song's theme, and using over-the-top language for aesthetic reasons. It reminded Mitya of drunk men in Chekhov's stories. They often talked weirdly and held each other by the button when drunk.

"I do, Uncle Petya," he lied, thinking that his father did not cherish him either.

"Good boy," Uncle Petya sniffled. "My Zhenya, here, does not cherish me enough. Just like her mother, who beats me up whenever she doesn't like something. She should listen to Tanya Bulanova. So many families without fathers today, and yet no one values a man who stays."

Zhenya did not react to her father's outburst. It was the usual refrain that she heard pretty much every day, and honoring it with a response was not something she was predisposed to do.

"See, Mitya?" Uncle Petya gestured. "And this is all because I don't make enough money. I would love to. But I work in the militsia department, I'm not out patrolling the streets. And when they bring in perps, they already have their pockets emptied out. Lyuba wants me to patrol the streets. It's dangerous! I am not a young man. Chasing those lowlifes! What does she think of me? She wants to risk my life for gain!"

"Speaking about your work, Papa. Do you remember the bomzh we had in the building? Valerka?"

"Valerka! Old soul. He was a good one. Never late with his payments."

Mitya did not quite understand but pressed on: "But where do you think he has gone?"

"Oh, he's been killed, Mitya. I was working that day but I don't know what transpired. They brought him in, said he had an altercation at Tsoi's Wall. He was badly injured. And then he didn't walk out again."

"Did he see a doctor?"

"Didn't have time."

"So he died at the precinct?" Mitya asked. The militsia precinct was close to their building, and right across the road from the playground where Valerka usually fed the birds. It was not relevant, but Mitya thought for a second: "Did the birds hear him die? Did they know it?"

"Yes, I suppose," Uncle Petya said. He didn't want to think about all the dirty business of the precinct now that he was in a wonderful, teary mood. He wanted to listen to more heart-wrenching songs and sing along with them. Perhaps have some pickled mushrooms in the fridge that his brother-in-law had made in Ryazan.

Once he heard the answer, Mitya felt a heaviness inside his chest, and his body started going numb all over. He had gotten a definite answer about Valerka's fate. Mitya had guessed earlier that he might indeed be dead. But the finality of it, the absence of a way out, was what hit him the hardest.

"Did you search for the killers?" he asked.

"I don't go searching for killers. I sit in the precinct."

"He means the other militsionery," Zhenya interjected. "Did they search for the killers?"

"I don't think so," Uncle Petya responded. What did they think the militsia was, some avenging superhero force, like in those cartoons his daughter liked to watch so much? "They don't get paid enough to solve bomzh murders, can't you understand? He's a bomzh. No one cares."

Mitya wanted to say that he did care, but it seemed unnecessary. He wanted to find out as much as he could, but it was clear that no one else in the world regarded this case as something worth pursuing.

"Where was he taken afterward?" Mitya asked.

"You mean the body?"

"Yes."

"The morgue. I called his wife. They always make me do the sad things that no one else wants. She said she didn't want the body, and nobody else would. But the morgue would call her later anyway and ask her to pick up the body."

Mitya had never thought about things that followed after death. His other grandmother died when he was small, and his grandfathers died before he was born. Uncle Seryozha, Vovka's father, too. What if Mitya died, and the militsionery called home? It would most likely be Yelena Viktorovna dealing with the morgue. Or maybe Alyssa Vitalyevna. She would certainly find a way to connect with people at the morgue and bring them bribes to make sure that they treated Mitya's dead body well. Doing what? He didn't know what they did in morgues. He was sure Alyssa Vitalyevna would get him a nice coffin; she often told him that she'd expect that from him if she died.

"So, what then?"

"He's probably buried now. What else could there be, Mitya?"

"What if she didn't take his body from the morgue and left him there?"

"Then the government has to take care of him. They bury the homeless in a special cemetery if the relatives don't. I think that's how it goes. What are you asking me for?"

"Don't you feel sorry for him, though?" Mitya asked and immediately bit his tongue. Asking something like that at home would land him in hot water with his father, and it was unlikely that Uncle Petya would appreciate it.

"You think I'm paid to care?" Uncle Petya asked, and turned back to the TV. "Investigating me. Like I'm a criminal. I'm the guardian of law and order," he mumbled to himself and raised the volume to hear Alla Pugacheva in a red wig lament about her love life to a girlfriend. Finally, the sweet abandon.

Mitya determined that this was all he could hope for, and he nodded to Zhenya to see him out.

"See, it's not helpful at all. My mama says he's a sorry example of a militsioner, and I agree, although to me most grownups are not the brightest bunch."

Mitya agreed but didn't say anything against Zhenya's father.

"What do you think I should do now?"

"What can you do? He's dead, Mitya. You wanted proof; there's that."

"But they don't even want to solve the murder."

"Solve it yourself," Zhenya chuckled. "You'd probably be way better at that than my papa and his idiotic comrades."

That night, Mitya put the money he had saved up for Valerka into the box with his milk teeth and buried it in the playground, beneath a tree, in a plastic bag. He thought about "Kroshechka-Khavroshechka," a fairy tale that Babushka often played for him on a vinyl record. In it, an evil woman ate her stepdaughter Kroshechka-Khavroshechka's favorite cow, and then, Kroshechka-Khavroshechka buried the cow's bones, out of which a beautiful tree grew. As Mitya buried the money, he hoped that something would grow, if not out of Valerka's bones, then out of his memory, a beautiful, shady tree on which the crows could rest.

FIVE

One night, as Koschei was sleeping, cozy in his nightgown and with two baby moles nested on his chest, he heard a bloodcurdling wail. At first, he didn't want to pay attention to it. But the cry repeated, and Koschei felt a pang of guilt. He carefully put the baby moles, in their deep slumber, aside, and ventured out of his shelter. A friendly firefly landed on his shoulder to show him the way.

There was some commotion where the healing spring was located. Upon reaching it, Koschei saw a human figure leaning over the water. When the firefly got closer, Koschei was able to make out a soldier's uniform, as well as the object the soldier was using to try to get water out of the spring. It was the top part of the soldier's own skull, cut off neatly, perhaps with a sharp sword. The pink-gray brain lay arranged on top of the soldier's head, like a dusty tangerine half. Though the soldier was scooping the water up, it kept spilling out before he could reach his improvised bowl to his lips and sip. Each time he realized his failure, the soldier grunted.

"What's the matter with him?" Koschei asked in a whisper.

"He's returned from the other world," said a saiga antelope, and a parliament of eagle owls nodded in agreement.

Koschei asked for clarification.

"He died but found that he belonged neither in heaven nor in hell," a jumping spider began to explain. "And now it turns out that he can't be on this earth, either, because nature rejects him for his otherworldly scent."

"And what happened to his head?"

"I heard it got caught in the golden gate when he was running away from heaven," a stickleback offered from the spring's waters.

"So, he'll die of thirst now?" Koschei wondered.

The animals shrugged their paws, wings, and legs. The fish released air bubbles. The creatures began disbanding, and soon it was only Koschei standing by the spring, his trusty firefly gently buzzing by his ear.

"It doesn't seem right," Koschei told him. "If I didn't know about this tragedy, it would be one thing. But now that I know, I can't in good conscience turn away."

Koschei approached the soldier, still accompanied by his glimmering friend. Immersed in his fruitless labor, the soldier did not notice.

"Here, let me help you," Koschei said. He cupped his hands and leaned down to the spring. Then he brought the water to the soldier's parched lips and let him drink. He wasn't sure this would work, but it did, and the soldier sipped greedily and, in a hoarse voice, asked for more. After the soldier had enough to *drink, Koschei poured some water on the cut in his skull. The flesh and bone started sizzling, and when Koschei placed the top part of the skull on the cut, it was welded shut.*

The soldier leaned back, exhausted, and uttered a satisfied chuckle. Now he had time to look at his vis-à-vis. After looking Koschei up and down with his gleaming red eyes, the soldier asked, disgusted, "What are you?"

As the soldier stared at Koschei's nudity gleaming through the nightgown, Koschei's skin started tingling, then itching, then burning. Red flames first engulfed his nightgown, then his body and skipped to the grass beneath, the nearby bushes, trees. In a couple of minutes, the whole island was on fire.

9

The next day at breakfast, someone rang the doorbell. Everyone thought it was Vovka coming back from a bender, but when Mitya went to answer, he saw Zhenya, dressed for school.

"My mama sent me. Your cousin is in KPZ, the holding cell in the militsia station. Your papa should go to work it out and get him."

Mitya immediately thought that what he had suspected had happened. Vovka was, indeed, Valerka's murderer, and he had finally been apprehended. But why would they be letting him out, then? Perhaps it was only for the time before the trial. Mitya was not familiar with any of the intricacies of law enforcement.

He was so happy, though, that he did not ask Zhenya any questions. He told her he'd see her later at school and went back to the kitchen to pass the message to his family. They had more questions about the situation. Yelena Viktorovna and Dmitriy Fyodorovich rushed to talk to Zhenya's parents. Dmitriy

Fyodorovich slapped Mitya on the back of his head before leaving. "Useless," he groaned.

Once they were left alone, Alyssa Vitalyevna took out a bottle of Armenian cognac from her secret stash and added a splash to her and Mitya's tea: she felt like celebrating. "What do you think he did?" she asked, beaming at Mitya.

Mitya relayed his version to her. Alyssa Vitalyevna listened with interest. But once Mitya was done, she raised her brows skeptically.

"I don't believe that he had anything to do with killing Valerka. He has 'fallen from the oak,' as the saying goes, that's for sure, but Valerka went missing during the days Vovka spent at Sveta's, remember? I noticed because I always took Vovka's cigarette butts to Valerka, but on those days I had nothing to give and wanted to give him some rubles for a fresh pack. But he wasn't there," Alyssa Vitalyevna said. Mitya nodded: it was around the time Dmitriy Fyodorovich managed to persuade Vovka to go and visit his mother again, this time for a whole week. He returned even more jittery and swore he would never go again.

Alyssa Vitalyevna got the calendar she kept in her wallet, and they counted the days. It turned out that Vovka did have an alibi, and Valerka had gone missing right in the middle of his stay at Sveta's.

"And I would assume that he lied about visiting her, but that darn woman kept calling me at work and asking me to give her son some magic drug to cure him of drinking. As if I'm a witch. I told her: code him. Like Cleopatra's friend's husband. He used to chase her with an ax across the apartment, and once shit all over the room. But now that she's coded him, he is mellow and sweet."

"What is coding, Babushka?" Mitya asked.

"Oh, it's this fantastic way of making sure a person doesn't drink anymore. They do a spell or something, say a special code, and then whenever the coded person drinks any vodka, they fall violently ill and can even die."

Mitya was fascinated with the idea. A way to make Vovka stop drinking! Stop doing horrible things.

"So Khristofor Khristoforovich can do it?"

"Doctors refuse to do it. Too bad, because half of them are drunks, and the other half are coded themselves. But there are special places. If she only wanted to take him. But Sveta wants this to resolve on its own, without her having to spend her precious time on that. As if there's anything so important that she's doing these days."

"Do you think Vovka could become a better person if he were coded?"

"I don't know. His soul seems to be rotting from within. As they say, 'A stubborn ass will only get fixed by the cudgel.' Besides, I believe our billy goat will not be affected by any medicinal means that work for normal people. He's too damn special."

Well, Mitya thought, in that case, Vovka could have some vodka and die from the effects of coding. It seemed a pretty foolproof way to get rid of him. At least, the evil version of him or maybe both of them: whatever worked first.

Alyssa Vitalyevna took another sugar cube out of the bowl and crunched on it. She looked at her grandson and could almost see the wheels turning inside his blond head, he was thinking so hard. She had noticed in the past few months that he had started to look better, too, the spitting image of Yelena at that age, a tender beauty. His hair was longer than a boy's should be. She liked it, mainly because she knew that her son-in-law didn't approve.

When his parents came home from the precinct, Mitya was in the WC, thinking. He realized that he was so caught up in all the drama that he had forgotten to leave for school. At least he had his backpack with him, so he could sneak out through the back staircase, which led to the street from the kitchen. He heard his parents go into the kitchen to talk with Alyssa Vitalyevna. Mitya froze inside and began listening in, while he stared at the shapes formed by the cracks in the wall tiles. What had happened was that Vovka had gotten so drunk and rowdy the previous night, he'd gone outside and, while wielding a hammer, broken the windows in three cars parked near their building.

"I'm telling them that he couldn't have done it," Dmitriy Fyodorovich said. "He can't do anything properly with his left arm, but the militsionery are happy to have a perp."

"They want to make us pay the damages," Yelena Viktorovna chimed in.

"Did you all talk to Petya?" Alyssa Vitalyevna asked.

"He is at home sick, and Lyuba did not let us see him."

"Okay, I'm going to have to make a few phone calls," Alyssa Vitalyevna said with resolve, and Mitya heard her storm past the WC door, followed by his parents.

"Maybe we should leave him to marinate? Surely jail will do the boy some good," Dmitriy Fyodorovich said to Yelena Viktorovna.

"That's what you said about the army. Now look at him. You want him to come back without his head?"

When he couldn't hear them anymore, Mitya slipped out of the WC and went out through the dark staircase in the kitchen.

———

Later that day, after school, Mitya waited for Zhenya so they could walk back home together. She didn't seem to mind. Mitya wasn't sure how to start the conversation, so he blurted out the thing that concerned him most.

"Do you think militsionery will ever solve who killed Valerka?"

"You have no experience with militsia. They don't—how do I put it mildly?—play by the rules. Take yesterday, for example. It was my father and Vovka, together, in the streets. After you left, Papa got drunker. I saw him leave; I heard him sing those idiotic Tanya Bulanova songs in the courtyard below. And today he is hungover and sick, and my mother was chastising him for damaging those cars. But he's a militsioner. Vovka isn't, so he's going to pay for all the fun they had together, alone. The same goes for Valerka's murder. If there is not enough incentive to solve, it will remain unsolved."

"Maybe I should go tell them what I know?" Mitya asked.

"Which is what?"

"Nothing."

"Exactly. Mitya, you can try to solve this on your own, have your fun playing detective, but don't get involved with the militsia. They're often laughable, but if you anger them, they can be scary. I've been around them all my life, can't count how many times they've gotten drunk, tried to throw me up in the sky as if I were a toddler, and dropped me. But the things I some-times hear from my parents speaking . . ." Zhenya looked at him meaningfully. "They think I'm an idiot and I don't understand, but I do. And it's all unpleasant. So let your parents bail your cousin out and don't get involved."

Zhenya's brows were knit and her eyes icy and severe. Mitya nodded: if she was so serious about this, he had no other choice but to agree. They had reached McDonald's by the end of the conversation, and he left her behind. He went down the Old Arbat, past the pastel buildings, past the archway that led to his building, past the post office. He passed the wall covered with tiles hand-painted by children: an initiative of an American artist to promote peace and love between the two countries.

A fleet of shaved men in floaty persimmon clothes and warm jackets passed Mitya. They were chanting "Hare Krishna, Hare Rama," and beating handheld drums. Mitya admired them, their clothes especially: womanly, but also genderless, like all religious garb. He had wanted to go over to them and ask them about their song, or their clothes, or both. But whenever he was with Yelena Viktorovna, she pulled him away from them, and when he was alone, he was too shy. Now he had the resolve but did not want to spend it on the wrong situation. So Mitya moved toward the brooding giant of a gray building with the store called Samotsvety on the ground floor. Gems, the least appropriate name for the dreary site. He turned to the right in front of it and reached Tsoi's Wall, an unsightly one-story windowless structure covered with graffiti. Mitya had never been this close to it. He saw a few people next to the wall and decided to move closer and observe them from a short distance, keeping them in his peripheral vision. It would be a way to quench his interest while also mentally preparing to speak to someone.

The paint was densely layered, and the writings were all different. The most distinct was a rough portrait of Viktor Tsoi, which made the slender half-Korean man look like a plump middle-aged woman with jaw paralysis. Mitya recognized a bunch of quotes from songs by Tsoi and his band, Kino, Cinema, written all over the wall: bits and pieces of the youth hymns that Vovka sometimes listened to. Mitya liked hearing them, too, only he never wanted to admit that he admired the same music as his cousin. "Death is worth living, and love is worth waiting for." "Our heart works like a new motor, we're fourteen, and we know all we should. We'll be doing whatever we feel like before you ruin the world." "And we know it was always like that, and that fate strongly prefers those who follow different laws and those who die young just because."

There were markings made by people who had visited: "Arthur Lesha Edik," "Polina, Izhevsk City," "Law school with you." A few of them had phone numbers and addresses attached, which first seemed like a significant clue to Mitya, but then he realized that there were too many, and he wouldn't be able to follow through on all of them. The majority of the messages on the wall, though, were repetitions of the same phrase: "Tsoi is alive." It had been transcribed by hundreds of hands over and over again with mantric resolve all over the surface of the building, as if it could resurrect the singer, who had died in a car crash at twenty-eight. It was affecting, but quite repetitive, and Mitya quickly realized that nothing on the wall could help him.

This meant that he now had no other option but to strike up a conversation with one of the people sitting on the dirty pavement next to the wall. Mitya stepped back from the wall and turned to face the people sitting there: there were three. He didn't want to talk to random people, but justice for Valerka beckoned him. So Mitya gulped down his hesitance and then started talking.

"Did you know a man named Valerka?" Mitya heard himself ask.

The three people all looked his way. They were two young men and a woman, about Vovka's age, all smoking cigarettes. One of the men was blond and wearing a black leather jacket and had a guitar lying on his lap. He looked exactly as Mitya had pictured someone hanging out by Tsoi's Wall would look, but he was also oddly clean, well shaved, and neat. The other man and the woman had darker hair and were dressed in simpler clothes, much like his parents would wear, but looked decent enough too. Cleaner than Vovka. Why had he considered Tsoi's Wall a scary place? These people seemed normal enough.

"What do you need, maloy?" the man with the guitar asked. Mitya realized that they did not understand what he wanted.

"There is this man, Valerka, he was homeless and he used to come here sometimes. I wonder if you know him?"

"Chuvak, there are hundreds of people coming here every day. Is he a Kinoman?" asked the other man.

Mitya pondered for a second whether Valerka did in fact like the cinema but then realized that it must be the name for people who liked the band.

"I don't know, really," he said. He could feel the truth surfacing, the truth that he didn't know anything about Valerka, and that looking for traces of him would prove to be incredibly difficult.

"What are you asking, Gleb?" the woman said. "If he comes here, he's most likely a Kinoman. Everyone here is a Kinoman, me, Sasha. Except for you, of course. But how does that narrow it down?"

Mitya noticed that she had freckles on her nose, ginger curly hair, and a metal stud in one of her nostrils. Mitya had seen things like that on TV; they usually signified someone so cool that they left home to start a life on the streets. He wondered if the woman was living on the streets. She looked nice.

"What is your name, maltchik?" she asked. "So that when he comes looking for you next, we know what to say."

The woman smiled and small dimples appeared on her cheeks. The men exchanged glances and snickered. Mitya was annoyed by them: they clearly did not understand what was at stake. He had to explain.

"My name is Mitya, but he will not come for me, because he is dead."

The smiles faded abruptly.

"Mitya, I'm sorry," the woman said. "What happened to your friend? Do you need help?"

"Yes, I need help. Somebody killed Valerka, and it was here, but the militsia don't want to do anything about it."

"Why would he be killed here?" Sasha asked. "People come here to sing and drink, not murder each other."

"My neighbor from the militsia told me it was here," Mitya said.

"So he used to hang out here? Sasha, Marina, do you remember anyone like that?" Gleb asked.

Marina shook her head.

"I vaguely remember someone like that," Sasha responded. "There was a homeless guy, barely talked to anyone, and stank a kilometer away. Sometimes he brought beer and shared with people."

"Until he got killed." Mitya was glad to have finally gotten the strangers' attention.

"What horror," gasped Marina. "And why do you care for this homeless man, Mitya? Was he, tipa, your father or something? It's sad, but maybe better this way, if he was homeless?"

"He wasn't my father, he was my friend." Mitya couldn't get why it was so hard to understand the basics of the situation and move on to the essential things. Like who killed Valerka.

Marina looked like she wanted to ask another question, but then she waved her hand, stubbed her cigarette out, and shrugged. "Go ahead, Mitya, ask us questions, we will try to help."

"Who do you think killed him?" Mitya asked.

"Hey, easy. How would we know? We're music-loving people, I live right in this building over here, and these two haven't been hanging out here for long," Sasha said.

"He's not asking you if you killed him, though, right?" Gleb looked back at Mitya. "It's a dangerous place here, especially at night. Your friend would be an idiot if he came here after dark."

"Why is it dangerous?" Mitya wondered.

"Because there are all kinds of terrible people here. Druggies, drinkers, thieves. Werewolves," Sasha said, and Mitya could see Gleb stick his nose into the sleeve of his jacket and convulse with restrained laughter. Marina slapped Sasha's arm.

"Please tell me about the dangerous people who come here," Mitya said. He thought that if he stuck to the point and was straightforward, he could get the info he wanted and start investigating.

"Are you crazy?" Marina said. "I didn't realize it was such a criminal den here. But we don't want to get you killed next, stupid, so no one will tell you what dangerous people to seek out."

"I'm not gonna get killed." Mitya was sure of it. They'd have to find the needle first. "And I know dangerous people too. Does Vovka come here by any chance? Army veteran with a missing arm?"

"Where are you hanging out with these freaks, patsan?" Sasha asked. "You look like you're from an intelligentsia family. Why all the homeless people and one-armed men?"

"Vovka is my cousin," Mitya said.

"Anyway, we don't know any one-armed Vovka. We weren't here; we didn't see the body," Sasha said and started plucking at the strings on his guitar. "There is a bunch of kids who come here sometimes, though. A bit older than you. They sniff glue and steal things, they're homeless and they're up to no good. But all the others are Kinomen, or hippies, or other neformals."

"Do you know if these kids knew Valerka?"

"You think we keep track of everyone who comes here?" Sasha said, annoyed, laying his guitar aside.

"Huh, I saw them hanging out by my metro station too, recently. Rebyata, let's help Mitya out. We should learn to be better friends to each other from him. Look how determined he is. Do your parents know you're out and about?" Marina asked.

Mitya wondered whether he wanted to lie or tell the truth. Marina's freckled face was so round and open that he couldn't bring himself to start on a lie with her, but at the same time, he knew that no one would want to get involved with a child who was missing from home.

"As if *your* parents know you're out and about," Gleb said, touching Marina's jacket lightly. She stuck her tongue out at him.

"Can't argue with that. So, Mitya, would you like to come ride the metro with us and see if we can find those kids? It's the Konkovo stop." Marina stood up from the ground and came up to Mitya. She took his hand into hers firmly, and he felt her skinny palm with chapped skin. Mitya wasn't sure how far Konkovo was from home, but he felt like going would be the right decision. The needle would make sure everything went smoothly.

"Wait, but we were supposed to go have a beer at my place." Sasha jumped up after her. "Come on, it's right over there, in that building, and there's only fifteen more minutes to go."

"I'm tired of waiting for your mother to leave the apartment. We'll see you tomorrow, Sasha. Maybe you can give us a ride in your papa's car? Let's go, Gleb."

Sasha's self-assured look faded from his face. He tried saying something, but Marina turned away from him and was already leading Mitya toward the Old Arbat. Gleb quickly shook Sasha's hand and ran after her, and as soon as they turned the corner, he put his arms around her. She leaned into his arm but did not loosen her grip on Mitya's hand. They walked to the subway in silence.

10

In the metro, Gleb hugged Marina and Mitya so that they could pass through the gate using one token for all three of them. Then, on the train, Marina sat Mitya down next to herself, while Gleb sat across the aisle.

"Don't you think he looks like Viktor Tsoi?" she asked Mitya, as Gleb grinned and made faces at her.

Mitya nodded. There was a vague resemblance.

"Don't tell him. He hates it! Says that it's not true and that he is Uzbek, not Korean, and I'm putting all Asians into one pot. But I think it's because he doesn't like Kino's music. Says it's too simple, govnorock, shitrock. He's into all these weird underground bands who perform in apartments. Keeps taking me to hear them, but I'm not into that sort of thing, I guess."

"I didn't know you could have concerts in apartments," Mitya said. He wondered how that worked. Did the musicians climb up on the kitchen table to perform?

"Are you kidding me? Even Tsoi started that way. There weren't too many clubs that would have rock musicians in the eighties. It's better now, but still. You have to rely on people to host concerts in their living rooms. And it's kind of nice. I mean, I went to see Yuri Shevchuk in Gorbushka, and it was way cool. But you can't get Shevchuk to sing to your ten friends. So I appreciate it, it's special."

"Can you take me too?" Mitya wasn't sure why he'd asked. He didn't particularly care to spend more time with Marina and Gleb, but he liked the idea of a living room where concerts happened. It seemed a more appropriate use of the space than the way his grandmother used it, to watch soap operas, or the way his cousin did, doing painful things to him. Maybe he could learn, and then he could do concerts in his living room too.

Marina nodded. "What kind of music do you like?"

"I like Bon Jovi," Mitya said. It was the only kind of rock music he could think of. He had liked watching their video for the song "Always" when he was smaller. The singer was quite beautiful, though Mitya couldn't figure out if it was him when he painted half-naked in the video, or if it was some other man. They looked alike, but the naked painter also had weird froggy lips that Mitya wanted to kiss but simultaneously found repulsive. "Not the music so much, but I sometimes kiss the singer in my dreams," Mitya shared with Marina for no reason at all. He never had such dreams, but he wanted to seem like he was also living an exciting life, and this was what he came up with.

"Wait, so you like men?" Marina asked. "That is so cool! I heard about golubiye and always wanted to meet them, but we didn't seem to have any. I knew I'd meet some in Moscow! Though you're so young. I thought it was a grown-up thing."

Mitya was taken aback. He knew what she was talking about, of course; he'd read about such things: the articles in his grandmother's tabloids, or some briefly mentioned plotlines in the soap operas, of men who loved men. *Golubiye*, sky blue. There were some in *A Próxima Vítima*. But he had never thought to consider himself in such terms. He wasn't a man, to begin with, just a child, who had nothing to do with romantic love as grownups described it. He loved his grandmother, his mother, sure, his father in some sense. Not Vovka. He loved Valerka and the crows. But he had never thought about romantic love. Would he ever experience it? For whom? Mitya had no idea.

"So where did you come to Moscow from?" he asked Marina, to change the subject.

"Donbass. It's in Ukraine. I'm from this small place near Donetsk. Boring and rural. No place for a seventeen-year-old girl in bloom."

"Did you run away from home to be here?" Mitya asked.

"You could say that," Marina said, laughing, as her eyes remained sad. "Some places are made to be run away from."

Mitya wanted to ask her what she meant. Was there a sure way to know that your home was not good enough for you? But before he could ask anything, they reached a stop.

"Okay, we're here." She pulled Mitya up by the hand and pecked Gleb goodbye on the cheek, as he would be staying on the train for another stop. As they walked down the platform and up the stairs out of the station, Mitya asked Marina if she missed home. "I do, but I came here for a better life. Not that it's started yet," she sneered. "I'm renting a bed from Vietnamese migrants, who are themselves renting in the National University of Science and Technology dorm. I live with two other girls in the room. I found some work selling lingerie at the market, but it's only when the other woman is busy with her grandson, and it pays kopecks."

They reached the top of the stairs and left the station, and Marina immediately whispered: "There's one of the boys you wanted to see." She gestured at a skinny boy with her head, barely taller than Mitya himself. He was dressed in soiled clothes and a beanie that covered his eyebrows. Marina said she had seen him at Tsoi's Wall, selling counterfeit lottery tickets to some tourists. Now he was holding a few packs of cigarettes in his right hand and offering them to passersby. A lit cigarette was smoldering in his left hand.

Marina led Mitya down the street toward the cluster of kiosks, where she stopped as soon as they turned a corner.

"Look, I'll wait here. They don't trust grown-ups, if you can call me that," she said coquettishly. "I'm going to stand in the distance and watch so that he doesn't do anything bad to you. Can't trust those wild boys, especially with someone as sweet as you."

Mitya shrugged and made his way back to where the boy was standing. He felt less nervous about approaching him because he had spent some time around Marina.

"Marlboros 4,000, L&M 3,000," the boy told him, flaunting the packs as Mitya approached.

"Can I please ask you a question?" Mitya tried to look the boy in the eyes, so as not to betray his nervousness.

"Slysh, patsan, either buy this or get the hell out of here, I'm working," he said sternly, menace in his eyes. But Mitya couldn't think of anything that the boy could do to him that hadn't been done before, so it didn't make him afraid.

"Look, I've heard you hang out in the Old Arbat, and I've been looking for my friend from there. Maybe you knew him?"

"I hang out wherever I want, that's what makes me free," the boy said, boastfully. Mitya saw that the skin around his nose was raw, and there were sores in the corners of his mouth. He realized he had to employ his previous tactics of speaking frankly and to the point.

"My friend was killed. His name was Valerka. Did you know him?"

"Why should I know your tsivilniye friends? Go back to your school, patsan, and eat Babushka's soup."

"He was a bomzh, this Valerka. And he kept birds. You sure you don't know him?"

The boy's face enlivened in recognition.

"Blya, you should have said so. Valerka . . . of course, I know him! Used to beg with my koresh Dlinniy next to the Old Arbat McDonald's, before Dlinniy died. Have you seen him, skinny chuvak with wounds on his body?"

Mitya briefly remembered seeing a slightly older boy with unhealing sores on his skin who asked for change next to the entrance, along with Valerka and the older woman from his building whose son beat her. Mitya asked Alyssa Vitalyevna why he had the sores, and she said that it was some cancer. But the boy hadn't been begging there for quite a long time. Mitya nodded.

"So, you say Valerka's dead too? You sure? Maybe he moved to a new place? I was never that comfortable on the Old Arbat. Too many militsia. But Dlinniy liked the tourists. Some fat American woman once wanted to adopt him. He stole like two hundred bucks from her and had to lie low for two weeks." The boy tittered as if he were remembering the funniest thing, and Mitya had to put some effort into not letting his brows rise.

"I know he died; that's what the militsia says."

"Why d'you trust the militsia, patsan?"

"I don't." Mitya quickly clarified, and it sounded about right. "But my grandmother does."

"See, I knew you were a grandmother's boy."

Mitya ignored that.

"Somebody beat Valerka up by Tsoi's Wall, and he died. I want to find out who did it."

"How should I know?"

"You know any other boys who hang out on the Old Arbat? Someone should know something."

"Maybe they do, but it's going to cost." The boy raised his palm upwards and rubbed two extended fingers against his thumb.

Mitya thought about it for a second but decided that he didn't want to dig out the money he had buried under Valerka's tree to give the boy. He wanted more time to see if the magic of planting the money would work.

"I don't have money, but I can bring you food. Or toys." Mitya said.

"Patsan, how old do you think I am? Two? I'll take vodka or glue, though."

"Okay, I can do that," Mitya said to the boy, although he wasn't sure how.

"Now we're talking. When you're ready, find me. Or ask other patsany for Chervyak."

"Chervyak?" Worm. Why would anyone want to go by such a nickname?

"I fit into places other people don't," Chervyak responded with a crooked smile.

Mitya did not ask further questions. He nodded to Chervyak, which seemed like a proper way to say goodbye, and went toward the bus stop where Marina was hiding.

"He doesn't know too much but has agreed to introduce me to the others if I bring him vodka or glue," he relayed to her.

"He's what, thirteen?" she said with horrified eyes.

"If not vodka or glue, he said he'd love money. But where can I get money?" Mitya wondered if she had any thoughts.

"I'll think of something," Marina replied. It was all coming together in her head. She wanted to help. As simple as that— the exact kind of impulsiveness everyone was always accusing her of. She didn't care. Kindness was not the same as meddling.

They decided to meet up the next Monday afternoon at the wall, and see Chervyak together afterward. Mitya wasn't sure why Marina chose to start helping him, but it felt nice that someone else was also taking part in his adventure. She probably liked being able to speak to someone who was not in love with her, unlike Sasha and Gleb.

SIX

After setting Koschei and his surroundings on fire, the soldier glanced around, and his red eyes spread the flames everywhere. Bewildered by the damage he had inflicted, he took off and ran away from the spring. As he disappeared into the woods, Koschei saw flames and plumes of smoke emerge in the distance, until the horizon was dense with gray fumes.

Koschei was on fire, too, so he submerged himself in the spring. The flames on his skin died down immediately, but the nightgown, now singed and shriveled, seemed to become one with his body. He tried prying it off, but it wasn't budging and covered his skin like scales, or scabs, concentrated around the neck area and below the ribs.

He helped the animals nearby form a chain to start passing water in buckets and splashing it on the flames. But though they were using water from the healing spring, the fire wouldn't let up. It burned for seven days and seven nights, and the island's *abundant greenery was reduced to nothing more than scorched earth and charred sticks, and the wail that persisted and seemed to become one with the wind haunted the desolate landscape. The animals with Koschei survived, but others, trapped deep in the thicket, were piles of ash. The beautiful house burned to a crisp, too, even though the twin baby moles took turns pissing on the flames to put them out. The only thing they managed to salvage was the moon-sun-stars crown, which they took to guarding with their little chubby bodies.*

With the vegetation burned, one could easily see across the whole island. Neither the soldier nor Leshy was to be found. Leshy's red slippers were retrieved on a faraway shore.

"Was he chasing the soldier?" Koschei wondered. There was no trace of the soldier, but he must have gone somewhere.

"I didn't see them, but I was too flustered," a sockeye salmon said from the water.

"Well, we're doomed," said a cuckoo, kicking the ash beneath her feet. "Whatever chance we had to salvage this island is gone with Leshy. He's the only one who knows how to replant and re-populate it."

"And it's all my fault," Koschei lamented. Some animals began reassuring him that it wasn't, not really, but the majority knew he was telling the truth. "I have to make it right, and I have to find Leshy for all of you," he said to weak affirmations.

Koschei waved at his friends the animals, inhaled deeply, pinched his nose, and jumped off the edge of the island into the water. The trench beneath him turned out to be surprisingly deep. Koschei breathed out so he could fall deeper and deeper. He exhaled, and exhaled, and yet the trench's bottom was nowhere in sight. He was reluctant at first, but then Koschei tried to breathe in, and it turned out that he could breathe underwater too. The scorched bits of his nightgown stuck to his body had turned into gills.

Because he didn't have to worry about his breathing anymore, and because he hadn't slept for seven days and seven nights, Koschei fell asleep as he continued down. He slept and slept, and woke up only when his body hit a hard surface with a thud. Koschei opened his eyes and saw that a snake with a crown on her head was sitting on top of his chest and staring at his face. When she saw him come to, she yelped and fell off. "Brother, he's awake!" the snake cried out excitedly, as she slithered away. "Come see!"

11

When Mitya returned home, he found the family at the kitchen table, drinking tea with varenye.

"I was able to negotiate Vovka's release," Alyssa Vitalyevna said with aplomb, as if she had set a crowd of hostages free from the hands of terrorists. "It all came together quite well: the head of the precinct has a mother who needs brain surgery, and Khristofor Khristoforovich happens to know one of the best neurosurgeons in Moscow. I got her a space in the queue, and your cousin is free now!"

Alyssa Vitalyevna sparkled with her accomplishment like a newly minted coin.

"So where is he now?" Mitya asked, trying to hide his disappointment.

"Drinking somewhere." Yelena Viktorovna made a helpless gesture.

"One would think that after such a smooth negotiation, he would at least try and thank me." Alyssa Vitalyevna put a whole preserved strawberry into her mouth. "I guess I shouldn't expect good manners from him. It's not in his genes." She cast a dirty glance at Dmitriy Fyodorovich, who turned on the TV instead of answering.

The next morning, a Saturday, Dmitriy Fyodorovich told Mitya that they were going to see Aunt Sveta, Vovka's mom. He had been postponing the visit, but now that Vovka had gotten himself into trouble, it seemed like they had to go. Mitya had not been to Sveta's apartment for a while, not since before Vovka came to live with them. She was a strange woman and, if Mama and Babushka's whispers were true, had become stranger lately: more secluded, less able to look after herself, more immersed in her obsession with following celebrities' lives. But Mitya was eager to see Sveta's friendly dog, Hector, an old basset hound who used to greet Mitya by standing on his hind legs and putting his front paws on the boy's chest. When Mitya was small, he couldn't hold Hector's weight, and they both toppled over. It made everyone laugh.

Previously, it had been only Yelena Viktorovna who went to see Sveta, loaded with a large thermos canister of soup and bags of kotleti and pirozhki. But then she said to Dmitriy Fyodorovich she wouldn't go anymore. It was time he took care of his relatives himself. Dmitriy Fyodorovich tried to counter the argument: after all, Yelena Viktorovna's mother lived with them, too, so it seemed like a shared responsibility for all relatives. But Yelena Viktorovna brought up his brother. She knew it was mean to do so, but she'd had enough of the crazy woman.

"You owe it to Seryozha to go," she said and saw her husband's eyes dim, his shoulders slope down.

Dmitriy Fyodorovich invited his son to come along. Not because he particularly liked the company but because Mitya seemed like a good buffer to install between himself and Sveta.

———

Hector leaped to the door with all his sleepy bulk and panted with excitement.

"Yelena cooked borscht," Dmitriy Fyodorovich pointed out instead of a greeting and ushered Mitya in with the package: a giant gingham polyester bag filled with containers of food. Carrying it made Mitya's back hurt, but he didn't say anything, hoping his father would notice his strength. At the same time, Dmitriy Fyodorovich wished he hadn't taken his son with him: he was so excruciatingly slow. He almost took the bag away, but didn't. The boy needed to learn to handle his responsibilities.

Sveta saw that Dmitriy Fyodorovich and his son were both wearing windbreakers, and realized it must be fall. She hadn't been out for a few weeks now, maybe a few months.

"How do you take care of him?" Dmitriy Fyodorovich pointed at Hector, who made circles around Mitya unloading groceries on the kitchen table. "Have you been working?"

"My students come over, and the neighbor girl walks Hector in exchange for help with her son's stuttering." Sveta was proud to have everything set up so well. "She is a lovely girl, and single now. Vovka used to like her when they were both in kindergarten."

"Has he called you?" Dmitriy Fyodorovich asked.

"He has not called since his visit."

"You know that he was in jail?"

Sveta clutched her chest. She knew she couldn't trust them with her son.

"It's fine; we got him out."

Mitya noticed how Dmitriy Fyodorovich was able to reclaim Alyssa Vitalyevna's victory in her absence.

Sveta sighed and calmed down. She didn't ask why her son had been in jail, how they'd managed to get him out. The less of the truth she knew, the easier it was. She invited them to sit down for tea with greenish cheese and stale biscuits.

"As soon as he left the joint, he went to go get drunk," Dmitriy Fyodorovich continued as he plunged down on the couch in the living room. "And now he's probably lying somewhere with his pants pissed, passed out, or even dead."

"Dmitriy, please . . . I tried calling that woman he had taken up with, but there was always some drunken noise on the line, and then silence. I thought about going to the Old Arbat and looking for him there. Maybe I will go next week?"

Sveta had been thinking about this for a long time now. She had almost been ready to go a couple of times, but first the psoriasis came in, and then there was a repeat of a documentary series on the lives of celebrities on TV. Perhaps because of Dmitriy's words, she felt her inner thighs flare up and patted them, hoping they would calm down.

Dmitriy Fyodorovich nodded, although he was not sure what he wanted from her. Everyone seemed to be powerless to stop Vovka's demise. What were they going to do if Vovka died? Dmitriy Fyodorovich asked himself. He had two responsibilities to his dead brother: to take care of the two people he loved most in his life. And now one was probably lying somewhere in a puddle of his own waste, and the other one was scratching herself like a mangy dog and not leaving her apartment.

"Do you think Vovka can come to see me again?" Sveta asked.

"I think he will come to you when he needs money. Did you give him money when you last saw him?" Dmitriy Fyodorovich looked at Sveta suspiciously.

She looked down into her cup and felt a tear stream down her cheek into it, as if she were a cartoon character.

"Did you?" Dmitriy Fyodorovich raised his voice.

"I don't want him to starve. And it wasn't much anyway, you know my pension is small and I don't make much tutoring."

She couldn't stop the sobs from coming. They sounded like hiccups.

Hector got out from beneath the coffee table and barked at Dmitriy Fyodorovich, who was now off the couch, frantic, screaming, pointing fingers. Mitya looked at the portrait of his uncle in his military uniform, hanging on the wall, and wondered what he would make of all this.

"Find him, Dmitriy," Sveta begged. "Tell him I need to see him. Bring him here. The neighbor girl, she's so sweet. She doesn't know he drinks, and we won't tell her. They can marry, and she'll take care of him, and they'll live with her parents. It's all clear to me now—the plan in front of my eyes. I need help, I need my boy to come back to me, and then I'll make sure it all works out. I'll watch her kid so they can date. I'll cook an apple pie and a potato pie. Or I can feed them whatever Yelena cooked, since I don't have the supplies anymore. Maybe they'll take Hector to live with them too. So sweet! A real family, with a son and a dog already."

In the metro, though Mitya felt that his father was angry, he tried to make him comfortable.

"Papa, was it long ago that Uncle Seryozha died? I was not born yet, right?"

"I had not met your mother then," Dmitriy Fyodorovich responded. There was a pulsating dot below his temple, which usually promised Mitya a beating. But not this time. Suddenly softened, his father began talking.

"Vovka was four, maybe less. Sveta was young, too, but they had been married for a while. We were all living together when the telegram came. He was captured by the mujahideen and killed soon after. We never got to know exactly how. The coffin was sealed."

Mitya thought that he ought to hold his father's hand in compassion, but fear and the alienness of such a touch made him freeze. Dmitriy Fyodorovich was staring straight ahead, into the rolling darkness behind the glass of the train car.

"Why weren't you in the army yourself at the time?" Mitya asked.

"I had been dismissed for a few weeks for my twisted ankle. Can you believe it? A twisted ankle. They never sent people back home for that, but the hospital was overcrowded." Dmitriy Fyodorovich gulped painfully. A wrong brother sitting next to his wrong son.

"I wish my father had lived to see Seryozha grow up, how brave he was, how strong. It's the goal of every father to see his son a hero in the fight against terrorism or fascism, decorated, even if it's within the coffin," Dmitriy Fyodorovich said to his son, eager to have the conversation over with.

They sat in silence for a long, gloomy while, shaking along with the train. Mitya thought about dead brothers, and strength, and realized, an emptiness widening inside of him, that his father would never stay alive long enough to see him growing strong, or becoming a hero. It just didn't seem likely to happen. Not in the way his father had hoped.

12

On Monday, when he reached Tsoi's Wall, Mitya saw that Marina was sitting there with Sasha and some other people in leather jackets, but no Gleb. When she saw him, her mouth stretched into a smile. She put her thumb up to say that everything was great and that she had done all that was expected of her. Sasha was playing a song by Tsoi, and the people sitting around, including Marina, sang along.

> And for two thousand years, there's a war,
> A war without reason or cause,
> This war is the business of youth,
> A cure against getting old.
> Flowing vermillion blood,
> In an hour, just regular soil,
> In two, there are flowers and grass,
> In three, it's living again,

Warmed up by the rays of the star
That we're calling the sun.

Mitya knew that song well. It was one of the most popular Kino songs, and Vovka liked it a lot. It was one of the songs he liked to scream at the top of his lungs from that woman's window early in the morning.

Once the song was over and Sasha stopped playing, Marina left the singing circle and walked over to Mitya. She waved good-bye to everyone else, and they waved back. Only Sasha got up. He nodded at Mitya and asked Marina:

"You sure I can't take you home?"

"No, stay, play, it's so nice here today, so many good voices," she said, gently patting him on the cheek. "I need to help Mitya with something, and he'll see me home."

Sasha was reluctant, but he kissed Marina on the cheek and went back to the circle, where people were taking beers out of a black grocery bag.

"I got 200,000 rubles," Marina said to Mitya, as they turned the corner and headed for the metro. She was excited to be in this position: a benefactor who gives her friend the money he so desperately needs. "That will buy him four bot- tles of vodka, I checked. Or a ton of glue. But I hope he buys something more useful. Here." She handed a plastic bag to Mitya. "I also put in a can of sgushenka. I hope he tries the condensed milk and decides he wants to have more sugar in-stead of bukhlo and kley."

Mitya nodded. "So how were you able to get this much in a weekend?"

"I have my ways." She said mysteriously. Marina didn't want Mitya to know the prosaic truth of how she'd gotten the money: it would make her seem less noble, and could even cause her friend to like her less.

Mitya took the bag from her and held it throughout their commute. Marina told him about her life back in Donbass: it was nice, but everyone was poor. Because of that, her father was often angry and beat her. So she wanted to try to make a life in Moscow, get a good job, or marry a rich guy, to be able to bring her mother and grandmother to live with her.

Mitya was reluctant to reciprocate by sharing his own story with Marina. Their lives seemed to have some commonalities, but he felt like the behavior of his father and Vovka was something to be ashamed of. He wasn't complicit, but still ought to protect his family's honor in the opinion of everyone else. That's what Mama and Babushka always told him: some things were only family things. And there was also that saying: "Don't take the trash out of the izba." Mitya never fully understood how one could keep up a proper household if one was not supposed to take the trash out. Wouldn't it make the house dirty, overflowing?

So Mitya didn't take the trash out and didn't go into many details about his family. Instead, he told Marina about Valerka: how he loved his birds and was gentle and sweet. Mitya was not sure if he wanted to tell Marina about the dress. She would be able to understand, but he was afraid of being misunderstood. And he also felt like she might diagnose him again, like when she concluded he was goluboy, the previous time. Maybe he was. He had been thinking hard about this ever since, but that was his call to make. He decided to start from a safe distance and then feel his way, maybe share more truth with her, tell her about the needle.

"I also like to dress up funny," Mitya said to Marina, "and grown-ups judge me for it, but Valerka didn't."

"What do you mean, dress funny?" Marina asked. She looked him over and saw a simply dressed boy, jeans and a sweater, a jacket, like everyone else.

"Well, like costumes. Sometimes like a clown. Sometimes like a girl." It seemed that if he buried the truth under layers of embellishments, it wouldn't stand out quite as much.

"You are so bohemian," Marina gasped. "This is what I expected from Moscow. Not from eleven-year-old boys, of course. But I thought that everyone here is weird and artistic, but the majority of people I encounter are as plain and boring as back in Donbass. Gleb has some friends that are like you, I think. You should definitely come along with me to a kvartirnik."

Once they arrived in Konkovo, Marina hid behind the kiosk again. She would follow Mitya from afar so that he wouldn't get in trouble, in case the homeless boy and his friends chose to take advantage of him, or something of the kind. Once she determined Mitya was safe, she would leave. She was sad that she wouldn't be able to participate more, but she didn't want to threaten the investigation.

Mitya was thankful to her. Surely, she had better things to do with her day, but she not only found money for Mitya to use but also wanted to make sure he would be all right. It was more than he expected any grown-up to do to help him and Valerka. Although, now he wasn't sure that he wanted to consider Marina an adult. She was more of a sister that he didn't have. Or the sister he wanted to be like.

———

Mitya found Chervyak at the same spot, only this time he was selling bananas. It took the homeless boy a minute to understand who Mitya was and why he said that he had brought something. Finally, when he remembered and Mitya handed him the contents of the bag, making sure to neatly fold the bag and put it away in his pocket, Chervyak's face lit up.

"Wow, I can get, tipa, ten bottles of vodka for this," he said, counting the yellow 10,000-, orange 5,000-, and green 1,000-ruble notes. When Mitya handed him the can of sgushenka, Chervyak licked his lips and said that it was his favorite treat in the whole wide world. He proceeded to open the can with a large rugged knife that he produced from inside his parka.

"A guy I ran with made it for me especially," he explained, as Mitya watched him place the tin on the ground by the curb and poke holes around the lid with the tip of the blade. "It's made from a car's leaf spring." He didn't have a spoon, so Chervyak proceeded to drink sgushenka right from the can. He slurped loudly and then seemed to roll the liquid around his palate. There was an expression of bliss on his face. Some of the substance was left on Chervyak's chafed lips, pearly, half-transparent, gooey, and Mitya had the strongest longing to go up to the boy and lick it off his lips. He fidgeted in place to shake off that weird feeling.

After swallowing sgushenka, Chervyak carefully closed the lid and put the tin in his inner pocket so that it stood upright.

Mitya thought about warning him that it might spill. But Chervyak's clothes were pretty dirty anyway, and this comment would only prove that Mitya was a boy with a home, someone who could get clean and had clothes worthy of care. It made him uncomfortable, to see the difference between himself and Chervyak so starkly. He tried as hard as he could not to call unnecessary attention to that. Mitya wanted Chervyak to like him, although, of course, there was no obvious way to establish whether he did or not, since money was involved.

"I'll bring this to the rest of the boys," Chervyak said, licking his lips. "They'll be so happy. We haven't had sgushenka since Komar's eighth birthday two months ago."

Mitya figured that Komar, a mosquito, was also a homeless boy, and was surprised to find out that there were homeless boys as young as that. How early did they start?

Chervyak put the bananas into a sack, lit a cigarette from a pack he had in his pants, and led Mitya down the stairs into the metro.

"You know the Cheremushki rynok? That's where we live. It's a ride away. I can't sell my stuff close to the market because they'll find out. Also, here I can raise the prices, charge the people for avoiding the trip."

He still had the cigarette in his mouth when they entered the metro vestibule. Mitya had never seen anyone smoke inside the metro, and he was appalled by Chervyak's moxie. No one seemed to be paying attention, though, when Chervyak jumped over the turnstile instead of paying with a ticket. Mitya hesitated and then followed suit, again afraid to show that he was coddled. But instead of jumping over, he crawled under, which proved quite uncomfortable. He felt that he must have dirtied up his outfit, but didn't check it: the dirtier he could get, the better he would fit in.

"What was it that you wanted to find out from my patsany? I forget," Chervyak asked.

"I wanted to find out if any of them know about how my friend got killed," Mitya reminded him.

"Right. We'll see. Some of these boys are pretty messed up. I mean, even I don't remember anything you've told me, and it was, like, a week ago? Some days ago?" Chervyak scratched his head. There was a fog inside his head that never cleared up. He believed it was from not sleeping enough. It must be the glue, Mitya thought, but he didn't say anything. Would Chervyak be just like Vovka one day, out of touch with reality, hurting people, sick?

"Have you lived in the market long?" Mitya asked.

Chervyak was eager to respond. Sgushenka had perked him up, and the story spilled out of him smoothly.

"Just a few months. Me and a bunch of other kids, we lived in an empty old building for two years, I think, not far from there. But they said the building was a mess, and the government khuynuli it this spring. Then it was summer, so we just lived in the streets. We went to this village where one of the boys had a grandmother. Swam in the river. It was nice." Chervyak half closed his eyes, dreamily, recalling his summer adventures. "There's also a bunch of places where the people come to their dacha only for the weekend. So we had places to sleep. But when the summer's over, it's not fun to be in the village. Only abandoned dying dogs. We moved back to Moscow. It was still warm, but Luzhkov, the suchiy mayor, was sending all the homeless away, or putting us in jail. He wanted to have his stupid 850th-anniversary celebration for Moscow without the homeless everywhere. So we couldn't sleep in the streets. We found this sweet hookup in the market. Something always works out. That's how freedom works."

Mitya was once again taken aback by the word he used. "Freedom." Did Chervyak consider himself free? He had no place to sleep, always had to look out for himself, and work, and steal. How was this "freedom"?

Chervyak had exhausted his chattiness and drifted off into the sweet memories of his summer, of swimming in the river and waking up to bird songs. He nodded quietly to the sugar crush.

13

When they arrived at the market, Chervyak led Mitya to the entrance. Mitya was not sure if he had been to the Cheremushki market before, but it looked familiar. Chervyak told him to wait next to the honey stall and went to talk to the Asian-looking man who sold nuts. Then, the two disappeared into the depth of the market rows. Mitya looked at the honey for sale, gooey, thick, of various shades of amber. He noticed a few plastic jars with what looked like the bodies of dead bees inside, and it fascinated him: Why would anyone want to buy a bunch of dead bees? The woman who was selling them noticed his interest and explained that it was called "podmore," you diluted it with hot water, and it was good for a long list of afflictions but cost 10,000 rubles per jar. Mitya said he didn't have any money.

"I'll give you a sample, and you can bring it to your parents, have them try it out. Tell your father it's good with manly might. He'll know what it means." With those words, she shook a few shrunken bodies onto a napkin and folded it into an envelope. Mitya received the gift and thanked the woman. He put the napkin into the inner pocket of his jacket.

Chervyak returned with a plastic bag, which Mitya immediately recognized had two bottles inside. Mitya did not think they'd be selling vodka at the farmers market, but then again, he also had not realized that boys lived there. Chervyak brought him to the rear of the market and through a door leading into the warehouse. It wasn't as well lit or as well cared for as the market hall, and the stench bordered on the unbearable. The stink of rotting vegetables commingled with some suffocating sweetness and the crisp, provoking mouse smell that reminded Mitya of Zhenya's hangout in their building's basement. Chervyak showed no sign of noticing the smells. Mitya thought that from living at the market he had become desensitized to it, as sanitation workers and plumbers become indifferent to the stench of their workplace.

After a long walk, they reached a remote corner with a pile of mattresses and clothes, shoes, toys, bottles, and scraps haphazardly thrown around them. This must be the nest for the homeless boys, Mitya thought, as he noticed that one of the mattresses, dirty and without linen, was occupied by a tiny figure covered by what looked like a burlap sack: a small boy, sleeping. There were also a few boys sitting on mattresses arranged in a square, playing cards. They looked older than Chervyak.

"Why aren't you at work?" Chervyak asked them, as one of the boys laid a card, a jack of spades, over a five of spades, clicked his tongue, called out, "Beat," and put the two cards away into a deck of used cards.

"We're waiting for Uncle Misha to figure something out with the Solntsevskiye, so we're off today," the boy who had beaten the card said. He had big eroded teeth.

Mitya knew that the Solntsevskiye, the Solntsevo bratva, was a mafia that controlled the majority of the south of Moscow. Sometimes when Mitya was eating breakfast, Alyssa Vitalyevna liked to turn on the small TV in the kitchen and watch "Road Patrol." It was a short, fifteen-minute segment on the morning news, in which the program's correspondents rushed to crime scenes. The crew filmed apprehensions of perpetrators, the scenes of car crashes, and, if Mitya was lucky, an occasional corpse splayed across a staircase, the sweater raised above the swell of the gut, blood seeping out. As he thought about it, he realized that they sometimes showed markets on the program too. That was where raids on counterfeit alcohol and drug busts were conducted. Did they link them to the bratva? Mitya wasn't sure. He even remembered hearing something about a brothel backed by the bratva. What could these boys, just a bit older than he was, be doing for the bratva?

"Who nakhuy is that?" a boy with a pitiful mustache asked Chervyak, stubbing out his cigarette. "Chervyak, we've told you to stop bringing random people to our headquarters, haven't we?"

"He's with me. Look, I've got us some vodka." He produced the bottles that he'd purchased earlier from the bag.

"Blya, Chervyak, you should have less vodka, not more," the boy with the teeth said. "You will get your ass whooped one day."

"Who's the mamenkin synok?" the boy with the mustache asked again. Mitya wanted to answer that he wasn't a mother's boy and had an important mission, but he couldn't think of a convincing way to say it.

"We're solving a crime," Chervyak said earnestly.

"You're an ebaniy clown. Your luck he looks harmless enough," said a third boy, who had a hat on, nodding to Mitya. "Slysh, Chervyak, give some vodka to Tsypa. Kostyl here tried to wake him up earlier, but he refused. Must be some awful hangover."

Tsypa did indeed look like a small chicken. Kostyl was thin and straight like a crutch. Mitya wondered what his name would be if he were to live among these boys. Would they get close enough for him to start dressing as a woman in front of them, for them to start calling him Devchonka? He couldn't see it all together: boys living in the market and working with the bratva, and the tenderness he strived for did not mix.

Chervyak got a cup and poured some vodka into it. He took it to the mattress with the body under the blanket. Mitya followed him because he felt awkward staying next to these bigger guys. Chervyak pushed the body awake, and a boy no older than seven emerged from the cocoon of the sack.

"Na, opokhmelis," Chervyak said, giving the boy the vodka to drink. Mitya was flabbergasted. The little boy took the cup and emptied it in one gulp, as if he were a professional drinker, and then smiled widely. Some of his teeth were missing, and there was an uncanny air about him. Did he look like a regular elementary-school-age kid, or did he resemble a down-on-his-luck alcoholic who'd lost his teeth? Mitya could not tell.

They went back to where the bigger boys were playing cards. Chervyak poured vodka into more cups and served everyone, including Mitya. He then pulled two plastic crates to the table so that the two of them could sit. Mitya understood that if he didn't drink the vodka and clink his glass with the older boys, he would not have their respect. It was the same old refrain, repeated by Dmitriy Fyodorovich when he tried to talk some sense into Vovka. Or cited by actors on TV: if you don't drink with someone, you don't respect them.

He took the stopka and emulated the movement he had seen so often: flipped it over into his mouth and swallowed the liquid in one gulp. It was acrid; it burned, and yet it was like someone hugged his insides from within. Another kind of warmth.

"So, Chervyak, will you explain why you're bringing outsiders here?" the boy with the eroded teeth asked.

Chervyak clapped his palm against the table so loudly that Mitya almost jumped out of his seat.

"Hey, don't be so loud," Tsypa whined from his bed.

"Patsany, my friend here is looking for a homeless guy with birds from the Old Arbat," Chervyak said.

"Why the khuy should we know anything about that guy?" asked the boy in the hat.

"He was a friend of my pal Dlinniy, remember, the crippled kid? So, a good guy. But he died too. Ego uebashili. And this guy wants justice."

"Admirable," the boy with the mustache said.

"But blya, he's hit a dead end," Chervyak continued. "I thought maybe some of the middles would know. They hang out in the Old Arbat sometimes, right? So I wanted to know if you'd mind."

The boy with the mustache scratched his head.

"Sure, yeah," he said, looking at Mitya. "I wouldn't have helped you—you're too clean. But justice is justice. You guys go talk to the middles. They're upstairs with the smalls, helping the rich tyotkas. With their groceries, but mostly to get rid of their wallets." He laughed uproariously. "Maybe you should join them too, Chervyak. Get yourself a titty to suck for a change."

Chervyak blushed, and Mitya saw clearly that he was below the older boys in the hierarchy. This must be what "middles" and "smalls" meant. Was Chervyak a middle? He wanted to see the other middles, to see if Chervyak fit. It was apparent that he was not in the top tier. If the older boys were even the top tier. They had to answer to some bratva men above them, didn't they?

Mitya quickly realized that this was also why they called Solntsevo and the other gangs "organized crime outfits." Everything was, indeed, implemented in a precise, organizational manner.

"Get the khuy out now," the boy in the hat said. "And blya, Chervyak, get a grip. You'll run into trouble being this careless." Chervyak and Mitya headed to the market's main area again. The vodka he had drunk untied Mitya's tongue, and he now felt brave enough to ask Chervyak some additional questions.

"So, this market is controlled by the Solntsevo?" he asked, casually, as if he knew all about it.

"No. This is Dagestan bratva territory," Chervyak said. "You notice that I'm Dagestani too? None of the other boys are. I'm hoping that Maga will recognize it. He runs things here. My papa was Dagestani. I didn't know him, but who cares. I think I might run this place one day. But now I'm still too young even to sell travka."

"Travka?" Mitya knew what it meant, but he wanted to clarify. Did they sell marijuana at the market? Or did Chervyak merely mean dill and parsley?

"Yeah. Only some middles do it. Not me, I think they're keeping me for more important things." He sighed as if talking about not getting a toy he wanted. "There's always some problem with the Solntsevo bratva, but it's good the bosses are away today. They wouldn't like me bringing you. I didn't think about it, though." He giggled. "Hey, I got some glue too," Chervyak said as he procured a tube of Moment glue from his pocket. "The older boys don't do it, say it's dirty and the kayf—the buzz ain't as nice. So they freak out when I bring some, but I know it will make the middles talk better. You want some? Us Dagestanis are a hospitable people."

Mitya shook his head. He wasn't sure whether the same etiquette that governed drinking also applied to sniffing glue, but he did not want to try it. "You can do it after," he said, trying to sound affirmative and solid. Oddly enough, it worked, and Chervyak nodded and put the tube away. It was always better to take care of business first and have fun later.

They left the market through the front door, the same way they'd entered, and then walked around the corner. There, Mitya saw a group of boys standing next to a pile of hand trucks that customers could rent. All of them were Chervyak's age or younger, some even younger than Mitya, and almost all were smoking cigarettes. Mitya had never seen so many children smoking, and it looked a bit surreal. In contrast to his earlier behavior, Chervyak once again looked more sage and confident. It seemed that among the middles and smalls, he held a respectable position.

"Patsany, this is Mitya. He has made a generous contribution to our well-being." Chervyak took the Moment tube out of his pocket and shook it in front of them. The boys cheered. "But before we can enjoy it, we have to help him. Which of you have ever hung around the Old Arbat?"

A few boys buzzed in response.

Chervyak tried to remember the situation but couldn't think of anything coherent to say, so he let Mitya talk. "He'll tell you," Chervyak said. Mitya started describing Valerka, and as soon as he mentioned his name and the existence of his crows, some of the boys became agitated.

"Valerka!" one of them squealed from the back. He was so short that Mitya saw him only when the other boys moved away. "Valerka always gave me money."

"He was the one who offered me a place to sleep my first winter," an older boy in a tracksuit and a beanie said and sniffled. "It wasn't in the Old Arbat though, but on Komsomolskaya square. I didn't realize he moved to Arbat."

"He was a cool guy for a grown-up," said a stick-thin boy with hair so fair and wispy, it almost looked like an old man's. He was slightly older than Chervyak, around fourteen, or maybe he looked older because of his height and hair color.

The boys around him, all those who had any idea who Valerka was, nodded in unison.

"I met him when I lived in the Kurskiy train station," the boy continued. "The militsionery always kicked him around because he was feeding the birds, and you can't have birds inside. But he never said a bad word to them. He planned on finding an abandoned attic somewhere to build a house for the crows."

Mitya was amazed by the feedback and by how little he knew Valerka. He was not sure what he had expected. Perhaps to meet boys who had become so wild and savage that they had killed Valerka. Perhaps he had expected to see one who had not yet reached a balance between milk and acid, who still clung to his innocence, and could tell him where to look for the murderer. But this—such unflinching respect for Valerka from a ragtag crew of boys who stole women's wallets and sold weed—this left him dumbfounded.

"Does he have an attic in the Old Arbat?" the elderly boy asked.

"He died two weeks ago," Mitya sighed.

The boys, again unanimously, gasped.

"Somebody killed him, and I'm trying to find out who. Maybe you know someone who had a bad relationship with him? Like some bratva people?" Mitya asked.

"No one in the bratva would touch him," the elderly boy said. It was now him answering Mitya's questions, the rest of the boys nodding along. "It's bad luck to hurt 'god's fools.' They know that much."

"Maybe some other boys? Older ones?" Mitya offered.

"What do you think we do here? We're all free; we don't need to mess with lives." The elderly boy seemed offended, and Mitya felt ashamed of the way he had asked his question.

"That's not what I mean. I want to find out who did it." He felt another stab of loss, and this time let the tears spill. He didn't feel comfortable crying in front of all these boys, who probably already thought him a total wimp, but at least it would show them the remorse he felt.

"That's okay." The elderly boy came up to him and patted him on the shoulder reassuringly. "Look, none of us know anything. Right, patsany?" He looked around him, and the boys all shook their heads. "Let's go get some hot tea from Auntie Tamara, and we can chat about this."

The elderly boy steered Mitya toward the entrance.

"Zolotoy, you don't want some glue?" Chervyak asked him.

"I'm good," the elderly boy said. His nickname meant Golden, and Mitya could see that, as his hair shone in the twilight. He followed Zolotoy, leaving the rest of the boys, including Chervyak, behind.

They got two glasses in metal holders from an older woman with a mustache who was selling pirozhki and weak, urine-colored tea. Mitya took his 1,000-ruble bill out of his pocket and tried to give it to Auntie Tamara, but Zolotoy gestured for him to put it away.

"We're all good with each other here," Zolotoy said.

"Except when your Dagestani friend steals my pies," Auntie Tamara said.

"He stole again?" Zolotoy asked, his forehead wrinkling in concern. "I'll cover it. How much?"

"Forget it, Ignatushka," Auntie Tamara said warmly. "Not your fault."

"I'll talk to him, though. Meanwhile, Auntie Tamarochka, can we sit down beside your stand? My friend and I need to discuss an urgent matter."

"Of course, Ignatushka." She smiled warmly and let the two of them sit down on the nearby crates.

"You are moya krasavitsa, Auntie," Zolotoy said, and being called beautiful made Auntie Tamara blush.

As she went back to her trade, announcing fresh pies and hot tea every once in a while, Zolotoy asked Mitya to tell him everything he knew about Valerka's death. Mitya did, while watching the boy's delicate, pale face that looked on in concentration, and his thin fingers that were resting around the cup, warming up. Zolotoy did not look like a street kid. His clothes were clean; his skin was untarnished; his teeth were decent and more or less white. His face reminded Mitya of the portraits of saints in their youth that he saw when Alyssa Vitalyevna took him to the Tretyakov Gallery.

When Mitya finished telling him the few details of Valerka's death that he knew, Zolotoy was silent for a while and sipped his tea. The longer he lived on the streets, the less impact he felt from sadness, but this affected him, especially because Valerka was one of the few blameless people he had ever met. Him and some of the younger boys.

"Listen, I don't know anything about what happens in the Old Arbat other than what you've told me. I've never lived there; I don't know anyone. But if I know how this all works, I'll tell you: it must have been the menty."

"Menty? Militsionery? But why would they kill a homeless man?"

"That's what they do. They clean the streets. Do you know how many they offed in preparation for the 850th anniversary? We're small, we're fast, worst-case scenario, they put us into orphanages. Some of us have relatives. So we, patsany, made it. But the older ones, the crazy ones, the drunks—especially someone like Valerka—they're doomed. He was too trusting. Perhaps someone from your building told them that they didn't like him sleeping there. So what do they do? Take him into their perpetual care? His wife didn't want him. He had nowhere to go. There are no orphanages for old drunks. So they offed him, and that's that. Blamed it one someone else. If you're off the books, no one cares."

Mitya drank his tea. It had cooled down enough that he could swallow it without burning his throat, but now Zolotoy's words stuck there. He had never thought particularly well of the militsia. Just men in uniform, like Zhenya's father. But the realization that they could be the ones committing the crimes was such an attack on his view of the world that he had to try hard to swallow it. He didn't say anything: whatever he said would show Zolotoy how sheltered, pampered, privileged Mitya was, in comparison with him, navigating the hard truth of life.

"Is there anything I could do in this case?"

"No," Zolotoy said with a faint smile of sympathy on his lips. "But you're good for wanting to. It's rare. Especially among the tsivilniye."

Mitya wanted to hug him right then and there and to cry long and hard about the things that were unfair in life. Zolotoy was a boy of charm and eloquence, and yet he was homeless, making a living in the market run by the bratva. Why did Mitya deserve more than him to live in a warm home? Why did Vovka and Dmitriy Fyodorovich, brutes that they were, deserve to be safe from the militsia, while Valerka, the kind and wonderful, magical Valerka, got killed?

As if he'd read his thoughts, Zolotoy said to him:

"Life is not fair. You have to make it fair. My mother beat me with the leg of a stool all the time. When I did something wrong, or when I did something right. There was no method to her beatings; I soon understood. I thought I could behave better and make her stop, but it didn't work. That's when I left. Now she doesn't know where I live and she can't beat me."

Mitya wanted to say that he understood what it felt like, but he didn't want to make Zolotoy's story smaller by his commiseration.

"Is living here better than at home?" Mitya said. He wanted to know all about it, and Zolotoy with his confessions made him feel like it was fine to ask him anything.

"In a sense. It's safer. It's never boring. And here in the market, we always have food. I'm not happy with the people who run it, but at least they have a code they follow."

"And you all have to work for them?"

"Yes. It's not bad until you're one of the older ones, and then they make you do some things that aren't nice. But I will run away before that."

"What will you do when you run away?"

"I'll tell you, but please don't tell Chervyak and all these guys. They won't understand." He lowered his voice. "There's this place, the pleshka, near the Kitay-Gorod metro station, where a boy can work with older men. You know what I mean?"

Mitya didn't, but he nodded.

"I'm going to go there soon. I'll have to figure out where to sleep. But I have to before they decide I'm too old for the middles. I'm tall as it is. I've been planning to go check the pleshka out for a while. I'm a bit afraid. What if there are menty? But I have to make a decision."

Mitya resolved to look up what it was, maybe go and see for himself. He wanted to know that everything would work out fine for Zolotoy, that he had a future ahead of him outside of becoming a member of the bratva. Whatever work there was in Kitay-Gorod, it had to be better than this.

"You come and see me there one day, okay?" Zolotoy told him when Mitya stood up to go and grasped two of Mitya's fingers, gently, lightly, as if in a half handshake. Mitya felt as if a bolt of electricity had gone through his hand, and then he looked into Zolotoy's eyes of the most radiant bright blue and promised that he would. He felt like it would be possible to follow him anywhere.

They gave the glasses back to Auntie Tamara and left the market. Zolotoy went around the corner to see if there were boys outside. Mitya walked past the fence surrounded by parked cars and made a turn, too, so that he could take one last glance at Zolotoy and his beguiling beauty. He saw Zolotoy join a few others and put some Moment glue into a plastic bag. He then held it to his face and inhaled deeply.

14

Mitya could not stop thinking about Zolotoy. He was so excited when he came home that night that he barely paid attention to his father pestering him. He swallowed dinner and tea without tasting anything. And when everyone went to bed and Vovka left the apartment, Mitya sneaked into the bathroom. There was no makeup and no girl clothing, but that wasn't going to stop him. Mitya took off his clothes and applied some iodine to his lips and cheeks. He pouted in front of the mirror and used his fingers to puff up the fatty tissue around his nipples. Would Zolotoy like seeing him like this? Would he accept him, as Valerka had? There was so much of Mitya, of Devchonka, that longed to be in the world, that was valid. Powerful, but powerless in his solitude, Mitya pulled his face toward the mirror and kissed his reflection. He parted his lips and spread his tongue forward, closing his eyes, as he'd seen in the movies. He felt the dustiness of the glass, something chemical, and his own breath, minty from toothpaste. But there was none of the warmth he so longed for.

———

Saturday came, and the family, except for Vovka, was gathered around the kitchen table for breakfast, watching *While Everyone Is at Home*. It was a TV show where the presenter went to the homes of celebrity families for weekend breakfast and was treated to stories and pies.

Mitya concluded that this gathering of his family around the table and the TV was the perfect opportunity to interrogate the adults about some of the things that interested him.

"Zhenya told me that her father got drunk with Vovka that night, before the arrest," Mitya said. "I'm surprised that someone in the militsia can get this drunk and damage people's property."

"What, were you born yesterday?" Dmitriy Fyodorovich snorted. "Menty are all drunks."

"Not all of them," Alyssa Vitalyevna corrected him. "When Yelena was young, she had a suitor, Kolya Smirnov, who was the son of an ex-militsioner. Broad shoulders, tall, beautiful blue eyes." She gave Dmitriy Fyodorovich a side glance.

"What's up with him now, I wonder," Dmitriy Fyodorovich retorted. Recalling all the potential suitors that his wife could have married instead of him was his mother-in-law's favorite hobby, but he wasn't handing it to her that easy. "He's either fat and rich because he feeds on bribes, or fat and drunk because he doesn't get enough of them."

"I saw him on TV recently," Yelena Viktorovna said. "He is quite chubby and not in the militsia. But he is an elected official in Zyuzino."

Alyssa Vitalyevna and Dmitriy Fyodorovich both looked at each other triumphantly. Neither of them was able to accept defeat or that there was truth to the other's words.

"Of course, his father is in the Ministry of Internal Affairs. Also a stocky gentleman, but always pampered and smells nice," Alyssa Vitalyevna said pointedly.

"Perhaps you should call him," Dmitriy Fyodorovich told her.

Fearing that this would get out of control, Mitya quickly tried to change the subject.

"Do you think they could kill a person?"

"Have you been watching all the detective films with Babushka again?" Yelena Viktorovna asked. She quite enjoyed them herself, but she knew that you weren't supposed to let your child see things like that on TV because it could mess up their psyche for good.

Mitya shook his head.

"Have you been reading 'Uncle Styopa,' then?" Dmitriy Fyodorovich guffawed, reminding Mitya of the popular children's poem about a kindly, tall militsioner. "Doesn't seem so realistic anymore, does it?"

"I'm wondering, if they're not as good as they're supposed to be, what other terrible things can they do?"

"You better not do anything to find out," Dmitriy Fyodorovich said and tried to pry out a piece of cervelat stuck in his jaw. "A sissy boy like you won't have fun."

"Stop scaring the child." Alyssa Vitalyevna glared. "Mitya, as one can imagine, the people who go to work in the militsia, like the people who go into the army, are people without higher education. They're ignorant and can barely read. Of course they can get into drunken debauchery, and of course, they can kill someone. Not a nice boy like you, hopefully, but not necessarily someone who deserves it either. So the main lesson you can take from this is that you need to study. And you're going to get your diploma from Moscow State or the Institute of International Relations, nothing less. Rest assured, Babushka has you covered."

"Let's see how this sissy will protect you with his diploma the next time someone decides to go to war with us." Dmitriy Fyodorovich put his teacup down on the table so hard that splashes of his lukewarm tea landed all around. Sometimes he thought that fighting with any of the insurgents was preferable to fighting with his mother-in-law. At least the fundamentalists had an agenda, something they believed in, and a military structure. The woman had a nasty tongue to her, and all this bile.

"He'll surely do it better than your nephew," Alyssa Vitalyevna retorted.

Mitya tuned out of the rest of the conversation. He'd heard enough: the fact that militsionery could potentially kill a person did not seem as asinine to the grown-ups as it did to him. Which meant that it was possible that law enforcement had indeed killed Valerka. Mitya felt as if he had stepped into a puddle that turned out to be deeper than he'd expected it to be, and was now covered in dirty puddle water head to toe.

Mitya went to Tsoi's Wall twice that day, once after breakfast and once in the afternoon, and only on his second attempt was he able to see Marina, who immediately said goodbye to Sasha and joined Mitya. Her eyes were lined with her everyday kohl, but it was smudgier than usual, and they looked red and puffy, as Mitya noticed, but chose not to ask. Instead, he told Marina about his trip to the market, as they walked down the Old Arbat. Marina seemed distant, as if there was something else on her mind, more pressing than whatever Mitya was telling her. Nonetheless, she listened attentively, like she was taking an interview, and offered her opinions, which pretty much lined up with Mitya's. As they walked past the post office, they saw a young man, around Marina's age, or maybe older, lying on the floor, with a middle-aged woman leaning over him. The young man convulsed, and his back arched and subsequently collapsed. There was foamy spittle coming out of his mouth, but the woman, probably his mother, was holding on to his face with all her strength.

Mitya looked at Marina to see if she knew what it was about.

"What, you've never seen them? But you live here," she said. "This boy has epilepsy, and he keeps getting attacks on the street. Scary, right? He also soils himself each time, and his mother has to clean it. It's pretty sad. Poor woman."

Mitya imagined himself doing this, and Yelena Viktorovna having to clean up after him. It didn't seem right, somehow. Then again, this was pretty much what happened whenever Vovka or, on rare occasions, Dmitriy Fyodorovich showed up drunk. At least the young man had a good excuse. Mitya looked at the asphalt tiles beneath his feet and thought that it must have been painful to fall on them. Did the man ever hurt his head? Mitya had read that it was harder to get injured if you were drunk. Perhaps the same applied to being epileptic?

"So, you were telling me about a guy named Zolotoy?" Marina returned Mitya to his story.

Mitya wanted to linger on this part, to tell Marina about him again and again because it felt so delicious to be talking about Zolotoy. As if by telling Marina about him, he could re-create talking to him. But when he described the way his hair did indeed look golden, and Marina stopped to look at a magazine stand, he realized that she was starting to lose interest and it was time to get to the important things before he lost her attention.

"Do you know what a pleshka is?" Mitya asked her. "It's a place or something near Kitay-Gorod. He was saying he wanted to go work there."

"No, we should ask Gleb. Or Sasha. I'm not from Moscow, I know less than you do." Marina shrugged. "So what did he say about your Valerka?"

"That it was probably the militsia who killed him."

"I wouldn't be surprised!"

"Really? Am I the only person who didn't realize militsionery are killing people?"

"Ugh, you're young. They keep stopping me every other day. Can't rub Ukraine off this mug, I guess. Or maybe it's my makeup. They let me go once they see my Moscow registration but still manage to pinch my butt or put a hand on my thigh. And Gleb. The chuvak was born and bred in Moscow, yet they keep hoping he's some Tajik Gastarbeiter. So yeah, stay innocent and Russian, I guess. Don't wear bright lipstick."

"That's terrible, but to kill someone?"

"Just one step further."

"But he didn't cause any problems. He was quiet, stayed out of trouble."

"You know how they kill stray dogs and cats? Some might bite, but who cares if the other ones are nice? It's easier to dispose of them. Or a mouse. Like, a mouse in your room. It doesn't do anything bad to you, you still kill it to keep your room clean. Although there was this guy back in Donbass who had his face eaten off by mice when he fell asleep drunk . . . or maybe it was rats?"

"But people are not mice!"

"That's what you think because you're sweet and delicate." Marina hugged him with one arm and leaned her head to the side to tickle Mitya with her hair. "But seriously, there's one thing we can do. Sasha's dad is some big shishka in the militsia. I'll try to work my charms to make Sasha ask around. I'm sure he can."

"Are you sure that won't be too much trouble?"

"Ah, don't think about it. I might have to marry that guy, actually. He's clingy, but financial safety is more important than personal comfort."

They had come to the metro station by this point. Marina stared into the distance for a brief moment, and the sadness radiating from her was palpable. She wanted to go home and cry all night, but if she did that, she'd be giving in to despair. That was not a thing she'd come to Moscow to do. She shook her curly hair and clapped her hands.

"You know what, Gleb invited me to a concert after work. Kvartirnik, like I was telling you about. This should be good. You want to come? We won't stay late, I promise."

Mitya nodded. His parents did not seem to care where he was all day, anyway. And he could call home and say he was running late. They entered the station and started their journey to Belyaevo, where the kvartirnik was about to take place. Each of them was lost in thought, and they spent the trip in silence.

15

Mitya and Marina arrived at the Belyaevo metro stop earlier than Gleb and had some time to kill. Marina was hungry, and they went to a nearby bakery. Mitya was delighted to play with the little spatula on a rope that you were supposed to use to check the bread for freshness. Marina got them what Mitya's parents called "three-kopeck buns," rounds of white bread with a thin crust. Then they went to a store next door and upon Marina's insistence got a cut of "doctor's sausage" and a bottle of kefir. Mitya had never had such a wonderful meal. He stripped away layers from the bun, imagining that he was eating crab, something he'd never had but assumed required finesse and dedication. The sausage was the color of Mitya's skin and the texture of soft rubber. It was salty and smooth and pleasantly ripped on his teeth. The kefir with which they washed it down seemed carbonated and left a tangy aftertaste.

"Is it true that kefir can get you drunk?" Mitya asked. He had read about road militsia stopping a man who had drunk too much kefir. The Breathalyzer test detected alcohol, which led to his arrest.

"I wish." Marina said through the crumbs. "Alcohol never tastes this good." Mitya agreed. Kefir was much tastier than vodka. Marina was more cheerful throughout the meal than she'd been on the metro, lost in her thoughts, but there was still something sad about her.

Gleb arrived with a bottle of wine to bring to the concert. He led Marina and Mitya to the apartment in question through the open plains of the residential neighborhood, where all of the buildings looked just like the other ones. Mitya instantly thought of the film *Ironiya Sudby*, which they always showed on New Year's Eve: about a man who got drunk and accidentally ended up in the apartment that was identical to his, in a high-rise with the same address, but in Saint Petersburg instead of Moscow. Mitya hoped that he wouldn't have to make his way back to the metro on his own because he would never be able to retrace his steps. Besides, it was already pretty dark, and the buildings blended together into one superblock.

He remembered about the thing on his mind when they were in the building, waiting for the elevator to get to the thirteenth floor.

"Do you know what a pleshka is, Gleb?"

"Yes, that's what Plekhanov University is known as. That's where all the rich kids go to study finance."

It didn't make sense that Zolotoy was talking about that place, so Mitya decided to ask someone else.

The apartment they entered was smaller than the one Mitya's family lived in, and it was crowded. There were shoes scattered all over the floor in the entryway, and it smelled like feet. They took off their shoes, too, and placed their coats on the bed in the dark room to the left, and then joined everyone in the bigger room. The furniture there was arranged so that everyone could see the "stage." Some random chairs and instruments stood in front of a wall of cabinets. There were a few guitars and some things that connected to them and looked technical. All the spots on the sofa and armchairs were occupied, so Marina and Mitya made a space for themselves on the floor. Then they waited there for Gleb to join them. He knew some of the people in the audience, so he had to say his hellos. If the people were in proximity, he introduced them to Marina and Mitya, which, in Mitya's opinion, was unnecessary. He misheard or immediately forgot everyone's names and was terrified that he'd be in a position to have to remember them.

Mitya was happy to sit there and look around the crowded, loud room. Thankfully this setup also suited Marina. Mitya did not want to pry or make her tell him what was wrong, so he concentrated on studying his surroundings. It was not what he had imagined an underground party to be. Everyone was dressed simply: pants or jeans, plaid shirts, and chunky sweaters. He had expected the bohemians to be dressed in flashy clothes. Mitya looked himself over. Everything that made him seem so poor among his classmates looked completely normal at this concert. Most of the people were older than Marina, but some were between him and Marina in age. The only difference was that they looked quite healthy, without the lesions on the sides of their mouths, or blue circles beneath their eyes. Their hair was clean and shiny, not standing in greasy tufts from where the beanie was. Everyone was drinking wine, its purple aroma filling the room like steam. Gleb brought a glass of wine to Marina too.

"I don't know if he should drink," he told Marina, pointing at Mitya. "So if you want, share?"

Marina looked at Mitya and concluded that it was up to him to choose what he wanted. She gulped some wine from the glass and then passed it to him. Mitya took the glass and sipped some of the liquid. It tasted remotely fruity, like unsweetened jam dissolved by water, but also had burning sourness that felt astringent in his mouth. He swallowed it and gave the glass back to Marina.

Mitya sat there, lulled by the loudness around him, and stared at a small stuffed fox that had been stuck on top of one of the cabinets. It balanced precariously on the cabinet's edge as if it were ready to plummet down on the humans at any minute. Its orange-and-white fur looked matted even from below, and Mitya thought that at least one creature in the room looked dismal, like him.

The concert started quite abruptly, without any introduction. Some people from the crowd came to the front and started playing. The songs had long complicated lyrics that did not always make sense and music that sounded as if it were coming down the pipes and the radiators. People around Mitya seemed pretty taken with the performance, reacting to certain lyrics with approval and nodding along to music solos, which never lasted too long.

The singer wore thick-rimmed glasses. Mitya thought that he could have easily confused him with a math teacher, definitely someone academically inclined, maybe even a mad scientist. The words he sang were interesting: poetic and beautiful, like something Mitya could have read in a book, but at the same time oddly current, with slang and colloquialisms. He often mentioned current events and contemporary everyday occurrences. The songs reminded Mitya of Mayakovsky's poetry, but they were even more alive. The man sang in a declamatory nasal monotone, which made Mitya wonder if he had any musical ability at all, or if his singing was just a way for the words to be born.

The ending of one of the songs particularly resonated with Mitya:

A white doe ran down the pavement at night.
A mentovskaya car pulled over, flickering its lights.
It's an unfair fight, but who's going to win?
Will everything go along with fate's whim?
It will be up to you, in the end, it seems.

As a woman sitting near Mitya sang along with the band, he felt like he was receiving a message from somewhere. Masked as a song, it was aimed at him, with ciphers that only he could decode. Mitya had never seen a white doe or any doe for that matter, but he conjured the image of a big-eared, graceful animal from one of his favorite nature books, and thought about Zolotoy's long face and albino hair. The mentovskaya car was where the militsia was loading Valerka to murder him. The unfair fight between the good and the bad, which only he could win, was, of course, the current situation. Mitya was the only person who could help the good win over evil because he was anointed with the needle. Mitya was eternally grateful to the singer for conveying this message, although he wasn't sure if the man knew what he was doing or merely served as a vessel. He moved on to the next song, seemingly oblivious of his prophetic words, and quite drunk.

After the band played a few more songs, they gave the stage to another band, which, to Mitya's surprise, was fronted by a boy who looked only slightly older than him. One of the musicians was a girl, which Mitya also found unexpected. The boy read a poem, then started singing to music. He sounded like a young boy calling out his friends to play soccer, though his subjects were all serious: hunger, politics, work, and war. There was nothing unusual about this boy; he looked like most of the boys at Mitya's school, and yet here he was, singing like a grown-up, receiving approval from the room. It was as if he had managed to break the mold that constrained everyone to their particular positions in life and become a grown-up without abandoning his childhood.

> Little foxes took up matches
> And set the azure sea ablaze.
> It's us the control point dispatches
> To settle the impending craze.

Mitya recognized the first two lines from a children's poem, in which the animals began rebelling against their ordinary behavior. But the rest of the lyrics were, he thought, the author's own. This mix of the old and the new struck Mitya. He didn't understand exactly what was implied by the lyrics. But it all still made perfect sense to him, because he saw the power of words put together this way. It was similar to what he felt when he became Devchonka, and when he descended the stairs to see Valerka as her. It was the feeling of truth and beauty conveyed through art, and Mitya realized that he wanted nothing else in the world but to keep re-creating this feeling.

After the performance, Mitya had to call home. Gleb asked the owner of the apartment, a brown-haired girl who looked at Marina with prickly eyes, to show Mitya the phone in the kitchen. Mitya told Alyssa Vitalyevna on the other end that he was at a concert, and she was so happy to hear that he was at a cultural event that she told him not to rush home at all. Besides, his father had gone out to see a friend and wouldn't return until later.

When he was done with the call, Mitya left to look for Marina and Gleb. He couldn't find them, and figured they were kissing somewhere. He heard voices from outside the apartment and went to check it out. The audience and the musicians had spilled out of the tiny apartment and gathered by the stairwell, smoking, drinking, and laughing.

He saw the boy from the second band next to the apartment's door. He was now smoking an unfiltered cigarette, a papirosa. They were cheaper than regular cigarettes, but even Vovka didn't smoke them. It looked kind of cool, though, at least the way the boy smoked it, his teeth clenched hard around its tip, as if he were an old-timey film star playing the role of a sailor.

"I've never seen anyone smoke those," Mitya said, smelling the smoke of the papirosa as it drifted toward him. It smelled almost like a regular cigarette but somehow worse, duller, with an undertone of something acidic.

"These are Kazbek," the boy said and showed a pack from his pocket, which was, unlike the usual cigarette packs, square, softer, and had a picture of a black silhouette of a horseman against a mountain range. "You want one?"

Mitya refused. He didn't want this acidity inside his mouth.

"I liked your performance," he said.

The boy inhaled the smoke sharply, which made his upper lip curl up.

"Some of the lyrics are so raw, most of them don't work," he said, exhaling.

"I think they were powerful."

"Yeah, what did you like?"

"I liked the one about foxes."

"That's our old one. See? It's good, but the other things are shit. I write well when my lyrics are from a girl's perspective, or when I fall in love. But that's why we're called Little Foxes, that song."

"I like the name too."

"It's the only thing that can describe our reality. Postmodernity, you know? We had so many stupid ideas for names, like Anarchic Broth, or Well-Being Palimpsest, you know, in reference to Kropotkin, but it's pretentious. So we stuck on this one."

Mitya nodded as he watched the blue spaces around the boy's mouth where he had shaved.

"Have you read *Lord of the Flies*?" the boy said all of a sudden.

Mitya shook his head.

"Read it. My favorite book. It shows how messed up we all are, how full of shit. Given the opportunity, we'd all want power. Little profit-hungry Yeltsins and Gaidars. I'm as bad as anyone else, but at least I'm so sickly that I'd probably end up dead before someone could kill me."

Mitya recognized the names, but still was not entirely clear on what the boy was angry about. He also wondered what kind of sickness was plaguing him, but didn't want to ask the impolite question.

"At least Boris here doesn't pretend to be noble." The boy pointed to the man in glasses smoking farther up the stairs. Mitya recognized the singer from the first band. "He gets piss drunk and breaks bottles over people's heads when he doesn't like them."

"I liked his songs too," Mitya said.

"Of course, he's the real deal," the boy answered. "I'm Seva, by the way." He extended his hand for a handshake.

"Mitya."

"I'll see you around, okay? I have to go now, my grandmother is waiting for me."

Mitya nodded. So, like him, Seva was here on permission from his grandmother. It seemed incredible. A boy only slightly older reading poems and singing in front of grown-ups, being taken as an equal and admired. And, moreover, someone who had talked to Mitya himself like they were equals. It was as if Mitya had left the ordinary world, where he was small and insignificant, and been transplanted to a place where such things as age did not matter. Then again, Mitya thought, Seva was talented, and he himself was ordinary, so it didn't seem like he would be able to command the same kind of respect.

Mitya watched Seva walk away, saying goodbye to everyone outside the apartment. Boris, when he wasn't singing, seemed more like a math teacher. A drunk math teacher. Mitya went inside the apartment to look for Marina and Gleb again so that he could ask them to direct him to the metro.

They were still missing, so Mitya used the WC and then wanted to get into the bathroom to wash his hands. It was locked. Mitya knocked on the door, and then knocked again after a brief pause. "It's Mitya," he said through the door loudly, in

177

case his friends were inside. Finally, the door was unlocked, and Gleb peered out of the room. He ushered Mitya in and locked the door again.

Marina was sitting inside the bathtub, and her face was a mess of smudged makeup. She had been crying, and her eyeliner and mascara had run in black smudges, which made her look kind of cool. Mitya still did not feel like he was in a position to pry. But since she was already crying in front of him, it seemed like it was okay to ask.

"What happened?"

"I don't think it's any of your business, but Marina is of a different opinion," Gleb said, putting his hand firmly on Mitya's shoulder.

But Marina sniffled and raised her voice.

"Don't talk to him like that, Gleb. It's not his fault. Mitya, I'm in big trouble. You're my friend, so I want you to know. The money I gave you for that homeless boy—it wasn't mine. I took it from the cash register at the lingerie stall at the market. Yours was a small portion only, I took much more, as I was short on my rent money and other things. I wanted to replace it. I was going to as soon as I could spare it. But my boss found out."

"Marina, I'm so sorry. I didn't realize." Mitya's first instinct was to hug her, but he felt a barrier that he couldn't cross, some block inside of him, so he stayed where he was and grasped his face with his hands.

"What were you thinking of, asking her for money?" Gleb reproached him angrily, and from the way his face was pained, Mitya saw how much he cared.

"I didn't; I didn't know."

"He didn't ask me," Marina interjected. "I offered. Where else was he going to get the money? If we don't help people, no one will help us, Gleb."

Gleb didn't say anything, and instead leaned back on the sink and took a big breath. His eyes were filling with moisture.

"And then my boss found out and wanted me to sleep with him. So I did," Marina said. Her voice was suddenly drained of all emotion, and it sounded dead, detached, when she said it. Gleb banged his fists against his thighs in impotent rage.

"I want to kill that Azeri ublyudok. I want to strangle him with my own hands."

"He is so well connected. I told you I had to do it. But I did it voluntarily . . . Mitya, I've been trying to make him promise that he won't do anything for the past hour."

Gleb was pale, as if he were a person in a black-and-white photograph.

"Promise me."

"Okay," Gleb said and turned around to land a massive blow against the sink. Mitya was surprised that it remained in place. "Okay, I won't do anything. What a magnificent way to find out your woman thinks you're powerless. And not worth anything. This is not how I pictured being in love. None of the romantic stories I know have the girl sleeping with her boss."

Gleb struggled with the latch for a minute and then, when he managed to open the door, stormed out.

"As if it's not enough to have lived through sex with that disgusting pig, I now have to deal with him. This is not what I expected from my free life."

Marina covered her head with her arms and sobbed quietly.

Mitya locked the door, went to Marina and touched her. He tenderly placed his hand on top of her hair and stroked it. She whimpered louder, but then calmed down. He stood over her like this for a long time. People kept knocking on the bathroom door, but Mitya kept shooing them away. When Marina had calmed down enough to go, he helped her get out of the bathtub and clean off her face with a wet towel, which wasn't that different from when Mitya took his makeup off.

SEVEN

It turned out that Tsarevna Snake and her brother, Tsarevich Toad, were in charge of hell. Koschei started asking them about the soldier with red eyes and about Leshy, but they claimed to have never seen either of the two. Koschei wanted to go looking for them, but Tsarevna Snake told him that she'd be mortally offended if he didn't stay for some dinner.

Koschei did not want to offend her and realized that he could be more useful in his quest if he had something to eat: after all, he hadn't eaten a bite for more than a week. So he agreed, and Tsarevna Snake jumped off the ground happily with all her coils.

"We don't get many visitors that come here voluntarily, you understand." Tsarevich Toad winked at Koschei. He was reclining on a sofa of water lillies.

Tsarevna Snake, Tsarevich Toad, and Koschei all sat down to eat. They were served by humans dressed in pristine white clothes starched so thoroughly, they resembled paper. Koschei felt uncomfortable with his nudity, but the humans did not seem to notice, as they kept bringing large plates loaded with gelatin molds. They also did not seem to pay any attention to the fact that loud human moans were coming through the walls, and neither did his hosts. Koschei thought it would be rude to mention it, so he asked instead: "So, are you happy running this place?" He took the jelly closest to him, filled with a pearl necklace and an oyster mushroom.

"Well, our dad wants us in the business," Tsarevna Snake sighed. "It's not that bad. Repetitive, I guess. Messy, as all factories are, and the workers like to rebel—we get the troublemakers, after all, not good quiet ones—but you get used to it."

"You must be wondering where our boiling pots are. They were banned recently," Tsarevich Toad added, piling his plate. "Health code violations."

"Why do you do this at all? Can't you stop accepting people?"

"Good question. The profits are shit: it's nothing compared to what Daddy is making selling oil." Tsarevna Snake waved her top part in lieu of a shrug.

"You should ask earth why they keep at it." Tsarevich Toad rolled his eyes. "They say they need to send their people somewhere, or it'll get overpopulated. And we have to honor a long-term contract. But who cares about us? You're the guest! Tell us all about yourself!"

"Well, I'm a Koschei. I don't know if you're familiar. We usually kidnap tsarevnas, but I'm not going to do anything that rude."

"How fascinating." Tsarevna Snake fluttered her eyelashes as she propped her head with her tail. "You know, I wouldn't mind being kidnapped by someone like you."

Tsarevich Toad hopped across the table and landed right next to Koschei's plate. He grabbed a bit of jelly from his plate, gulped it down, and also fluttered his eyelashes at Koschei.

"Maybe he's into kidnapping tsareviches."

It took a while for Koschei to explain his situation. And when he was done, the jellies had melted, and Tsarevich Toad said with a yawn: "Perhaps you should stay here for the night. We'll have a bedroom prepared."

Koschei yawned: it did feel like he could spend some more time with them. There was something about Tsarevich Toad's lips that beguiled him to kiss them.

"Yes, you can't leave at this late hour," said Tsarevna Snake, although it was impossible to tell what time it was underwater, and there was no clock anywhere. "Feel free to wander around, but keep in mind, whatever you do, don't go into the room with three iron latches."

16

Mitya did not know Marina's telephone number, so the only way to get in touch with her was to go to the wall. And he went, almost every day for the next three weeks; however, he never saw her, nor did he see Sasha or Gleb. It was mid-November already, getting colder every day, and it was apparent to Mitya that no one wanted to hang out outside if they could do anything about it. Mitya also kept thinking about the boys in the market. It must have been terribly cold in the storage spaces beside it. He imagined Chervyak freezing, Zolotoy shivering, paler than he already was, and felt an urge to go and see them.

He went down to the place where he'd buried the money in Valerka's memory and took some out to give to the homeless boys. It was clear that the tree wouldn't grow out with the soil around it frozen. And Valerka would not mind him taking the money, either, Mitya was sure. Valerka knew full well how bad it was to be outside in the winter.

But when Mitya arrived at the market, it was unapproach-able. The entrances were all blocked; there were militsia cars everywhere. Mitya asked one of the gawkers what happened, and it turned out that the militsia was raiding the market be-cause of its connection to illicit trade. It was as if the militsia and Mitya coexisted side by side, with their crosshairs on the same people and places.

He wondered if Chervyak and Zolotoy were okay, if they had been able to hide or find a new place to sleep. Powerless-ness once again descended upon him like a heavy blanket. He thought about the first time he visited the market and remem-bered the sample he'd received before Chervyak took Mitya to the warehouse dorm that he shared with the other boys. The bees. He had left them in his pocket and completely forgotten about them. When he arrived home, Mitya took his windbreaker out of the wardrobe, where he'd put it once the weather was too cold for him to wear it, and found the envelope with the dead bees inside. When he spilled them out, they had remained un-touched, as far as he could tell: small hairy bodies with crunchy fragile limbs and wings that looked like the membranes inside sunflower seeds when you shelled them. He didn't want to drink the bees, because the hot water would surely ruin the integrity of their well-preserved bodies, but he wanted to do something with them.

He took a piece of drawing paper from his old school pad, some glue and pencils, and had the idea to draw the market as he'd seen it, from memory. As he drew, he was amazed by how easy it was to re-create the details of the buildings, and how good his drawing was. He arranged a few bees next to the building as if to symbolize the boys sniffing glue. Mitya drew the carts around them, as well as smoke from the cigarettes, and then attached the bees with glue. When he finished, he still had bees left, so he made a drawing of the place where the boys slept, and arranged a small bee in a bed, and the bigger bees sitting in a circle as if they were playing cards. Though he had re-created everyone in the room, there was one extra bee, still. He thought about attaching it to the first drawing, along with the other bees, but there was no way to do it well. So he made another drawing, with a building, and trees, and crows, and made this bee Valerka.

It all looked funny, but also made him sad. He thought about how Valerka had died, and how the boys, including Zolotoy, had probably died too, just like insects.

One day Mitya decided to find out the truth about the pleshka place that Zolotoy had talked about. It was not as hard to find things out as it used to be because there was internet at the library, and Mitya was getting better at using it with every passing day. He put words into the search engine Rambler, and the results appeared.

When he searched for "pleshka," he first saw a lot of references to the Plekhanov University that Gleb had mentioned. That couldn't be it, so he kept looking. Then he struck gold. It was a slang term used to refer to a meeting place for homosexuals. As the website Gay.ru informed him, there were two pleshkas in Moscow: one right next to the Bolshoi Theater, which was then closed for renovation, and another one near Kitay-Gorod, currently open.

Mitya was confused by this information. Did it mean that Zolotoy was gay? Did it mean that he wanted to go there to have goluboy sex? And if Mitya could not stop thinking about Zolotoy, did it mean that he was gay too?

———

It was the end of November when Mitya finally saw Marina. After school, he went to the pet shop to stare at the puppies. It was right in front of Tsoi's Wall, and even though looking at the pets for sale always made Mitya upset, he thought that at least being there for them could be helpful. Marina and Sasha were in the cat food aisle when Mitya saw them. Marina was happy to see him and immediately hugged him, a wave of her perfume washing over Mitya. It was familiar, and yet not having experienced it for a few weeks, Mitya felt it anew, fleshy, powdery, all woman. When she pulled away, Mitya saw Sasha staring at him with annoyance.

"I'm so happy we ran into you, Mitya! Here, take my number and call me tonight." Marina took a notepad and a pen out of her purse and scribbled some numbers on one of the sheets. "We have to go feed Sasha's cat, or it will eat us instead." She joked, and Mitya was happy to see her smile.

There was still something sad about her, but at least she didn't look as miserable as she had after the concert. Mitya wanted to ask whether Sasha had been able to inquire about the militsia, but thought that he could wait until the evening.

Mitya hated nothing more than making phone calls. He did not have to make them often, thankfully, which was a benefit that came with having no friends. When there was an unknown addressee, with the possibility of someone else picking up the phone, Mitya felt crippling anxiety and tried to avoid the call at all costs. This time he felt like he owed it to Marina to call her, and even when he had to ask her roommate to pass the phone to Marina, it didn't seem quite as bad.

When they talked on the phone, Mitya noticed how prominent her accent was. Though they were speaking the same language, the way she said her soft *g*'s and rounded up her *o*'s made it seem as though they were speaking different ones. It was somehow enhanced on the phone line, and Mitya wanted to bathe in the warm sound of her voice. It was odd speaking to her without seeing her. Now that he had a blank canvas in his imagination, he imagined Marina not as a girl in a leather jacket and dark makeup but as a woman from one of his mother's *Krestyanka, Peasant Woman*, magazine covers. He saw her hair in a heavy braid, barely any makeup on her face, a shawl modestly thrown over her shoulders.

Mitya did not want to be the one to bring up the subject of her fight with Gleb, so he hinted at it, pointedly asking how Gleb was doing, and let her choose whether she wanted to pick up the subject. She didn't.

"I haven't talked to Gleb since the concert," she said.

"Is that good or not?" Mitya asked. He felt like it was more honest to ask her what he should think, rather than assume.

"I don't know. Good, I think. Because I don't have to choose between him and Sasha anymore. So that's easy. Hey, I missed talking to you. It seems terrible that you're the only one I can talk to about boy problems since you're, tipa, an eleven-year-old boy . . ."

"What about your roommates? Do you like the one who passed the phone?"

"Oh, she hates me because I'm skinny. Or because I'm from Ukraine. I'm not sure. She's Moscow born and bred, and she still has to share her room with a Gastarbeiter."

"I thought Gastarbeiter could only be from Central Asia."

"Who even knows. If I end up marrying Sasha and get a prop-iska in Moscow with an Old Arbat address, we'll see who's talking."

"You think you might?"

"I don't think I have another choice," she said, quietly, and then abruptly changed the subject. "So what's new with you? Any new leads?"

Mitya thought that this was as good a time as any to ask about Sasha's potential help, especially since Marina was so close to him now.

"No, it doesn't seem like I can find out anything from the outside. Did you have a chance to ask Sasha?"

"I asked him, but he must have forgotten. I will ask him again. Don't worry. You're my only friend, so that means not only boy talk but my eternal, unrelenting care. You'll be asking me to get off your back soon!"

Her face was radiant. Mitya had no idea how could it be that such a beautiful, grown-up, self-reliant girl was, like him, friend-less. Maybe it didn't mean anything about him then, it wasn't that he was somehow deficient. It was the way things worked in life. You didn't have people, and then you found people.

Asking Marina about the inquiry into the militsia's dealings for the second time did not prove fruitful either. A week passed, and there was still no news from Sasha. Mitya called Marina to find out how she was doing and discovered that she was sick with the flu. Though her voice sounded coarse and snotty, she said that she was having a fantastic time and did not have to go to work because her boss was afraid of infections. She suggested that to speed things up, Mitya talk to Sasha himself: she gave him the number. Mitya did not think it was a great idea, but he didn't want to argue with Marina while she had the flu.

Sasha seemed to not understand what Mitya wanted from him but Mitya played nice and patiently relayed all the information to him, from Valerka's disappearance to how he had thought Vovka killed him and to Vovka's alibi. This made Sasha perk up a bit.

"Your cousin, he wants you to think he has an alibi, but I think he's just 'putting noodles on your ears.'"

"But my aunt seconded that . . ."

"Why wouldn't she? So that her child would go to prison? Anyway, I will ask around some more, but beware, if it was indeed your cousin, Moscow's noble militsia will make sure he gets what he deserves."

That evening, Vovka dropped in at home. He was not yet completely drunk, and coherent enough to make it possible for Mitya to start questioning him, fueled by the suspicions instilled in him by Sasha.

"Vovka, did you know Valerka?"

"The homeless man with the birds who slept on the stairs?" Vovka asked.

Mitya nodded.

"I'll miss that guy. He was a decent muzhik to drink with."

It was a weird thing to hear. The way that Vovka said it, without any malice, and with a soft nostalgia, was surprising. Mitya could not imagine his cousin ever saying anything as sincere about someone around him. Mitya was immediately full of warmth and could not for another second think that it was Vovka who had murdered Valerka. The way Vovka showed his vulnerability allowed Mitya to let his guard down as well. So he felt brave enough to ask Vovka about the murder and hoped that he knew something.

"Vovka, you know he was murdered, da?"

"Yeah, that's what I'm saying. I'll miss him."

"Do you maybe know what happened to him?"

"Menty did him in. Uncle Petya told me when the two of us baragozili. Said that Valerka arrived at the precinct badly injured by some high-up chuvak. There was an order to do Valerka in, and so they did. Then Uncle Petya started crying. I guess he was sad about Valerka. Or maybe because he didn't get in on the action," Vovka said, smirking.

17

There was no word from Sasha throughout the next week. Marina was still sick, and she seemed to be enjoying her time away from Sasha. Outside of nudging him on the phone, she couldn't be of much use to Mitya. Mitya concluded that a week was a long enough wait period. It was time to give Sasha a reminder with a polite call.

"It's Mitya. I wanted to find out if there have been any developments in the case of my friend Valerka's murder?" To raise the urgency of the inquiry, Mitya felt like it was necessary to remind Sasha of the fact that Valerka wasn't just a homeless person but someone's friend.

"Mmm, yes," Sasha muttered, and then there was some loud banging on the other end of the line. "Look, I'll call you back, okay? I have the number identifier; I got your number."

He hung up. Mitya assumed that he must have been distracted and couldn't talk. He paid it no mind, hoping that Sasha would call back soon enough, before Mitya's parents returned home. Dmitriy Fyodorovich wouldn't like some man calling and asking for his son.

Sasha called back in about an hour.

"Okay, so the case has been investigated, and it's known who the murderer was. I'm sorry to say, but it's your cousin. I warned you that if it's his fault, the police will get him, and there you go."

"But I know he is not guilty."

"Well, you don't work for the militsia, do you? Anyway, they're preparing to take him in at the OVD Arbat. You wanted justice: there you go."

Mitya did not know how to continue this conversation, so he thanked Sasha, though it was unclear why he would thank him. He hung up. Mitya thought that while Vovka deserved to go to jail for some of the things he had done that didn't mean that he could be blamed for Valerka's murder. You didn't put a person in jail just to have someone in jail. You had to find the murderer so he wouldn't do it again. That was especially crucial when a case like this one was considered, with militsionery breaking the law themselves: punishing bad people in the law enforcement seemed extra important.

He would have wanted to find Vovka and warn him, but as usual, Mitya didn't have the slightest idea of where his cousin could be.

"Sasha framed my cousin for Valerka's murder," Mitya told Marina on the phone that night.

"Why would he do that?"

"I wanted to ask you the same thing. My cousin was away at his mother's home, which my father always makes him do.

They fought about it a lot, then he went. Babushka and I even checked the calendar, so it's not like I'm confusing days or something. But most importantly, when I talked to Vovka, he seemed to be really fond of Valerka and upset he was gone. He drinks too much, I don't think he's able to pretend."

"And what about now, is your cousin in jail already?"

"I'm not sure. He didn't come home, but he never does anyway. He might be drinking."

Marina stayed silent for a second. "Okay, let me think about this overnight. Let's talk tomorrow."

The next day Mitya arranged to leave for school at the same time that his grandmother was heading for her trolleybus to work. The trolleybus stopped at Smolenskaya Square, halfway between their home and his school. On their way, Mitya tried to vaguely explain the situation with Vovka to Alyssa Vitalyevna, without giving too much away.

"Can you please find out if he's been arrested?" he asked her before they parted ways.

Alyssa Vitalyevna promised to do so. After all, she had to pretend to be busy all day. That way, if people she didn't want to interact with wanted something from her, she would always have an excuse.

Meanwhile, Mitya tried to find out something from Zhenya. But after approaching her and lingering around for the entirety of the first break, Mitya found out that she didn't know anything.

"It reminds me of something, though. Last year, while you were still at the elementary school, we had bomb threats here, and the school had to be evacuated almost every day for two weeks."

"Why would someone want to bomb the school?"

"They didn't. It turned out some boy was calling in the bomb threats because other boys had made him do it."

"And they found this boy?"

"Yeah, they said his parents were supposed to pay for each time the special forces came to school. It cost a million rubles. And his father is an Afghan War vet, like yours. But he also has no legs or something, so they're really poor."

"What about the other boys?"

"They were rich boys, and one was a teacher's son. No one did anything to them."

"But it's not fair!"

In response, Zhenya just rolled her eyes.

But Mitya understood what she was trying to communicate. Sometimes when someone wanted the crime to go away, they made sure that someone else was at fault. But who was the perpetrator in the case of Valerka's murder? Mitya had talked to Sasha, Sasha was supposed to go to his father, and Sasha's father—to investigate within the militsia. It was the militsionery—unless, of course, Sasha himself knew who the real perpetrators were and was trying to shield them from harm.

When he returned from school later that day, Mitya called Marina. When they started talking, it turned out that both of them had independently reached the same conclusion: that there was some conspiracy at play.

"I've given this some thought, and I've decided that we have to wait to clarify what's going on with your cousin," Marina said. "Will you be able to find out?"

Mitya told her about his grandmother's promise to call the militsia.

"All right, well, if Vovka is detained, I'll start squeezing Sasha's balls and make him free your cousin. I don't want to do it in case this was all a farce or a mistake, but I am resolved, so trust me."

"How are you planning to threaten Sasha?"

"I think I have an idea. But I don't want to tell you yet. You might be against it."

Mitya didn't like it but told himself that it was okay if he didn't know more.

When Alyssa Vitalyevna came home, she had news. Though Vovka had not been apprehended yet—because his drunken routes were unpredictable and the militsionery were lazy—she had managed to find out some more information. Uncle Petya was the person on telephone duty that day, and he told her that the directive to arrest Vovka had arrived from somewhere above. When she tried to dig further as to whoever would be interested in framing her son-in-law's loser nephew, Uncle Petya got confused and refused to talk more.

"He's pretty stupid but not stupid enough, unfortunately," she said.

But for Mitya, it reaffirmed what he had discussed with Marina earlier: that people directly involved in the murder had framed Vovka. Someone in the police, to be precise.

———

After two days, they learned that Vovka had been apprehended. Alyssa Vitalyevna ran into Uncle Petya in the elevator after work. He told her that the militsionery had picked up drunk Vovka as he slept standing up in a phone booth.

As she told this to Mitya upon his return from school, Alyssa Vitalyevna was most of all interested in establishing how it was even possible for Vovka to fall asleep while standing upright.

"I think that maybe anything is possible if you're drunk," Mitya mused. "Don't they say you can't get hurt if you're drunk?"

"You don't work at a hospital; otherwise, you would have seen that it is, in fact, very easy to get hurt this way. But I have no explanation for his sleeping habits."

"Are you sure you can't ask someone to help get Vovka out?"

"Mitya, Petya told me there is a criminal case open. What can I do if your cousin interfered with someone important? I'm powerless. He should have known better. Besides, it's Friday, and no one is going to do anything. It will serve do him good to sober up. Maybe he'll catch the 'white fever,' delirium tremens. We don't want him at home like that, it's dangerous. Some people murder their whole family when they have it."

Talking to his grandmother did little to ease Mitya's anxiety. He felt overwhelmingly guilty that he had given out Vovka's name to the wrong person. But at the same time he was glad that Vovka would not be around him when he got the white fever.

He called Marina after that, but she must have gotten better and gone back to work because her roommate said she wasn't in. He asked her to tell Marina to call him back as soon as she came home, and even made the girl take down a note because he was pretty sure that otherwise, the message would not reach Marina.

With just Alyssa Vitalyevna at home, Mitya felt more at ease because he didn't have to pretend that he didn't know around her. Then, Dmitriy Fyodorovich showed up, and Alyssa Vitalyevna told him about Vovka's arrest, as if she had just received the phone call from the precinct and had not been waiting for the news for quite a bit of time. Mitya wondered how he would have to act so that his father did not grow suspicious. But it turned out that Dmitriy Fyodorovich didn't even pay a bit of attention to his reaction. He didn't seem to care about the reason for Vovka's arrest, either, and didn't ask. It seemed as though Vovka's previous arrest had made him used to the idea.

Alyssa Vitalyevna told Dmitriy Fyodorovich to call Sveta right away. He refused, saying that Vovka might be set free soon, so why worry the woman needlessly? He was upset that Yelena Viktorovna was not home yet and he couldn't charge his wife with the task, under the pretense that feminine softness would work better in conveying such information. Listening to Sveta cluck on the line was unbearable to him. What else did she expect? That all of a sudden, her son would stop drinking and become a decent person again?

EIGHT

Koschei's bedroom for the night had an underwater design. He lay down on the large, puffy yellow sponge that served as the bed, covered himself with an extra-large nori sheet, and was prepared to fall asleep. But he kept thinking about the door with the three latches that Tsarevna Snake had warned him not to open. So Koschei got up and explored the room. He sat down at the vanity and found that it was filled with delectable makeup in all shades of blue and green. Koschei put it on, and admired his extravagant new look. He tried watching the TV, but it only showed fish float-ing in the water. So finally he left the room and went to explore the hallways. If someone caught him, he'd pretend to have gone looking for something to drink. Koschei giggled at how funny that sounded when he was underwater.

The walls were covered with long yellow kelp plants that shimmered in the darkness like gold. However, all the doors Kos-chei encountered as he followed the corridors were a dark deep blue. There was nothing red in this part of the tsardom anywhere, and he soon grew weary.

"I wish I could find the door with the three latches already," Koschei groaned. It was chilly in the corridors, and he wasn't sure he'd be able to find his way back to the bedroom.

"I'll help you if you help me!" he heard a tiny voice say.

Koschei looked around and couldn't find its source. But then a small, elaborate animal appeared in front of his nose. It was a seahorse, the same color as the kelp.

"I am pregnant, and I need you to help me birth my children," the seahorse said, and Koschei noted that he had a large swollen belly.

Koschei had never worked as a midwife and had never seen a male animal give birth. He was prepared to learn a new complex ritual, but it turned out that he simply had to press on the seahorse's belly from two sides, and the babies would be released. It felt funny, like popping a pimple, but soon, a slit in the seahorse's tummy opened, and tiny curls of seafoals started appearing. The father neighed, as the release must have tickled. When the final seafoal was released, he closed his slit and pushed Koschei's hands away.

The seahorse dad produced two tiny bottles of beer with his tail from somewhere, and they shared a refreshing drink.

"So, you're looking for the door with the three latches?" the seahorse asked, holding back a burp. "Here it is."

And indeed, Koschei turned around and realized he was right in front of a giant vault-like door locked by three heavy latches. The seahorse swam away and Koschei busied himself with the door. He was expecting that the latches would be further obstructed by locks, but it looked pretty straightforward. He opened them one by one, taken by curiosity, and pushed the heavy door open.

At first, he couldn't see inside because of the darkness. But as soon as the kelp shimmer got inside, he saw that there were a whole bunch of other Koscheis held by large rusty chains covered with sea moss. He didn't know any of them personally, but there could be no doubt they were his relatives: skinny, long-haired, pale with a bronze glow.

It took a while for them to open their eyes, which were covered with barnacles.

"Hey, kid, have you come to save us?"

Koschei shrugged. He looked around the chains, as the other Koscheis bombarded him with questions about his origins and whether he had defeated Zmey Gorynych, the serpent who had imprisoned them. Koschei did not respond and pretended to be busy with the chains. He wasn't aware who the zmey was, and did not want to acknowledge his relationship to his father, in case they'd heard about their fight.

After studying the chains, he was able to locate a spot where they were all linked. He didn't have any tools to cut them with, but the moment he touched them, the chains' whole length disintegrated immediately, setting the Koscheis free.

"He has the magic touch," the Koscheis whispered, incredulous. They quickly regained their strength and lined up next to Koschei.

"She looks strange. I thought lady Koscheis didn't exist!" said the smallest Koschei, who only came up to Koschei's waist.

"Must be one of those European Koscheis we keep hearing about," another Koschei said, scowling.

"What an abomination," a third Koschei said, shaking his head. "Well, anyway, we don't have time for this, men. Let's get free!"

They stormed off in a noisy swarm and left Koschei standing there alone. He wasn't surprised that his encounter with relatives had ended this way again. Koschei sighed and suddenly felt someone's hands cover his eyes from the back.

18

It took until late next week for Marina to work her magic. She refused to tell Mitya what exactly it was she had done. "I don't want to jinx it, but the gears are turning."

On Wednesday Marina said that Sasha had promised her to have Vovka released the next day. Mitya kept away from home all day on Thursday in case Vovka was released before the grown-ups had returned, so that he wouldn't have to be around him alone. But when Mitya came home from the library for dinner, Vovka still wasn't there. Not being able to know what was happening—or what to expect—made Mitya nervous and annoyed.

The minute the family put their forks into macaroni "navy-style"—pasta mixed with fried ground beef and onions—the bell rang, and Yelena Viktorovna rushed to answer the door. Dmitriy Fyodorovich gave Mitya a dirty look, but Mitya didn't care. He didn't want to answer the door for so many reasons that they canceled out the fear of his father's wrath.

Yelena Viktorovna returned with Vovka. He looked sallow and tired, but seemed perfectly sober.

"Oh!" Dmitriy Fyodorovich exclaimed. He wasn't sure if he was more disappointed by his nephew's return, or relieved that he wouldn't have to talk to Sveta about it.

Yelena Viktorovna rushed to put a plate with dinner in front of Vovka. He ate half of it amid everyone's intense expectation. Then he wiped his mouth with his only hand and started talking. "Uncle, Aunt, Alyssa Vitalyevna. I don't know how you managed to get me out, but I'm grateful!"

Everyone shrugged. Mitya feigned innocence and noticed with pleasure that he was invisible to his cousin. Vovka did not realize that Mitya had any agency or influence on the situation.

"I don't know why they got me, why they thought it was me who killed Valerka," Vovka said, his eyes fixed on a glass of apple juice in front of him. "The militsionery said they had an error in the paperwork or something. But I see how I have brought it upon myself. And I understand that I was unbearable to you, and my mama."

They all stared at Vovka in silence. Even Dmitriy Fyodorovich was reluctant to interfere.

"I had a terrible few days breaking out of that . . . fog, and I wanted to smash my head against the cell. But I didn't, and now I want to turn my life around and pay you back for all the kindness you are showing me. Uncle, Aunt, Alyssa Vitalyevna."

Now Mitya was irritated that Vovka had not listed him in the dedication of his apology. Didn't he deserve the biggest one of all?

"I will go get coded like Mama always tells me, and I will live a good life," Vovka said, and Mitya saw that he had tears in his eyes. Mitya didn't quite believe their sincerity, but it was touching. "And you, Mitya." Vovka looked at him, and though there didn't seem to be malice in the look, Mitya did a little jump in his seat. "I will be a much better older brother to you."

Vovka had had a lot of time to think about his life, and he was now sure that he finally had the power to fight the corruption that made him do things to his small cousin.

"Well, they say the army changes people, and prison changes people too," Dmitriy Fyodorovich boomed and slapped his nephew on the back. "I guess you needed this in your life, even if it was jail for a few days!"

Vovka snickered, still averting his gaze. Yelena Viktorovna offered him a second helping of macaroni, complaining how he'd grown much thinner. Alyssa Vitalyevna rose from her chair to make some tea and kept looking at Vovka from the side of her eye.

Because Vovka was dry now, he had no intention of going anywhere for the night. So he started preparing to sleep next to Mitya again, top and tail. Mitya had not considered this to be a possibility: he had expected Vovka to come from jail and immediately get drunk, to disappear into the night like he always did. He had even considered trying to dress up as Devchonka, which he hadn't done for way too long now. The new development put Mitya in a state of anxiety that made it impossible to concentrate.

Vovka showered to wash off the jail and then wanted to go to bed as soon as everyone was done with the TV. For a while, Mitya hid out in the bathroom, but soon he grew cold sitting on the enamel of the bathtub. He returned to the bed and lay on his side of it, pretending to be engrossed in a book with his flashlight, although he wasn't even sure which book it was, something he had picked up blindly. He wasn't following the text, just sliding his eyes over the letters and letting his mind race with scenes of what could come in the night. Vovka seemed to be sleeping peacefully and didn't even convulse in his sleep as much as he used to. Mitya didn't notice how he fell asleep himself, and woke up only when it was already morning and someone was in the kitchen clinking teacups.

At breakfast, Vovka said that he was going to visit his mother that day and together they'd book an appointment for coding. Meanwhile, he would look for a job that he could do, even if it meant something stupid and menial. Dmitriy Fyodorovich promised to ask if there were openings at the store, and Yelena Viktorovna made Vovka cheese sandwiches for lunch on the go. Alyssa Vitalyevna stayed silent.

On her way to work, she waited for Mitya, so that they could walk together.

"How long do you think he's going to last?" she asked as they headed down the Old Arbat.

"What if he has changed?"

"People don't change. They learn to pretend." Alyssa Vitalyevna sneered. "Coding works, but I don't think Vovka has the will."

"I do think he may have changed," Mitya said. "I change all the time."

"Oh, Mitya." Alyssa Vitalyevna smiled. "Nu khorosho. Sure. But you're talking about yourself. Your cousin is a different species. Watch and learn how wise your babushka is."

As Mitya saw her off to the trolleybus station and continued his walk to school alone, he wondered if that was true. Alyssa

Vitalyevna, being older and more experienced, knew the world better. He didn't have a problem with that. What bothered him was the prospect of being proved wrong about the world again. It was enough that he felt like a complete failure after his investigation led him to a dead end and caused so much trouble for everyone involved.

After school that day, Mitya headed to the library again and stayed there until it was safe to go home for dinner. From the public phone, he gave Marina a call. She once again refused to disclose what she had done to get Vovka out of jail. Instead, they arranged to meet the next day, Saturday, at noon by the wall.

Vovka didn't come for dinner. Sveta called when everyone was around the kitchen table. As Dmitriy Fyodorovich talked to her on the phone, Alyssa Vitalyevna had a triumphant look about her. When Dmitriy Fyodorovich returned, he said that Vovka was still sober and staying over at his mother's for the night because they had booked a coding procedure for the next day.

"Does anyone even perform legitimate medical procedures on the weekend?" Alyssa Vitalyevna exclaimed, clearly unhappy about the news.

"It's an urgent matter," Dmitriy Fyodorovich reasoned, "so she said you could do it anytime, as long as there's the will to do it at all."

"What do they do during the procedure?" Mitya asked.

"Sveta said they would insert something inside his skin that will make him sick if he ever drinks, and then perform some psychological work. And after the procedure, he has to recuperate and rest, which might take some time. So he'll be coming here afterward."

"Perfect," Yelena Viktorovna said in a quiet, angry voice. "Sveta still managed to turn this around in a way where she doesn't have to be responsible, and we have to do the whole thing."

"Sveta can't take care of him when she's ill; you understand that. And you didn't like it when he drank, but you still don't like it now that he's getting treatment?" Dmitriy Fyodorovich raised his voice.

Yelena Viktorovna didn't say anything. Alyssa Vitalyevna wanted to interject, but she stayed silent too.

Mitya thought about having to sleep with Vovka again. He was still worried, though the previous night nothing had happened, and there was a night free of his cousin ahead of him. What had to happen so he wouldn't have to share the bed with Vovka anymore? Maybe something during the treatment could go wrong and send Vovka to a hospital?

Mitya looked at Alyssa Vitalyevna and wondered: Did he want her to be right, or did he want her to be wrong? Because as much as having drunk Vovka around him was unbearable, at least this made him go away from home most of the time. If he sobered up, there was a threat of him staying at home.

The next day, when he went to meet Marina at the wall, Mitya noticed that she looked sad, kind of like she had on the day of the kvartirnik.

"Are you okay?" he asked her, and Marina nodded.

"Let's go eat ice cream? Have you ever been to Pingvin?"

Mitya hadn't, although he had wanted to. The shop's sign featured a cocky penguin wearing a cap and a bow tie, embracing a cone filled with ice cream scoops that looked like balloons. But he couldn't afford it and only ever had the vafel-niye stakanchiki from the kiosks.

"Isn't it super expensive?"

"I know the guys who work there," Marina said. "They drink in the café after hours, and they like to have girls come in. They said I could have free ice cream whenever I want to."

They went to the café and joined a long line in front of it. Once it was their turn, Marina chatted up the young men behind the counter, while Mitya held a space at one of the few tables in the café. She brought two cones, both piled with brightly colored scoops of ice cream.

"I promised them I'd come back late tonight, after they close! Now let's share and see which ones we like best," Marina said.

Mitya liked the chocolate best, and she preferred the pistachio.

"What was it that you did to make Sasha have Vovka released?" Mitya asked Marina once they finished the ice creams and the runny cold liquid leaking out of the cones wasn't distracting them.

"I threatened him with my boss." Marina grinned. "Told him that if he didn't let your cousin go, I would have the Azeri mafia come after him. No one wants that, but Sasha was reluctant at first. So I made my boss call him. Then Sasha quickly agreed. Frankly, I'm offended that doing it for me was not enough." She smiled, but this time it was like she was putting on a face for the sake of Mitya's comfort.

"Are you still going to date him?" Mitya asked her.

Marina immediately turned sad, but nodded.

"Sometimes it feels like getting rid of him could prove impossible. He's so close to the corrupt militsia, it seems like he can do anything."

It sounded scary but Mitya didn't push her about it. Instead, he told her about Vovka's decision to get coded.

"It'll work, I'm sure of it," she said. "My aunt back in Donbass was coded, and she hasn't been drinking for what, thirteen years now? It works. They do something to you that makes you super sick if you drink, so sick that you can even die. Before that, she used to get drunk and give her husband black eyes, but now she is afraid of the bottle, and he runs the family."

Mitya tried to imagine his mother beating his father, but couldn't conjure such an image. He could imagine Alyssa Vitalyevna beating Dmitriy Fyodorovich, though; somehow that seemed like a thing that could happen. In his mind, Alyssa Vitalyevna sat on top of Dmitriy Fyodorovich like the men in action movies and beat him on the head. Her shoulders went flying back and forth as if there were a motor inside of her.

Mitya and Marina left the café and took a stroll along the Old Arbat. Marina was supposed to see Sasha afterward, and she didn't seem to be in a rush to leave, so Mitya walked with her until they reached his building. As they hugged goodbye, Mitya noticed how downcast she looked, and hugged her twice as hard.

Mitya returned home to find his mother and grandmother in the kitchen, "scratching their tongues" about his aunt. Apparently, at the last minute, Sveta had backed out of getting Vovka to the coding place and asked Dmitriy Fyodorovich to take him instead. He swore loudly and made a dent in the bathroom door, but then went to meet Vovka at the doctor's. There was no way to persuade Sveta that she had to make this sacrifice for her son.

"Maybe she can't force herself to leave home?" Mitya asked.

"Oh please, she was here in the summer for your father's birthday, wasn't she?" Yelena Viktorovna groused. "She doesn't like it when she has to be proactive. She wants someone else to solve all her problems, and won't lift a finger to do it."

Mitya did not want to argue. He could understand not wanting to leave the apartment if you had a face that looked like it had been skinned, like Sveta with her psoriasis. Or if your son was drinking himself to death. But he also knew what his mother was talking about. Sveta had resigned from Vovka's life and was making them deal with him instead.

As he sat down and listened to Alyssa Vitalyevna and Yelena Viktorovna discuss it further, he wondered what would happen if his family concluded that Mitya would be better off living with Sveta. In the way of a barter, an exchange of sons. Could it work to his advantage? Of course, he would probably have to cook everything for Sveta and be in charge of the apartment, but at least he could have a dog this way and be able to do whatever he wanted. Since she didn't seem much inclined to take care of anyone, it didn't appear like a real possibility. Mitya thought that the best option for him would be if Alyssa Vitalyevna moved in with Dr. Khristofor Khristoforovich Kherentzis and took him with. But there were issues with Khristofor Khristoforovich's family, his daughters especially. They didn't like Alyssa Vitaly-evna, so it was out of the question.

In the late afternoon, Dmitriy Fyodorovich showed up with Vovka in tow. They had come in a taxi, because as soon as he left the doctor's office, Vovka turned pale and started feeling weak and dizzy. The taxi had to pull over twice on the way so that Vovka could vomit out of the open door. He also had a feeling that someone was choking him, which made it hard to breathe. Yelena Viktorovna helped Dmitriy Fyodorovich put his nephew down on the sofa in the living room. They put a basin on the floor next to him and closed the door to let him have some privacy while they sat down for dinner in the kitchen. Dmitriy Fyodorovich didn't have much information: he wasn't in the doctor's office while Vovka was being coded, so he didn't know what happened to him there. Yelena Viktorovna had a lot to say about the situation, warmed up by all the gossiping with her mother, but it didn't seem right while Vovka lay there sick, so they mostly stayed silent throughout dinner.

Mitya was waiting for someone to acknowledge the fact that Vovka was in his bed. At some point, Mitya would have to go on in there too. Didn't they see a problem? Perhaps it wasn't the best idea to leave the boy there next to the convalescent cousin. But no one said anything. As soon as the grown-ups were done watching TV in the kitchen and went to their rooms, Mitya was left with no choice but to go to his. Vovka was sleeping there quietly, and because in the rush no one had closed the curtains, Mitya could see the lamplight from the outside on his cheek. Vovka's eyelashes were lit up by the yellowish glimmer. He looked young, innocent, just a boy, and Mitya felt a pang of sorrow in his chest. If only there was nothing that had come before, and this was all there ever was.

19

Vovka slept through the next two days, and then emerged for dinner. He looked pale and nervous but had a good appetite, and eagerly ate everything that was on his plate. In a week's time, he gained more weight and had some color to his cheeks. The husband of Sveta's childhood friend who had a business office somewhere in the center of Moscow had agreed to take Vovka on as the night guard. Mitya was thankful because he now had the room all to himself from dusk till dawn. He had to avoid being at home in the daytime, when he was at school anyway or could stay at the library.

But even when he was around Vovka, it was as if his cousin had become a different person. Quiet as usual, Vovka became soft-spoken, concerned with his work, and polite to Yelena Viktorovna and Alyssa Vitalyevna. He seemed not to notice Mitya unless it was to ask him to pass the bread or kompot. That both appeased Mitya and made him a bit wary: if he didn't feel like he had to assuage his guilt in front of Mitya, perhaps Vovka did not feel like he had done anything wrong to his little cousin. And if there was nothing wrong, why not repeat it?

Everything was going along smoothly, and the only disturbance in the world seemed to be concealed within Mitya himself. Because there wasn't as much to worry about, he felt adrift, and uncomfortable thoughts got into his head. These thoughts were almost as bad as Vovka himself, and when there were too many of them, it sometimes felt like his head might blow up.

Valerka's murder remained unsolved, and Mitya did not know what to do next. Alyssa Vitalyevna warned him not to get involved whenever he mentioned it to her. Marina said the same thing. Mitya understood that they were worried about him. But he didn't want to let his cowardice be the reason for Valerka's real killer to go unpunished. He wanted to do something, take the next step. What could it be?

If only he could ask someone for advice. No one seemed to care about finding justice for Valerka. When it came to justice, Mitya thought, everyone seemed to be acting the same way as his aunt Sveta during Vovka's coding. They liked the idea of justice but did not want to be involved directly.

Because Marina and Alyssa Vitalyevna were too preoccupied with his own well-being, Mitya decided to ask Zhenya for advice.

"Why don't you let it go? You'll never find your answer," she said, as she munched on a french fry.

The rats had outgrown the bucket, and the girls let them out of it to roam the building. Zhenya still went through the McDonald's routine, though, putting half her loot in the corner for the rats to snack on, if they felt like it, and consuming the rest with Dasha.

"We'll stop in the springtime. Now it's cold and hard for the rats to find food on their own, so we need to keep feeding them for a while. But this can't last too long. They will need to learn to look for their food."

"Aren't you afraid they'll get poisoned or something?" Mitya asked. It seemed odd that they had spent so much time in bringing these rats up and were now letting them live the dangerous life of rodents.

"There's nothing we can do about it." Zhenya shrugged.

Mitya wasn't convinced. It seemed like such a waste to him: to care about the rats first, and then let them go, with no oversight, into the danger. It was unsettling to think that those you once loved could end up being out of your sight, out of your life, out of this world even. He didn't like this idea one bit. And if he were in Zhenya's place, he would make sure that the rats would always be under his watchful gaze.

It made him think about Chervyak and Zolotoy. He had them in his life for a while, and he started caring about them. But now they were gone, like Valerka, probably murdered too. His life was a set of random encounters with friendly people. But instead of staying in his life, these people kept disappearing forever. Who could he ask to exchange them all for one Vovka? Vovka, of all people, was a constant in his life, who didn't seem to be going anywhere, no matter how hard Mitya needed it.

Mitya felt weak, powerless, inadequate, and terrified of being alone. Doubts seeped through the thickness of the night, through silence, through the lines in a book he was reading.

They filled his brain with a choir of resentment. Mitya tried to numb it by ignoring, shifting his mind to other things. But even when the thoughts were gone, the nagging feeling stayed behind, a permanent reminder of how weak he was. Was he even special anymore? Was the needle still protecting him, or had it given up on him, seeing his uselessness?

Mitya changed into Devchonka at night, and the minute he saw his made-up face in the mirror, he felt a semblance of peace and was able to forget what a failure he was. But then it all came rushing back in, twice as powerful. Sometimes his brain stopped working altogether, overloaded with thoughts, and Mitya felt as if his consciousness had been switched off for a second. As if he'd fainted, though he clearly hadn't.

———

December was coming to an end and with it New Year's Eve and the following seven days of vacation were approaching. That, along with the korporativ, the office party at his new job, was to become the most significant challenge to Vovka. Alyssa Vitalyevna was watching over him, waiting for him to slip, like a hungry python over its prey. Mitya was expecting that any minute ominous music would play, and Alyssa Vitalyevna would start bending her body into rings and hypnotizing Vovka, as the python Kaa did to monkeys in the Soviet *Mowgli* cartoon. Vovka wanted to skip the korporativ altogether, and it seemed like after this decision Alyssa Vitalyevna gained some respect for him: the adversary was not as straightforward as she had expected him to be, and that made her even more excited about the challenge.

On New Year's Eve, Sveta came to celebrate with them. There was a lot of cooking, so the three women were in the kitchen all day. The day before, both Yelena Viktorovna and Alyssa Vitalyevna had expressed their doubts that Sveta would come, let alone help with the cooking. However, she seemed rejuvenated by her son's resolve, and even her psoriasis didn't look as bad.

Vovka had arranged to go to his shift a bit later so that he would be present at the New Year's Eve dinner. Mitya helped Dmitriy Fyodorovich assemble the big dining table and carried the dishes with celebratory food from the kitchen along with his mother. The basin that had served as the emergency vessel for Vovka's rehab was now full of Olivier salad: a mushy whiteness with bright specks of carrots and peas. Herring hid under a "fur coat" of white mayonnaise, psychedelic pink beetroot, and bright yellow yolks. Meat à la French languished in the oven under a thick layer of mayonnaise and grated cheese.

From her bribery compartment, Alyssa Vitalyevna donated a tin of salmon caviar for the open-faced sandwiches, thickly spread with butter and sprinkled with the tiny orange balls. A tin of salmon was used to make Mitya's favorite stuffed eggs. They tasted like they were something corporal, not meant for human consumption, and yet so scrumptious. There were also two tins of sprats, the ubiquitous Latvian fish, with a black-and-gold wrapper that both reflected the patina of the headless carcasses submerged in a puddle of oil within, and made the product seem more classy.

Sveta had brought canned pineapple that she'd had in her pantry. She made a salad that she'd seen on TV, with chicken, prunes, mushrooms, and pineapple smothered in mayonnaise.

"Promise you won't eat it," Alyssa Vitalyevna said to Mitya. "Who knows how long that pineapple was there? Besides, it looks pretty vile."

Sveta was not convinced that the table was festive enough and produced from her bag a skinny magazine of poor-quality paper that she had received in her mailbox. Inspired by one of the suggestions in it, she began making animals from the bread and the sausages that were meant for the cold cuts plate, attaching slices with the use of broken matches. She found a jar of sliced black olives that had been in the fridge forever because no one liked them or used them, along with leftover pickles from the Olivier, to make eyes and noses. Mitya watched her at work, fascinated. It made him think of the art he had made with the dead bees. He resolved to hide a few of his aunt's creations and see how they aged. He could experiment with sausage too. However, because of the way Alyssa Vitalyevna looked at the charcuterie menagerie, Mitya refrained from publicly acknowledging his admiration for Sveta's art.

They sat down for dinner at nine. Everyone drank vodka except for Vovka and Mitya, who shared a bottle of RC Cola. Mitya was wondering if Alyssa Vitalyevna would try to cause Vovka to crave alcohol more, but she did not instigate anything. *Ivan Vasilyevich Changes His Profession* was on TV: the beloved comedy sci-fi film about a timid building superintendent who swapped places with Ivan the Terrible using a time machine. Everyone was engrossed in the events of the film and sang along to the songs in it.

Vovka left for work at eleven. At six minutes to twelve, President Yeltsin came on screen.

"He looks sick," Dmitriy Fyodorovich commented. "Maybe he should get coded before he drinks himself to death at this age."

"Yes, he has always been a slow talker with heavy enunciation, but this is worse," Alyssa Vitalyevna affirmed.

It was unusual for his papa and babushka to agree on Yeltsin. Usually, Dmitriy Fyodorovich would call him a bloodsucker who had ruined the country, and Alyssa Vitalyevna defended him, saying he was a man of dignity. Mitya watched the president with puffy cheeks deliver his labored speech. He seemed old, much older than when he climbed the tank to make the government change and the Soviet Union disappear.

Now, Yeltsin was saying that their country had turned seven years old, that it had to move forward and overcome growing pains to take its place in the world.

Was that what Mitya needed to overcome too? He was a few years older than the country, but did he even have a place in the world? It was unclear. Mitya thought about the year that had passed, and he was filled with sadness. He had messed up everything.

When the Kremlin Kuranty watchtower clock began to toll, it was time to make a wish. Mitya wished to have a place in the world, and for the needle to make him special again.

The celebratory programming started with a comedy sketch based on the film they had just watched. Ivanushki International, a boy band, were singing and dancing dressed as gentry from Ivan the Terrible's time. A new year had come, but everything was pretty much the same.

Though he was full, Mitya took a sprat out of the open tin and dismembered the tiny fish on his plate, eating the dirty-looking morsels together with the pliant spine. Then he ate a clementine. The citrus mixed with the gasoline aftertaste of the sprat oil in his mouth was the authentic flavor of a new year.

Alyssa Vitalyevna gave Mitya a bunch of books, a neat envelope with money, and a colorful carton chest with assorted candy inside. This was her usual gift to him, each New Year. He had gotten the first candy box at the yolka, the New Year's celebration at the Kremlin. Alyssa Vitalyevna took little Mitya there the year of his fateful needle accident, to assuage her guilt. It turned out to be a pandemonium full of badly behaved, sweaty children who had had candy on an empty stomach, and their provincial parents, as Alyssa Vitalyevna called them, who did not hesitate to slap a bare bottom in front of an audience. Mitya was so freaked out by the surroundings he pissed his pants, and Alyssa Vitalyevna swore never to set foot at such an event ever again. She thought that the gift component, a box full of candy, was enough to keep the holiday magic alive in the years to come.

Now Mitya spilled the contents of the chest on the sofa in front of him and sat there, sorting the candy by type. The idea was to count how many of each sort there were. Then you had to make a hierarchy, where the amount, type, and preference all factored in. The most important were the chocolate ones, the least important, hard candies. But Mitya could never make up his mind whether he wanted to eat the good ones first or wait to eat them later while starting with the less desirable assortment. And then there were iriski, toffees that were not especially valuable but could not be left until later, because they quickly became rock-hard.

Mitya settled on having the lowest candy in the hierarchy first, and eat up to the top from there. Waiting for the prize meant something. If he ate all the good chocolates from the start, what did he have to achieve after that? He sucked on a mint candy, which got the weird taste of sprats out of his mouth, and wondered if life was like that, too, and the unpleasantness of the present moment would pass and his real life would start. He had to have the patience and wait for it.

As he put away the rest of the candy, Mitya's gaze fell on the name of the toffee, Zolotoy Klyuchik. Golden Key. In *Buratino*, the Russian version of *Pinocchio*, the golden key was what everyone was after. And when Buratino found zolotoy klyuchik before everyone else did, everything was resolved, and good won over evil.

Suddenly Mitya knew what he had to do. He had to find Zolotoy, after all, and for that, he would go to the pleshka. He was so happy to have found a new path forward that he immediately ate the toffee and decided to use the wrapper in art later.

He felt calm enough and had a feeling that 1998 would be a good year.

———

Sveta didn't stay for the night and left in a taxi at around four in the morning. An hour later, when everyone was already in bed, Vovka showed up. He was drunk and covered in vomit, did not take his street shoes off, and barged into the living room loudly. Mitya awoke and ran for the bathroom to hide there. From inside, as the cold tiles stung his bare feet and ass through his pajamas, he listened to Vovka rambling about noisily. Then he heard Dmitriy Fyodorovich wake up, discover his nephew, and throw him out of the apartment, enraged, to Yelena Viktorovna's weak protests and Alyssa Vitalyevna's cheering.

The door closed with a loud bang, the booming of Dmitriy Fyodorovich's frustration concluded a bit later, and then, finally, Mitya was able to emerge from his hiding place in the quiet apartment. He was grateful that no one tried to soften the shock of what happened with a rinse from the bathroom sink. He lay down on his bed, thankfully untouched, except for a lingering smell of vomit in the room. Maybe tomorrow Vovka would be back again, but for now, Mitya was safe.

———

Dmitriy Fyodorovich did not change his mind, to Mitya's happy fascination. At breakfast, over holiday leftovers, he announced that Vovka had relapsed and that it was the last straw.

"He is not allowed inside of our home, and if any of you let him in, you can leave together."

Mitya was okay with this setup. Alyssa Vitalyevna kept looking at him triumphantly. Yelena Viktorovna seemed to be the only person against having Vovka banished.

"We can try to help him again," she said. "Maybe it didn't stick the first time."

But Dmitriy Fyodorovich was unapologetic.

Later that day, Sveta called. It appeared that before returning home drunk, Vovka had also managed to open fire in the office with the gun he had been given as part of his guard equipment. No one was hurt, but there was some damage to furniture and computers. Her friend's husband who had hired Vovka for this position was kind enough not to ask for money to cover the losses, but Vovka's future employment was out of the question.

"She wanted me to go look for him in the streets," Dmitriy Fyodorovich told the family. "But I said that she could do it on her own."

"We'll see how soon she starts." Alyssa Vitalyevna grinned, and Dmitriy Fyodorovich laughed along with her.

Mitya was amazed at how having a common adversary brought his father and grandmother together.

20

Mitya did some research before going to the pleshka. All the info he could find was disappointingly vague, but Mitya figured that anything related to illegal activity would not be overly descriptive. The website just said that one had to go to the monument to the heroes of Plevna in Ilyinsky Gates Square close to the Kitay-Gorod metro station. But there was no information on what one was supposed to do upon arrival. It made Mitya very anxious, but he calmed himself down. He'd been through a lot already, and it had only given him strength.

He chose to go on the first Sunday of January because that day everyone was gone from the apartment. His parents had gone over to their friends' for dinner, and Alyssa Vitalyevna was out with Dr. Khristofor Khristoforovich Kherentzis. Mitya was sad to miss such an excellent opportunity to be alone and dress like Devchonka, but he wanted to act on his resolution to find Zolotoy as soon as possible. And it was good that he wouldn't have to explain why he was out and about after dusk in winter.

The weather was mild for that time of year, and everything around was covered in a thick layer of fluffy snow. Mitya thought that the monument would be a large bronze statue. It turned out to be a squat towerlike structure in the middle of the square in front of the metro station. It had doors and windows and was covered with gilded details and topped by a crown with an intricate cross on top. As if someone had cut off the top part of an Orthodox church and dropped it on the ground.

Mitya came up to the structure and for a minute forgot about the reason for his visit. The monument was so odd, so beguiling, unlike anything else he'd ever seen. Mitya read the golden letters that described its dedication to the memory of soldiers fallen in the Russo-Turkish War in the nineteenth century. A relief depicted a struggling man on his knees, who clutched at the chain binding a standing woman's arms. Mitya had no idea what the Russo-Turkish War was, or whom the figures represented, but he was still affected by the pathos.

A voice behind his back broke him out of the enchantment.

"Hello, my dear girl!"

Mitya saw a man of Alyssa Vitalyevna's age in a dublenka and a fur hat. His face was covered in craters on the sides, and the hair beneath the hat was bright red.

"You've got me confused with someone else," Mitya blurted out and retreated from the monument, almost falling down the steps. There were benches everywhere around the square's perimeter, and he sat down on one of them.

People walked through the square on their way from the metro, men and women alike, but none of them stopped, rushing home to their leftover Olivier salad. A group of men occupied the benches on the other side of the square, conversing loudly and drinking something from plastic glasses. They looked like they were having a lot of fun. But they seemed like men who liked vodka, not necessarily men who liked other men.

Suddenly, another man approached Mitya's bench. He had curly black hair and a fuzzy mohair scarf in wild colors wrapped around his neck.

"Is it okay if I join you?" the man asked. Mitya nodded and watched him wipe the snow off the bench and take a seat. It was starting to get chilly.

"How are you doing tonight?" the man asked as he crossed his legs. Wasn't crossing your legs something that only gay men did? Dmitriy Fyodorovich had reprimanded Mitya for emasculated sitting quite often.

"I'm fine, thank you," Mitya responded. "How are you?"

"Not bad either," the man answered and switched his legs.

They sat for a bit in silence. Mitya wanted to ask about Zolotoy, but he wasn't sure how to do it. With Valerka, it was pretty straightforward: there was only one homeless man with birds who'd gotten murdered. But with Zolotoy it was a bit more complex. Surely, he was special to Mitya, but to others—merely a face in the crowd. Even if he had distinctive hair. Then there was the matter of whether the man would even know anything. Was he a passerby who paused to sit for a while in the snow, or did he come here a lot? Mitya glanced around the empty benches next to them and wondered why the man had asked to sit down in that spot.

"May I ask you an indelicate question, please?" the man uttered after a minute of silence and switched his legs again. Mitya noticed that his voice was high, which, according to his father, could also be a sign of his being gay.

"Yes," Mitya answered. Was his own voice high? It was hard to judge. It hadn't broken yet, so perhaps it didn't matter, anyway.

"Skolko? How much?" The man moved in closer to Mitya, and Mitya could smell cigarettes on his breath.

"How much what?"

"How much do you take for one go?"

The man had taken him for a prostitute, Mitya realized. It made him feel many complicated things at the same time. He was happy to have been chosen, deemed worthy, pretty, desirable enough to be a prostitute. But he was also upset because he didn't want to be considered something that he wasn't.

"I'm not here for this," Mitya responded.

"Are you sure? I could give you 50,000 rubles."

It was the cost of a bottle of vodka, as Mitya knew now. He felt offended but thought that the man owed him an answer to his question after being this rude.

"Do you know a boy who comes here called Zolotoy? He is skinny and has fair blond hair."

"No, but tell him about my offer, when you find him," the man said, and laughed a bizarre fake laugh, as if it was the funniest thing in the world.

Mitya stood up and walked away from the benches. He felt disgusting after talking to the man and resolved to go home immediately. As he walked down the stairs into the metro station, he noticed that quite a few people were standing along the walls in the vestibule. They all looked like they could know something. There was a fat older man who was wearing plastic bags over his shoes, a soldier, a tall, big man with a mustache wearing a suit beneath his coat, and a pair of younger men who talked to each other in loud voices, almost shouting, so it was hard to figure out what they were saying.

"Excuse me," Mitya addressed the younger men. "Do you by any chance know a boy called Zolotoy who comes here?"

"Sestra, look how tiny and cute she is," one of them said, and Mitya was thrilled to hear himself referred to as a cute girl, though he wasn't happy that his words were, as usual, ignored.

"Blyad, you'd better get your cunt away from here," the other one said to Mitya, and then addressed his friend: "Dura, these tiny and cute ones make us look like we're expired goods."

"You're right. Kysh, get out of here." The first one waved his hand at Mitya as if he were a stray cat.

Mitya was perplexed and felt his cheeks flush. He wanted to find his friend. He had not expected this much unpleasantness from the magical pleshka that Zolotoy had told him about. He veered away from the two figures scowling at him.

"I'm sorry, young man, are you looking for someone?" The tall man with a mustache came over to him. The two effeminate men stared at him, and one of them said: "I told you so, dura!"

"Yes, I'm looking for my friend Zolotoy. He is a tall blond boy, who might work here."

"I might know something about him," the man responded. He was big and powerful and reminded Mitya of his father.

Something told Mitya that he could trust him. "Would you like to follow me so we could find out together?"

"Can't you tell me here?" Mitya was pretty fed up with how grown-ups always needed to overcomplicate matters and insist on so many unnecessary movements.

"Of course I can, but I'm hoping that we can go and find him together," the man said, smiling through the mustache. "What if he's out there right now? Imagine how happy he'll be to see you too!"

It didn't seem likely, Mitya thought, but the prospect of seeing Zolotoy was too good to resist. Besides, the man looked like he knew what he was talking about. Finally, something was going right. Mitya walked out of the station after the man and felt his heart beat faster because he might be seeing Zolotoy again.

The man led him past the monument and into the depth of the square. It hadn't even occurred to Mitya to go there on his own: he'd assumed that everything that could be happening would take place around the monument. The paved paths meandered farther away, and there were more areas covered with snow, mostly pristine but with some garlands of footsteps or black silhouettes of trees and bushes here and there.

They stopped, and Mitya saw that the square was much longer than he'd realized. The monument disappeared on the horizon. All around them were trees, with buildings on both sides of the square. Why was it even called a square? Mitya thought. More like a boulevard.

"It doesn't seem like your friend is here, but I think it's time for you to make a new one." The man smiled widely and clapped his hands. Mitya wasn't sure what to answer. He did not want to offend the man by refusing his friendship but also wanted to indicate that he had more important things to do.

But before he could think of something, the man was suddenly right in front of him. He sank to his knees in the snow, and as Mitya looked at him, he saw that the snow was littered with small sail-like green things. Leaves or seeds. Where did they come from to land on top of the freshly fallen snow in January?

The man raised the bottom of Mitya's jacket and began undoing the zipper on Mitya's pants. It was so wild and unexpected that for a moment, Mitya froze and could only watch him. But then he regained his senses and tried to shake the man's hands off his clothes.

"Da perestan." The man resisted. "You're going to like it."

He tugged at the zipper again and pushed his fist into the softness of Mitya's groin. As his fingers grasped Mitya's penis and testicles over the fabric of his briefs, Mitya felt a sharp, searing sensation. He had never had anyone touch him like that, and it felt nice. But it also felt mean of the man to do it like this. They had come to look for Zolotoy, and now the man was touching Mitya's privates.

"Aren't you afraid someone will see?" Mitya asked as he looked around, thinking that it would bring the man to his senses. There were no people, but there were the headlights of cars passing in the distance.

"Relax and let dyadya take care of it," the man said. Mitya squirmed at the word "dyadya." He couldn't accurately point out why, but it made the thing seem even more wrong. Someone pawing inside his underwear was not supposed to call himself an uncle.

"And what about if militsionery see us?" Mitya reasoned. He wanted to stop this, but he didn't want to offend the man. He wanted him to end it all on his own.

"Don't worry, sladkiy, I'm a militsioner myself," the man said, as he placed his palm around Mitya's penis, took it out of the briefs, and moved his mouth toward it.

For a second Mitya thought that he was joking. But then Mitya realized that it could be entirely possible for him to be a militsioner. If militsionery were capable of killing someone, why wouldn't they also put little boys' penises in their mouths in the middle of Moscow? He felt like he was hit with a zap of electricity. He leaned away from the man and kicked him in the chest. The man lost his balance and toppled over into the snow. Mitya had expected him to look angry, but he seemed more surprised. Before the man could get up and attack him, Mitya straightened his underwear and charged toward the metro station, zipping his pants as he ran.

Over the next few days, Mitya kept trying to make sense of what had happened. It was clear to him now that there was a conspiracy by the militsia against him. He was being warned to stay away, but his conscience was telling him that he couldn't give up. There was nothing he could do to help Valerka, and the murder investigation seemed to have hit a wall. But there was still hope to find Zolotoy, to not lose him forever as he had Valerka. Mitya understood that the need to have Zolotoy in his life was selfish, but he still felt like it was a worthy thing to do. Everyone he was encountering was proving to be a terrible person, so he wanted to keep tabs on the few good people around him.

He went to the market once more, before school started again, and this time it was fully operational. Instead of entering, Mitya walked around the side of the building to where he had first met Zolotoy. Many boys were scurrying around the carts, but all of them told Mitya that they hadn't seen Zolotoy at the market for a long time.

"I heard he was killed, but I'm not sure if that's true," said a boy with a shaved head beneath his beanie. Some of the other boys repeated the same opinion, but no one could say for sure from whom they'd heard it. When Mitya asked about Chervyak, it seemed that no one had seen him for a long time either. Perhaps because this time Mitya had no chaperone, the boys didn't seem as talkative as before, and he gave up on trying to find out anything else from them.

It occurred to Mitya that there was one more person he could ask in the market. He went inside and found Auntie Tamara, who was selling tea and pirozhki. She was open to talking once she heard Zolotoy's name.

"Oh, Ignatushka." Auntie Tamara frowned. "He's gone missing before, but never for this long. We returned after the shakedown, and he wasn't here. Still hasn't returned. Some other boys, too, like that Dagestani sorvanets." Mitya figured she was talking about Chervyak. "Poor boys. They get mixed up in some horrible bratva dealings, and then there's no way back. I miss Ignatushka so much. I even considered adopting him, you know, but I'm not young, and I have my ailments, my knots flare up all the time."

Auntie Tamara sighed and poured Mitya a glass of tea, for which she refused to take his money. It was nice to see someone else who cared about Zolotoy like he did, but Mitya did not want to ask her about Zolotoy's plan to go to the pleshka. He was pretty sure Zolotoy wouldn't have related his prostitution plans to her. He finished the tea, thanked Auntie Tamara, and left.

In a phone call with Marina, Mitya told her about the new developments, although he chose to leave out the parts about the prostitution and the mustached militsioner.

"That's how things work in this world," Marina said when he complained about constantly losing nice people in his life. "You can't get used to anyone. I've had this happen to me in the market too: one week a girl is there, she's selling something, and then she gets deported back home, or takes up prostitution, or has been killed by Nazis somewhere. And there's nothing you can do about it, and no one cares."

"But even if this is how things work, I don't want to allow them to be like that," Mitya disagreed.

"I don't think you have a say," Marina responded, solemnly. "You're a kind boy, and I know you want to make the world better, but maybe sometimes it's better to stop? After all, we're just tiny people in this city. Nothing changes whether we're here or not."

"It's sad," Mitya said.

"It is sad."

"Can you at least not disappear, please?"

"I promise," Marina laughed weakly.

NINE

"Who's a naughty Koschei?" A beautiful human girl with emerald eyes and curly brown hair was standing in front of Koschei. She was as naked as him, except for a crown on top of her head.

"Don't you recognize me?" The girl grinned.

He didn't. It turned out she was Tsarevna Snake.

"I shed my skin, and voilà," she said, and Koschei realized they had a lot in common. He looked at her and admired her softness: it wasn't something a skinny Koschei could ever aspire to.

"So why do you have all the Koscheis?" he asked, trying to stick to the important stuff.

"Oh, it's just that they kept trying to kidnap me. And Papa doesn't like that."

"I'm sorry. As I said, I'm not into that sort of thing."

"Well, who knows? Maybe it's in your nature. Want to go to my room?"

Koschei followed Tsarevna Snake while admiring the swell in her thighs from behind. Her room was similar to the bedroom he'd been appointed, but it was much bigger and had a large fireplace with real flames within. The tsarevna sat Koschei down on the coral sofa, offered him a plate of lily pod seeds and a pot of sea buckthorn tea to snack on, and left for the bathroom, to freshen up.

As Koschei crunched on the popped seeds, he saw that a snakeskin glittering with green hues lay on the floor in the middle of the room. He tried it on, to see if he could become a snake, but he turned it in every direction, enjoying the dry, scaly surface, and couldn't figure out the opening.

When the tsarevna emerged from the bathroom, Koschei quickly threw the skin to the ground and pretended that he was stretching his legs.

The tsarevna sat him back down on the coral and sat next to him, too close for comfort, her breath, which smelled like plankton and raw blood, hot on his cheek. She put her arm on his thigh. Koschei didn't mind being next to Tsarevna Snake, but he'd so much prefer to look at her supple body instead of having it shoved into him.

"Will Toad be joining us?" he asked to lighten the mood. He wondered if Tsarevich Toad could also become a boy.

"We don't need him. We can do perfectly well like this," the tsarevna said and produced a large, red and spiky sea cucumber from somewhere behind her back.

As the cucumber whirled in Snake's hand, Koschei looked in her eyes and saw the same red glint he'd already encountered. It scared him, and he jumped away from the couch.

"Is something wrong?" the tsarevna asked sweetly.

"No, I feel a stomachache coming. I should go back to bed."

"Oh, my friend can help with that too." The tsarevna started coming at him with the cucumber in hand, gyrating her hips.

Koschei tried to pass by her, but then Snake's eyes lit up with red, and she shot a firebomb right next to him. She seemed to be much better versed in the operational technique than the soldier before her, and the firebomb lightly grazed Koschei's leg.

"I don't think I need to explain what the consequences will be if you don't come with me right now," the tsarevna said.

Koschei stepped back and almost tripped over. It was the snakeskin, which he seized. Maybe if he threatened to take it away, the tsarevna would stop?

"Let go of it right this minute." She started shooting firebombs to both sides of Koschei while moving in closer.

Koschei hesitated for a moment because it was in his nature to respect other people's belongings, but then he turned to the fireplace and threw the snakeskin into the flames. It shriveled up quickly and then disappeared.

Snake's eyes turned back to emerald right then, and she couldn't attack anymore.

"What have you done?" Tsarevna Snake weakly threw the sea cucumber at Koschei and burst into tears. "Papa won't let me work in hell anymore: if I come as a human, the devils don't listen. Now everything is going to stupid Toad!"

She stomped her foot, ran to her bed, and plunged herself into the sponge, her body rocking with the sobs.

"I'm sorry, I . . ." Koschei started, feeling like he had to make amends. He had wanted her to stop, not lose her job.

Suddenly he saw the door to the room open and three green heads, which looked a lot like the tsarevna in her Snake incarnation, peek in.

"I returned early, my dear," one of the heads said tenderly, as the other two nodded along. "Why does it smell like this? Are you about to eat the human?"

"He's a Koschei," Tsarevna Snake corrected, as she turned around and sat on the bed. "Papa, he wanted to kidnap me, and when I tried to resist, he burned my snakeskin!"

And then red glimmers lit up in all six eyes that belonged to the creature, and Snake's papa, the serpent Zmey Gorynych, came into the room and breathed fire out of his nostrils into Koschei's face.

21

The holidays were over, and Dmitriy Fyodorovich had gone back to work. But Mitya's school still hadn't started, and Yelena Viktorovna and Alyssa Vitalyevna had some free days too.

Alyssa Vitalyevna was about to go to a health retreat with Dr. Khristofor Khristoforovich Kherentzis. They couldn't go during the holidays because he had been on another health retreat getaway with his daughters.

"It's like I'm the other woman," Alyssa Vitalyevna complained. "His wife has been dead for over a decade, and yet we can't be together as a couple because his sister Pupa doesn't approve of me being Russian."

"Why is he listening to his sister Pupa? Isn't Khristofor Khristoforovich seventy?" Mitya asked.

"That's the other side of him being a good man. He's not only good to me, but he's also good to other women in his life. Too good, if you ask me," Alyssa Vitalyevna scoffed.

"See, Mama, at least Dmitriy doesn't listen to anyone but me," Yelena Viktorovna said, immediately plugging into their ongoing dialogue about her choice of Dmitriy Fyodorovich as a life partner.

"He doesn't listen to you either. So, where is your khabalka now that you have the days off?" "Khabalka", a vulgar woman, was Alyssa Vitalyevna's name for Lana, Yelena Viktorovna's latest boss, for whom she cleaned.

"Canary Islands," Yelena Viktorovna responded.

"Just yesterday she shit into a hole in the ground, and now she's pretending to be a refined socialite, vacationing in Spain," Alyssa Vitalyevna hissed. It was still not easy for her to accept that her daughter, an heir to a scientist, engineer, and inventor, had to wash the parvenu's dirty clothes. "Besides, she's not even really Jewish. 'Mountain Jews' are not the same as the rich, smart ones; they're more Azeri than Jewish."

"Well, that doesn't interfere with her husband being very smart and rich, as well as a much respected, high-level member of some Jewish organization."

Yelena Viktorovna didn't dare admit this to her mother, but despite Lana's bad temper, she admired her. The two women were the same age, but one would think that Lana was much younger than Yelena: not only did she know how to use makeup to her advantage, she also had all the money she could burn in various salons. It allowed her to have flowing, bouncy waves and perfectly shaped brows at all times of day. Yelena Viktorovna did not feel like her own tiny body deserved such care: her hair was too thin, her spine curved too far forward, and her face was too plain. Lana, meanwhile, was tall, with the posture of an empress, a thick mane of hair, and large, juicy features: sensual lips, big eyes, and a chiseled down nose. Lana was beautiful and deserved to be even more so.

"Did I tell you that she had another breast enhancement?"

"Again?" Alyssa Vitalyevna raised her eyebrows.

"Yes, apparently they were not big enough." Yelena Viktorovna shrugged.

"How big are they now?"

Yelena Viktorovna extended her palms in front of her chest, imitating a sizable bust.

"What does it mean?" Mitya asked.

"There's a surgery where they cut the flesh of the breasts open and put in silicone balloons to make them bigger," Yelena Viktorovna explained.

Mitya was intrigued.

"Would they be able to do it to someone who had tiny breasts?" Mitya did not want to cause suspicion by asking if this was something that could be done to a man.

"I'm sure they could."

Mitya wondered for a minute whether he would want to do something like that. To have breasts that filled out his shirt? It made him excited, but also a bit scared. He liked having the option of attaching breasts, but this way, there would be no free choice.

"I think she's considering doing it for Kristina too," Yelena Viktorovna said. Kristina was Lana's daughter.

"How old is she?" Alyssa Vitalyevna asked skeptically.

"Fourteen. I don't think you're allowed to do it until you're sixteen though. But it will not help much. She might have

Lana's temper and figure, but she looks like her father: cystic acne and bug eyes."

"That's unfortunate." Alyssa Vitalyevna spread a piece of bread with cherry varenye. "But it won't matter much since she's the only heir, and potential fiancés will be able to overlook her appearance to get their hands on that money."

"I don't know. There seems to be something wrong with her. Did I tell you how she flew into a rage about the grandmother taking her computer away? It was before New Year's."

Alyssa Vitalyevna shook her head.

"Kristina said that the robotic mind inside the machine was scaring her, so she wanted to throw the computer away. She put it in the kitchen next to the trash. The old lady took the computer, and she now uses it to play some card game she likes. Well, Kristina forgot all about getting rid of it herself, and accused her babushka of stealing it."

Mitya and Alyssa Vitalyevna were both aghast. Yelena Viktorovna felt the delight of having discovered new gossip she hadn't previously shared.

"I thought I'd told you about it. The girl is crazy. Remember how she used to lock herself in her room all the time? So quiet, so reclusive. Well, things have changed. She's just reached puberty, as I can tell from the bloody underpants she keeps leaving everywhere."

Mitya knew that girls bled from their privates when they reached a certain age, and the detail fascinated him. He wanted to ask Yelena Viktorovna more about the underwear, and what else was happening to Kristina, but he didn't want to seem like a creep.

"And now something broke inside of her," Yelena Viktorovna continued. "She gets angry and starts shouting at everyone for no reason."

"Does she shout at you?" Alyssa Vitalyevna asked crossly.

"No," Yelena Viktorovna lied. Some of the wrath was addressed toward her. And one day Kristina had even accused Yelena Viktorovna of spying on her in the shower and slapped her. Once she came to her senses, she didn't apologize. Instead, she asked Yelena Viktorovna not to tell her parents and gave her 500,000 rubles, her whole week's allowance. It was meant to be spent with friends she didn't have at cafés she didn't visit. Yelena Viktorovna hadn't been planning on telling the parents, but took the money anyway.

It was such a juicy detail, but sadly Yelena Viktorovna couldn't tell this part to her mother and son. There was enough deliciousness to go on.

"She has also taken to going around naked all the time. Even in front of me, or Maxim, the driver. She has a good little body, I have to admit. It's such a shame for the girl to be so beautiful below the neck, and so unpleasant above. Her eyes are dull; she dyes and straightens her hair all the time, so it looks chewed up. But if you don't look above the shoulders . . ." Yelena Viktorovna drew an hourglass in the air with her hands.

"See, her parents need to find her a nice boy who likes money and 'crawfish style.'" Alyssa Vitalyevna giggled, and Yelena Viktorovna joined in.

Mitya wasn't sure what she meant. "Crawfish style" meant leaning over, but he didn't understand how this was related. He was intrigued by Kristina, though. She wasn't beautiful or nice, but she lived a mysterious life.

"I wonder if maybe she'll outgrow all this," Yelena Viktorovna wagered. "I don't know how much money you need to
cover the crazy when marrying her out."

"I'll tell Khristofor Khristoforovich about her. Maybe he
knows what's up. Isn't paranoia a sign of schizophrenia? I hope
you get out of their apartment before she starts running around
with a knife."

Yelena Viktorovna wasn't too scared, though. To the con-
trary, she enjoyed being around the psycho, as she called Kristina
in her mind. The unfortunate spawn of a gorgeous woman and a
brilliant man made Yelena Viktorovna feel a tang of pride for her
own genes. Maybe she wasn't attractive herself, maybe Dmitriy
was not the sharpest man, and maybe Mitya had been in his ugly
duckling phase for a bit too long. But now the swan in her son
had clearly begun to emerge.

Yelena Viktorovna looked at Mitya now, as he pressed his
finger against the jam circle in the middle of a kurabie cookie
and then admired the fingerprint on the surface. His hair was
almost to his shoulders now; the bangs had stopped getting in
his eyes and revealed a high forehead. His face seemed full of
angles: the prominent cheekbones, the strawberry curve of the
chin, the straight nose, sleepy eyes under a furrowed brow. A
nymphet, Yelena Viktorovna thought. He didn't even need to
apply makeup to look like a girl. Perhaps that was why she saw
him do it less and less.

Seeing that delicate, heartbreaking face was for Yelena like
finally looking in the mirror to find herself beautiful, as she'd
wished before going to bed back in her youth. Mitya looked
like her, if she had been attractive, and he was not only passable

but impressive. Yelena Viktorovna noticed how men stared at him with lust, and women with envy, as he stood, oblivious, in line to buy bread. She often delayed coming back home after work to try and catch a glimpse of her son in a nearby store, or in the metro, and see the glances he attracted. It allowed her to feel, for a second, that somehow, by association, she was beautiful herself.

"I don't think they want to see doctors for her, because if she gets diagnosed . . ." Yelena Viktorovna returned to Kristina's misfortunes. "It's one thing to marry off an ugly daughter with a bad temper. But marrying off a diagnosed psycho might be too hard."

Alyssa Vitalyevna nodded.

"Maybe she can find someone who loves her despite the way she looks," Mitya said. He felt sad about the girl, and the more his mother and grandmother talked about how undesirable she was, the more compassion he felt toward her. He would want to love someone that everyone else deemed unlovable.

"Look who's a true romantic." Alyssa Vitalyevna petted Mitya on the cheek. "Since when are you so knowledgeable on the workings of the human heart?"

Mitya blushed.

"Ahh, our little boy is growing." Yelena Viktorovna said in a singsong voice. "There is someone who has caught your attention too, right?"

Mitya felt a fever on his cheeks but did not say anything.

"Well, we respect your privacy, but do tell us when you feel like it," Alyssa Vitalyevna said.

"Sometimes situations are more complicated than you'd want them to be, Mama," Yelena Viktorovna countered, nodding at Mitya. "Besides, why would he tell you, when you're so judgmental?"

Mitya was impressed by the accuracy of his mother's assessment of the situation. How could she know? Perhaps it was true what they said: a mother knows what the child feels.

"Me? Judgmental? Just because I don't approve of your choices doesn't mean I'm against everyone else's!" Alyssa Vitalyevna protested.

"That's before you actually find out what they are," Yelena Viktorovna said and smiled at Mitya.

Mitya felt a warm feeling of kinship and was almost ready to tell the women in his family about Zolotoy. But then he realized that he couldn't be too forward.

"I wonder if sometimes these things feel like they're not meant to be," he said, vaguely. "Like the whole world is against love."

"Of course! Why do you think there would be so many stories of star-crossed lovers otherwise?" Alyssa Vitalyevna responded. "So, does this mean our Romeo has found his Juliet? Our Onegin his Tatiana?"

Mitya averted his eyes and did not say anything. He wanted to tell, but the fear of being misunderstood was stronger.

"Mama, don't get into his business. He'll tell us when it's time, right, synok?" Yelena Viktorovna tore a morsel of Rossiyskiy cheese off a slice and ate it.

Mitya thought that the time would probably never come, now that he wouldn't be able to find Zolotoy because of the militsia's interference. But he felt acknowledged, seen and understood, and it was something.

———

A week later, Lana and her family had returned from the Canaries, and Yelena Viktorovna headed to work. Alyssa Vitalyevna was practicing the ice-skating chops of her teenage years somewhere in the Moscow region, while Dr. Khristofor Khristoforovich Kherentzis watched her and imagined the horror of her bones collapsing if she fell. School started again, but that day Mitya didn't go and instead stayed at home.

He wasn't dressed as Devchonka, but he was sitting at the kitchen table, hard at work drawing outfits she could wear. It was an ordinary day, yet something was off. The air seemed charged with electricity, a disturbance lurking. So when Mitya heard someone open the door with a key and enter, he felt a strange peace inside. The premonition he'd been feeling was correct.

Mitya watched his cousin come into the kitchen as if it were happening in slow motion. Or as if Mitya were observing from within a fish tank. Vovka approached him, breathing the sweet and sour of hangover and new inebriation over the picture of a female figure in a tight-fitting dress that rose above the paper in folds and waves of brown modeling clay.

"You're doing it again, bratish?"

Suddenly Mitya felt boredom. He was rarely bored, loved spending time on his own, and always had things to do. But this feeling, he realized, was precisely that: melancholia that constrained his limbs with passive revulsion. He knew exactly what was coming. He could see no fun in it, no surprise, no exodus: So why experience any feeling at all? He didn't respond to Vovka, walked from the kitchen to the living room sofa, lay on it, and closed his eyes.

He let it happen, while he thought about other dresses to make, or where Devchonka could wear them. He thought about Zolotoy, Marina, and Valerka, who could all wear them too, and fly over the golden sun on giant bumblebees like ancient chariots. That made him even more bored. The things happening to his body were those of hell, and that world he imagined was of heaven. But outside of his imagination, heaven could not exist. It made him weary and forlorn, and then, at the most terrible moment, Mitya thought he would choke or die from the sadness that minute. Maybe both. The inside of his head got hot and tingly, and he lost consciousness.

When he came to his senses, Mitya saw Vovka eating a vafelniy stakanchik next to him on the sofa. His cousin's pants were back on, and he was flipping channels on the TV. Vovka was acting so casual that for a second Mitya could almost believe again that he had made it all up. But no, his throat felt singed. It had happened.

"How did you get in? I thought you didn't have keys?"

"I have my ways." Vovka said, smirking, and tilted the waffle cup with a piece bitten off toward Mitya. "You want some?"

Mitya shook his head and lay back down.

That winter, Mitya had to avoid going home again. He figured that Vovka would never show up when Dmitriy Fyodorovich was present in the apartment, so he started timing his arrival to coincide with his father's return from work. He rushed home when Dmitriy Fyodorovich was about to return: a development in their family dynamic that he could never have anticipated.

Dmitriy Fyodorovich did not acknowledge this change. But as Mitya waited for him while peeking out from behind the building next to the playground, he noticed that Papa began slowing down after entering the courtyard every day. He'd linger by the entrance and look around, as if expecting his son, not willing to go up without him. Even though they went upstairs in the elevator in silence, they still did it together, and that made Mitya feel a sort of warmth. Because of this new shared ritual, Mitya almost dared to tell Dmitriy Fyodorovich that Vovka had the key. But the whole spectrum of consequences for Mitya that would stem from such an action could not be wholly predicted. His father loved going on and on about how it was unacceptable to be a snitch, and Mitya thought that was a good enough clue. He was also wary of telling his mother or grandmother about Vovka's visits. Neither of them seemed to be aware, and he was afraid that they'd tell Dmitriy Fyodorovich if they found out and present him as a snitch anyway.

22

Mitya and Marina had been meeting up occasionally for ice cream, which seemed like such a decadence in the winter. From bits and pieces, and the way she sometimes omitted details in her stories, Mitya figured that she was still seeing Sasha. It was okay, as long as she was happy and Mitya didn't have to communicate with him. The last week of February, Marina invited Mitya on an outing.

"There is a concert that some of Gleb's friends are doing somewhere to the south of where I live. Do you want to come with me? These people are all so intellectual; I can't bear them. But it'll be easier with you."

Mitya was surprised to hear that she was doing something with Gleb, whose name he hadn't heard from her for a long time, but he agreed to go with her. They planned to meet in the subway and then go to the concert together with Gleb. It was taking place in an abandoned building and getting there on their own could prove challenging since neither Mitya nor Marina knew Moscow well.

When Mitya arrived at their meeting point, Marina and Gleb were already there. Marina seemed to have blossomed: Mitya had almost forgotten how pretty she could be when happy. She looked at Gleb with such tenderness and longing that Mitya almost became jealous. He didn't want Marina to look the same way at him, no, but he wanted someone else to do it.

Gleb was also excited about the event they were about to attend and kept talking about it. It was an annual celebration of the Unknown Artist's Day, which happened every first of March, or Pervomart. The previous year it had taken place at an abandoned hospital, and this year they'd picked a high-rise building that had been ditched mid-construction.

"So who is the unknown artist?" Marina asked.

"That's the point. The true artist is unknown," Gleb explained.

"Why is he being celebrated, then?"

"It's not a he. The unknown artist has no gender, and no name. It's not a man or a woman at all."

Mitya was interested. Would he want to become an unknown artist, then? If he understood Gleb correctly, you couldn't be an unknown artist, because it was a concept, a metaphor. Mitya wanted Gleb to elaborate about the gender, but he couldn't think of the right question to prompt him.

Marina became interested in something else entirely: she wanted to know how they would be able to get into a construction site and not be caught. Did Gleb worry that someone was going to get hurt? Gleb answered her questions with vague condescension as if she were a loved but ignorant child. Marina didn't notice or preferred not to notice.

Though Sasha was one of the most abhorrent people he'd ever met, Mitya felt like he was at least more genuine in his approach to Marina. He seemed to be in love with her. And Gleb, while smitten too, showed signs of annoyance.

The building was not guarded at all, but to get to the twenty-second floor where the performance was taking place, they had to climb concrete stairs that looked solid enough but seemed to float from floor to floor precariously. They made pit stops every few flights or so, usually prompted by Marina, who would run out of breath quickly and flushed from the exertion. Gleb appeared restless and wanted to smoke during most of these stops, especially when someone passed them by as if it were a race.

When they made it to the performance floor, Mitya discovered that the genderlessness to which Gleb had alluded was also merely a concept. The people there looked pretty much like those he had seen at the apartment concert, only dressed more warmly, most of them in leather or puff jackets and jeans. Some men had long hair, but there was nothing there that he hadn't seen on the Old Arbat before. There was no particular showcase of genderlessness.

Gleb went to mingle with the other visitors. They all seemed to be his friends and acquaintances. So while he was occupied, Marina urged Mitya to stand to the side.

"I honestly don't understand what they're doing here," Marina confessed. "But don't tell Gleb, because I think he's already ashamed of having come with me. I'm not as smart as all these girls that he's studying with." She nodded at a bunch of young women, who were wearing glasses and were dressed like they were middle-aged.

"You're much prettier than all of them," Mitya said earnestly, and Marina was delighted, because she thought so too.

Neither Mitya nor Marina enjoyed the performance much. The music was amplified by some boxes that the participants attached to their guitars. The sound filled the cavernous space with an echo, and Mitya could not make out the words. The bass line was loud, and it kept making Mitya's throat vibrate. It was a weird, ticklish sensation. The rhythm was enough to provoke the majority of men in the audience to jump around, banging their bodies against each other. Gleb, an eager participant in it, later told them that jumping like that was called "slam." Despite the cold, some men were so energized that they shed most of their clothing for the duration of the slam.

"Looks painful," Marina said, squirming, and Mitya nodded.

Even when Little Foxes, whom Mitya was happy to recognize, went on stage, it was not the same as when he saw them at that apartment. Perhaps because the intimacy of the small space was lost, Seva seemed to be too concerned with providing the right kind of feeling to the slamming crowd. His energy was palpable, but a few minutes in you could see a strain in the fragile boy. He drank something from a thermos as if to try and regain some energy, and Mitya saw how hard it was for him.

When Marina and Mitya went to track down Gleb, they discovered Seva and Gleb talking to each other. It turned out that Seva was interested in chemistry, and was asking Gleb's advice about preparing for his school exams.

"How did you like it?" Seva asked Marina and Mitya. "This was your first Pervomart, right?"

"I loved it," Marina lied, and Mitya saw Gleb's eyes brighten. He had not been expecting her to appreciate it but was thankful for this answer, even if he also knew she wasn't telling the truth.

"I thought it was too loud. I so much preferred the apartment concert," Mitya said.

"Oh, me too. But we have to get out of our usual space to create a sustainable counterculture. At least, that's what the guys keep telling me." Seva smiled. "I just want to be able to do it for as long as I can. I don't want to be popular or anything."

Though the concert was over, the crowd was still enflamed with the excitement of the slam. A bunch of guys began dislodging a cast iron bathtub from a place where it was attached to the floor. Once they were able to pry it off the ground, they picked it up and threw it over the edge of the building. From where Mitya was standing, he couldn't see the fall, but when it landed, what seemed like a half a minute later, there was a loud noise.

"I hope they don't kill anyone." Marina knit her brows.

"This is the energy we need to cultivate. It can start revolutions," Gleb said, and Seva nodded along.

"Do you want a revolution?" Marina asked.

"Of course we do. Do you see where the country is going?" Gleb's eyes narrowed as if he was again suspicious of Marina.

"When has it ever gone anywhere good?"

"Exactly," Seva said calmly, which seemed to ground both Gleb and Marina. "Once the revolution is over, everyone is always proclaiming that the people participating in it were wild, bloodthirsty, and excessively violent. That the way to do it would be through a peaceful referendum. Only the next peaceful referendum will never solve anything."

"Marina's from Donetsk and her father is a miner. Which makes it even more strange that she doesn't understand the urgency of change," Gleb said, and Mitya saw how much this annoyed Marina.

"Then, by all means, she knows more than we do," Seva said, peacefully, though Marina's face was a flame of anger next to his pale one. "Anyway, I have to go, my blood sugar's getting low, and I don't like to keep Babushka waiting. I'll see you around, guys," Seva said, and shook their hands.

Once Seva had left, Marina erupted at Gleb.

"Maybe I don't have time to think about the urgency of change because I'm too busy earning money to send back home?"

Gleb shrank back.

"I didn't realize you did that," Mitya said. He thought about the money she'd given to him, and shame, hot and sticky, clung to his skin.

"Of course I do. There's no work back home. Papa keeps drinking. Mama was fired. My sister is pregnant again. And my brother-in-law is on a measly pension because he hurt his eyes in the mine. We don't even know if he'll regain his sight, if he'll ever be able to work again."

"You never told me that, Marina," Gleb said, a mix of hurt and accusation in his voice.

"As if there's nothing better to talk about."

"Is that why you had the thing with the boss? For money?"

"Of course, the khokhlushka is also a prostitute. I had the thing with the boss because I'm a free woman, and you should respect that, with your revolutionary vision."

"I'm sorry." Gleb reached out for her but Marina walked a few meters away from them and lit a cigarette.

"But why is this happening?" Mitya asked. "Why are people losing jobs? It seems so unfair."

"They've privatized everything, that's why," Gleb answered. "Where did your parents work before the fall of the Soviet Union?"

"Rubin factory. Where they make the TVs."

"Are they still working there?"

"No."

"See, that's not a coincidence. Do you know why they were fired?"

"No. I didn't ever really think about it," Mitya confessed.

"Because the government has sold everything that it owned to rich guys. And the rich guys don't care if your mamochka and papochka have jobs. They want to hire new people for less money or sell the whole thing to someone else. So they fire everyone. What does your mother do now?"

"She cleans apartments."

"And your papa?"

"He's a guard at a supermarket."

"At least they have that. My father has been out of a job for two years now since his research institute closed, and I don't think he'll find another job soon." Gleb looked down, clearly pained by the thought. "Meanwhile, the government is not helping, because it has no income now: its factories and research facilities are not there anymore to bring in the funds! It's all a vicious circle, where only the rich get richer."

Mitya had never considered any of this. His parents seemed to him abstract entities who existed by particular arrangements. But he had never tried to describe them through the same notions that he used to apply to himself, like justice or truth. And now that he saw what had happened to them, and what had happened to Vovka, it seemed self-evident that something was massively wrong with the system that was in place.

They stayed in silence for a while. Marina, smoking in the distance, was visibly upset. Gleb looked uncomfortable. Mitya wanted more time to think. A group of people, including some of the musicians, started to head out, and Mitya, Marina, and Gleb followed them. The stairs looked even more precarious on the way down. Gleb joined some other people ahead because Marina refused to take his hand. So Mitya was the one leading her. It was nice not to have to talk, but Mitya's mind was overcrowded with thoughts.

He felt small. Not in terms of age, or stature, but his whole existence suddenly felt insignificant. He had thought that he was concerned with many important things, like Valerka's murder, Zolotoy's life, Marina's well-being, and his inability to be safe at home. But everything was so much bigger and more dire than he had imagined. Besides, he hadn't had any success with the murder investigation or tracking Zolotoy. He had to hide in the library to avoid Vovka. And, as it turned out, he had only made Marina's situation more uncertain by accepting her money. It seemed like the whole world was a web of sticky injustices that you couldn't avoid at any turn. What was the reason that people kept on enduring this?

They walked in a small crowd even after they'd descended the stairs. There was only one way to the elektrichka, the commuter rail. Gleb was walking slightly ahead with his friends, while Mitya and Marina tagged along behind, still holding hands, though the ground seemed less dangerous. It was not paved, and the areas covered in snow could hold something terrible beneath them. Mitya thought about reading in the newspapers how once the snow melts in the spring, people keep discovering bodies. They usually called them "snowdrops," like the tiny white flowers that bloom before the thaw. Mitya wanted to tell this to Marina, but the mood didn't seem right at all.

They didn't speak throughout the walk or the ride on the elektrichka. At one point Mitya overheard some guy ask Gleb why his girlfriend was so gloomy. He must have thought that she wouldn't hear it over the wobble of the train, or didn't care. Mitya heard, and Marina must have heard, too, but she didn't show it. Gleb, however, answered that it was none of the guy's business, and that made Mitya respect him more. And he hoped that Marina noticed it too.

After they reached the Paveletskaya station and got on the Koltsevaya metro line, Marina told Gleb that she wanted to take Mitya home before going to her place.

"It's only six o'clock," Gleb said. "Don't you want to hang out more?"

"I know, but I'm tired. You can go ahead with the guys from the band or something," she reassured. "I'll be fine."

Gleb seemed anxious to join the musicians, so after some back-and-forth, he agreed. Once Marina and Mitya were the only people from the event left in the train car, she said that she was in the mood for a party. They left the metro on Park Kultury, earlier than the stop they needed to transfer.

"It's nice out; we'll walk you home down the boulevards. Have you ever walked down the boulevards?"

Mitya shook his head.

"See, that's perfect. Have you ever heard any songs by Yanka?"

"No."

"I love her. I'm sure those guys think it's a bit too main-stream, although she was a real punk, Yanka. She committed suicide the year after Tsoi died. And she was even younger than him. And more talented."

They emerged into the crisp air. The temperature had only dropped to zero Celsius by night, so it was comfortable enough. Marina led Mitya over to where the street was at its widest, with the cars speeding to their left, and started singing.

Why don't you join me for a promenade of the railroad
    trackside?
We could sit on pipes at the bottom of the city beltway.
Our warm wind will be the exhaust from the factory
    smokestack.
Our guiding star will be the yellow plate of the traffic
    light.

If we both get lucky until dark, we won't return to cages.
We must learn to dig ourselves into the ground in just
    two seconds,

To stay lying there when gray cars ride over our bodies,
Carrying away those who couldn't and who wouldn't
    mess around with dirt.

Passersby noticed them, cast strange glances, and hurried off into their busy lives. Marina's voice rang like it was made of crystal breaking against the air. She kept looking at Mitya, not smiling, but not frowning either, a calmness that fit her face like the freckles did.

If we are on time, we'll keep on crawling on the rail-
    road forward.
You will see the sky and I will see the soil on your shoe
    soles.
We must burn our clothes in the furnace if we're to
    return there,
If we're not greeted on the threshold by the blue-
    capped people.

If they greet us, you stay hush about our promenade of
    the railroad trackside.
That's the first sign of a crime or of mental disorder,
And Iron Felix will be smiling from his portrait.
It will take so long, but it will be so justifiable.

A punishment for promenading on the railroad trackside.
A justifiable punishment for promenading on the
    railroad trackside.
We'll be killed for promenading on the railroad trackside.

"That was amazing," Mitya said. "Now I can say I was at a real concert."

Marina punched him on the shoulder lightly.

"Me too. And now I feel like getting drunk."

23

Marina bought a bottle of wine and a bag of sunflower seeds in a convenience store. She walked sipping from the bottle and spitting out the sunflower shells. They proceeded down Zubovskiy Boulevard as multiple lanes of cars sped by them. Mitya squinted at the car lights as they blended with the neon signs of the still-open stores, and felt peace and beauty.

"Thank you for taking me on this walk. I feel like I don't know Moscow at all," he told Marina, trying to shell the seeds using only his fingers.

"Dance while you're young, boy," she quoted from a pop song. "I like it too. It's as if I didn't have to think about my life. Just you, and the city, and wine. And sunflower seeds. Ooh, I love them. But the best thing is something you don't have here in Moscow but we have in Donbass. Milk sunflower seeds. It's when the sunflower is almost ripe: the seeds are tender and you can squeeze them out of the flower head. Chyort, I miss it."

She drank from the bottle some more. They had reached the traffic light, and Marina looked at Mitya with eyes that seemed wet.

"You know, I'm becoming desperate. My life is not what I planned for when I came here. I wanted to help my parents and have some fun, I had a vague idea, but I did not think it would be so hard and so complicated."

The light turned green, and they began moving forward. Mitya wasn't sure how to respond. Which aspect of her life was she talking about precisely? He wanted to help, but he felt so useless and naive.

"Can you marry Gleb?" he finally asked. "You seem happy with him."

"I wish. I mean, I love him, I do, but he doesn't understand some of it. And his parents don't want him to marry some village broad; they think I'm after the propiska—Moscow intelligentsia at their finest, chyort poderi. And I expected them to understand at least somewhat, because they're from Uzbekistan originally. But he doesn't reason with them, or anything. So if we do get married, we'd have to find another place to live, so we don't crowd them. And his salary, you know how much he makes at the university doing his PhD? I make the same selling this stupid underwear part-time. The only difference is his boss isn't grabby, like mine." She sneered and drank more.

Mitya stayed silent.

"I know it could be worse. I've met some other Ukrainian girls here who have to prostitute themselves. And they're not gorgeous putanas like on TV shows. They're gross. Ugly, beaten up, some underage. It's nauseating to see them. They come and buy lingerie from me, and then wear this cheap lace against their bruised popa, it's sad. At least I don't have to do that."

Mitya caressed her arm.

"I wish you were older." Marina smiled. "You would marry me, and you could be a model, rich and famous, and I would wear fur coats and drink champagne all day, and at night we'd take these walks."

"I could never be a model," Mitya corrected her. "They have to be manly and strong."

"You're so silly. You are way more beautiful than you can ever imagine. Don't you see how people look at you, in the subway? Sometimes I'm jealous, I swear. I thought I was pretty. But you're like a star child, an alien. They can't stop staring; they want more."

"It doesn't mean I'm beautiful. It means I'm strange. People stare at freaks."

"Say what you want. But as your model manager I prohibit you from slandering my client," Marina said, pretending to be stern, and Mitya felt grateful because she managed to do it so easily: to say good things about him, but at the same time, to make it light, like a joke, so that he could choose to believe it or not.

They crossed from Zubovskiy Boulevard to Smolenskiy Boulevard in silence. Mitya decided he could talk to her about everything he wanted. First, he told her about the needle and how it was protecting him from harm. It came easy, and Marina responded to the story really well: interested, trusting. So Mitya carried on sharing.

"Remember how I tried to find Zolotoy?"

"Yeah, you told me you went looking and didn't find him, right?"

"I think he is a prostitute too. When I went to the pleshka, that place he mentioned, many men wanted sex. One of them was a ment, and I barely made it away."

Marina snatched him by the wrist and leaned down to him.

"Never go to places like that without me! What if something happens to you?" Her eyes were serious for a minute, but then she snorted with laughter again. "Or what if I miss all the fun? But wait, about Zolotoy. You didn't tell me he was also . . . ?"

"I'm not goluboy; I don't think." Mitya blushed.

"Yeah, it doesn't matter. You'll figure it out. But I like the idea of you having a crush," she chuckled. "I didn't know men could be prostitutes too, though. It makes sense. Men and their sex. What will they not do to get their ballsack empty? Back in Donbass, all the boys I knew were sex-obsessed by the age of ten or something. 'Urine in their brains' . . . Oof, I'm sorry, you don't deserve me, I'm so indecent."

"I touch myself," Mitya said, without looking at her. He didn't want her to think he was a child, but he also couldn't look her in the eye.

"Good, it's healthy. Better to touch yourself than touch others."

"I want someone to touch me, though, but I don't think anyone ever will."

"Is this some weird way of asking me if I'll take your virginity?" Marina's eyes were so round and horrified that for a second Mitya thought she was serious. But then she cackled.

"No, I mean someone else." He felt his face grow hot with blushing.

"Like Zolotoy?"

"No!" Mitya protested so defiantly that they both giggled.

"Don't think about it too much. Goluboy, not goluboy. People should be allowed to have sex with whomever they want."

"What if someone wants to have sex with me and I don't?"

"Has someone been hurting you?" Marina asked.

Mitya didn't have the heart to admit it and shook his head.

"Never let people have what they can't have. And if they try, kick them in the balls. Like this." Marina stopped walking and began kicking the air furiously. When she grew tired, Mitya noticed tears coming out of her eyes.

"You know, I'm one to talk," she said quietly. "I have been sleeping with my boss again. I try to stop it, but he gives me money. Says that he loves me, and his wife is fat and sick, so she doesn't give anything to him. Don't I have any compassion? It's not like he forces me. But I don't want it. I feel so dirty."

"Does Gleb know? What if Sasha finds out about him too?"

"Oh, Sasha. That's the best part." Marina took a big gulp from the bottle. "Remember how I threatened him with the Azeri gangsters when he had your cousin in jail? Rokovaya zhenzhina, femme, blin, fatale, starting wars between factions."

"Wait, there is a war among the bratva?" Mitya said, worried that Zolotoy and Chervyak might be in the crosshairs.

"No. I mean, there could be. But not yet. Just if you read somewhere tomorrow that menty are battling the Azeri, don't be surprised. Think of me."

Mitya was relieved.

"I wish they would kill each other, though," Marina continued with disdain. "Like, you know, in the kids' poem: 'Wolves were so afraid, they ate each other's heads.'"

"I think Sasha loves you," Mitya said. "He would never do anything to hurt you. I see it in his eyes."

"Oh, Mitya, but it's not about me. There's more that you don't know. I didn't want to tell you, because you'd think less of me, or resent me. I should keep myself from getting involved with these shady men. Well, I'm drunk now, so khuy s nim, I'll tell you." She drank the last few gulps from the bottle and made a weird sound, as if her voice cracked from emotion. "You want to know who killed Valerka?"

Mitya felt tingles all over his body. He nodded.

Marina closed her eyes and started sobbing louder. Her face turned ugly, and yet it was the most beautiful thing in the world for Mitya. He felt angry and powerless because there was nothing that he could do to make her not cry.

"Sasha told me, when I was pushing him to investigate."

She started sobbing again, and Mitya, as he waited, felt her pain as if it cut through his wrists. But at the same time he knew that she was about to say something that would make him hurt even more.

"It was him. Sasha . . . He accidentally—he says that it was an accident, at least, I don't know—ran him over with his father's car, when he wanted to park it in the courtyards of the Old Arbat, right between his apartment and Tsoi's wall." Marina paused, waiting for Mitya's reaction, hoping that he would somehow make it easier for her to say this. He didn't. "It was late and dark; he freaked out and told his father. He says that he didn't want this, but because his dad is this big shishka, he called the militsionery and told them to take care of it. Valerka was not dead yet, but they finished him. Because that's what they do."

Mitya was stunned. It all made sense, but everything was just as he had anticipated it to be: terrible, or maybe even worse. Mitya didn't say anything. He couldn't find the words that would accurately describe what was inside of him at the moment and still not hurt Marina.

"I didn't want to tell you because then what does it make me? I still ebus with Sasha. And it's so horrible that I wanted to shelter you from this. I don't want you to know how fucked up the world is, though I feel like you're catching up fast. But Mitya, you are like the only good, pure thing in my life that isn't tarnished by this shit, and there I go, drowning all faith in humanity left in you."

"Was he at least sorry?" Mitya felt a wave of weak, fizzling anger inside of him. Not rage, but more of an irritation that didn't make him want to do anything but wallow in his helplessness.

"He was. He cried. But if he's so sorry, why did he ask the menty to do this thing with framing your cousin? Khuynya kakaya-to. It doesn't solve anything, Mitya. But I'm the worst, you know. I keep sleeping with him. I hate him so much, but I think that he may be my one chance at a decent life here. I don't think I have a choice. And it's pretty rich coming from me when I say that the world is shit because I'm part of the problem."

Mitya wanted to say so many things, but he didn't know where to start. He put his arms around Marina, breathed in her smell mixed with that of wine, and held her. She had told him the truth, and she cared enough about him to want to shield him from the truth. That was way more than any other grown-up in the world had ever thought of him. And though he couldn't have thought of a worse explanation for Valerka's death, the relief of knowing was immense. Mitya felt as if he were recovering from an illness: he still felt weak, and everything hurt, but at least he had the strength to move now.

They stood like that, hugging, under the lights of the Ministry of Foreign Affairs, for what could have been hours, or maybe mere minutes.

Finally, Marina pulled away from him.

"Thank you. I've never had a friend like you."

"Me neither," Mitya said through the tears.

"I'm glad we have no secrets anymore. Secrets poison friendship, and what we have is too good to lose."

Mitya hesitated for a moment, but then figured that if he didn't say anything at that point, he would never admit to it. He had to take the leap.

"I do have a secret, though."

Marina squinted at him.

"This night is getting curiouser and curiouser. What is it? Spill it."

"Remember how I told you that I like dressing up? Like a girl, for instance. Well, I don't just dress up like a girl."

"What do you mean?" Marina sniffled and wiped the bottom of her nose with the sleeve of her leather jacket.

"I like to *be* a girl. Sometimes. Not always."

"See! I knew you were goluboy! Such a pretty boy can't be normal."

Mitya shrugged.

"Or wait, do you want to become a woman? Like, surgery and all that? My roommates were watching that stupid talk show with the guy with the mustache, you know, *Moya Semya*? And there was a guy who came on wearing the golden mask; they let people wear it for embarrassing stories. He said that he was born a boy but became a woman through surgery. I couldn't see if he looked like a woman, though, because of the mask. But he had man hands. You can always tell by the hands. So do you want to be a woman?"

"I'm not sure. I like it sometimes. I wish I could do more things like that."

"I'm sure you could pull it off!" Marina said and took one of his palms into hers. "See, even your arms are not manly. Maybe it's because you're little. But still. Wait, has anyone ever seen you? What do they say? Are you convincing?"

Though it felt nice sharing things with Marina, it grated Mitya that she approached everything in such a way, without sugarcoating it. He had never considered whether he looked convincing enough as a woman. It didn't seem to matter. He wanted to dress up his body and put makeup on his face, not become someone else.

"Valerka. I don't know. I think he thought it was me dressed differently."

"Well, he wasn't in his right mind, was he?"

There it was again. Mitya ignored that comment.

"My father beats me up for it. So I do it in secret. And Vovka, my cousin . . . Vovka beats me up too."

Again, Mitya did not dare make the final step. He couldn't tell her about the other experiences between him and Vovka. Owning up to Devchonka was one thing. It was a happy part of him. But the darkness where Vovka's attacks tortured him was not a place where he wanted to take anyone, especially not after he'd learned about the circumstances of Valerka's death.

"What right do they have?" Marina became aggrieved.

"They say it's shameful."

"They're shameful. Just let your child explore, be himself, play around, experiment. It's your son, who cares if he's wearing a dress or pants? Makes me so angry."

Mitya did not know what to say in response. But it was interesting that Marina noted that it made her angry. It never made him angry. Sad, yes, because in the beatings he saw shame, he understood that what made him happy would never be allowed to exist. But Marina's indignation shifted this view. It allowed him to be angry, too, and that was a welcome change.

"Wait, so why have I not seen you as a girl yet? Should I feel offended? Here I go telling you you're my best friend and get nothing in return, 'a fig with butter'!"

She didn't smile, but the earnest way she said it was so comforting, Mitya hugged her again.

"Okay, you will, I promise," Mitya said into her hair.

Marina kissed him on the top of his head and retreated.

"Otherwise, you better beware!" She threatened him with a clenched fist. "But seriously. Thank you for sharing this with me. We'll work it out together, okay? If you need to be a woman, or if you're gay, we'll work through it together. I know. And I know that while you're by my side, it will all be good. I will sort it out for myself too. I will find a new job, won't have to see my boss anymore, and I'll move out of that apartment with those suki who hate me. I will break up with Sasha. And I will make Gleb be a man and face his parents. I will fix everything. And then I will have enough free time to manage you when you're a bit older and even more stunningly beautiful. Female model or male model. Whatever."

"Khorosho," Mitya agreed and smiled weakly.

Mitya saw Marina to the metro and walked home. Before going up the stairs, he took a detour to Valerka's playground. It was empty and still, only a bit of glow coming in from the lights on the building next door.

"I'm sorry," Mitya said out loud, hoping that Valerka, wherever he was in spirit, could hear or feel it. He had thought it was so simple that there would be one, maybe two murderers who could be caught and apprehended. The bad apples who caused things to go wrong. But instead, it was all a system, rotten and screwed, in which little people had no chance. Especially if they were as kind and innocent as Valerka.

Mitya did not want to be kind and innocent, either, but there wasn't much he could do about that.

TEN

As Zmey Gorynych approached him, Koschei leaned down to pick up the sea cucumber that Tsarevna Snake had dropped. It was limp in his fist but could do the job. Koschei slapped the zmey's three heads with it. As the cucumber hit them, it exploded white goo all over the heads, covering the zmey's eyes and making it impossible for him to shoot fire. The tsarevna rushed to her father to help him clean it off, and Koschei dove beneath the serpent's giant body and leaped out of the room.

Koschei retraced his steps back to where Tsarevna Snake had approached him, next to the room of trapped Koscheis, then made it back to his bedroom. Then he reached a giant hall where the corridors crossed. There were around twenty corridors. He had no idea which one to take and had to decide quickly.

Suddenly, something jumped out at him from the side, and Koschei recognized Tsarevich Toad, who must have been reclining on his water lily sofa, and was now sitting on Koschei's shoulder.

"Looking for a way out?" the tsarevich whispered in Koschei's ear and tickled his ear with his lips. Koschei felt hot and excited but did not show it.

"Are you going to start shooting fire at me like your sister and father?" Koschei growled and tried to shake Toad off himself.

"What? No!" Toad held tight with his webbed hands. "Can't you see I don't even look like them? I'm a bastard from Papa's chance encounter with a turtle. But she was always more interested in vacationing with younger lovers than raising a kid, so I have to make do here. I have no one else but them. But that doesn't mean I have to help them with everything."

"Can you show me the way out of here, then?" Koschei asked.

"If you promise to reciprocate with a favor sometime when we meet again."

Koschei agreed. As Toad led him through more corridors and made sure they ducked every once in a while to evade being followed, Koschei asked him about the fire-shooting power.

"You can only get it if you eat enough human flesh. I've never had any, but Papa and Snake always eat it. Now that they can't boil people, they have to be sneaky, amend paperwork to make people 'disappear.' And then they go to the shooting range together and bond."

Koschei decided to ask about the soldier again. Perhaps Toad would tell the truth when he wasn't with his sister.

"Sorry, we had to lie," he responded. "We had a soldier here recently. He was sent to heaven because the rules on earth right now are that soldiers go to heaven no matter what. But he didn't like it there—his words, not mine—and he found his way here. He got into the factories, raped some workers, and found Papa's secret kitchen, where they cook people. Snake found him and started shooting, tried to wound him. But because he could shoot, too, he managed to get away."

"Did you see him again after that?"

"No, I swear."

"I think he might have gone to heaven again."

"Well, then you'll be able to find him there. Because that's the entrance."

The corridor they were following came to an end, and they were now standing inside a large cave, which was filled with some sticky brown residue that smelled horrible. Overhead, on the ceiling was a rosebud-shaped anemone, which kept vibrating, contracting, and widening. Every once in a while, more residue fell out of it.

"Is this . . . ?" Koschei began to ask, and Toad quickly nodded.

"This is the only way, and you have to go up. Here, I'll help you." With those words Toad started breathing in, which made his chest inflate, and he grew bigger and bigger. When he was so big he filled the cave halfway, Toad invited Koschei to climb up on his back, from where it was easy to reach the opening.

Koschei grabbed the tender rim around it with both hands and stretched the sides out to open. A bunch of brown stuff fell out on top of his head, but he brushed it away and kept stretching. Finally, it was big enough for him to fit, and he first put in his legs, then pulled in his body. As he let go of the flesh, and the anemone began to close, Koschei thanked Toad, who in turn waved his webbed hand at him, while letting the air escape his belly.

Koschei realized that he hadn't asked Toad whether he, too, could turn into a human.

To climb up toward heaven, Koschei had to place his legs di-
agonally across the passage, grasp at the tissue to his other side,
and pull up. This way, zigzagging, he went and went, until a
bright light appeared above him.

Koschei climbed out of the passage, looked back at the hole and
saw a curved beak close around it, and then open again with a loud
cracking sound. A burp. He jumped back, and saw that the passage
to hell was in fact just the throat of a very large bird. The bird
winked at him with a matte black eye. Koschei curtsied, to thank
the creature for letting him travel inside of its body, and rushed
away: he didn't want to make it awkward for either of them.

There was only one way to go, and Koschei found himself in
a cave again, but this one was all white, lined with a rubbery
white material, and full of dense foam that smelled divine. Koschei made his way through the foam, and as he walked, it cleaned
the brown off his body and refreshed it.

This cave did not lead into a corridor but to a balcony with a
view over the entirety of heaven. Heaven was full of humans, too,
but they were all naked and didn't have to do anything strenu-
ous. Some of them reclined on lush lawns; others frolicked in the
meadows. Silver chariots with large bumblebees in the harnesses
passed by, and inside they were carrying more humans. Koschei
stood on the balcony and admired the view.

24

After Mitya's confession, Marina made it her mission to make sure that he would be able to be a girl in real life. She approached the project with unexpected zeal, possibly because she felt guilty about the business with Sasha.

Mitya himself did not want to bring it up with her. He didn't even care much if she was still dating Sasha or not. This reality could exist somewhere in the background, not acknowledged by either of them.

To start with, Marina concluded, Mitya had to have real girl clothes that would allow him to pass for an ordinary female. On a Saturday, she took him to Manezhka, an underground shopping center next to Red Square, which had just opened and boasted numerous boutiques with desirable clothing. There were many beautiful things, dresses, skirts, blouses, in the windows, but they all cost too much.

"Are those telephone numbers or prices?" Marina asked as they admired a dress with a floral pattern in one of the stores. Whenever they liked something, they checked its price tag.

Then, while Marina treated the two of them to a large packet of fries and chocolate sundaes at McDonald's on the ground floor, Mitya estimated how much each dress or skirt was in milkshakes, burgers, fries, chocolate sundaes. The majority of the items were in the ballpark of 350 McDonald's dishes—a whole year of scraping the chocolate fudge off the sides of the plastic container.

His new money box was filling up ever so slowly, so Mitya would never be able to afford anything. But Marina told him that they weren't in Manezhka to shop, anyway.

"It's for inspiration," she said. "We need to figure out what you want, and then we can go to the market where I work and buy everything there. It's all the same, made in the same factories, using the same materials, by workers on their 'third shift.' See, this is your first lesson in being a woman. Smart women don't overpay!"

She licked the salt off her fingers and smiled.

After lunch, they went back to the stores and walked into one of them, with rows upon rows of feminine outfits. At first, only Marina was picking up dresses to look at, but then Mitya got braver too. When the sales assistant approached them and asked if the young gentleman wanted the men's section, Mitya told her that he wanted to buy a gift for his twin sister. It wasn't something he had been planning to say, just the first thing off the top of his head.

"What a good brother you are," she said, smiling. He thought about his classmates, the Nariyan twins, and their identical

Mickey Mouse tracksuits. Mitya wondered: If he had a sister, would they share clothes? It seemed likely.

"That is an ingenious idea," Marina told him, once the shop assistant left. "You can pretend to be your twin!"

"I'm not sure it will work," Mitya said. "Everyone I know understands that I have no sister."

"Not everyone. You're growing up and meeting new people. We could go to one of these kvartirniki with you like a girl, and no one would be the wiser. Even Gleb, although he has seen you so many times. People, in general, don't pay much attention to the details, so as long as you're insistent, your truth will prevail."

Mitya liked that idea, so he tried to pick out the girl clothes. But as much as he liked the feminine lace, florals, and satins in the windows, he did not feel anything when he held them in his hands. They seemed to be suited for someone else, for older women maybe. Marina was frustrated with this apparent contradiction.

"So how come the female clothes are not female enough for you?"

"But you wouldn't wear them yourself, would you?"

Marina hesitated. She used to have to wear dresses and skirts back in Donetsk, especially when around her grandmother, who always reprimanded her for wearing torn jeans. But in Moscow, she hadn't worn a skirt once.

"Or the other girls at the kvartirniki," Mitya continued. "None of them are dressed in skirts or dresses, but there is never any doubt that they're female. So what is it that makes the difference?"

"Now that you're asking, I don't even know."

They stood in front of the mirror and stared at their reflections. The two of them were quite similarly dressed, in dark tones, baggy pants, tops, jackets, and scarves. Only Marina's clothes conveyed her affection for rock music, with Viktor Tsoi's face on her chest.

"You're not even wearing makeup today." Mitya pointed to her face. "And your hair is not that much longer than mine. What is it that makes you a girl, then?"

"Apart from the fact that you have a penis in your pants?" Marina rolled her eyes. "Well, my boobs? But you most likely wouldn't have them at your age if you were a girl either. Or my hips. My mama used to tell me I have childbearing hips. But some girls are skinny; models, for example. I think the difference would be more distinct if you were older, shaving and stuff. But right now you look like a girl without girl clothing. Do people confuse you for one?"

"All the time."

"See, that's where we should have started. You don't need dresses, I don't think. We should doll you up a bit, and tell everyone you're a girl. We'll see if it works."

Marina promised to think about ways of subtly dolling him up for next time, and said she'd find a kvartirnik to go to, so they could try it out.

"What will your name be?" she asked. "I mean, the best girl's name in the world is obviously Marina, but we're not going to share a name."

"Lena?" Mitya said. It was the short version of his mother's name, and because he looked so much like her, it seemed right.

"I like that, podruga," Marina said, calling him the female version of the word *friend*.

———

Another week passed, and Marina invited Mitya to go to a kvartirnik as his twin sister Lena. Mitya was anxious but calmed himself down by thinking that out of the many different crowds, Gleb's underground punk friends were the ones most likely to tolerate weirdness. He put on his regular clothes but made specific changes: he put on a few extra pairs of underwear to make his hips seem more prominent, tucked his sweater into his jeans, and tied his hair in a ponytail. He looked in the mirror for signs of boy or signs of girl, but everything had become so muddled, he couldn't tell anymore.

Marina asked him to meet up at the Smolenskaya Mc-Donald's so that they could do some additional tweaks in the restroom. It was his first time in the women's restroom, and Mitya expected a revelation. But it smelled bad like the men's bathroom, and everyone was too busy to pay him any mind.

Marina brought him lip gloss, hair clips shaped like butterflies, and a girl's pink sparkly scarf, all of which she had handpicked at her market. Though those things did not change anything about Mitya's appearance, they gently navigated the decision about the person's gender in the eyes of observers. As they were exiting the bathroom, Mitya bumped into a fat man, who shouted back: "Watch where you're going." He called Mitya "dura," stupid girl, instead of a stupid boy, durak. It wasn't nice of the man, but it made Mitya happy, and Marina cheered back at him.

The kvartirnik was at a different apartment than Mitya's first time, but it was concealed deep in a residential neighborhood again. They walked down a long street, with smaller side streets branching out and disappearing in the depths of residential buildings. Gleb was as aloof as usual, and was unfazed by the introduction of Mitya as Lena. He only had eyes for Marina, anyway, and looked at her little friend from above, indifferently.

Because the majority of the people at the kvartirnik weren't aware of Mitya's existence, they skimmed over Lena without pause. But what had Mitya expected to happen? For someone to start beating on him? Or to praise him for being a beautiful girl? He wasn't sure, but the lack of any feedback felt anticlimactic. As Marina and he sat down on the rug in front of the "stage," Mitya noticed Seva at the other end of the room, talking to Boris. Seva was deeply engaged in the conversation and didn't seem to notice Mitya. Mitya wondered if he would see him and recognize him later.

Three bands were playing that night. The first one consisted of all girls, and Mitya thought it was symbolic that he saw that band on his exceptional day. Then, Little Foxes performed. Mitya was glad to have Seva back in a confined space. Unlike during the abandoned-building performance, he seemed to have enough breath to make the proclamations of his songs powerful. The final act was Boris and his band, Solomenniye Enoty, the Straw Raccoons. And again it seemed like they were performing for Mitya, with words that spoke right to his experience, and which only he could understand fully.

I greet life with a bash in the mug.
My hero is Captain Zheglov.
I'm the best ment of an exemplary city
And your heads will be falling off.

Not everyone knows on this planet
How hard life is for a ment.
I place in jail pedestrians and poets
And all similar kinds of dregs.

There are too many of us who are proud,
The leashed ones, and the free-range,
But let the dead bury their dead ones,
We'll bury the living instead.

Mitya felt goose bumps on his skin and a tingling somewhere between his eyes and nose as he heard Boris sing that. Dusk descended behind the lacy pattern of the shade. Boris was upright but antsy, stepping from one foot to the other and playing with his hands as if he didn't know where to put them. Finally, he crossed them on his chest, on top of his tight-fitting T-shirt with foreign words. There was nothing prophetic about him at all, drunk, half-blind behind the thick-lensed glasses. And yet, due to an inexplicable link with the cosmos, Boris knew precisely what was happening in the world and sang the truth without even realizing it.

After the concert was over, Mitya followed Marina out of the living room. There were people everywhere, drinking, smoking, talking, but Mitya, though he wanted to be around people as a girl, began feeling uncomfortable. He sensed that

Marina wasn't having fun either. After all, she didn't know any-one well and was cautious around this crowd.

"Let's find Gleb," she whispered to Mitya with wine on her breath, and he nodded.

Mitya was delighted when they found Gleb outside the apartment, on the staircase, talking to Seva. They were dis-cussing chemistry again. When Marina and Mitya approached, Seva seized the conversation, though Gleb seemed eager to continue without including them.

"You look familiar." Seva squinted at Mitya.

Mitya was so excited that he almost blurted out that they had met before. But he took a deep breath and braced himself.

"You must be confusing me with my brother. I'm Lena, and I've never been to one of these concerts before."

"Oh, welcome. I'm Seva. So did you like it?"

"Yes, everything my brother has been telling me about kvartirniki was true. And you do indeed make great music."

"Can I ask you a thing?" Seva said to Marina and Mitya. "I need the female opinion. The first band that played, where the girl was singing, what did you think about the lyrics?"

"I liked them," Marina responded. "Especially the one where she didn't want to open the door, even if god was com-ing. I feel that."

"I liked them too," Mitya said, and hoped that it sufficed as an answer. It seemed that an inability to answer a question demanded of a girl could be his downfall.

Seva was more preoccupied with his part of the story. He wrote all his lyrics from the girl's perspective himself, and was concerned with making them seem authentic.

"I would love to see you at the concerts again and to discuss this. I need as many different women's opinions as I can get to be able to write as a woman." Seva smiled.

"Why don't you ask a woman to write?" Mitya asked. "Like the girl who sings."

"I'm not exactly sure that she understands it all the right way," Seva responded.

It didn't make sense, but Mitya chose not to argue. He was observing the way Seva was watching him. It wasn't drastically different from before, but there was something new. It was as if a flicker had lit up in Seva's eye, and instead of talking to the person in front of him, he was reacting to them, the exchange inducing a sort of heat. Mitya couldn't quite describe it or say how he felt it, but it seemed similar to the way Gleb and Sasha looked at Marina: a longing look that bathed Mitya in energy. It was the first thing that felt different from being a boy, and it was immensely pleasant.

Seva talked more, but Mitya wasn't listening. As a boy, he would listen, because there wasn't anything else. But now he wanted to take pleasure in the gaze, and watched Seva's eyes move as he tried to give all his interlocutors equal attention but kept slipping back to Mitya, to Lena.

"I'm sorry, but I have to go, I need to study for the exams," Seva finally said, and made a point of shaking Mitya's hand. "I hope to see you here soon."

Mitya smiled because he noticed how Seva did not mention his blood sugar or his grandmother. He wondered if this was because Seva liked Lena and did not want to seem like a child in front of her.

The three of them left, too, soon after. In the metro, Marina talked Gleb out of taking them, insisting that she had to bring Lena home to her parents and it would take too much of his time. Once Mitya and Marina were alone, Marina almost started shaking him to extract his impressions. Mitya told her that not that much was different, and shared his thoughts on the warm energy he'd felt from Seva.

"He likes you, that's for sure," Marina said. "Do you like him?"

Mitya couldn't say. Feeling the attention was nice, but because he had the previous encounters with Seva to compare it to, he knew that this energy wasn't directed toward him in general, just Lena. And what if he wanted to feel the same while remaining a boy? What if he wanted to send it toward someone while remaining a boy?

Marina noticed him lost in thought and squeezed his arm.

"It's okay; it's too much for the first time, I know. But I wanted to show you that you can be whatever you want. Don't ever think you can't, okay?" Marina sounded like a movie character, a kind teacher who helps children realize their true potential, or make life decisions.

Mitya was grateful to her for showing him that. But now the issue had become even more complicated, instead of less. He didn't know what he wanted to be.

25

It was in April that Alyssa Vitalyevna determined that it was a good idea to take Mitya with her to a birthday celebration for one of Dr. Khristofor Khristoforovich Kherentzis's daughters. She was saying that it would do Mitya good; however, she planned to use him as a sort of human shield, because of the precarious position she was in with Dr. Khristofor Khristoforovich Kherentzis's family. Mitya did not want to go, but Alyssa Vitalyevna lured him into it with the promise of buying him something new to wear. Mitya hoped that he would be able to purchase something that wasn't too boyish, or too girlish, all at the same time.

Alyssa Vitalyevna also wanted a dress for herself. She needed to look splendid for the occasion, and a quick survey of her wardrobe revealed that she had absolutely nothing that would make *the daughters* embrace her as their new mother-in-law and fear her at the same time.

Because shops would be too expensive, they went to a clothing market. Mitya tried to persuade Babushka to go to Konkovo, where Marina worked, but Alyssa Vitalyevna said that it was not a quality market. They went to Olimpiyskiy instead, which was located inside the former Olympic stadium. Cleopatra had told Alyssa Vitalyevna that her daughter bought Dior and Dolce & Gabbana clothes there for a fraction of the price. They were not real, but you couldn't tell the difference. Perhaps they were even the same clothes, marked differently with tags that the company did not approve.

The market was sprawling and seemed endless. Alyssa Vitalyevna said that it was necessary to know what you were looking for before you started. The stalls with the good clothes were inside the stadium, not outside, and she had a booth number saved and a particular woman named Valentina to ask for. She did not want to make herself known yet, and they spent about an hour walking around the stalls near Valentina's.

Mitya did not mind at all; he loved looking at all the different dresses. Unlike the ones he had previously seen, some of them seemed pretty straightforward in their design, and he realized that he wouldn't mind wearing them himself. The boy clothes on offer were not bad, either, and Mitya kept looking for something that would be fitting for any gender.

After a while, they approached Valentina, who turned out to be a heavyset woman with flaming makeup. She immediately found everything Alyssa Vitalyevna asked for and made great suggestions: for instance, that Alyssa Vitalyevna would look good in a pencil-shaped skirt. Mitya didn't understand why it was called "pencil-shaped," but he was fascinated by how

good his grandmother looked in a dress. He was so used to seeing her in A-line skirts below the knee and cardigans that when
she put on that first dress she had decided on, the sight took his
breath away. The dress had thin straps and a leopard print, and
the way she filled it up with her breasts and hips was stunning.
Her waist, meanwhile, looked wispy and cinched. Would he be
able to look like that when he grew up? Perhaps he would enjoy
wearing leopard pencil-skirt dresses when he got older.

"I think you're going to be the star of the party," he said to
her, and Alyssa Vitalyevna smiled. She knew that she would,
but wasn't sure it would be for the right reasons.

For Mitya, they chose a pair of slim black trousers and a
black shirt. Alyssa Vitalyevna said that she had seen Brad Pitt
wear something like that in a photograph. Mitya knew that
Brad Pitt was a handsome actor, with a girlfriend who looked
like his twin and had a similar haircut, so he didn't mind.

When he started putting the clothes on, it turned out that
the men's and boys' pants were either too wide for Mitya in the
legs, or too short in the ankles, and the shirts hung excessively
on the arms and torso. After a dozen rejected options, Valentina offered to have him try the trousers and shirt in women's
sizes. Though the buttons were facing the other direction, the
clothes fit perfectly, and Mitya couldn't tell if it was a boy or a
girl staring back at him from the mirror. As Valentina wrapped
their purchases, Alyssa Vitalyevna told Mitya to keep this from
his parents.

"I'm sure indyuk won't pay too much attention to the buttons anyway."

Mitya nodded.

The party was at a restaurant owned by one of Dr. Khristofor Khristoforovich Kherentzis's nephews. The seating was prearranged. When Alyssa Vitalyevna and Mitya arrived, they were sad to discover that they were seated away from each other. Moreover, Alyssa Vitalyevna was not seated next to Khristofor Khristoforovich, as she had hoped, and as would be proper due to their relationship. Instead, she was placed at the table with older women, including Khristofor Khristoforovich's sister Pupa. "They're trying to show me my place," she thought and resolved to work with the situation and make sure that the old ladies were enamored with her. After all, her late husband's mother had been a big fan, hadn't she? So Alyssa Vitalyevna sat down and got ready to impress. She began by covering herself up with her shawl so that the grannies couldn't give her plunging décolleté the side-eye.

Meanwhile, Mitya was placed at the children's table. It probably wasn't any more diverse in the represented age groups than the old women's table, but because everyone was more or less under sixteen, the difference in the ages was noticeable. Mitya's chair was between a curly-haired little girl and a gloomy big-nosed teenage boy in glasses, who seemed to be the oldest person at the table and twice as big as Mitya. He had never met them in his prior interactions with Khristofor Khristoforovich's family.

"Kostya," the boy said, introducing himself, and Mitya shook his extended hand. The boy was dressed in a full suit, with a vest and a jacket, and Mitya realized that his own outfit looked a lot like what the servers were wearing, albeit more stylish.

"So, you're not from the family, are you?" Kostya asked.

"No, my grandmother is Dr. Khristofor Khristoforovich Kherentzis's friend." He wasn't sure he was allowed to talk about the relationship before he had established whether the boy could be trusted. "Do you know him?"

"Of course! My mother is his cousin's daughter"—Kostya pointed to a table somewhere to the right of theirs—"and my father is somehow related to him through his father, but honestly, I can't remember myself, because I never met my grandfather, and we don't speak about him at home."

Mitya was amazed. At least this explained how Khristofor Khristoforovich's family was able to fill a party with a hundred-odd people, while he would have extra fingers if he counted his living relatives. Did Vovka even warrant a whole finger?

"And the one next to you is Nika, but I don't think she likes talking to boys," Kostya said. "She is Khristofor Khristoforovich's great-niece, by the way."

Mitya turned to the little girl, who looked back at him with her huge brown eyes and said, with or without malice, it was hard to tell: "You look like a girl!"

"Don't pay any attention to her," Kostya said. "She is spoiled. Here, have some of this khachapuri, it's fantastic."

Mitya allowed Kostya to serve him a slice. The melty cheese in it was so good, he wanted to eat it every day for the rest of his life. And he also wouldn't mind sitting next to the little girl, with her thick curly brown hair, because she inadvertently seemed to get him.

Mitya looked out for Alyssa Vitalyevna and saw her a few tables away, busy in a conversation with an older woman. She seemed to be having a good time. In the center of the room, a white-haired man picked up the microphone and began toasting the birthday woman, Maria. He soon shifted his narrative and began to recall his life in Sukhumi before the war. Mitya knew that Sukhumi was a place in Abkhazia where a lot of Khristofor Khristoforovich's relatives lived before the war started but had never learned the details.

"Have you been to Sukhumi?" Mitya asked Kostya, hoping he would shed some light on the matter.

"We used to live there when I was small but had to flee during the war. We were running to a ship to take us to safety under the gunfire, and I lost my shoes," Kostya said, pensive.

Mitya pictured Kostya running on the shore toward a ship, barefoot and, for some reason, naked. Like the little Vietnamese girl in the war photo that Mitya had seen somewhere. Who was firing at him? Why was there a war? Mitya didn't know the details, but he was sure that Sukhumi was not in Chechnya or Afghanistan. How many wars were there around them? Mitya imagined soldiers shooting at the naked heap of Kostya's body, making sure he didn't make it to the boat. The body fell on the shore, the trickles of blood mixed in with the salty water, and Kostya died.

Though it was his imagination, and the real Kostya was sitting next to him safe and sound, Mitya shivered and wanted to hug the boy. Instead, he stayed respectfully silent.

The servers swapped the dishes for the main course: plates of pieces of lamb on bones arranged among vegetables. Mitya had never eaten lamb, and did not even know what it was: Kostya told him of the meat's provenance. When he put a bone against his lips, it smelled like his wool scarf, with meaty smokiness. It was delightful, especially because Mitya could imitate Kostya and eat with his hands, peeling off the filmy connective tissue that attached the meat to the bone. It was rubbery, crunchy, and especially delicious for this weirdness.

The meandering toast finally came to an end, and music took its place on the loudspeakers.

> You're a very classy lady
> And your daddy serves as an ambassador.
> You're obsessed with Dostoevsky
> Even though it's time for you to be a wife now.

Mitya recognized the velvety baritone of the young crooner Valery Meladze. People started dancing between the tables and in the specially allocated spot in the middle of the room. First, there were a few middle-aged women; then they were joined by some children. Mitya saw Khristofor Khristoforovich invite his birthday daughter, Maria, to dance too. Mitya looked at Alyssa Vitalyevna to make sure she was okay and saw her looking on at the dancers with a smile frozen on her face. Perhaps it wasn't that bad: after all, it was Maria's birthday, and it was only fair for her father to invite her.

"Girls from the higher society often struggle with their loneliness silently," went the chorus.

"Kostya, dance with me." Nika reached right over Mitya and tugged the older boy's sleeve. Kostya patiently stopped eating his lamb chop and wiped his hands with the cloth napkin. Once they reached the dance floor, Kostya helped Nika put her little feet on top of his dress shoes and started moving his legs while bobbing from side to side, so that she moved around like his puppet.

The song now playing was Irina Allegrova's "Empress."

Burn up this town, oh feisty empress,
Forgetting all that matters in the young companions'
    embrace
As if the night were to last forever,
And disillusionment would not become the dawn of
    the new day.

This was the cue for more women to enter the dance floor and flaunt their empowerment. A lot of them, from tiny girls like Nika to hunchbacked older women, danced along to Allegrova's throaty vocals and made sweeping gestures with their arms. Mitya noticed that everyone from his table had gone, either to dance or somewhere else, and he was sitting alone, surrounded by plates heaped with lamb rib bones. He thought about the elephant cemetery in *The Lion King*, which had made him uncontrollably sob for an entire evening. The bones looked sad, but also kind of beautiful. Mitya looked around and, satisfied that no one was watching him, snatched the bones from the surrounding plates and stuffed them into his pants pockets. He wanted to save the bones, to make something with them, but he didn't yet know what exactly. Since Valerka's tree had failed to sprout in the spring, Mitya didn't believe in burying things to have them regrow anymore. But he had started believing that art could give anything a second life.

After a few more songs, the dance floor grew sparse. Most of the kids returned to the table, including Nika and Kostya. Kostya had rivulets of sweat coming down his temples. Nika was hot too. She sat down on the floor and started fanning herself with the hem of her dress, so that everyone could see her white tights and the gaping hole in their crotch.

"You don't dance?" Kostya asked Mitya.

Mitya shrugged. He wanted to, but it didn't feel right.

"Where did you learn to dance?" he asked Kostya.

Now it was Kostya's turn to shrug.

"We do it all the time," he said.

Mitya wondered what his father would say if he were to participate in such a party. Would he dance too? Would he invite Mitya's mother? Or would he find the dancing men effeminate, no matter the amount of hair on their chests or the strength of their jawlines.

A tall skinny woman in glasses came up to Nika and took her somewhere, telling her it was impolite to sit like that. When a slow song came on, Khristofor Khristoforovich asked Alyssa Vitalyevna to dance. She leaned into him gracefully as they moved. Mitya watched the couple dance, mesmerized: despite being next to their relationship for a long time, Mitya had never realized that it was a romance, in fact, full of passion, and youth.

"Is that your grandmother?" Kostya asked Mitya as he watched the dancers. "She looks so young. Not like my grandma." He pointed to someone at the table where Alyssa Vitalyevna had sat a minute ago. Mitya wasn't sure which one was Kostya's because they were all quite old. But now he realized that they were all looking at Alyssa Vitalyevna and Khristofor Khristoforovich and talking about them. Mitya looked for Maria, the birthday woman, and found her at her seat at the main table, her lips pursed. Just as she had told his mother, his grandmother was not liked by this big family, and it made him sad and defensive. At least his neighbor seemed to genuinely think his grandmother was beautiful.

Nika's mother brought her back and sat her straight on the chair. Once she left, the girl turned to Mitya. "My mama said that your babushka wants Khristofor's money," she told him, deadpan, and turned back around to look at the dancers.

Mitya did not quite know how to respond.

"Don't pay attention to her," said Kostya. "Only seven and already causing trouble." He tapped the girl on the shoulder. "Nika! Be nicer to my new friend, or I'll eat all of your cake when they bring it out."

Nika showed him her tongue.

"They don't like her, do they?" Mitya asked. He immediately regretted it, but it was Kostya, stuffing his face again, so lovely and welcoming, who made him want to be honest.

"Don't think about it. We're a big family; no one likes each other, what do you want them to do with strangers? And non-Greeks, especially." Kostya waved his hand and poured more cola into his and Mitya's glasses. "They always keep my father out of things because he is a proctologist and not a dentist or surgeon like everyone else."

"What's a proctologist?" Mitya asked.

"A doctor who heals butts."

Mitya inadvertently spat a bit of his cola on the plate with some leftover slices of potato and eggplant. Then he was terrified that Kostya would be offended by his reaction. "I'm sorry!"

"You think I don't know it's funny? Relax. And go dancing before you miss the chance. This is sirtaki; we will all be
dancing, you should join," Kostya said as a new composition
came on. It was string music that resembled loud, rhythmical
dripping.

The people on the dance floor formed a circle and began
moving together, like a ripple in the water. They each put out
one leg to the side, then the other leg, and then threaded their
legs one behind the other to take a step. Every once in a while
the circle broke, so that one of the participants could pick up
someone from the adjacent tables. Mitya watched Kostya join
the ring, then Khristofor Khristoforovich, then Alyssa Vitalyevna. She was not as sure of her movements as the Greeks, but
it was apparent that she'd been practicing. The music sped up,
and the dripping became a quick string melody.

When the circle was close to the children's table, Alyssa Vitalyevna reached out to Mitya and gestured for him to join the
circle. Mitya was reluctant, but he felt a push from behind: it was
Kostya reaching out from the dancing circle. In a second, Mitya
was dancing along with the others, trying desperately to copy
their movements. It was hard but incredibly fun, especially as
the music sped up more and more.

They served cake after the dance, white, fluffy, with pieces
of fruit. The teenage girls at the table offered their pieces to
Kostya because they were minding their figures, and he shared
them with Mitya.

There was more dancing after the cake. Mitya watched
Kostya move elegantly. He chose not to participate in the dance
himself. Mitya liked Kostya, and wondered if the boy would

have admired him had he come as Lena. This raised a wave of longing in Mitya that he didn't know how to quench.

He wanted to be alone for a moment, so he went to the window closest to their table, sat down on the wide windowsill, and looked outside. It was dark in the street, but people still rushed up and down in the lamplight. Mitya looked at them from his second floor and felt like a god, perched above humanity. He saw them, and they would see him, too, if they only looked up. That was until a young man passing by stopped right beneath where Mitya was sitting.

He had thick brown curls and dark, impressive eyes, and for a moment, Mitya thought that he was Greek too, someone from the party. He looked a bit older, but not by much, maybe fifteen. He stared right into the window where Mitya was sitting and had a vague smile on his lips. It seemed like he could be looking for the restaurant, but he didn't express recognition or move, just stood there. Could he see Mitya? The room behind Mitya was lit, so most likely, yes. The boy seemed to direct his gaze right into Mitya's eyes—or even deeper. He smiled more openly, and Mitya smiled back, although he couldn't know for sure if the boy could see it. Though they were separated by glass and height, Mitya felt the same kind of warm, enveloping energy as he had previously with Seva. But this time, Mitya wasn't a girl, and yet still warranted it. Was the boy goluboy?

Mitya felt the urge to run down the stairs and out of the restaurant and ask the boy. Or at least introduce himself. But he realized that before he'd be able to reach the street, the boy would be gone. The boy smiled at Mitya some more, and then rotated on his heels and walked away fast. Mitya felt a renewed longing for him, the need to find out, to resolve it, to run after. But then he felt the heaviness of all his losses and realized that some moments were precious just because they existed, even if you could never latch on to them, or reproduce them.

At least now he knew that he could be noticed.

———

Soon after the cake plates were taken away, Alyssa Vitalyevna told Mitya it was time to leave. Khristofor Khristoforovich had called them a taxi, and it was already there. Kostya heartily shook Mitya's hand, as if they had become best friends over the few ex-changed phrases, but when Mitya glanced into his eyes, he saw his loneliness reflected in them. Still, he was jealous of Kostya. Even if he belonged to a family that was so mean to butt doc-tors and non-Greek grandmothers. At least he had one. He could come to a place where there were little nieces to dance with, and cousins to share their cake, and grown-ups to look up to. Mitya had no one, only the microcosm of his apartment, where some were suffocated, others suffocating, and, apart from his grand-mother and mother, there was no one to admire.

Perhaps that was why he wanted to be a woman.

In the taxi, Alyssa Vitalyevna slumped in the soft back seat. She was happy to finally be able to stop trying to maintain her posture enough, but not too much, so that everyone would see that she was of good stock, but not snobbish.

"How did you like it?"

"It was fun," Mitya said, honestly, inhaling his grandmother's wine breath, "and I liked the lamb."

"Did anyone say anything to you about me?"

"No," Mitya lied. He didn't want his grandmother to worry about it.

"I was trying my best, and still some of these aunties were giving me dirty looks," she said. "And his daughters. That's why he asked the taxi to come so early, you know, so that I would be able to say thank you to the birthday one in front of everyone and she would have no way to act out. She still gave me the 'chicken's asshole,'" she said of the woman's pursed lips.

Mitya was amused with the expression.

"I think you were the most beautiful one there," he said.

"No, it was you! I saw how some of the girls were looking at you. They may have olive skin and big eyes, but no ponti Greek has ever boasted blond curls." She put her fingers through Mitya's hair. "Never cut it. I know your father doesn't like it, but he's an idiot. This is true beauty. And everyone will like it. *Girls and boys.*" She winked.

Mitya smiled shyly. He hoped so. He had no idea whom he would prefer to like him, but the thing that he knew for sure was that he desperately, overwhelmingly wanted to be liked. And the fact that Babushka understood it, with nuance, with ambiguity, was extraordinary. Mitya felt seen.

26

When it arrived in all its balmy beauty, May made Mitya hopeful. Though not much had changed in his life by then, he had a particular feeling that it would soon. For one, warmer weather made it easier to avoid home during the grown-ups' working hours. Along with Marina, he went on walks around the city that the two of them didn't quite know but were learning to love. They often strolled down the Boulevard Ring, Mitya becoming distracted by conversation so that he couldn't exactly tell which boulevard was which. But he liked their green chain that stretched around the whole city and could always bring him home. There was a comfort in predictability.

Sometimes Mitya wore his girl accessories, of which he accumulated more, outside. There was no method to it; it depended on how he felt at any given moment, and whether he wanted to look like a girl or preferred to be a boy. Marina did not ask him any questions; she smiled at him either way. Depending on what gender the day was, Marina either tousled Mitya's hair or shared her lip gloss as they looked at their reflections in a shop window.

Mitya was reading *The Petty Demon*, a book he had gotten from the library. In it, Lyudmila, a gorgeous young woman who liked to laugh and smelled like lilacs, sought out Sasha Pylnikov, a fourteen-year-old orphan, because he looked like a girl more than a boy. Their relationship developed, they kissed and caressed each other, and at one point Lyudmila dressed Pylnikov in a kimono so that he could attend a masked ball as a geisha. Mitya was all aflutter at how resonant it was. In his life, Marina was the Lyudmila. Thinking about her, soft and curvy, sweet-smelling, gentle, even made him feel a sore longing. When he saw her, this longing didn't appear. Otherwise, it would be too uncomfortable.

One day, Mitya even appeared in his accessories in front of Zhenya and Dasha. He didn't warn them or say anything, just entered the small space of the caretaker's closet and asked them if they wanted to play "it" outside. It was one of the first warm days, and it seemed a shame to stay inside.

Initially, Zhenya did not want to go out. She was fixing a remote control–operated car that she'd found outside. She said that once it was done, she'd be able to put rats inside and take them for rides. But Dasha insisted, and then they were outside, running after each other, dizzy from the sun. Zhenya was not a great runner, because of her club feet, but she seemed to be enjoying it a lot too.

"Are you wearing lip gloss?" she asked Mitya as she caught up with him in Valerka's playground.

Mitya nodded.

"Ty vodish," Zhenya announced, tagging him "it."

Upon his return home, Mitya took out his lipstick stash, the few precious tubes he had bought at the kiosks by the metro, and went into the bathroom. He put on more gloss, and pouted and bit his lower lip seductively, and admired the girl he saw in front of him: long dirty-blond hair, mostly clear skin, large blue eyes, thick eyebrows. Mitya was becoming pretty. He thought that this must be the needle's doing too: it had finally had enough time in his body to take root and make him special on the outside, to match the inside.

His classmates still didn't see it. They were used to him as the scrawny boy sitting in the last row, reading books he hid beneath his desk. But he had started noticing grown-up men and older boys stare at him in the streets, in the metro, in line at Dieta, the store around the corner, where Mama would send him to buy milk, cola, or bologna. Some of the men would try to start a conversation. "Devotchka," they called him, girl. And they were right, in a sense. Previously Mitya hadn't responded and stared down at the floor, picked at a zit, or clutched his change, 1,000-ruble bills, with his sweaty palm and rushed back home. He'd liked the attention but hadn't been ready to receive it.

The encounter with the curly-haired boy through the window filled Mitya with a new resolve. So the next time a man passing by called him a beautiful girl, Mitya didn't turn away. It was on the steps of the Oktyabr Cinema, defunct and filled with small stores, in one of which Mitya had bought a vatrushka. He looked up at the man, into his face. The man was probably a bit younger than Papa and Mama; thick-framed glasses, greasy brown hair, his face cute but a little idiotic. Mitya smiled back at the man and tried to mimic Lyudmila, to imagine her contagious laughter. The man hadn't expected that. He took a step back, his cheeks flushed, and then he turned around and started walking away.

Mitya felt as if a gust of wind swept him off the ground and elevated him above it. He felt so mighty. He took a bite of his cottage cheese–filled pastry and, skipping, giddy with his inherent ability, made his way to the Moscow House of Books. He spent two hours there: stared at expensive notebooks on the ground floor and read Daniil Kharms's absurdist poetry on the second.

Marina was seeing Gleb and seemed happy about it. They still hadn't brought up the subject of Sasha, but Mitya assumed that he was no longer in the picture. Mitya accompanied Marina and Gleb to a few more kvartirniki. If Mitya came as a girl, and Seva was there, Mitya relished the energy that he got from the boy.

He also saw Boris get drunk and break a bottle over a person's head, as Seva had described. The man wasn't seriously hurt and seemed thrilled.

"A stroke of genius hit me," he exclaimed, wiping the blood and beer from his face.

Mitya was becoming more and more mesmerized by Boris's poetry and prophetic vision, but Boris the person scared him quite a bit. Marina shared this opinion, but whenever she brought it up with Gleb, he always countered that a genius like Boris had a right to behave in any way he wanted. Mitya wasn't convinced. But the more he listened to the songs of Solomenniye Enoty, the more he understood that Boris in general did not like following the rules. He viewed the world as something foreign to his existence. Or was it his existence that was foreign? Mitya wasn't sure.

In one of Mitya's latest favorite songs, "Poplar Blood," Boris sang:

There'll be all!
They'll be all!
Sun will shine, and dew will fall,
Dogs will bark, districts will grow,
In the icons, god will glow,
And prosperity for many years to come,
But by then we'll be forever gone.

Mitya understood what Boris meant, and he could see why someone who would be gone from the world and not able to hear the dogs bark would treat the universe with such carelessness.

———

June came, and one day Marina didn't show up when they were supposed to meet. Mitya waited by the Smolenskaya metro station entrance for half an hour, then called her from the pay phone. But her roommate said she hadn't seen Marina for the last few days. It was unexpected. The previous time Mitya saw Marina was four days ago, and she seemed content. She said that Gleb had invited her to go on a camping trip later that month with his university friends. She wasn't keen on camping and predicted that insects would crawl into her ears and lay eggs inside. But she was also grateful to be included.

"I think this means that he wants me to be a part of his life, you know?" she said. "And it doesn't even seem like he's afraid that I won't be smart enough around his friends."

Mitya spent the rest of the day in the library and tried to call Marina a few more times from the phone there. The girl on the other end of the line seemed to be getting annoyed with him, and the last time he called, no one picked up. Mitya thought that he was confused. He must have remembered the week of the camping trip wrong. He'd thought that Marina had said they were going later that month, while in fact she'd said that she'd be leaving soon. Meanwhile, Marina had forgotten about their meeting and departed on the trip without telling him or her roommate.

He went to bed marveling at his confusion, and Marina's forgetfulness, and spent the next two days calm. On the third day, a Thursday, in the morning, when Alyssa Vitalyevna and Dmitriy Fyodorovich had already left, and Mitya was drinking tea with Yelena Viktorovna, their phone rang. Mitya picked up the receiver to hear Marina's trembling voice. She said she was sorry to have missed their meeting, but something horrible had happened. They agreed to meet in an hour by the metro, and Marina promised to tell him everything.

Marina was twenty minutes late, but she came. Her eyes were red and puffy, and as she greeted Mitya with a hug, she continued crying.

"Oh, sorry, you've got my snot all over your hair," she said and wiped it off. Mitya didn't mind; he was more concerned with the reason she was crying.

Marina did not want to tell him everything straight away and insisted they walk down Karmanitskiy, a side street, away from the hustle and bustle of the Old Arbat. As they passed the English pub John Bull, Mitya noticed Vovka smoking with a man dressed in the pub's uniform out on its service porch. Mitya turned away and hoped that his cousin did not see him.

There was a pocket park to their left, and Marina led Mitya to sit on the bench inside.

"I don't even know where to start. Everything is such ebaniy pizdets," she said and started sobbing. Mitya leaned toward her and hugged her shoulders. They sat like this for a while, but then Marina pulled away and turned so that she was halfway facing him. She started talking, and though she kept sniffling, she spoke with fierce energy and made jokes.

"Okay, let's go one by one. First, I'm pregnant. And I have no clue whose it is. I was with Gleb mostly, but I also slept with my boss." Marina fell silent and averted her eyes. "And Sasha. Blyad, I didn't want to tell you, because I'm such a shval, but, there, I didn't break up with him as I promised. I wanted to, but then I kept thinking that maybe this relationship could come in handy. Well, not really sure it can."

"What do you mean? Maybe it's his? At least his family is rich; you won't be suffering."

"I wish it was that easy. You know the joke where the woman gives different instructions to the doctors depending on whether the baby is black or white? I'm that ebanaya woman. I can't take a gamble and hope for the best because I'm not even sure which race it will be. It will either be Asian, or all hairy like my boss, or pale and blond like Sasha, but there's no way that any of them won't be able to tell that the baby's not theirs. When you grow up and fuck around, make sure to choose people who at least remotely look like each other . . . Wait, I forgot, you can't get pregnant. So, yeah, fuck around all you want, I guess. Maybe being a girl isn't that great." Marina grabbed the hair above her forehead, and her face collapsed as she started crying again. "Oh, I also forgot that student. He was a Tatar and had red hair. I'm like a VDNKh exhibition, hosting men from all ends of the Soviet Union." She snickered bitterly.

"Well, can't you give birth to the child and see what it looks like, and then tell the man that applies?"

"I won't be able to afford it. See, when I found out, I took all the money from the register at work, and some from my boss's emergency fund, and ran. I'm staying with this woman from the market now, but I will have to move out soon. But the doctors all cost a fortune. Even an abortion. No more free medicine for us. If you don't want to get skewered like shashlik without anesthesia, you need to be able to pay them."

Mitya thought about Alyssa Vitalyevna's bribe compartment and decided that he could raid it to help Marina. He'd give her all those doctor offerings along with all the money he had.

"Another great thing is that I also have syphilis." Marina wailed loudly as she said it. "I think, at least. So that's more bad news or good news, I don't know, because maybe my child will die, or maybe it will be born with four heads, and each of them different. That'll be helpful!"

Mitya gently embraced Marina, and let her cry on his shoulder. She emitted a mixed array of sounds, ranging from crying to laughter, and Mitya realized that this was precisely what hysteria sounded like.

"You know, I was always so proud of myself that I'm not your regular khokhlushka in Moscow. I'm not a shlyukha, I have my passport, no one beats me up, and the men I see are all promising: a militsia head's son, a scientist, a business owner with connections to the mob, a student. I think the Tatar boy studied economics or something. And yet I end up like every other migrant whore: pregnant, infected, desperate. Maybe someone can beat me up for good measure. It would serve me right. Can you beat me, Mitya?"

Mitya stroked her hair, and repeated the sound "shhh," which was something that Yelena Viktorovna did when he fell as a toddler. It was supposed to calm down the crying, and it worked with Marina because pretty soon she wasn't making any sounds. He could tell that she was still crying only by her hot breath on his shoulder.

"So what are you going to do next?" he asked. "You need to get treatment and have a doctor see the baby. Maybe I can ask my grandmother to direct you to one of the doctors in the hospital? After all, she works there. And she can't refuse if I beg her."

"No, I can't do any of that. I have to return to Donbass. It's all been wrong since I came here. I shouldn't have. I mean, I am grateful to have met you, but the rest of it is just nightmare after nightmare. I have this talent for ruining everything. You're the only thing I haven't messed up here."

"But what will you do in Donbass? You said there were no jobs, nothing."

"Not that different from here, though. And it's much cheaper, at least. I'll have my mama helping me. My sister. I wanted to start my life anew here, but maybe I'll have to start all over back home. Sometimes you have to understand if something is not working out. And clearly, Moscow and I are a recipe for tragedy."

Marina stopped crying and seemed peaceful. It was clear that she had made her decision and was prepared to stand by it.

"Can I go with you?" Mitya asked before he even had a chance to think about it. He was surprised as he said it and froze as the words left his mouth.

"Why would you want to go with me?" Marina stared at him in bewilderment.

"I can work. Help you. Take care of you. Do I need to learn Ukrainian?"

"No, we all speak Russian actually." Marina shrugged. "But why would you want to leave your life here in Moscow and go to khuykino zazhopye? I know it might seem difficult sometimes, you're a sweet boy, but it will pass. You have a family here. You have an apartment. Study, grow up, get an education, and life will be wonderful. Then you can find me in Donbass. Or maybe I'll already be done solving all the problems I've accumulated in Moscow and come see you again. With my four-headed child and a fancy husband. Maybe I'll marry a Ukrainian rock star, and we'll come on his tour."

"You'll never meet any rock star if you don't have someone to babysit your kid," Mitya countered.

"Tochno." Marina wiped her eyes. "But still, tell me, why would you even consider going with me to change my bastard child's diapers?"

"I need to start afresh," Mitya said, somberly. From where they were sitting, he saw Vovka, telling something to the guy in the uniform. Vovka's friend gave him a plastic bag, and Vovka was eating something from inside of it, while holding it between his knees.

"Why would an eleven-year-old boy need to start afresh?"

Mitya looked at Marina. He didn't want to take away from her story by sharing his grief, but she could never understand unless he told her everything. So he did. He pointed Vovka out in the distance by the pub, and Marina was most impressed by the fact that he was indeed missing an arm.

"I thought you were embellishing," she said.

"I feel so trapped. I have to avoid going home. I have to hide. And you are the only good thing about my life. If you're gone, I'll have nothing. Only the library and books."

"Did you try telling your parents about it?"

"Why? They will defend him, or say that I deserve it."

"Even your grandmother? I didn't think she liked him that much. Didn't she refuse to get him out of jail?"

"But they didn't even think about me when I was stuck sleeping in the same bed as him after the coding. It's like with the militsia. You think you're supposed to go and tell them when something bad happens, but we both know that's not how it works."

Marina sighed.

"I could have never imagined something like this to be happening to you. You're a boy from a good family, living in the center of Moscow; everything is supposed to work out fine for you."

"Maybe it can still work out fine."

Mitya knew, somewhere deep within, that it wasn't a sustainable plan, that he would never be able to move to Donbass and live with Marina there. But the more they talked about it, the more resolute he became. He couldn't back down from this, not now.

"I guess it could work. Maybe you could go there and live like a girl? Mama still keeps all my teenage clothes."

Mitya was intrigued by the idea. He hadn't considered the fact that starting a new life would imply making radical changes to the formula of his old life. But what was there to prevent him from it? He could tell everyone he was a girl, and Marina would back this up with her witnessing. And he would be able to live as Lena. He wouldn't have to wait for the right mood, or for the right kind of opportunity to be girly. He wouldn't even have to conceal himself at home.

"Anyway," Marina said, interrupting his vision. "I'm going to buy train tickets. I'll leave as soon as I get some things I might need for the child. You can't buy them in Donbass. If you want to go too, you can go. I'll get a ticket for you too. It's twenty-eight hours to get to Donetsk, and then we'd have to get a ride from the station. And they might be checking documents, like, whether your parents have authorized your departure, so we'll have to get money for the bribe. But think about it. It's very different. There is no McDonald's, no kvartirniki, nothing; it's so incredibly boring."

"I think I would prefer boring," Mitya said, making lines in the dust with his sneaker. Vovka had finally left his field of vision, but not his mind.

ELEVEN

Koschei looked at all the people in heaven, so comfortable in their nudity, and thought that, perhaps, he'd feel at home there. He got lost in thoughts and didn't notice when a bumblebee chariot pulled over next to him. It had a coyote sitting at the wheel and howling in place of a siren. Three eagles in blue uniforms got out of the vehicle and flew over to the balcony. They took out guns and aimed them at Koschei.

"We've been warned of an intrusion. What are you doing here?" said the eagle at the front.

"I came out of there." Koschei pointed back at the opening behind him.

"You have authorization?"

"No, but Zmey Gorynych tried to kill me, and I had to run."

"Well, you can't be here without authorization, human. If you've been sorted to hell, you should stay in hell even if they're trying to kill you. These are the rules."

"But I'm not a human. I'm a Koschei."

"Oh. You don't look like one." The front eagle lowered his gun and studied Koschei for a bit, and then he must have deemed Koschei legitimate since he gestured for the other two eagles to put away their firearms. "Are you with the earlier group? They've already left for earth."

"No, I'm on my own. Did you, by any chance, also have a soldier with fiery eyes running through here? Or Leshy, a wood spirit?"

"If you have inquiries you need to make, we can take you to the information bureau. Otherwise, you'll have to be transported to earth immediately."

"Take me to the information bureau, I guess," Koschei said.

One of the eagles carried him to the car in his talons. Koschei was placed in the back, where the silver leather of the seat clung uncomfortably to his thighs. The eagles dropped him off at a building with many columns and embellishments gracing its exterior. It looked like a palace. However, when he entered it, he saw only one big room, which was full to the brim with old, faded folders of yellowed paper piled up to the ceiling. In the middle of the room, between two equal mountains of old documents and dusty nuts, sat a gray-haired, bespectacled squirrel, who also looked powdered with dust.

Koschei introduced himself politely and asked the squirrel if he could answer some of the questions he had.

"I can answer anything, but you will have to fill out some forms," the squirrel said and threw a thick wad of papers in front of Koschei. "Here, make sure you print; my eyes are not what they used to be." The squirrel wiped his glasses with his fingers, only making them grimier.

"And when I'm done with the paperwork, what happens?"

"You go back to where you came from and wait."

Koschei tried to argue and explain the situation. The squirrel was firm in his position: Koschei had to fill out the paperwork, be escorted back to earth, and wait for an answer, which could take anywhere from six months to 140 years.

"I only have a few questions for you, which you could answer in under a minute, but you want me to waste all that time?" Koschei felt frustration crawl all over his body. *"You're worse than hell!"*

As he said those words, he saw the squirrel's face contort.

"How dare you?" the squirrel screamed. *"Officers!"*

As the officers entered the building, Koschei rushed to the pile of nuts and pulled out one near the bottom. The whole structure collapsed, and an onslaught of filberts rushed like a wave toward the eagles. As they tried to avoid falling and flailed the wings they didn't use much, Koschei moved past them and made it through the doors.

Outside the information bureau, he saw the coyote in the police chariot and wondered if it was a good idea to ask him for a lift. No, he would probably arrest him and give him to the eagles. There was nothing else around them. Like the entrance from hell, the bureau of information was suspended in the air, and you could reach it only via flying chariot. Koschei heard something rattle behind him and saw that one of the eagles was coming out of the building.

Koschei climbed the enclosure surrounding the porch and looked below, where he saw greenery and naked, happy humans. He was not meant to join them, after all, but it would be his decision, not someone else's. As the eagle flapped his wings and told him to stop, Koschei took a step forward and started falling. He saw a flash of silver in his eyes, and then nothing.

27

June 1998 turned out to be one of the hottest months ever recorded in Moscow. It got hotter with every passing day, and when he walked outside, Mitya felt his sneakers, bootleg Abibas, sink into the melting asphalt. He had a sallow city tan, and there was a pink rash around his testicles. Shops and metro trains were smothered with the stench of unwashed bodies, bad breath, liberally applied perfume, dust turning to moist grime. The air was so thick, Mitya expected it to detonate with any brisk movement. Watching the news became a family routine, and yet the meteorological center failed to promise rain, again and again, morning after morning. Mitya was still unsure if he'd made the right choice to depart with Marina, but he was sticking to it. He conceded that nothing was going to grow out of the money buried in the playground, and dug it up. He didn't want to go to Donetsk and force himself upon Marina's family; he needed a safety net.

He packed his things in secret, taking only those in which he would be able to be a girl, and leaving the rest behind. What he wanted to take he put into an empty duvet cover, which he would then tie on the top and carry. Sometimes he thought of the prospect of living as a girl with excitement; sometimes it filled him with claustrophobia. But the best way to approach this issue was not to think about it excessively. Instead, he concentrated on taking in everything that he would miss. He walked around the Old Arbat every day, and maybe because of his premature nostalgia, or because of the heat, the buildings around him seemed to blur in front of his eyes.

Though he wouldn't be saying any goodbyes, Mitya still needed to have some closure with the people in his life. He didn't want to tell Zhenya and Dasha he would be leaving, in case they spoke of it to their parents, so he bought them Hematogen and chocolate. He couldn't go to a kvartirnik, not without Gleb's involvement, but he recited Boris's songs in his head.

Alyssa Vitalyevna and Yelena Viktorovna were the ones he'd be missing most. So each day after dinner, he lingered around them. Alyssa Vitalyevna liked to take her tea languidly. Yelena Viktorovna joined her most days, as they talked about different things and watched TV. Mitya joined them, too, instead of drawing in the corner. He realized that soon enough, he wouldn't be able to see them again. However, because he could never bring up his plans, these teatimes became repetitive, anticathartic, and he almost wished to be gone already, so he could start missing his mother and grandmother for real.

Marina finally bought the tickets. They would leave on a Saturday, the train to Donetsk departing from the Paveletskaya station late in the evening. They calculated how much time it would take for Mitya to get there from home, so he could escape smoothly.

For dinner on the night of his departure, there were two packs of pelmeni with vinegar. After they'd eaten, Dmitriy Fyodorovich was drinking vodka in the kitchen. Alyssa Vitalyevna, Yelena Viktorovna, and Mitya sipped pale tea with sushki in the living room. All the windows were flung open, and yet there was no draft.

Mitya put the little bread rounds of sushki on each of his pinkies like rings and licked their surfaces. They were slick as if lacquered. He wondered if that was what lips felt like when you kissed someone. Then he took dainty bites of the crusty bread, which tasted like wood.

"Tea is good for you in the heat; that is what the Uzbeks say." Alyssa Vitalyevna slurped the liquid from the saucer and bit on a sugar cube. "They drink tea all day, and sweat it out in their padded robes."

She had been saying this every day of the heat wave, yet when Mitya asked if she had ever been to Uzbekistan, Alyssa Vitalyevna shook her head. She just knew it, and this made it right. She and Yelena Viktorovna were both wearing light, colorful robes instead of padded ones, and their heavy breasts hung down, unencumbered by bras. They were watching reruns of *A Próxima Vítima*, the Brazilian soap opera about the serial killer. They had already seen it the previous year and knew who the killer was, yet their interest did not diminish.

"Cleopatra is telling me that this time it will end differently," Alyssa Vitalyevna said.

"Why would it end differently?" Yelena Viktorovna asked, more to continue the conversation than to argue.

"Because they filmed a new ending for the Russian audience. We are more sophisticated; we have different tastes, you know."

Mitya wished they could talk about something else for a change. But he couldn't think of anything to say to prompt a conversation. Besides, he was getting fidgety. His stomach started cramping, and he had to go to the bathroom. When he returned, the living room was empty. He heard voices coming from the kitchen. There was a strong draft down on the floor, as he approached, and it took a hard push to get the door open. Mama, Papa, and Babushka were all gathered in the kitchen in front of the window that opened to the front yard. It wasn't that late, yet the sky had suddenly turned dark, and the wind outside was blowing in strong gusts.

"Look, Mitya, it's colder," Mama said as he approached them. She put an arm around his shoulder, and her fingers went through the loose strands of his hair.

"It's going to rain any minute," Papa said, holding down a belch. He had put too much vinegar on his pelmeni, which was now returning in acidic waves.

They heard the hollow sound of thunder in the distance.

Mitya wondered how the hell he was going to get to the metro in this wind.

"Count the time between thunder and lightning, multiply by the speed of light, and you'll know how far away the lightning is," Alyssa Vitalyevna said, shaking a finger. Her late husband had taught her that, although it wasn't an exact method.

The lightning struck a second later. With the next peal of thunder, Mitya started counting.

"They're three seconds apart, Ba."

"Too near! We should close the windows to avoid balls of lightning."

"What are balls of lightning?"

"It's when electric currents form a ball that can, in turn, burn everything it encounters. If it gets in the room, we'll all be dead."

Dmitriy Fyodorovich always found fault with Alyssa Vitalyevna's ideas, but this time, he reached for the handle on the window frame and pushed the window shut. Mitya remembered him telling about the time he was struck by lightning, during his army training, in the middle of a Kazakh steppe. The grown-ups then went to close all the windows in the other rooms in their apartment and turned off the TV so that the lightning couldn't get through the power lines.

Mitya stood by the window and put his face against the glass to see better. The wind had gotten stronger and was now carrying a string of leaves, sticks, and empty chip bags in a whirl. Occasional droplets were falling from the sky. The glass was getting colder, and as he kept on breathing, he could smell his breath and the smell of glass, which he hadn't realized existed. Maybe it was just the dust trapped on its surface, a cold, powdery smell.

"I wonder where that khuy is in this weather," Dmitriy Fyodorovich said, as everyone returned to the kitchen, turned the lights off, and assumed their positions beside Mitya, looking out.

"Probably kosoy, as usual," Alyssa Vitalyevna clucked. "Must be shlyaetsya with his drinking buddies."

"Ah, bedniy, he might get soaked," Yelena Viktorovna said, sadly. "One wouldn't even let a dog go outside in such weather."

And as soon as she said it, it started to rain.

"Oof, maybe that'll teach him. He's worse than a dog." Papa scratched his belly beneath a white sleeveless shirt.

Yelena Viktorovna shrugged. Her fingers were back in Mitya's hair, braiding it nervously. Usually, she didn't dare touch his hair in front of Dmitriy Fyodorovich, since he did not approve of its length. But at that moment they were all united against the forces of nature.

And this was when Mitya knew that he wouldn't be going to Donetsk that night. Not because it was impossible to get to the metro through the developing storm, but because it was the first time Mitya had ever felt a part of a larger unit, backed up by his family. It felt surprisingly good, and though they all merely stood there in silence and watched the weather unravel—they were together.

It took only five minutes for the rain to become a full-fledged thunderstorm. The wind got stronger and banged the open windows in the opposing building. It picked up random litter and carried it as high as their seventh floor. Mitya couldn't peel his eyes away from the window. Papa asked him not to lean on the glass, as his nose was leaving oily marks on it. Mitya wiped the grease marks with a kitchen towel, and then took a step back and watched the power of nature, so dark, so menacing, so strangely beautiful.

The universe had given him a sign, and he had received it. He only hoped Marina would understand and forgive him. He would send her money to Donetsk. Mitya had gotten the

Donbass address from her, which he was planning to leave for his parents to find after he was gone. Now he was glad that there was another use for that piece of paper.

There was a noise in the hallway, and the family went to investigate as if the storm had merged them into one unified entity. Vovka was standing next to the front door, with his keys lying on the floor next to him. He was drunk and held himself up against the wall with his only hand, barely upright, oscillating.

"Vmphmph," he uttered.

"Moodak ebaniy," Dmitriy Fyodorovich spat out and tried to shut the door, but Vovka stuck his arm out.

"Uncle Dmitriy, let me in," Vovka said with an effort, his tongue heavy inside his mouth.

"Go to your friends and drink yourself stupid with them. Do you think I took your key away for nothing?"

How he wished he could give his nephew a beating. But he wasn't even worth it anymore. Not like this.

"Uncle Dmitriy, strelyayut." Vovka snatched Dmitriy Fyodorovich's arm, afraid that he might not provide shelter from the hell outside. "They're shooting." His eyes were wide and crazy, welling with tears.

"You want me to push you down the stairs?"

"Dmitriy, come on." Yelena Viktorovna tugged at her husband's arm. "He must be so drunk; he thinks it's gunshots, not thunder."

She imagined how it must be, to be chased by visions of the horror he had seen in Chechnya. Vovka was, after all, a boy too, only a little older than Mitya.

Vovka stared at her with gratitude.

Dmitriy Fyodorovich banged the door open, picked the keys off the floor, and stormed off toward the kitchen. He wanted no part in this female charity. No one wanted to listen to the master of the house anymore.

"Mitya, help your mother," he said without turning around and then began muttering under his breath. "Alkash. Baba." Alcoholic. Woman.

Yelena Viktorovna and Mitya helped Vovka into the hallway and to the bathroom. Alyssa Vitalyevna stood to the side and observed them with unmasked disgust on her face. She didn't even want to pretend to care. He wasn't her relative.

Once they placed him in the bathtub, Vovka dozed off. They left him and switched off the light. Babushka and Papa were in the kitchen, looking at the storm. They both pointed at something outside.

"Yelena, Mitya, look, an enormous tree branch flew into a car; the wind is nightmarish." Papa summoned them to the window, and they saw a car with a smashed roof. It was something expensive, a Saab or a Mercedes, and it made Dmitriy Fyodorovich feel good that someone rich was getting to suffer for a change.

"And Vovka's friends have left their windows open." Alyssa Vitalyevna pointed up, toward the top floor of the opposite building where that horrible woman lived with her son. "Probably passed-out drunk."

Everyone was excited, mesmerized by the tempest. The family stood in front of the window for half an hour or so, pointing out objects that flew past them, cardboard boxes, plastic buckets, McDonald's cups. Someone they didn't recognize from above, a man with a shopping bag on his head, ran into the courtyard from the street. The wind was so strong that the man could barely keep himself from being pulled away. He was finally able to take shelter by entering their building, with a lot of effort. Throughout all this, the four of them exchanged observations. It was as if they were watching a sports competition between nature and the material world of humans, rooting for the latter.

Never had Mitya felt that he belonged to a family as much. Never had he felt such warmth. It was already past the train's departure time. He knew that Marina was going back home to Ukraine at that moment, lulled by the clamor of the wheels. And he wasn't with her, because he was already home.

But then it was over.

After the storm ended, Alyssa Vitalyevna went to her room to try and reach out to Dr. Khristofor Khristoforovich Kherentzis, to check if he was all right, and then call Cleopatra to compare their observations of the events that unfolded in their respective courtyards. Yelena Viktorovna started cleaning the dishes. The television had been switched on and reliably droned in the background. Mitya wanted to prolong the warmth and asked her if she wanted him to help.

"What are you, a baba?" Papa asked, knocking over a stopka of vodka. "Instead of doing women's chores, better have some of this. If you learn how to handle your bukhlo with your father, you'll never have problems like that cousin of yours."

He poured vodka into the stopka and pushed it toward his son, prepared to hear some sorry excuse.

Mitya looked at him, not sure if he was serious. Papa seemed earnest. Mitya glanced at Mama over by the sink, but she was busy soaping dishes with Fairy. Mitya played along and pretended like he'd never had vodka. He brought the stopka to his lips, and gingerly turned it over into his mouth.

"Here, zakusi." Papa gave him a piece of black bread. Mitya still looked like a girl, almost indiscernible from Yelena when Dmitriy Fyodorovich had met her. But even if he looked like a sissy, at least he was at home and tried to be helpful. It might have been the weather, or his nephew passed out in the bathtub, but Dmitriy Fyodorovich felt like his son hadn't failed him as much for a change.

Mitya bit on the bread and let it absorb his bitter saliva.

"Muzhik," Papa said in approval. A man. He patted Mitya on the back, then poured himself another stopka and drank it. "Now go to bed."

Mitya came out of the kitchen with the happiness of vodka surging through his limbs. He felt a tingle in his thing: he had to pee. As he fumbled for the light switch next to the WC, he remembered that Vovka was still in the bathroom and decided to take a look. Vovka was sound asleep, his withered, bruised body in the bottom of the bathtub like a weird, misshapen fetus inside the womb. Mitya pitied him. And yet, he hated him, for all the hurt he had brought to Mitya. It felt like the boy that Vovka had abused in the nights was not the same Mitya but a smaller, weaker one. And Mitya, the new, grown-up, resolute Mitya, wanted to protect his past self, and to punish his aggressor.

Mitya unzipped his trousers and pissed all over Vovka. His cousin kept sleeping. Mitya shook off the remaining droplets, tucked himself back in, and turned to the sink to brush his teeth. They were white enough, like the teeth of an actress, and he grinned like a maniac. It was to see his teeth better, but mostly because he was enjoying himself.

Suddenly, and too quickly for his inebriated state, Vovka emerged from the bathtub and jumped at Mitya. He grabbed Mitya by the throat with his only hand and pushed him against the mirror.

"Suka, kak ty smeesh," Vovka roared, as the smell of fresh urine, not pleasant, but not quite a stench either, reached Mitya.

But Mitya felt brave. "Do you know that it was me who saved you from jail?" he said to Vovka. "It was me, I did. If it weren't for me, you'd still be there. Because I'm a good person, and you're govno." He spat in Vovka's face.

Vovka bellowed and toppled him over. Mitya fell on the floor, almost hitting the edge of the sink with his head. Vovka landed on top of him. In a practiced gesture, Vovka unzipped his pants. Mitya let out a scream. Vovka must have been disoriented by the unexpected reaction, because Mitya was able to shake him off and run out of the room. He made his way past the WC and to the kitchen, and Vovka followed, slowly, wobbling, but with the determination of a wounded animal. Yelena Viktorovna and Dmitriy Fyodorovich had left the kitchen, but a bottle of vodka was still standing on the table. Mitya grasped it and froze with it in his hands in front of the same window where they had previously watched the storm as a family. Vovka approached, his penis still sticking out, his eyes mad. He wasn't even saying anything anymore, just making weird bellowing sounds. When he reached Mitya and was close enough for him to smell the urine again, Mitya landed the blow. He did exactly what he'd seen Boris do, only his bottle was bigger, and had more liquid inside. It didn't break but landed on the top of Vovka's head with a dull thud. Stunned, Vovka fell to the floor. There was no blood.

Still holding the bottle, Mitya fell back on the windowsill and felt as if the curtain of the irreversible covered him. He had killed his cousin.

Dmitriy Fyodorovich was the first to enter the kitchen, followed by Yelena Viktorovna and Alyssa Vitalyevna.

"What happened?" Dmitriy Fyodorovich shouted. He approached Vovka and turned him over, recoiling first when he smelled the urine, and then when he saw his nephew's penis hanging out.

"He attacked me," Mitya heard himself say clearly. He would have expected to be crying hysterically by that moment, but he was oddly calm, clasping the bottle's neck.

"Did he piss all over himself?" Dmitriy Fyodorovich winced.

Mitya did not answer. Alyssa Vitalyevna rushed through to him and took him in her arms. Mitya felt his hands and the bottle tremble against her, but the rest of him felt collected and cool.

Yelena Viktorovna took a small vial of ammonia from the kitchen cabinet and leaned with it in front of Vovka. As soon as Vovka inhaled it, he opened his eyes.

"What happened?" Dmitriy Fyodorovich boomed, and Mitya saw spittle land on Vovka's face. "How the hell did you get the keys, and what did you do to my son?"

"Dmitriy, calm down." Yelena Viktorovna was screwing the cap back on to the bottle. "I gave him the keys. I felt it was wrong that he had to be in the streets."

"Suka, what is, blyad, wrong with you? You want him to kill our son?" Dmitriy Fyodorovich took Yelena Viktorovna by her wrists but immediately released her. "Mitya, what did he do to you?"

"He wanted to rape me," Mitya said, simply. Just an hour ago it seemed like he would never be able to say that out loud to his family, but now he uttered it, and the world didn't fall apart into small pieces. Instead, he felt good, unbearably light but also filled with a steely resolve. Mitya looked down at the bottle he was holding and felt the ring of aluminum around its neck. A sharp edge from where the cap was attached poked his finger. Like a needle, Mitya thought, and instantly felt the warm glimmer of protection from within, although he wasn't sure he even needed it anymore: he'd learned to protect himself.

"You blyadskiy pervert," Dmitriy Fyodorovich roared and began landing blows on Vovka, who stared around him, disoriented.

"Dmitriy, perestan, he might be hurt." Yelena Viktorovna tugged at his arms. Dmitriy Fyodorovich backed away and sat down next to his nephew on the floor.

"He probably didn't even feel it. You know how drunks are."

"I'll call the emergency brigade I know." Alyssa Vitalyevna released Mitya from her grasp and reached for the kitchen phone.

Dmitriy Fyodorovich groaned: "What did we do to deserve this? Isn't it enough that Seryozha is dead, now his offspring has to be this, too?"

Yelena Viktorovna briefly touched Dmitriy Fyodorovich's shoulder and stood up to walk over to Mitya. She put an arm around him, and he felt her fingers playing with his hair again.

Mitya loosened his grip on the bottle, and it fell to the floor with a metal clink.

Once Alyssa Vitalyevna had called in the emergency, she reported: "We can leave him outside, next to the door. They'll pick him up there. They know we don't want him. I'll help you, Dmitriy." She approached her son-in-law and picked up Vovka's legs. Dmitriy Fyodorovich grasped him under the armpits, and together they carried Vovka out of the kitchen.

"Uncle Dmitriy," Vovka muttered, "Alyssa Vitalyevna!" But it was impossible to make out anything else he was saying.

When Yelena Viktorovna and Mitya were the only ones left in the room, she kissed her son's temple.

"I thought you two were getting along fine," she whispered.

Mitya stayed silent. He had no strength in him to protest, or to guilt his mother for not noticing enough.

Dmitriy Fyodorovich and Alyssa Vitalyevna returned to the room. They both looked somber.

"I have taken away the keys, and if you ever let him in again, Yelena, I swear I will kill you both," Dmitriy Fyodorovich said to his wife with metal in his voice, and then turned to Mitya. This time his voice was almost tender: "If he ever comes home, if he, or anyone else, tries to do anything to you, tell me first, at any time of night or day. Don't risk it."

Alyssa Vitalyevna stood in the corner as if she was hugging herself. As Mitya looked around the room at the grown-ups in his family, each of them drained of emotion, in this moment, they all seemed to have aged by a decade.

All the next day's news was about the tragic events of the previous night. They watched it as a family and were brought together again. No one mentioned Vovka, as if the storm had been the ultimate event of the previous night and there was nothing else to acknowledge. It was fine by Mitya; he had nothing to add.

Ten people were killed, and two hundred had been hurt in the storm. Tens of thousands of trees had fallen, and two thousand buildings had suffered irrevocable damage. Even the walls of the Kremlin were affected. Yelena Viktorovna gasped, thinking of all the poor people stranded in the storm. Dmitriy Fyodorovich exclaimed, angry with everyone and no one. Babushka was skeptical: she wasn't sure there was anyone to trust. Everyone was blaming the country's meteorological agency that had failed to warn the city government and the people of the upcoming catastrophe, in decay, like every other institution around them.

After breakfast, Mitya went for a walk. The air was crisp, cold; it was easy to breathe. Everywhere he went, he had to navigate fallen trees, debris, and in some cases, volunteer brigades equipped with saws and axes, hacking away at the blockades. Mitya stepped around them to stare and admire the precision with which tree trunks were sawed into chunks. Thoughts about Marina, and Vovka, and everything else, entered his mind every once in a while, but he preferred to keep it empty, unoccupied. There was nothing except for the neat circles of the trunk being cut in front of him.

28

Every day for the rest of the summer Mitya woke up guilty about not going to Donetsk with Marina. She didn't call, and her former roommate hadn't seen her, so he knew she wasn't in Moscow. But had she made it home safely? Mitya wrote a letter to her using the address she had given him. He put most of his Valerka money into the envelope and thought that it only made sense for Marina to receive it, after all. He also drew a picture of Marina rocking out with Viktor Tsoi, and an infant of vague ethnicity showing the sign of the horns with its plump fist next to them. Mitya made the clothing for all three out of black sunflower shells.

He tried to persuade himself that his worries were unnecessary. What could have happened on the train? Surely, she had returned home, to her family, and he hadn't needed to return because he was already home. It was now Mitya's firm belief that everyone returns one day. You might feel miserable at home, but at least you know how things work there. Or you're close to figuring it out.

Still, Mitya couldn't shake the feeling that he had betrayed her. Not by staying back, but by not becoming a part of her life moving forward. He liked to think that his role in Marina's life would be different from the roles of Gleb and Sasha, but here he was, in Moscow, like them, instead of helping her. But then he thought that it was better that way. Imposing himself on her family, who could barely make their ends meet, was presumptuous of him. It would even be shameful for him to go live with other people when he had a home.

A home that was, thankfully, not threatened by Vovka anymore. He had been released from the hospital without any damage reported, as Alyssa Vitalyevna told everyone, and he did not dare return.

Mitya became more relaxed with Dmitriy Fyodorovich, although little in their daily interactions showed that same care that had radiated from the father's face as he punched Vovka for hurting his son. Mitya was reading *The Brothers Karamazov*, a long book he had found on his grandmother's bookshelf and had planned on reading for a long time. It was a hard one to read and had so many characters, mostly men, with problems. There was a father, and a son also named Mitya. The Mitya in the novel wanted to kill his father. Would the real Mitya kill his father, if given the opportunity? Previously, perhaps. But not after the incident with Vovka. It was as if all the hurt was softened. He still wouldn't want to appear as Devchonka in front of Dmitriy Fyodorovich, but at least he knew that his father cared for him.

It turned out that the storm wasn't the only tempest of that summer. First, in early July, an army general turned politician, Lev Rokhlin, was killed, allegedly by his wife. He was a prominent figure in both the Afghan and Chechen Wars. Dmitriy Fyodorovich took his demise to heart: he drank a lot and angrily ranted that Yeltsin's special forces had the hero general killed because he was a threat to the regime. He especially liked to direct his raving at Alyssa Vitalyevna as if she were part of the special forces operation to take down Rokhlin.

Then, one Friday in August, Mitya woke up to find all the grown-ups gathered in the kitchen, sober but worried.

"I'm telling you, Cleopatra's son works for a man in the Duma, and he is saying that it's dangerous," Alyssa Vitalyevna said with her usual arrogance.

"I don't trust the gossip," Dmitriy Fyodorovich replied in his booming voice. "They are banks, not pyramids. Banks shouldn't go bust, that's where the rich keep their money."

"Maybe it's safer to get the money?" Yelena Viktorovna asked quietly. She didn't want to argue; she wanted to do something.

"Cleopatra's son knows everything! He knew that Yeltsin had a heart attack before others!" Alyssa Vitalyevna could not believe that the indyuk would even risk losing the money he had before he would listen to her.

"And your beloved Yeltsin said there'll be no devaluation!" Dmitriy Fyodorovich did not trust the government at all, but was even less inclined to listen to his mother-in-law.

"Maybe I should try the branches in the area, see if they have cash?" Yelena Viktorovna asked. No one responded. She was already dressed, in black jeans and a crisp white blouse, a look that made her look younger, skinnier. She put on a pair of shoes, grabbed her purse, and was out of the apartment. Alyssa Vitalyevna and Dmitriy Fyodorovich argued in the kitchen for a while, each refusing to capitulate to the other.

Mitya listened to the arguments coming from the kitchen, Dmitriy Fyodorovich's voice a roar, Alyssa Vitalyevna's higher pitch keeping pace with him. Yelena Viktorovna returned much later when both Dmitriy Fyodorovich and Alyssa Vitalyevna had left for their work shifts. She had many banknotes in her purse, which she had managed to get after standing in lines to seven banks in the area. Most of the banks' clients had not yet caught on that there was a risk of losing their savings, but the lines were still pretty long.

She asked Mitya to help her sort the cash. They hid it in the books, sticking banknotes between the pages.

"Mama, why do you have all these rubles?" he asked.

"There will be a bank collapse," Yelena Viktorovna responded. "Your father doesn't believe it, but there is clearly a lot of commotion going on, and some banks are closing down. Luckily Lana made a card for my wages, so I used the machine. I only got a small part of our money. I'll try again tomorrow."

On Saturday more people were crowding by the machines, as only a select few branches were open, and it was even harder to get any money. Yelena Viktorovna took Mitya with her to stand in lines while she checked out other bank branches, hopping on and off buses. More remote areas were a better bet, but that was how the thinking of other people went too. They got some money, but not much. As they took the metro back home, Yelena Viktorovna leaned back against the chocolate brown of the seat and sighed, exhausted.

"I have been so fed up at work lately. Lana is always recovering after her surgeries. Kristina has been acting crazier lately. She terrifies me. I thought I'd start looking for a new job. Well, good luck to me keeping this one now. The rich folk keep their money in the banks too. It's been seven years, and yet this country will never cease sucking us dry."

That evening, the grown-ups convened in the kitchen again. They had powdered mashed potatoes with canned peas and sosiski for dinner and everyone except Mitya had vodka. He wouldn't have minded having some, but Dmitriy Fyodorovich didn't offer. His parents and babushka were concerned with getting the money back. It was settled that on Monday no one would go to work, and they would spread out to cover as many bank branches as possible. And then they'd buy supplies. Mitya would go with Mama again. He didn't mind.

Having to wait in lines gave Mitya enough time to consider the things he had avoided thinking about. He assumed that the bank collapse would not touch Marina since she was in a different country, and that calmed him down. To distract himself further, he read *The Brothers Karamazov*. And then, to distract himself from the dense reading, he stared at the people. Unfortunately, no one admired Mitya in the bank queues; no one thought he was a beautiful girl. They were all too preoccupied with their money and talked about how the ruble would keep depreciating. Mitya asked Mama, and she explained that it was becoming cheaper but was still valuable. They didn't get rubles that day, except for some on Alyssa Vitalyevna's part. She put the money away into a sock and beneath her mattress.

"I know the tellers at our branch, and they helped me," she boasted to Dmitriy Fyodorovich at dinner. Dmitriy Fyodorovich did not answer. He poured more vodka and chewed on the grilled chicken drumstick Yelena Viktorovna had bought at a kiosk.

———

Over the next month, Mitya's parents and babushka tried to get money again numerous times but to no avail. The government announced something called "sovereign default," and everyone was talking about it, Babushka on the phone with Cleopatra and Dr. Khristofor Khristoforovich Kherentzis, Dmitriy Fyodorovich with his drinking buddies. The prime minister was fired. And then, Dmitriy Fyodorovich was too.

On the day before school started, Mama and Mitya spent the whole morning and afternoon buying new school supplies at the Pedagogical Bookstore in the center of Moscow. The other children with their parents, who had all kept this until the thirty-first of August, formed endless lines. They were clutching at the lists of what kind of stationery they were supposed to get, and what books to buy.

When that was done, it was time to buy a bouquet of flowers for Tatiana Ivanovna, his homeroom teacher. Though Mitya's parents never gave her gifts, it was unimaginable to show up to school on the first of September, Teachers' Day, or her birthday without flowers.

"It's the worst timing ever," Mama said to the woman behind them in line to the flower shop, hoping to find someone to commiserate with. The woman was holding her little daughter by the hand. The girl was so small it was hard to believe someone that size could be going to school. She had a pink allergy rash on her cheeks.

"And these *urody* are raising the prices through the roof too," the woman responded, and then pulled hard at her daughter's arm because the child was bored and had started spinning around. "Stop this right now, or I'll give you to the gypsies."

"Mama, why don't we go to the Nariyan sisters' kiosk? It should be cheaper there," Mitya asked.

"They'll fleece us like the rest of them, Mitya. Such are the times," Yelena Viktorovna replied.

When it was their turn, Yelena Viktorovna bought a bunch of red gladioli and sighed as she paid. She let Mitya carry them home.

When they arrived, Dmitriy Fyodorovich was there already, drinking vodka. It wasn't his custom: on Mondays he returned only at dinnertime, and he normally never started drinking before dinner.

Mitya went to the living room to sort through his new possessions. He didn't have Mickey Mouse notebooks or shiny gel pens, the things that his classmates so enjoyed, but he still had some nice new things. He had neat green notepads with plastic covers to put on them, pencils with erasers on their tops, blue pens with transparent stems. He even had a wooden ruler, which he knew he would put into his mouth during classes, and feel the bubbles come out of the moist wood and hit his tongue.

Then he read *The Brothers Karamazov* for a bit: he had made it through the elder Zosima's endless musings, which he had been attempting all month, and realized that it had gotten dark and they hadn't had dinner yet.

Mitya went to the kitchen and saw his father sitting alone, crying. He had never seen him cry, not even when Lev Rokhlin was killed, and now here was a striking sight. Tears streamed down Dmitriy Fyodorovich's meaty cheeks; his large, hairy fist rubbed at his eyes.

"What happened, Papa?" Mitya asked him, but Dmitriy Fyodorovich grunted and threw his stopka against the wall next to him. He did not want his son to see him like this.

Mitya slipped out of the room and looked for Mama and Babushka. They were nowhere to be found until he thought of looking outside, in the staircase. Both of them were smoking, where Vovka had usually smoked. It was another surprising sight. When she saw Mitya come out, Mama threw her cigarette on the floor and stepped on it with her shoe to put it out, hoping he hadn't noticed.

"Why is Papa crying?" Mitya asked.

"He lost his job again, and now we'll be even poorer," Alyssa Vitalyevna said spitefully. "We're the only breadwinners in this family now." She also put her cigarette out and went past him back into the apartment.

"Mama, is this true? We don't have enough money?"

"We don't, Mitya. But don't worry. We'll think of something."

She wasn't so sure herself, but making Mitya worry would only make him grow up, and she didn't want that.

Yelena Viktorovna ushered him into the apartment, and as they passed the kitchen, Mitya saw Dmitriy Fyodorovich still sitting at the table, still crying.

In the living room, Mitya counted the banknotes that remained in his Valerka fund after the care package to Marina. Only a little more than 500 rubles remained. One hundred dollars before the devaluation, with the present currency, it was a mere twenty-five dollars. It wasn't enough. So Mitya gathered all his new treasures: the pens, the pencils, the notebooks with their covers, even the textbooks. Then he brought them to the kitchen along with the money bag.

"Here, this is money, and we can sell these too, Papa," he said, placing the pile on the table. He was overwhelmed with pity for this big man, who was so menacing but could not do anything about this situation. "We won't starve."

Dmitriy Fyodorovich pushed the pile off the table with a brusque movement. The notebooks fluttered their pages; the pens fell all over the floor; the money bag landed quietly. He wanted to make his son disappear, along with his shame.

Mitya slipped out into the corridor. Mama came and led Mitya into the living room, where she sat him on the sofa and held him. She felt powerless. She hadn't saved their money; she hadn't saved her husband's job; she hadn't protected her son from disappointment, yet again.

"It will be all right, everything will get better," she whispered. "He doesn't mean it."

But that was what she always said, Mitya thought.

Next day at school, Mitya had to write his name on the covers of notebooks that were wrinkled, torn, and wavy with spilled vodka. He didn't care. He finished *The Brothers Karamazov* over the next few days to discover that the Karamazov father was indeed murdered by his son, but not the one called Mitya.

In the following weeks, Dmitriy Fyodorovich drank a lot and swore a lot. He promised to find Vovka and kill him for his crimes, but he never did, because the angrier he got, the closer he was to a blackout. Mitya never saw him cry again. He never saw his bag with the money, either.

———

Marina responded to Mitya's letter in mid-September. She was doing well, she wrote, and she had taken care of her syphilis. The baby was growing inside of her, and seemed fine. She was eating her grandmother's borscht with garlic every day. She had never received the money that Mitya mentioned in the letter because someone at the post office must have gotten to it first.

"That's too bad," Marina wrote. "We could have used it. Ukraine is feeling worse and worse after the default in Russia, and the hryvnia has fallen hard. No one in my family has a job. I don't want to sound mean, but I'm glad you didn't come with me."

Mitya wrote his answer to Marina in one of his wrinkly composition books, while the teacher droned about math. He still felt guilty, but not as much, as the recession was taking its toll.

———

Yelena Viktorovna was fired in early October after a fascinating workday.

She was Lana's kitchen, ironing the boss's shirts and watching *The Streets of Broken Lights*, the new TV show about the adventures of militsionery in Saint Petersburg. The boss's mother was there, too, cooking some mountain Jewish dish from spinach and eggs for lunch. Kristina came in to cut the label off the new top Lana had bought for her and took the scissors from the kitchen cabinet. When the grandmother said that the dress top was too revealing, Kristina methodically and quickly stabbed her in the eyes.

Lana ran in from the living room and instructed Yelena Viktorovna to call the ER and the psychiatric emergency services, but not the militsia. Yelena Viktorovna got on the phone while trying to stop the bleeding from the elderly woman's face with a kitchen towel. Meanwhile, Lana managed to wrest the scissors out of Kristina's hand, despite the mad, primal strength that filled the girl.

After an urgent surgery, the grandmother survived but lost vision in both of her eyes. A few days later, Kristina was diagnosed with schizophrenia. And though the family now needed even more help at home, Lana did not want to continue the employment of Yelena Viktorovna.

"You understand, of course, it's a delicate matter," Lana told her a week after the incident.

"'It is a delicate matter,'" Yelena Viktorovna fumed to her mother and son that night. "I keep having nightmares. Some of them have the livid Kristina stabbing her grandmother, but the majority are about trying to find a new job in the recession."

Alyssa Vitalyevna was the only one in the family who got to keep her job, because of her relationship with Dr. Khristofor Khristoforovich Kherentzis.

"I never thought I'd be making a career 'through the bed' at sixty," she said, leering. Her paycheck had shrunk, but at least there was the safety net of the best healthcare available in Moscow.

TWELVE

Koschei came to his senses and saw a man's face hanging over his own. The man was young, had green eyes and curly hair, and smiled widely when he saw that Koschei was waking up.

"I'll do it again to make sure." He leaned in and kissed Koschei on the lips.

Koschei had to admit to himself that he liked the feeling of the kiss, but he was scared that the man was with the heaven police. So he crawled out from beneath him and jumped to his feet, ready to attack.

As he backed away, Koschei saw that he was on the shore of the island from which he had previously jumped to hell. Many of his animal friends were gathered around him and cheered as he rose. The man stayed on his knees. Now Koschei saw that he was naked except for a crown on his head.

"Are you Tsarevich Toad?" Koschei asked, incredulous. The man seemed familiar, but the main giveaway was the lips. So Koschei had gotten to kiss them after all!

"Tsar Toad." The man smiled. "Quite a few things happened while you were out of it."

It turned out that the silver flash Koschei had seen after the fall was the flying dog Semargl. Semargl was the only way to get from heaven to earth, but you could only ride him if you were good. When the soldier ate all the human flesh in hell and got the fire-shooting ability, he returned to heaven and threatened Semargl with fire. Since all dogs are afraid of fire, Semargl obeyed and brought the soldier to earth's surface. And as the soldier was burning the island, Semargl scampered through the sky in shame and wailed. It was Semargl's wail that haunted the island, not the soldier's. But that was discovered only after Koschei dove into hell, when Semargl got tired of running around and crashed on the island's shore. The twin moles found him, heard his story, and sent him back to heaven to look for Leshy or Koschei. When Semargl finally found him, Koschei was falling from heaven. The flying dog caught him, and brought him back to the island.

Semargl was now lying on the sand, licking his balls, with the twin baby moles sitting on his neck and hugging the flying dog's fur. It's a known fact that moles adore dogs and vice versa.

"But where did the soldier go, then?" Koschei asked, after hearing the illuminating story.

"We're not sure. Perhaps your friend Leshy sacrificed himself and led the soldier off the grid, where they fell off the face of this world together."

"That sounds like something he'd do," Koschei said, somberly. The animals all nodded.

"And this is why we have to replant and repopulate this island, in his honor," Tsar Toad said. "You've been lying here breathless for so long, some have already started."

He pointed, and Koschei saw that birds were flying around and dropping seed bombs from their beaks. Land animals, led by the carpenter hare, were busy building Koschei's new house. Meanwhile, a bunch of heavily pregnant mice were lying in a field hospital, ready to give birth. They were the only animals who had had enough time to bring their new pregnancies to term, and they were surrounded by rows and rows of unhatched bird and reptile eggs awaiting their term.

"But you, how come you're here?" Koschei turned back to Tsar Toad. "Aren't you supposed to stay in hell? How did you get your father and sister to let you out?"

"Let's say I had some help making sure that hell did not exist anymore." Toad smiled.

"So, there's no hell anymore?"

"None."

"And where do humans go?"

"To heaven. We're working on setting the eagles straight, but bureaucracy-backed military rule can take longer to defeat than a tyranny."

"But why did you do all that?" Koschei asked.

Tsar Toad got off his knees, walked over to him, and kissed him on the mouth. Finally, when they split their lips, he explained:

"Because I knew that I wanted to be with one particular tsarevna."

And so they lived together and gained good together. They resided in the new house, which was better than the previous one, on the island, which grew verdant and lively again, in full *harmony with all its animals, with the twin baby moles by their sides, and the flying dog Semargl at their feet. And they changed the way heaven worked, too, although it took a while, but that's a story for another time.*

Meanwhile, our fairy tale runs out like a trickle. Whoever listened is a lovely pickle.

29

In early 1999, the Noskovs had to put their apartment on the market. They sold it by summer and started their move to a much smaller apartment in a residential district in the deep south of Moscow called Chertanovo. The man who bought the Old Arbat apartment was working for the mayor's office. He didn't seem to have been affected by the recession in the slightest. The family had a lot to say about him behind his back. He was the closest thing they'd encountered to the physical embodiment of their strife, but they had to remain civil to seal the deal.

Mitya liked to think about the name of his new neighborhood, Chertanovo, which he was convinced stemmed from the word *chert*, the devil. It sounded fun. After studying the map, he realized that Chertanovo was close to the area where he'd attended the concert in the abandoned building. It was also in the south, the same direction where Marina used to live, where Chervyak and Zolotoy's market was, and where the kvartirniki happened. Mitya considered this all to be a sign. Unlike everyone else in his family, he was excited about the move.

The majority of the bulky things were moved by a truck that belonged to Dr. Khristofor Khristoforovich Kherentzis's younger brother's construction company. In the recession, they were glad to do some moonlighting, even if it was at a reduced rate. The rest of the things had to be moved by metro. Because Alyssa Vitalyevna was at work, and his parents were out looking for new jobs, it was often Mitya's responsibility to cruise back and forth between the Old Arbat and Chertanovo. Mitya had to be sneaky because he was using Alyssa Vitalyevna's subsidized metro card, but no one ever checked.

He didn't mind taking the trips because this way he was able to transport all the girly things. There were so many of them, accumulated and hidden across the apartment in places no one would ever look. For example, his lipsticks were in the old jar of bay leaf branches that his parents had brought from their honeymoon in Tuapse. There was a newer jar of bay leaves that Yelena Viktorovna used to make soup, but she still kept the old one for its sentimental value.

She saved many things like that: old, useless, dusty, unopened for the last decade, but things that brought a stir in her heart. Yelena Viktorovna did most of the packing for the move. Alyssa Vitalyevna refused to participate, and no one even asked Dmitriy Fyodorovich, but Mitya obediently helped. They managed to pack everything they had in the old apartment, even in the pantry, and then Mitya began to transport it. Each time, he added something of his, hiding it beneath his shirt when he left the Old Arbat and taking it out closer to the metro.

It was Mitya's duty to help his mother unpack too. Sometimes they did it together, sometimes Mitya was on his own. He noticed new hiding spots: among his old toys, in boxes of clothes that didn't fit anymore, in bags filled with broken Soviet kitchen utensils. His treasures would be safe.

———

It was a pleasant day in the middle of August, a Friday, and Mitya was taking his last haul to Chertanovo. They would get the remainder of the belongings from the Old Arbat together as a family over the weekend, and then they'd relinquish the keys to the new owners. For now, Mitya had two heavy bags loaded with pots and pans, and the yurt-like sculpture he had made from lamb ribs salvaged from the Greek party was thrust on top of them. A jar of lipsticks was tucked into his pants. He would have put it into one of the bags but there wasn't any space. He had to take two metro trains and then a bus or a tram to get to his new home, but as long as there were spaces to sit, he'd be fine.

Mitya was reading *Lord of the Flies*, the book that Seva had recommended to him some time ago. Mitya liked it, it had a lot of boys he imagined to be cute, but the atmosphere of the island scared him. Besides, he kept getting distracted by his thoughts. He was making plans for the fall ahead of him, when he would start at the new school in Chertanovo. Because no one knew him there, Mitya could see a massive number of possibilities for reinventing himself. He wouldn't need to be invisible anymore. In his head, he practiced what he would say to his new classmates. He imagined them and imagined himself, universally liked, and acknowledged. Mitya thought of things he and his new friends could do together. He had never been invited over to a classmate's apartment before. He had never gone kart riding. Mitya thought about opening up to them about Lena, Devchonka, or whatever he wanted to be. He wondered if they'd like her too. He was sure they would. He wasn't yet sure how to present her, but he knew it would all work out.

After all, the needle was, once again, giving him a chance to start his life anew. And it would be safe. None of the horrors would follow him. Most importantly, Vovka would stay on the Old Arbat to continue his unsuccessful, slow attempt at dying.

Calmed by the sweet thoughts and the rhythmic movement of the metro train, Mitya was almost lulled to sleep. But suddenly through the window to the next car, he saw something that caught his attention: a head of wispy, light blond hair. Mitya couldn't make out whom the hair belonged to: it was definitely someone tall and skinny, most likely a guy, but the person had their elbows on their knees and their head in their arms, and so the face was concealed. Could it be Zolotoy?

Mitya moved closer to the window but kept enough of a distance so that the person wouldn't see him. It was still unclear whether it was Zolotoy. The clothes seemed like they couldn't belong to a homeless boy, but then again, Zolotoy was pretty neat. Besides, he could have stopped living on the streets, for all Mitya knew.

Mitya resolved that he would switch train cars during the next stop, but position himself farther away from the sitting person so that he could observe them first. He stood in front of the doors to be able to get out as soon as the train stopped; from there, he could still see into the next car through the window. But as the train started approaching the station, he noticed that the other person had also relocated to the doors. There were two tall men standing by the doors in the other car, and Mitya couldn't see the blond person clearly. There was not enough time and not enough space to maneuver to the window and back to the doors again in time to get out at the station, so Mitya had to trust his gut and assume that the blond person would be leaving at the next stop too.

When they reached the platform and the doors opened, Mitya hastily stepped out of the train. He was about to go to the left when the jar with the lipsticks slipped out of his pants and fell to the floor of yellow and gray granite. The glass collapsed in a million sparkles, and the lipsticks rolled in every direction as the ancient bay leaves crumbled among them. Mitya instinctively reached down and got on his knees. But then he realized that he wasn't sure if the blond person had gotten off the train, and by trying to pick up the lipsticks, he could miss the chance to get back on. Mitya winced as a piece of glass tore through the knee of his pants and began raising himself, like a sprinter from a low start. Everything seemed to be happening in slow motion, as if within an aquarium. And as Mitya was getting up, he saw the person with the blond hair walking down the platform in the distance. The person also started turning around in his direction, perhaps because of the sound the breaking jar made.

Mitya removed a piece of glass from his knee and looked down at his palm to see red blood on his fingers. He raised his eyes just as the blond person did the same, and he smiled, ready

to explain the lipsticks and his blood. He'd have to tell Zolotoy how he had been looking for him everywhere, how he kept
returning to the market, and how he was approached by the
ment with the mustache on the pleshka. He would also need
to mention how he had almost left for Donbass with Marina.
Would Mitya feel comfortable talking about Vovka? After all,
it was behind him now, and it couldn't hurt him anymore, so
why not share? Or maybe he would start at the very beginning,
with the needle?

As Mitya debated where to commence telling Zolotoy his
story, their gazes locked, and their faces were flooded with the
lamplight reflected off the indentations in the station's ceiling.
With blood dripping from his knee to the granite, Mitya rushed
forward toward Zolotoy.

Zolotoy rushed toward Mitya.

ACKNOWLEDGEMENTS

This is a list of people, animals, and groups to whom I'm grateful for the impact they had on my life as an author and a citizen as I worked on this novel.

Ritoozik. Tanechka and Yurochka. Vanya and Oma. Nataliya Ivanovna and Vladimir Sergeevich. Fesya, Vinya, Mika and Moka, all the Masyuki. Jin Auh, Elizabeth Pratt, and Alexandra Christie. Masie Cochran, Becky Kraemer, Nanci McCloskey, Craig Popelars, Diane Chonette, Elizabeth DeMeo, Alyssa Ogi, and everyone else at Tin House. Anne Horowitz, Jill Twist, and Jaya Miceli. Lena, Thomas, Franka, and Cash Stenzel. The Sagaydakov 3 generations. Ruth and In. Afina, Lena, Misha Anastasiadi, Anton, and Misha Bolshakov. Sergey Radchenko. Tanya Denisova. Polina Zemlicka, Anastasia Chukovskaya, Nastya Matrokhina, Anna Koubeeva, Kalouda Saginidou, Ivan Smekalov, Katya Nikitina, Daniel Kashnitsky and family, Fabrice Kanda and kids, Dmitriy Mironenko, all friends found and lost in time. Francesca Giacco, Jenessa Abrams, Madelaine Lucas, Afia Atakora, Raluca Albu, Adrianne Bonilla, Siobhan Southern, Danny Tehrani, Olivia Ciacci, Supipi Weerasuriya, Miriam Kumaradoss, Courtney Campbell, and all the kind hearts of the Coven and Morningside Heights. Julia Szyndzielorz, Daniel Martini, Mariah Whelan, Harriett MacMillan, Freddie Gilder, Sam Brett, Gabrielle Mowat, Jana Casale, Maya C. Popa, and all the beautiful Moodlers. Irina Tataurova, and all the smokers of Parsons. Nour Sabbagh, Charles Billot, Rawan, Talal the pickle, and the Communititties. Lauty, Ceci, Kolya Rackers, Gera, Lyusya, Boilek, Henry Hakamäki and Safie, Nemanja Lukić, Gosha Rogov, Giovanny Simon, Kayla Popuchet, Jonathan, Lily Lynch, Anna Tse, Evgenia Kovda and Yasha Levine, Marlon Ettinger, Laura Ruggeri, Esha Krishnaswamy, Ivan Shogolev, Daur Dbar, Anton Pleschyov, Alexey Sakhnin, Yury Smirnov, Anatoli Ulyanov, Roderic Day, Denis Lavinski, Zaina Arekat, Favour Jubilee, and all my wonderful comrades near and far. Alexander Chee, Darryl Pinckney, Paul Beatty, Hilton Als, David Ebershoff, James Cañón, Karim Dimechkie, Erroll McDonald, Ellen Umansky, Greg Baxter, Brenda Wineapple, Binnie Kirschenbaum, Clarence Coo, and John P McShane. Elise Valmorbida, Jamie Nuttgens, Marti Leimbach, Amal Chatterjee, Frank Egerton, Rebecca Rue, Clare Morgan, Jane Draycott, and Jenny Lewis. Alice Peinado, Frederique Krupa, and Mark Tungate. Manana Kerimovna, Olga Pavlovna, and the man who taught me to read. Inez Wade and Barry. Irina Morozova, Ilya Kulyakin, Oxana, Małgorzata. Drs. Bertini, Dolman, Cooperman, Benvenisty, and all their wonderful assistants. Folks at 200C, 34D, 7D, PD and 61B, and Antonio. Solomenniye Yenoty, Lisichkin Khleb. RIP Boris Belokurov-Usov. And above all, thank you to all those on the periphery, the wretched of the earth, those who labor and toil to build our world, those who remain unseen. It is because of you and for you that I see and write, and my eternal loyalty is to you.